The Assembly of the Severed Head

A small monastic outpost in 13th-century Wales is rocked to its core when a gruesome discovery is made on the nearby shoreline: a severed human head. It's the first of several to wash up along the surrounding coast.The holy brothers stumble across the ruins of a bardic school. Inside there is a heap of decapitated corpses. Only one survivor, barely alive, is found hiding nearby. He is Cian Brydydd Mawr, the greatest bard of his age, who holds in his head the four 'branches' of an ancient, epic Welsh myth cycle: The Mabinogion. Physically weak but strong willed, he asks the monks to put aside their rigid Christian doctrine and commit his tales to parchment. And as the old poet tells his tales of spirits and shape-shifters, spells and curses, passion and vengeance, no-one in his audience will ever be the same again.

The Assembly of
the Severed Head

The making of the Mabinogi

Hugh Lupton

propolis

ISBN: 978 0 99294 605 0

This paperback edition published 2020
First published in 2018

by Propolis Books
The Book Hive,
53 London Street,
Norwich, NR2 1HL

Cover: Studio Medlikova

The right of Hugh Lupton to be identified
as the author of this work has been asserted
by him in accordance with the Copyright,
Designs and Patents Act, 1988

A CIP record for this book
is available from the British Library

Printed and bound by TJ International, Padstow, Cornwall

For Daniel and Marion

This is the night

when the second official
wearing his best orphrey'd jacket, must sing from his Liber
Mandatorum (which is the New Mandate) the beginning of the
Mabinogi of Mabon the Pantocrator, the true and eternal Maponos,
and of ... Rhiannon of the bird-throats, was it? Spouse of the Lord
of Faery? Matrona of the Calumniations, seven winters at the
horse-block telling her own mabinogi of detraction?

Modron our mother?

Ein mam hawddgar?

Truly!

That we must now call MAIR, MARY.

David Jones (from The Anathemata)

An oral poem is not composed *for* but *in* performance ... Singer,
performer, composer, and poet are one, under different aspects
but at the same time. It is sometimes difficult for us to realize that
the man who is sitting before us singing an epic song is not a mere
carrier of the tradition but a creative artist making the tradition ...

But there is another world, of those who can read and write, of
those who come to think of the written text not as the recording
of a moment of the tradition but as *the* song. This becomes the
difference between the oral way of thought and the written way.

Albert Lord (from The Singer of Tales)

Contents

Cian Brydydd Mawr

Monday August 15th 1211

It was Dafydd, who found the first head.

He was bucketing sea-water into the wooden tank where the hides were steeping. At first he thought it was a round stone washed up on the shore, but there was something about the agitation of gulls and crows. They were haggling and vying for a taste of something good. He dropped the leather bucket, waved his arms and strode towards them. They flew up in a ragged cloud.

It was lying on its cheek. The eye sockets had been pecked hollow. The tongue, lolling out of the open mouth, was mostly eaten away. The sodden black hair, where it wasn't half buried in sand, was pasted to the skin. The cut was clean, as though the neck had been sliced by a butcher's cleaver.

With his toe he pushed. It rolled face-upwards. Yellow liquid dribbled from the severed windpipe. The hair fell back.

"Jesu."

The hairline was shaven. He dropped to his knees. With his fingers he combed the hair away from the forehead.

He was muttering to himself:

"Christ Jesu – is it one of the holy brothers?"

Nothing was impossible in these troubled times.

But it wasn't a full tonsure. It had been shaved only to the top of the head so that the blank-eyed face had an egg-shaped, elongated brow.

Dafydd crossed himself and sucked the air between his teeth.

He fetched the bucket and gently rolled the head inside.

Then he heard the bronze bell in the little tower above him ringing for Lauds. He dropped to his knees on the shingle.[1]

"We beseech Thee, O Lord, forgive the sins of thy servants, and may we be saved by the intercession of the Mother of thy Son, our Lord, who with thee liveth and reigneth. Amen."

He crossed himself again. There could be no disturbing the brothers at prayer, and no amount of hurry or alarm would wake the severed head. There was time for him to drop a few heavy stones onto the newly flayed calf hides. They sank under the salt water to the bottom of the tank.

"Good."

Now he could kneel at the Eucharist knowing that the work of the morning was properly completed. A lay brother's devotions were always tempered by the demands of the day.

He picked up the bucket and hurried along the deep lane to the little stone church with its scattering of cells and its thatched refectory.

The Cistercians had rebuilt the monastery on the ruins of the old Clas that had been founded by Saint Beuno six hundred years before.[2] Behind it loomed the slopes of Bwlch Mawr and Gyrn Goch.

The bell began to ring again. The door opened. The brothers came blinking from shadow and candlelight into the hot August sun.

It was the feast of the Assumption of the Virgin Mary. Only three days had passed since the humiliation of Gwynedd. The brothers were silent, as they always were, but there were stories in the air that made it hard for them to keep their minds and hearts attuned to the consolations of prayer.

Even Dafydd, who was rarely troubled by the world beyond his round of work and devotion, could sense a grim agitation beneath their habitual pieties. The burden he was carrying in his leather bucket would do nothing to ease it.

Brother Deiniol was the last to leave the church. He had guests from the Mother Abbey. They had arrived from Aberconwy late the night before and he would be eager to talk with them. It would not be easy to make him stop and listen.

"Brother!"

His white woollen robe brushed past Dafydd. His head was down, his hands folded.

"Brother, a word!"

His step was unhurried but he showed no sign of stopping.

Dafydd had no choice. He lifted his robe and ran. He overtook Brother Deiniol and tipped the bucket upside down. The head rolled into the path. It came to a halt at the brother's feet. He stopped and stared.

"Holy Mother of God."

He looked at Dafydd.

"Where did you find it?"

"On the sea-shore."

"Go and fetch the visitors. Ask them to come straight away."

Soon a circle of monks were standing shoulder to shoulder, staring down at the head. Among them were the Sub-Prior and the Cantor of Aberconwy.

Dafydd crouched down and combed the hair with his fingers so they could see the shaven brow.

They crossed themselves.

The Cantor spoke what they all knew.

"He was a bard."

By late afternoon, when Vespers had been celebrated, four more heads had been brought to the church of Saint Beuno. Two had been caught in the nets of a fisherman working in the deep waters off Trwyn y Gorlech. Some boys from Cappas Lwyd had stumbled across another as they chased seals in the bay. The fourth had been found by an old woman searching for shellfish in the rock pools by Ynys Fawr. They were laid in a line against the church wall. Three had the shaven brows of bards. The other two – little more than boys – were unshaven.

The Cantor, Brother Selyf, was a regular visitor to this little outpost of the Mother Abbey. He came to oversee the preparation of hides for parchment and vellum. Dafydd was the foreman of the Abbey Farm. They'd often walked the low-lying pastures together, and climbed to the rougher grazing in the hills.

Brother Selyf knew that a book carries the living word of God. He knew its preparation is an act of prayer; when finished it becomes a vessel, a reliquary, a tabernacle and a testament. He knew that nothing could be achieved without the finest vellum. His Scriptorium at Aberconwy depended on it. To him, Dafydd's husbandry was the bedrock upon which the holy citadel could be built.

Brother Selyf was a man of profound learning. He had studied in Paris and Dublin. Dafydd could neither read nor write. He had a handful of prayers and psalms by heart. Latin to him was a mystery. It was a babel of spells and charms.

The two men took pleasure in each other's company.

Sometimes Brother Selyf would bring one of his decorated books with him when he came to visit. He would lend it to Dafydd. After Compline, when the brothers were snoring in their cells, Dafydd would open it. He would pore over it by candlelight. He would trace the mysterious script with his blunt fingertips. He would press his lips to the gilded images. Then he would sleep with the book under his head as a pillow, easy in the knowledge that every blessed word was pricked and spelled onto the skins of beasts he'd raised and slaughtered with his own hands. Those nights he would dream of angels.

After Vespers, as they were walking towards the Refectory, Brother Selyf caught Dafydd by the arm.

"Friend, do you recall a time some years ago when you and I climbed to the high pastures below Yr Eifl?"

"I remember it well. The cloud came down and you lost sight of me. You blabbed like a babe that has lost hold of its mother's skirts."

"I merely called your name."

"Called! You bleated my name."

"Be that as it may, the sun came through and the mist cleared. We looked down into a hidden valley. There were fields and what seemed to be a homestead."

"I know the place you speak of – Nant Gwrtheyrn."

"And you told me, if I recall, that it is a Bardic School."[3]

Dafydd smiled.

"And I said it runs contrary to your ecclesiastical schools, for though they train men to be scholars, they know no more of book, pen or parchment than the birds of the sky or the beasts of the field."

"Yes, that is what you said, and now it occurs to me that ..."

"And your thoughts are the very echo of my own, Brother."

"... it occurs to me that the killing has reached even as far as that hidden place."

"Yes Brother, and bear in mind that every severed head with shaven brow once held as much knowledge behind its forehead as any of your libraries of parchment and vellum."

"True enough, though I fear the greater part of it would have been the work of the devil and his imps."

"That is your opinion, friend. Our Lord Llywelyn would hold otherwise."

"And you?"

Dafydd kicked a stone and said nothing.

The evening meal of gruel and bread was eaten in silence.

There was a reading from Ecclesiastes:

"And so was I established in Sion, and in the holy city likewise I rested, and my power was in Jerusalem."

The only sound was the rise and fall of Brother Deiniol's voice and the scraping of knives against wooden plates.

"And I took root in an honourable people, and in the portion of my God was my inheritance, and my abode was in the full assembly of the saints."

The other seven brothers who were resident at Clynnog Fawr chewed and listened. Above them sat the two guests. Below them the eight lay brothers paid more attention to their food than to the indigestible Latin that carried only occasional glimmers of meaning.

"In plateis sicut cinnamomum et balsamum aromatizans odorem dedi: quasi myrrha electa, dedi suavitatem odoris."

When the tables had been cleared the Sub-Prior stood. He leaned forward with his knuckles on the bare scrubbed boards.

"Brothers, the Abbot, our father in Christ, has sent me to this house of prayer to speak of our situation. For not without reason did the psalmist sing: 'O God, you have tested us, you have tried us as silver is tried by fire.'

"You will have heard that Gwynedd is fallen. Bangor has been burnt to the ground – cathedral and city alike. Bishop Rhobert has been taken prisoner. King John has set the price of his ransom at two hundred falcons. Our Mother Abbey in Aberconwy is become a barrack for English soldiers. They sleep in cloister and refectory. The brothers are ousted from their dormitories. John himself sleeps in the Abbot's bedchamber. The holy brothers are forced to serve them at table. But despite all this they are not denied the offices of the day and John himself kneels at the Eucharist each morning. The word of God is not altogether forgotten."

"What of our Father Abbot?"

"He is fled across the Straits of Menai to the palace at Aberffraw. He ministers to our Lord Llywelyn and Lady Siwan. He teaches them to endure the humiliations of defeat. It will be hard for them, we must offer prayers on their behalf."

"And you?"

"We were away from the abbey when John's army crossed the river from Deganwy. We have not returned. From the hills we have watched their wanton destruction of our lands. Among the little oaks we have spoken the offices like saints of the golden age."

"And Llywelyn has offered his surrender?"

"Three days ago he went to Aberconwy. If it hadn't been for the intercessions of Lady Siwan – who is, after all, John's bastard daughter – he would doubtless have been hanged. Llywelyn knelt and offered his sword. John had his blacksmiths bend and buckle it before his eyes. It is said that Llywelyn wept to watch it. The fickle Welsh lords stood by and saw all – Gwenwynwyn of Powys,

Maelgwm and Rhys Gryg of Deheubarth, Hywel of Merioneth. They will, I fear, live to curse the day they sided with the English king.

When the sword had been destroyed, John forgave Llywelyn in mocking terms, as though his gwladgarwch, his love for his native land, was a sin to be confessed and absolved. And the settlement John has demanded is a harsh one."

"What is it?"

"All of Gwynedd that is east of the River Conwy goes to the king, as do the four cantrefs that are called Perfeddwlad."

"That is half the realm!"

"And that is not all. John demands thirty hostages to ensure an enduring peace. They must be the sons of the noblemen of Gwynedd and must include Llywelyn's own first-born, Grufydd."

The brothers shook their heads.

"And that is not all. He demands forty war-horses, sixty hunters and ten thousand head of cattle."

This was too much for Dafydd. He jumped to his feet.

"Ten thousand head of cattle! How can so many beasts be found? By Christ and all the Saints, does the English king mean to starve us until the flesh drops from our bones?"

The Sub-Prior shook his head.

"In a flood of words you will not avoid sin."

His neighbour pulled Dafydd back down to the bench.

"Shhhh."

"Brothers we must cast aside all pride and give what has been demanded. These monastic lands – pasture and grazing – were granted to us by Llywelyn and his forefathers. We must pay what we can. Every bull, cow, ox and calf must be handed over."

Dafydd was up again.

"And not a hide to spare for calf-skin vellum?"

Brother Selyf stood and met Dafydd's outrage with a solemn stare.

"Sheep and goats Dafydd, like Jacob we will be keepers of sheep and goats."

By the time the bell rang for Compline two more heads had been brought from the sea-shore and laid beside the others.

Lingering by the church wall the Sub-Prior asked:

"How long in the water would you say?"

Brother Deiniol scrutinised them.

"Three days, four at most."

They went inside. The psalms were sung and the Virgin was honoured:

'O clemens, O pia, O dulcis Virgo Maria.'

After the Blessing, seven of the brothers left the church. They lifted the severed heads in their hands. One behind the other they processed through the west door and up the aisle. They gently laid them in a row before the altar. Outside the birds were singing their dusk litanies.

Brother Selyf opened his bible and read from the Book of Job:

"My bone cleaveth to my flesh, and I am escaped with only the skin of my teeth.

Have pity on me, have pity upon me O ye my friends, for the hand of God hath touched me.

Why do ye persecute me O God, and are not satisfied with my flesh?

Oh that my words were now written! Oh that they were marked down in a book with an iron pen! Or graven with an instrument in stone!

For I know that my redeemer liveth, and that he shall stand at the latter day upon the earth.

And though my skin is destroyed by worms, yet in my flesh shall I see God."

Tuesday August 16th

It was still dark when they assembled for Vigils next morning. The air in the church was rank with the sickly stench of decay. It was eased only in part by the incense and the smoke of wax candles.

When the psalms had been sung the Sub-Prior whispered to Brother Deiniol:

"Today the heads must be laid to earth."

"Yes, at Lauds we will sing the Office of the Dead."

"And they cannot be buried in hallowed ground. We must not forget the interdict."[4]

"Brother have pity. Pope Innocent would not begrudge us a little hole in the corner of the churchyard. It is John he seeks to punish. As John's enemies surely we can allow ourselves this small indulgence."

The Sub-Prior bowed his head.

"So be it."

Later Brother Selyf asked permission to visit Nant Gwrtheyrn.

"The heads we are finding would suggest a massacre."

"But why?" The Sub-Prior was frowning, "Why would they seek out and kill these men who by law are allowed to cross borders and move from one court to another. What is the threat from those who have only the sharp and comely word as their weapon? Unless, like foxes among hens, the English have tasted blood and cannot rest until they have slaughtered the whole coop. And if that is the case, then how safe are we?"

"I do not know brother, but I will find out what I can."

"You have my blessing."

"And one more thing. Can I take Dafydd with me, the lay brother who oversees the farm? He knows every fold of these hills as though they were his mother's face."

"Very well. Take as many of the lay brothers as you need. But leave me one man with pick and spade to dig the grave."

First light was breaking when four of them set out. Two were monks. Brother Selyf the Cantor and Brother Pedr were carrying leather satchels with chalice, wine and flat-bread so that they could celebrate the Eucharist when the hour came. Dafydd and Rhodri, both lay brothers, carried wicker baskets filled with bread, cheese and small ale to break their fast afterwards.

The lay brothers, dressed in brown, led the way. They stepped from stone to stone along the old track above the sea-shore. The monks, in their white woollen robes, followed.

It would be some hours before the sun climbed over the mountains to the east and dried the dew.

"Ease your pace, Dafydd! Or we will break our legs on these wet stones before we ever reach the hills."

As they approached the bay at Trefor they could hear the distant sound of the church bell behind them. It was ringing for Lauds. They knelt on the sand and prayed. Then they made their way through Elernion, past the cluster of thatched cruck-houses and round-houses. There was a barking of dogs. A little naked girl stood in a doorway and watched them solemnly.

"Dydd da."

"God bless you."

They began to climb. Pasture gave way to gorse and heather.

The path led them between the two mountains. The greater, Yr Eifl, sloped up to their left.

Brother Selyf threw down his satchel.

"We are out of earshot of the bell, but my stomach tells me it is time for the Eucharist."

He poured the wine into the chalice and balanced it on the springy turf. He laid the bread on a flat stone.

"Hear us O merciful Father, we most humbly beseech thee; and grant that we, receiving these thy creatures of bread and wine, according to thy Son our Saviour Jesus Christ's holy institution, in remembrance of his death and passion, may be partakers of his most blessed Body and Blood."

He sipped and ate, then ministered to the other three. They knelt in a row on the path before him and took their communion. For a while they were silent. Brother Pedr broke the spell:

"Now Dafydd, in God's name, break open the bread and cut the cheese! That gruel we ate for supper is a distant memory."

They got up and brushed the twigs and crumbs of turf from their knees. They settled back into the springy heather and shared food. The stoneware flagon of ale was passed from mouth to mouth.

When they had eaten they followed the path until they could see the hidden valley of Nant Gwrtheyrn below. There was a cut with a narrow trickle that tumbled down the slope.

"Do we climb down here?"

"Further on. It winds but it is the quickest way."

They stumbled down into a vision from Hell.

It was the smell that struck them first.

The grazing horses in the rough grass looked up at them as they passed.

The brothers came to a stone homestead. As they approached they could see it was a small hall. There were cells around it, not unlike the cells the monks used. The door of one was open. Inside were two wooden pallets covered with bracken. There were woollen blankets and skins. A cloak was hanging on the back of the door.

The smell was overpowering. It was the second time they had endured it that day. This time no amount of incense could have masked it.

Brother Selyf was the first to enter.

Seconds later he was out again. He doubled over and retched onto the grass. He was crossing himself frantically, over and over.

Dafydd was next in. As a tanner he was all but immune to the stink of decay. But nothing could have prepared him for what met his eyes.

The floor was open and flagged with stone, like the floor of a barn or hall. There were benches against the walls.

In the middle was a heap of bloody corpses, one thrown on top of another. Legs and arms were askew. Grey stiff twisted hands jutted out of the heap. Feet pointed both upwards and downwards. Six or seven ravens were hopping over it, sinking their heads into the carrion, tugging out pieces of flesh and lengths of pale intestine. The floor was sticky with dried black blood.

Every head was gone.

Dafydd came out into the light of day. He took several deep breaths of clean air. He looked at the others and said nothing.

"How many?"

"Christ have mercy on their souls – fifteen, maybe twenty."

In one of the cells they found a linen undershirt. They tore it into strips. They soaked the pieces of cloth in the stream and wrapped them around their faces. Then all four entered the hall. One by one they dragged the headless corpses out of the hall and laid them on the grass. There were twenty-one.

The midday sun was fierce above their heads. They took off their masks and washed their hands and faces. They knelt under an alder tree at the stream's edge. Brother Selyf sang a psalm for Sext.

They found wooden spades and, watched by the solemn-eyed horses, they started to dig a long shallow grave, cutting neat turfs out of the pasture.

It was as they were working that the boy appeared.

He seemed to come out of nowhere. Suddenly he was standing at the end of the trench.

"Help me."

His voice was an urgent, hoarse whisper. Dafydd guessed he was twelve or so years old. He was filthy, his face pinched with hunger. His eyes had the haunted look of a child who has seen more than he can tell.

"Who are you?"

"I am Tomos."

Brother Selyf nodded to the basket.

"Give him food."

Dafydd went across. He took out the last of the loaf. He broke it in half. He cut some cheese.

The boy seized the food and crammed it into his mouth. He ate furiously, his eyes fixed, almost unblinking, on the watching brothers. Then, as if remembering himself, he stopped. He dropped the last of it into his shirt.

Dafydd offered him some water. He smiled.

"Drink. Eat it all – there's more."

The boy lifted the cup to his lips and gulped it down. He wiped his mouth with the back of his hand. He gestured with his thumb to a heap of rocks at the foot of the slope that led up from the pasture.

"There is another. I need food for him also."

Then he buried his face in his hands. He was trembling. Tears began to run between his fingers. When he lowered his hands and looked at them again, his filthy cheeks were mottled with tears.

"I'm afraid ... I think he is dying."

"Show us."

Tomos had made a rough shelter. He'd laid branches across two fallen boulders and covered them with bracken. Underneath he'd spread blankets and skins. Curled up on them lay an old, white-bearded man. His brow was shaven. He was shivering and muttering to himself. Between his shoulder and his neck there was a deep wound. It was clogged with congealed blood and crawling with fat grey-white maggots.

"When the soldiers came he was the first they found. They struck him down. Then they ran into the hall. I saw he was alive. I had time to hide him."

The boy was chewing bread, spitting it onto his hand and pushing it into the old man's mouth. He lifted the cup of water to his lips. The old man swallowed.

"You did well lad. Tell us who came?"

"I don't know. They spoke a tongue I had not heard before."

"French?"

"No, they were neither Norman nor English."

The boy shuddered.

"Nor were they Irish. Those accents I would recognise. They came by ship."

Brother Selyf turned to the others.

"Mercenaries! I'll warrant they were John's Flemish mercenaries who are indifferent to mercy."

"There was one who seemed to lead the way."

Dafydd narrowed his eyes.

"There's always one. He could only have been Welsh, and local too. They would never have found their way here otherwise. And dazzled no doubt, like Judas Iscariot, by thirty pieces of silver. Now lad, eat some more, there's plenty of bread and cheese. We Brothers of the Holy Church are raised on fasting, you needn't worry about us."

Brother Pedr looked mournfully at the last crust. The boy ate. They waited for him to ease his hunger.

When he'd finished he wiped his mouth on the back of his arm. Brother Selyf asked:

"So are you apprenticed here?"

Tomos shook his head.

"I look after their horses. I cook sometimes. My mother and father were killed in a raid. Irish pirates. These people took me in."

"So when the soldiers came ..."

"I was with the horses, over there, they didn't see me."

"You were lucky."

"Christ spared me. I didn't see what happened in the hall, not until afterwards. I heard it though. I tried to block it out with my fingers in my ears ... but the shouts ... the screams. I will never forget. They fought, but there were too many soldiers. The killing took a long time. Then they found the mead."

Tomos fell silent.

Dafydd reached across and laid his hand gently on Tomos' shoulder.

"There is no need to tell us any more."

But the boy continued:

"This old man has always been very kind to me. His name is Cian. When the soldiers came out of the hall he was groaning. I crouched low and pressed my hand over his mouth. Even so I could see what they were carrying."

"We know, Tomos."

"They were laughing. Some could barely stand. The tide was high. The little rowing boats were waiting to carry them back to their ship. They took the heads to the edge of the slope – over there where the grass is sparse – and rolled them down into the water as though they were playing skittles."

Suddenly the memory was too much for him. He buried his face in his hands and rocked backwards and forwards.

"Pray with us, lad, pray with us."

It was – Brother Selyf guessed – the hour of None.

The brothers knelt.

"Restore again, O Lord, our fortunes, as the torrent in the south.

They who sow in tears shall reap in gladness.

Euntes ibant et flebant, mittentes semina sua.

Venientes autem venient cum exsultatione, portantes manipulos suos."

It was early evening when they left the valley.

They had dug a long shallow grave and heaped loose stones onto the turfs that covered the corpses.

"It will be enough to keep away ravens and foxes."

At Vespers they had prayed for their souls.

With poles and blankets they had made a stretcher for the old man. They lifted him and covered him with skins from the huts. Brother Pedr washed his wound. He was delirious, his teeth chattering.

They made their way out of the valley. The lay brothers carried the stretcher. Dafydd was in front, Rhodri behind. Tomos walked alongside. He leaned over from time to time to cool the old man's face with a damp cloth. The monks followed in silence.

When they reached the high point of the path and could see Trefor Bay below them, Brother Selyf said:

"Now rest. Pedr and I will take the load."

The monks took the weight of the stretcher.

They had eaten nothing since morning. They were light-headed with the demands of the day. When they came to the houses there was smoke drifting through the thatch. They put down the stretcher. Brother Pedr knocked at a door.

"In God's name is there any morsel of food you could spare?"

"Come in, brothers, come in, we've had a good catch of mackerel, we can throw some more into the pot."

"Bless you."

They sat by the fire. The woman gutted more fish. She sliced them and flung them into the iron cauldron that was hanging over the flames.

"He doesn't look so good. The one outside."

"He is, at least, alive. There has been killing at Nant Gwrtheyrn."

She nodded to the man who was sitting in the shadows on the other side of the fire.

"It was my husband who caught two heads in his nets."

"What else have you seen?"

The man shook his head.

"Not much. Just a ship. Sailed past us four days since. Coming from Bangor. Early morning. With a foreign cut to its sails. It never returned, must have sailed on along the coast."

The stew was ladled into bowls.

Brother Selyf whispered a hurried grace. Then bread was broken. They lifted the bowls to their lips and ate.

The woman broke the silence.

"There is something else. Rhys Drwyndwn 'Broken-nose' from

Tan y Graig came down from Yr Eifl that night. He was staggering like a new-dropped calf, sick with drink. They say he's been squandering money."

Dafydd scratched his cheek.

"Has he by God. He's worked for me that one. I remember him well. He didn't get his broken nose for nothing."

The last part of the journey was the most difficult, carrying the stretcher along the rough track in the dark. It was midnight when they reached Clynnog Fawr.

Tomos would not be separated from the old man. The brothers found them an empty cell, gave the boy blankets and left them to sleep.

"The wound will have to wait until tomorrow."

As they were separating, Brother Selyf said to Dafydd:

"This has been the little wound. The greater one has been inflicted on our Lord Llywelyn. And he does not yet know that he has received it. I fear it will fall to me to tell him. It will cut him very deep, very deep indeed."

"Brother, I have never been to Aberffraw. Only once have I seen Lord Llywelyn and never Siwan. If you need company, and another witness to give weight to your story, then I would gladly go with you."

"Listen, friend, he is a man of turbulent mood and unpredictable humours. The bards have been dear to his heart. The bringer of bad tidings, especially in these times, is never welcome. Take my advice. Stay here."

"Take it or leave it, Brother, the offer remains."

"God be with you, Dafydd."

Wednesday August 17th

After Eucharist the brothers sat down together in the refectory and broke their fast with bread and dried fish. Brother Selyf sat between the Sub-Prior and Brother Deiniol. He told them all that he had witnessed the day before.

"The old man's wound is festering. Unless his doctoring begins today there is small chance of his survival."

The Sub-Prior turned to Brother Deiniol.

"Is there anyone among the eight brothers living here who is skilled in medicine?"

"Brother Pedr oversees the herb garden. He has some small skill as a bone-setter. Otherwise there is no-one."

"Then Brother Selyf and I will stay for one more day. Tomorrow we will journey to Aberffraw and break the news to Lord Llywelyn. Two mouths will serve that purpose better than one."

"What will you need for the healing?"

"A branding iron to clean the wound. Linen thread that has been waxed for the suture. Honey and strong mead for the mending. Strips of linen for bandaging. And as many jugs of water as can be carried to the cell to slake his thirst and keep all clean. All must be blessed."

"And helpers?"

"Brother Pedr and the boy Tomos will be ample – and one of the lay brothers to fetch water."

Brother Deiniol cast his eyes across the refectory.

"Dafydd."

Dafydd looked up from his platter.

"What is your task of the day?"

Dafydd winced.

"Cattle, Brother. I have sent word across the abbey farm, up to the hafods, where the boys are overseeing the summer grazing, that every bull, cow, ox and calf must be driven to Clynnog Fawr. The herds we have bred and nurtured must help to pay John's fine. Tomorrow they start their journey."

The Sub-Prior said:

"Put your trust in God. Remember his vengeance upon the ungodly: 'The Lord rained upon Sodom and upon Gomorrah brimstone and fire out of heaven; and he overthrew those cities and all the plain.' Be patient Dafydd – suffer, pray and trust in his mercies. The guilty will not go unpunished."

Dafydd bowed his head.

"And," said Brother Deiniol, "before you go down to the farm, be good enough to bring water from St Beuno's well, as many leather buckets as you can fill. We will need holy water if we are to cure the old man's wound."

Tomos opened the door of the cell. The brothers could not tell whether the old bard was asleep or awake. He was curled up under the blankets. No-one had dared lift him from his makeshift stretcher. Brother Selyf lit a candle and held it to his face. What they could see of him was ashen-grey. The Sub-Prior knelt beside him. He reached forwards and gently folded back the blanket.

He started back.

"Christ Jesu!"

He got to his feet and hurried out into the light. Brother Selyf followed. The Sub-Prior's voice was urgent with alarm.

"Did you not see who he is?"

"I have never set eyes on him before."

"He is Cian Brydydd Mawr."[5]

"You are sure? How do you know?"

"Sure? I am certain! When I was a youth, before I was called to serve God, I was a scribe at the court of Rhys, Lord of Deheubarth. Many times I have been called upon with pen and parchment to scratch his songs onto the page."

Brother Selyf whistled through his teeth.

"The Great Poet. I never imagined I would see him face to face. Did you ever hear his exultation for Gwynedd?

'I love its fields under the little clover,

Where honour is granted a secure joy.

I love the nightingale in the wild wood,

Where two waters meet in a sweet valley.'[6]

And now his life is in our hands."

They hurried back inside.

"Tomos blow some life into the fire. Brother Pedr fetch a bucket of charcoal and a branding iron. This will be a long day for our guest."

Dafydd came to the door of the cell. Over his shoulders he was carrying a milk-maid's yoke. On either end of it three slurping buckets of water from the holy well were swinging. He gently lowered the yoke to the ground. He lifted two buckets and brought them in, pushing open the door with his knee. His face was met by a wave of dry heat.

He saw that Brother Pedr was crouching beside a bed of glowing charcoal. He was turning a branding iron over and over, thrusting the tip of it deeper into the fire. Brother Selyf was tearing an old cloth into rags.

The Sub-Prior had a cup of mead. He was dipping a swab of linen into it and cleaning the wound in the old man's shoulder.

At each touch the old man sucked his breath between his teeth.

"Ah Dafydd, good, put the buckets down here by his head."

It was as he was setting them on the ground that the old man opened his eyes. Dafydd saw a hand reach out from under the blankets and seize the Sub-Prior by the arm. His voice was little more than a whisper.

"Oswallt."

The Sub-Prior was taken aback.

"That was my name before I renounced the world."

"Who broke his father Rhodri's heart by running away from court and taking up the white mantle of the Christ."

"Some things we do not choose. I am Andras now."

"And whose grandfather was Beda the Saxon who fled the Marches and made his name in the warband of Madog ap Maredudd."

"How do you know that?"

"It is my business to know, and I could tell you more – but answer me this. Do you still set traps for the living word with quill and ink?"

The cell was quiet. Brother Selyf was leaning away from the fire to catch the conversation.

"No longer. I am become Sub-Prior."

He gestured to Brother Selyf.

"But my Brother here oversees the scriptorium where the holy word is made into manuscript."

He nodded to Dafydd.

"And our vellum and parchment is the work of our lay brother Dafydd and his men on the Abbey farm."

The old man turned his fierce blue eyes on Dafydd.

"From where?"

"Carnguwch Fawr."

"Ah, the foot of Breast Mountain, whose father was Dafydd and whose grandfather was Dafydd also. And whose great great grandfather killed a Viking and nailed his skin onto the barn door."

Dafydd looked at the old man in amazement.

"True?"

"True."

"It is my duty to know these things."

He lowered his head and closed his eyes for a while. His fingers were still digging into the Sub-Prior's arm.

"We need to mend your wound. It will cost you a good deal of pain."

"Come closer."

The Sub-Prior leaned towards the old man's mouth.

"Listen. I am old. I was dying before I received this wound. There is something that is troubling me."

"You wish to make a confession?"

He laughed, a thin rasping laugh.

"Confession, ha, no – I have lived, I have loved, I have striven to give tongue to the music of what is – I have nothing to confess."

"What then?"

"There is a Matter that – in the wake of the killing at Nant Gwrtheyrn – I alone hold in my head."

"Your verses, odes, praises, laments?"

"Those! No! They are spent! Kings, lords and noblemen have honoured me at their tables for a well tempered song. Armies have gone to war with my urgings ringing in their ears. Women have welcomed me to their beds for the caress of my verse. Some have been set on the page by scribes. The rest are scattered on the breath of the wind."

"Then there is something else?"

The old man was silent. His breath became slow and easy. The grip of his hand loosened.

"He is asleep. Bring the iron."

"Wait."

The blue eyes opened and bored into the Sub-Prior's face.

"I have followed the old way. As Pencerdd I have been the Great Poet who knew neither bound nor master. As Bardd Teulu I have served in the retinues of lords and noblemen. As Cyfarwydd I have mastered a thousand tales."[7]

The Sub-Prior nodded.

"That is the bard's journey. What is the matter that troubles you?"

"They will not let me rest – those old tales. As a boy I learned them when my training began. They were old when Meilyr was born, who, as an old man, taught me. They are not the vanities of bards, but the very ground upon which our poetry is built."

"You speak of Arthur?"

"Arthur will not die. The Normans have developed a taste for Arthur. Every half-baked cerddor sings of Arthur."

"What then?"

"Older, older, older. Older than Arthur, older than the saints of the golden age."

He closed his eyes.

"There were eight youths, broad-browed, nimble-tongued. I had taught them all I knew. Now hermit crabs are setting up house in their brain-pans."

From outside there came the sound of the midday bell.

The Sub-Prior got up to his feet.

"It is time for Sext. When we return we must apply the iron."

"And I will die ..."

The brothers exchanged glances. Tomos lifted a cup of water to the old man's lips.

"I will die unless ..."

"Unless what?"

"Unless you promise ..."

The old man's head sank back onto the stretcher.

"... to scratch onto parchment ... with quill and ink ... this Matter that will otherwise crumble to dust as my flesh crumbles ... and be silent as my breath falls silent."

The Sub-Prior shook his head.

"Without the blessing of our Father Abbot we can make no such promise. The scriptorium is the preserve of God's holy word. Every letter is an act of prayer. What truth can be gleaned from this Matter of yours? Maybe there is a divine purpose in oblivion."

He left the cell. Brother Selyf and Brother Pedr followed him.

Dafydd found he was alone with the old man.

He hadn't expected to drop to his knees.

He was surprised to find himself kneeling beside the stretcher and reaching for the hand of Cian Brydydd Mawr.

He pressed it to his lips.

"I promise."

The old man opened his eyes and looked at Dafydd for a long time.

"I promise that every word will be set down."

Dafydd felt the thin, trembling fingers tightening around his hand. The voice was a whisper.

"Can you write?"

"No."

"Read?"

"No."

The old man smiled.

"Dafydd ap Dafydd ap Dafydd – I have decided to live."

He closed his eyes again.

"And I will hold you to your promise."

He loosened his grip on Dafydd's hand.

"But please – not on Viking skin."

Dafydd got to his feet. He hurried across to the church. The first psalm was coming to its end. He bowed his head in prayer.

When the monks returned to the cell, the mead cup was empty and the old man fast asleep.

"Where has it gone?"

Tomas nodded to him.

"He drank it."

"Maybe that is no bad thing."

Brother Selyf gently prized open his mouth and put a piece of wood between his teeth. He put his arm around the old man's head and knelt so that he was ready to put all his weight onto the good shoulder. Brother Pedr took the other arm by the wrist and stretched it outwards. The Sub-Prior pulled the iron from the fire. The boy twisted the white beard in his hand and drew it away from the wound.

There was a hiss and a stench of burning flesh.

The wordless scream was like the death-cry of an animal.

It startled the monks from their prayers and the lay brothers from their labours. The old man flailed and struggled.

With all their weight the brothers held him down.

The iron was heated again. The second time it seared deeper into the corrupted flesh.

He fell back onto the stretcher. Tomos turned to Brother Selyf.

"Is he dead?"

"No. No. Now quick, fetch the honey."

They spooned honey into the wound. The Sub-Prior threaded a needle. He pierced the firm skin and drew the sides of the wound together as though he was lacing a shoe.

"If he shivers keep him warm. If he sweats wash him. Give him water to drink. Brother Pedr stay with the boy. Pray."

"And the bandages?"

"For the time being let the wound breathe. Keep him free from all flies. At dusk bandage him."

From the byres of the abbey farm Dafydd heard the old man's scream. He crossed himself and whispered a hurried prayer.

Word had gone out that the cattle were to be driven in from the pastures and the high summer grazing on the hills.

Throughout the afternoon they came. Herd-boys with spike-collared dogs drove cows with their calves, long-horned oxen and hillocky bulls into the field below the church. The air was filled with lowing and bellowing. Hurdles were put in place to keep the bulls apart. The lay brothers rounded them up. As the bell rang for Vespers, Dafydd counted them. He notched them in tens onto a piece of wood: forty-three cows, sixty calves, twenty-two oxen and five bulls. All of them in good heart after a full summer at grass.

It pained him to look at them. Despite his vows of poverty he still had a farmer's eye for healthy stock. He leaned on a hurdle and smelt their breath, their flanks and their wet steaming dung. He prayed aloud:

"Blessed be the God and Father of our Lord Jesus Christ, the Father of Mercies and the God of all comfort, who comforts us in our afflictions."

He was still standing there when Brother Selyf made his way down from the church after Vespers.

"Idleness is the enemy of the soul!"

"If the raising of a hundred and thirty head of cattle is idleness, then show me what work is?"

"I was joking friend. Even I can see that they are beautiful. At Vespers we sang: 'Our sheep are teeming with young, abounding on their pastures, and productive are our cattle. There is no breach in our walls, no opening, nor is there lamentation in our streets.'"

"There is lamentation on these streets."

"All that lost vellum. And tomorrow you must drive them to the byres of our enemy."

"It is more than vellum, Brother, it is a tide of living blood."

"Now you are sounding like our poet."

"We must drive them to Bangor. The Normans will be making their tally there. It is a harsh tithe."

"Dafydd, I have been reconsidering. The Sub-Prior and I set off tomorrow for the Llys at Aberffraw. We will walk with the cattle for the first day. Then we'll take the ferry across the narrows to Traeth Melynog. You expressed a wish to see Llywelyn and Siwan. Why not come with us. Let the other lay brothers drive the cattle to Bangor."

"It would mean leaving them before they had forded Afon Seiont."

"They are not fools. Besides we will need you. The roads are overflowing with English foot soldiers. Most are penniless. We'd be glad of an extra pair of eyes and your strong arms. Come with us to Llywelyn's Court."

"And Llywelyn's rages?"

"His grief will be softened a little by the news that we have rescued Cian Brydydd Mawr."

"How is the old man?"

"His eyes are still closed. To tell you the truth I doubt he will ever open them."

Dafydd knew that he would. His certainty surprised him.

"Very well, I would be pleased to come with you."

"Good – and bring a stout quarter-staff."

Thursday August 18th

It was a two day journey from Clynnog Fawr to Bangor. The hurdles were taken down after Vigils and by first light the long line of cattle was making its way along the track that followed the low-lying lands above the sea-shore. Two of the Clynnog Fawr monks, eight lay brothers and twenty herd-boys with their dogs on leashes walked to either side. They had goads to hurry the beasts along and whips to keep them in line. Four pack-horses followed behind, loaded with food and blankets. Behind the horses Brother Selyf and the Sub-Prior walked in silence. At Lauds, Tierce, Sext, None and Vespers they stopped to pray and eat. The boys found grazing for the cattle and squatted on their heels, listening from a distance to the rise and fall of the psalms and prayers. They relieved the boredom by flinging pebbles at one another.

They forded Afon Llyfni and Afon Gwyrfai, driving the cattle through the rushing water.

They camped at Fynnon Faglan. The boys collected wood and built two fires. They tethered the dogs in a wide circle. The cattle were gathered inside. They milked the cows.

Brother Selyf led the psalms for Compline.

Then the horses were brought into the circle of light. Their packs were unfastened. Food and fresh milk were shared.

The monks and lay brothers sat round one fire, the herd-boys round the other.

One fire was silent, the other rowdy with talk and laughter.

The sky overhead brightened with stars.

The Sub-Prior broke the reverie:

"What is the likelihood of wolves?"

"Slight. They seldom come down from the hills in summer, except maybe to scavenge on the sea-shore."

They sank into silence again. The dome of the sky was cloudless. Brother Selyf's eyes were fixed on the heavens.

"Let there be lights in the firmament of the heaven to divide the day from the night; and let them be for signs, and for seasons, and for days, and years."

"Amen."

Dafydd noticed that the herd-boys were quiet. It had been a long day. He yawned and got up to fetch a blanket. He wrapped it around himself and stretched out in the firelight.

Then the howling began.

First one cry, high and plaintive, then another. Soon the sound was coming from every side. The lay brothers jumped to their feet. Their backs were to the fire. They drew knives and seized staffs. They peered into the shadows. There was a cracking of twigs.

The wolves were coming closer.

Dafydd lifted his quarter-staff and ran out into the night.

Brother Selyf shouted:

"Come back! Are you mad!"

They could see him swinging his staff.

"Owwww!"

The wolf howls were becoming howls of laughter.

Dafydd came back into the light carrying one of the herd-boys over his shoulder. He flung him onto the ground.

"Skin him!"

The boy scrambled to his feet and ran across to the other fire.

The Sub-Prior was shaking with rage.

"The devils should be whipped and sent home to their fathers. If they were novices they would be lying on the chancel floor with their faces to the ground for this."

Dafydd grinned.

"The joke was on us, Brother. Didn't you hear? Neither dogs, horses nor cattle fell for it."

He lay down again and drew his blanket up to his chin. Around the two fires herd-boys and brothers were doing the same. He closed his eyes and smiled. In a moment he was asleep.

When Dafydd opened his eyes the fire was reduced to glowing embers. Clouds had moved across the sky and darkened the stars.

There was a low murmur of voices. He turned his head.

The Sub-Prior and Brother Selyf were sitting up.

Brother Selyf threw a handful of sticks onto the dwindling fire.

They blazed. Dafydd could see their faces clearly.

Brother Selyf's was long and narrow-nosed. It was both shrewd and strangely horse-like. The high brow was folded with thought, the eyes amused. The Sub-Prior, in contrast, reminded him of a brewer or baker in a lord's kitchen. He was full-cheeked, with small quick eyes. No amount of austerity could burn away the plump sheen of his skin. His hands were small and delicate. He was using them to give added weight to his argument.

"It is a crusade we are fighting, Brother. The light must defeat the ancient darkness of our forefathers. Is it not written in the psalms: 'Awe inspiring wert thou in thy brightness from the eternal hills, all the foolish of heart were dismayed'?"

"So you are saying that our war is against the foolish of heart?"

"I am."

"And how does this relate to Cian Brydydd Mawr? The greatest of our bards is no fool. Nor has he turned his back on the teachings of the Holy Church. In his poem Ynys Enlli he says ..."

Brother Selyf voiced the words with affection.

"'Christ, his cross foreknown, will know me also,

32

Will lead me past the pains of hell,

And the Maker who made me will greet me.'[8]

These are hardly the words of a heathen."

"I have no argument with Cian Brydydd Mawr. It is his calling that I question."

"Tell me more."

"The Bardic Schools. What are they founded on? Did he not say that as a youth he mastered a thousand tales? Did he not speak of passing them on to his nimble-tongued apprentices, may Christ have mercy on their souls?"

"He did."

"And how many of those thousand tales are drawn from the Holy Scriptures?"

"I begin to follow your argument."

"I would venture a guess – none."

"They would have included some Saints maybe, some Miracles."

"Maybe."

There was silence. Then the Sub-Prior continued:

"The Bardic Schools, unlike our ecclesiastical schools, make a virtue of the ancient disciplines of memory."

"They do, Brother."

"It seems to me that Almighty God works in mysterious ways. He has given us a sign. Twenty-one bards are dead. One survives. I do not begrudge him his life or deny his genius. I would not have tended to him otherwise."

"Nor I."

"But this Matter, this ancient Matter that he speaks of and would have us preserve – it is my opinion that it should not outlive him. It should have no life beyond that which it has always had among bards – in the memory and on the tongue."

"What do you know of this Matter?"

"I remember fragments and shards from his entertainments at the court of Rhys: enchantments, wars, elopements, shadows of old gods. It is the beguiling work of the Devil. It would draw the foolish of heart into sin. It is best forgotten."

"So what of this request to set it down on the page?"

"Tell me, what is the life of a page?"

"They say vellum will last for more than a thousand years."

"Precisely. We will say nothing of this request. Even our Father Abbot will be spared the knowledge of it. The Matter will perish."

Dafydd listened.

He thought of the blood of the redeeming Christ, the holy Mother, the Sacrament, the Latin spells of Prayer and Psalm, the promise of Heaven, the winged Angels of his dreams. He thought of his vows of renunciation. His heart was filled with the Glory of God.

But the hard Welsh ground beneath his back told another story, the warmth of the dying fire, the lowing of the standing cattle, the cool southerly wind that smelt of the mountains, the sounds of the sea.

He knew he would keep his promise.

Friday August 19th

It was still dark when Brother Selyf woke them with the little travelling bell. They washed their throats with water and knelt for Vigils. Their psalms woke the herd-boys. Half dazed with sleep they shook off their blankets and fed the dogs.

After the service the boys ate. The brothers touched neither food nor drink. They had to wait the six hours until Eucharist.

At first light the cattle were made ready to continue the journey.

Dafydd called together the monks and lay brothers who were to drive them to Bangor.

"You know where you are going?"

"The open fields beyond the cathedral."

"The English are making a tally there. There will be cattle coming from every farm. They are swimming them across the Strait from Môn."[9]

The Sub-Prior came across to them.

"Everything in Bangor is reduced to ash. We looked down from the hills and saw the destruction. It will be hard to follow the old streets. The cathedral is a carapace of stone and scorched timber. The people fled into the mountains. They returned to devastation. Give them what you can. Milk the cows before you hand them over and give it away. If you can lose some cattle among the hungry, so be it. But be careful. Norman reprisals are swift and brutal."

"And," said Dafydd, "brothers, one last thing, the ford across Afon Seiont is treacherous, the waters will be low but keep your wits about you."

"God bless you."

The tide was out when the three of them came to the sands of the Bay of Foryd.

"We'll have to cross Afon Gwyrfai a second time – here, before the river forks."

Dafydd, Brother Selyf and the Sub-Prior disrobed at the water's edge. They waded stark naked through the river, holding their clothes and satchels above their heads. There was a soft wind. They stood for a while drying their skin on the far side, turning backs and chests to the rising sun.

They heard the sound of cackling laughter. A clutch of women had been cockling on the wet sand. They were peering over the dunes.

The brothers pulled on their clothes, crossed themselves and carried on walking. When they came to the beach, the women were waiting for them and were kneeling. The Sub-Prior had no choice but to bless each of them in turn. Then the brothers continued. From behind them the laughter bubbled up again.

"A pity the water was so cold!"

"Or do the Holy Brothers stay shrivelled as a winkle in every weather."

It was time for Lauds when they came to the little jetty.

They knelt on the bleached wooden boards.

"For truly, O Lord, Thy enemies, yea, Thy enemies shall perish, and all the evil doers shall be scattered. But my horn, like that of the unicorn, shall be exalted; and mine old age will see the bounty of thy favour. Mine eye looketh down upon my enemies, et in insurgentibus in me malignantibus audiet auris mea."

Dafydd understood not a word, but he noticed a flicker of a smile on Brother Selyf's lips. When the service was over Dafydd saw him go down to the beach. He saw him choose a stem of seaweed with a stone clutched in its roots He saw him kneel on the shingle and whip it hard across his back ten times.

When the little ferry-boat came to the jetty the tide had turned.

The ferryman shouted up to them:

"The current will be strong, brothers. You'll have to help with the oars. And when we get to the far side don't waste any time. The sea will chase you across Traeth Melynog."

Abermenai Point, across the water, seemed barely a stone's throw away, but it was a hard crossing. The four of them strained their backs and arms against the swell. They heaved at the oars to keep the boat on course. When they came to the mooring place the ferryman pointed across the expanse of sand:

"Now, quick! That way!"

The Sub-Prior tossed him a coin. The brothers lifted their robes and ran.

It was a two mile race across Traeth Melynog with the advancing tide lapping at their heels. At Pen Lon they knelt for the Eucharist. Then they broke their fast, grateful and ravenous in equal measure. They walked the seven miles to Aberffraw, stopping only to kneel at the wayside for Sext and None. The few ragged soldiers they encountered knelt for a blessing.

The Llys had been built over the square foundation of a Roman fort. It was walled and moated. The gateway was guarded by soldiers.[10] Beside it was a little porter's lodge. Beyond they could see Lord Llywelyn's high hall. The timber frame loomed over them.

"We are two monks from Aberconwy, and we have with us a lay brother from our sister foundation at Clynnog Fawr."

The porter looked them up and down.

"Are there instructions for your welcome?"

"There are not. But we have come, in God's name, with news for your Lord."

"Any traitor can don white Cistercian robes and shave the top of his head – and I see your friend has deepened the brown of his robes with cow-clap."

Dafydd clenched his fists, muttered a prayer, and then loosened them.

The Sub-Prior was outraged.

"I am the Sub-Prior at Aberconwy, and my companion is the Cantor, if you do not believe us then fetch our Father Abbot and all will be made good."

"If you were Pope Innocent himself I could not fetch him."

"Why not?"

"He is at Vespers and deep in prayer. You'll have to wait."

The porter retired to his thatched lodge.

The brothers knelt on the hard cobbles outside and sang the Vespers psalms. It started to rain. Time passed. The rain thickened. They saw the Abbot hurrying across from the little church. He disappeared through a side door and entered the hall. Smoke rose through the thatch as the fires were lit.

They were soaked to the skin.

"Will you please fetch the Abbot?"

The porter came out again.

"Why didn't you ask before? I had clean forgotten you."

He held a piece of leather over his head and ambled across the courtyard to the hall. A while later he returned. He was chewing something. He wiped his mouth with the back of his hand.

"He'll be with you shortly."

They waited. At last the Abbot appeared.

"Father!"

"For pity's sake! Brother Selyf, Brother Andras, I had no idea. Come in, come in."

They nodded to the porter.

"But we told him we were here."

"A little boy came to me saying something about mendicant friars seeking alms. Come out of the rain in God's name. Who is this?"

"This is Dafydd, a lay brother from Clynnog Fawr. We wanted some protection on the road."

"Of course, come in all three. Dry yourselves by the fire."

The porter unlocked the gates and held them open. Dafydd hurried through behind the other two. He slipped on the wet ground. He fell against the porter, who buckled under his weight.

Dafydd scrambled to his feet. He offered his hand and pulled the porter upright.

"I'm sorry, friend. I seem to have covered you in horseshit. I'll offer up prayers for your recovery."

Then he saw his sin, saw his old unredeemed self laid bare.

He dropped to his knees in the mud.

"Forgive me in Christ Jesu's name."

When they had warmed themselves in the hall the Sub-Prior said:

"Father, is there a place where we can talk alone."

"Yes, yes, of course, come to the church."

They crossed the courtyard, bowed their heads beneath the low stone arch of the doorway.

"Sit down, what is it? Have there been more desecrations in our holy house?"

Brother Selyf spoke:

"Father, as you know there have been many bitter sorrows. You have suffered as deeply as any. We are come with news of another."

The Abbot's face was drawn, pale with alarm.

"What is it?"

"I think I am not mistaken when I say that our Lord Llywelyn is both a patron and a lover of the old high poetry."

The Abbot lowered his voice to a whisper:

"He is. It is both a virtue and a flaw. Like many he struggles to find a reconciliation between the old ways and the pieties of the holy church."

"Father, there has been a massacre. In the Bardic School at Nant Gwrtheyrn, in the mountains behind Trefor."

"A massacre?"

"Twenty-one are dead. Bards and their apprentices. They were killed by Flemish mercenaries, their heads thrown into the sea."

The Abbot got to his feet. He walked to the altar. He knelt and closed his eyes. The three brothers sat in silence. When he stood his cheeks were stained with tears.

"Is there no limit to the savagery of these times? Llywelyn will take this very hard, very hard indeed. Only yesterday he sent away his thirty hostages. First-born sons. Not one of them was older than fourteen years. The youngest was seven. His own boy was among them. It broke my heart to see them parting. And now this."

He was silent for a long time.

"Father, when should we break the news?"

"Straight away. There can be no virtue in delay. We will celebrate Compline. He will come to his feasting hall soon after we have sung the office. Tell him before he eats. Do not fear him. The bearer of bad tidings is never welcome, but he is no fool, he will neither blame nor harm you for the news you bring. His rages are all against himself. He has never laid a finger on Siwan – except in love – and she the daughter of the hated English king."

They knelt in prayer until the bell rang for Compline, and then they took what solace they could from the psalms.

'He will rescue thee from the snare of the fowler, and from the sharp word. With his pinions he will shelter thee; and under His wings thou shalt be secure; like a shield His truth shall guard thee: non timebis a timore nocturne.'

Llywelyn, his wife and his retinue were already seated at the high table when the brothers entered the hall. He was impatient to eat.

"Father Abbot, quick, bless this food before it gets any colder and the grease stiffens it to a standstill."

The Abbot hurried to the high table.

"My Lord, before we eat there is a message that cannot wait. Two brothers are come from Clynnog Fawr."

Llywelyn turned to him.

"No message that comes between me and my meat has ever been welcome. Bring them to me."

Brother Selyf and the Sub-Prior walked forwards with their heads bowed as though they were supplicants. They dropped to their knees. Llywelyn's brooding presence loomed over them, the blue cloak thrown over the broad shoulders, the thick golden torc glittering around his throat. He looked down at them.

"Well?"

"Lord, there has been a killing."

Llywelyn reached for the Abbot's hand. His voice trembled.

"Not the boys. In God's name tell me it is not the boys."

The Abbot pressed his hand.

"Not the boys, my Lord."

Llywelyn stood. He leaned forwards on the table. His black moustache bristled beneath the hawked nose. His voice was so enormous in the hall that even the crackling fire seemed to hold its breath.

"Who then?"

Brother Selyf looked up and fixed his eyes on the king's face.

"Bards."

Llywelyn closed his eyes.

"Bards?"

"At Nant Gwrtheyrn. Twenty-one of them, Lord. Flemish mercenaries came and ..."

"Enough!"

Llywelyn's sword was out. He raised it above his head and brought it down against the table of polished oak with the full strength of both arms. A wedge of wood flew between the heads of the kneeling monks. The newly forged blade lodged deep in the timber.

Siwan turned away from her husband. She gathered her skirts and hurried out of the hall.

Llywelyn stood as though frozen into stone. He stared down at the jewelled hilt of his sword. Runnels of tears were streaming down his cheeks. His Distain, with gesturing arms, wordlessly urged people to leave.[11]

One by one the members of the royal household got up from their seats and benches. They filed out of the hall in silence. Their food was left behind. Only the dogs remained.

The two monks were still kneeling. They could hear the sharp intake of Llywelyn's breathing.

The fat was whitening on the surfaces of the cauldrons and tureens when Llywelyn lifted his head. He slowly uncurled his fingers and left his sword jutting at a sharp angle from the high table.

The brothers heard him walking across to the fire. From the corners of their eyes they saw him drop to his knees. He picked up a stick and stirred the grey-white ashes. One of his dogs crossed the hall and nuzzled his neck with its nose. He lifted a hand and caressed it.

Brother Selyf and the Sub-Prior slowly got to their feet.

They crossed themselves and left the hall.

They didn't see Llywelyn lie down beside the embers. They didn't hear him keening himself to sleep like a mourner at a graveside.

Saturday August 20th

The next morning, after Lauds, the word came that Llywelyn wished to speak further with the monks. The Abbot led them into the hall. Llywelyn was sitting on the floor by the fire. Siwan was seated beside him. His head was in her lap and she was combing the ashes from his hair.

He gestured to a bench on the far side of the hearth. Brother Selyf, the Sub-Prior and Dafydd sat down. The Abbot stood behind.

It was the first time Dafydd had properly seen Llywelyn's wife. He was struck by her youthfulness. Her skin and braided hair – which was covered by a fine net of embroidered silk – were dark. Most of all he was struck by the tenderness between husband and wife. He had expected distance and formality. But an arranged marriage with the daughter of a mortal enemy had proved no barrier to affection.

Llywelyn's voice was deep and weary.

"Tell me everything."

They told him about the severed heads and all that they had found at Nant Gwrtheyrn. He listened in silence. Then he whispered:

"I sent them there."

"Lord?"

"I sent them to their deaths."

He stared at the flames. Siwan stroked his cheek with her fingertips.

The row of monks waited for him to speak again.

Llywelyn lifted his head.

"When John and his English army came into Gwynedd I mustered a war host. To each company of warriors I designated a bard. Every man rode into battle with the old words firing his blood. Every ambush and skirmish had its echo in the hero tales of our ancestors. My soldiers were sung into war frenzy by the high speech of poets. The Sovereignty of Wales, Unbeiniaeth Cymru, rang from every crag and valley."

Llywelyn closed his eyes. His voice intoned the old words:

"The dragon of Môn, how reckless in battle!
Around Tal Moelfre a thousand war-cries,
Spear upon spear, terror on terror,
The Menai's ebb-tide blocked by bodies,
The water boils with the blood of strangers,
Grey armoured men in the swoon of calamity.
The fame of those with the stern swords,
The proud hawks who breach the battle-line,
Shall rise again in seven-score tongues
And ever be sung in the halls of heroes."[12]

He let the verses sink into the silence of the hall.

"It is the old way. It is our keenest weapon, our deepest solace. The first time the English came we drove them back with words and swords. But when they returned in greater numbers we could not defeat them. I saw them crossing the water from Deganwy and I knew we were overwhelmed. I sent word to every bard that he should leave the ranks of warriors and retreat to the hidden valley at Nant Gwrtheyrn. I wanted them to be safe. They carry in their songs the secret heart of this land – just as you, the holy brothers carry its soul, and the clerks and upholders of the ancient laws of Hywel Dda are the bearers of its mind. The three entwined are the triad that makes us who we are."[13]

Tears filled his eyes.

"And now they are dead. John has hacked open the broken body of the land and torn its beating heart from its breast. He could not have done me a deeper harm."

The Sub-Prior leaned forwards.

"Lord, the songs will not be altogether forgotten. There are other bards in other places."

Llywelyn leapt to his feet. He seized the monk by the shoulders and shouted into his face:

"Other bards! What consolation is that?"

Siwan came forwards. She rested her hand on her husband's arm.

"My Lord, you are biting the hand that reaches out to you."

Her Welsh, with its Norman inflection, was soft and strangely alluring. Llywelyn bowed his head.

"Forgive me."

He sat again. His voice was trembling.

"There are indeed other bards. But these were the bards of Gwynedd."

He wept openly, looking across the fire at the monks.

"And there were men I loved among their number. Two had been Bardd Teulu, had ridden into battle at my side."

Tears streamed from his eyes.

"And one was the greatest poet of his age."

"You are speaking of Cian Brydydd Mawr?"

"I am."

Llywelyn wiped his face with his sleeve.

"He was blessed by the awen and matchless in eloquence. There was nobody more deeply steeped in the histories, nobody with a greater mastery of awdlau and englynion. I cannot bear to think of his old head, that bore so much, broken from its body. Or of his tongue become silent."

"Lord," said Brother Selyf, "there is one fragment of good news that can be salvaged from this tragedy."

"What is that?"

"Cian Brydydd Mawr lives."

Llywelyn looked into the monk's face, as though he was scrutinising him for falsehood. He whispered:

"He is alive?"

"He is wounded almost to the point of death, but living still. We carried him to Clynnog Fawr, we have done what we can for him."

"Thank God, thank God."

Llywelyn made the sign of the cross three times upon his chest.

"Tend him, nurture him. I will give you money, anything you need. If he could only live – then there would be some breath of sweetness in this bitter defeat. Only to hear his voice would give me strength."

"He is weak, Lord, and even should his wound heal, I fear he is not long for this world."

Outside the hall the church bell began to chime for the Eucharist. Llywelyn turned to the door.

"Now, Father Abbot, brothers, it is time for us to go and see what prayer can do."

Dafydd watched Llywelyn and Siwan walk forwards to the altar to take the mass. He saw the chalice lifted to Siwan's lips. He saw how she closed her eyes and swallowed. Then he saw Llywelyn as the chalice was tipped to his mouth. He seized it in both hands. He poured the wine down his throat until there was none left. He gave the empty salver back to the Abbot. He fortified himself with the blood of the Saviour as though it was mead from a drinking horn on the eve of battle.

After the service Dafydd was hurrying to break his fast. There had been no supper the night before. He was ravenously hungry. He was amazed when one of Llywelyn's chamberlains drew him aside.

"My Lord wishes to speak with you. He says you must not fear for your belly, there will be victuals to hand."

He followed the chamberlain to a private chamber. Llywelyn was seated at a table. Beside him was a scribe with pen and parchment. Several men at arms stood behind.

"Sit down."

Dafydd sat. A pitcher of wine, warm bread, salted pork, cheese and apples were set before him. He pushed away the pork.

"Nothing with four legs my Lord."

Llywelyn reached across and broke the bread. He gave half of it to Dafydd.

"Eat!"

They ate together. Llywelyn's eyes watched Dafydd's every movement from hand to mouth with a fierce scrutiny. When they had finished he said:

"You are a lay brother?"

"I am."

"From?"

"I was born at Carnguwch Fawr, close to Llanaelhaearn."

Llywelyn hit the table with the flat of his hand.

"I knew it! When I saw your face and your shit-smirched lay robes I guessed you were a local man. I need your help."

"How can I help you, Lord?"

"King John is no fool. He caught wind of the service my bards were rendering. He knew their loss would wound this kingdom to the heart. He ordered the cursed Earl of Chester to fill a ship with mercenaries. This much I have surmised. But there is a question."

He paused. Dafydd waited for him to continue. The scribe dipped his quill into an inkhorn.

"Nobody could have found the valley at Nant Gwrtheyrn without being shown the way. Someone led the killers. It must have been a man with local knowledge. Do you have any idea who he might have been?"

"Lord, I do, and I have been biting my tongue and waiting for the right moment to tell you his name."

The scribe was scratching at his parchment. Llywelyn was gripping the edge of the table. His knuckles were white.

Dafydd summoned all the courage he could muster.

"Lord, when I have spoken, will you give me your solemn word that you will listen a little longer? There is another matter."

Llywelyn was impatient.

"Yes, yes, in the name of God you have my word. Now," he leaned forwards, "what is the traitor's name?"

"His name is Rhys Drwyndwn from Tan y Graig. Ask any farmer or bondsman in Clynnog Fawr or Llanaelhaearn and he will point him out to you."

Llywelyn was on his feet shouting at his scribe:

"Do you have it down? By Christ!"

He turned to his men at arms.

"Did you hear his name?"

They bowed their heads.

"Yes, Lord."

"Come."

He led them outside and closed the door. Dafydd heard muffled words and the sound of horses' hooves clattering against the stone cobbles of the courtyard. He waited.

Llywelyn returned and sat down. His eyes were hard and blank as stones.

"A broken nose will be the least of it."

He lifted the pitcher of wine and emptied it into his mouth.

Dafydd shuddered.

Llywelyn looked across at him, as though surprised to see him still there.

"You can go back to your psalms now."

The scribe leaned across the table and whispered into Llywelyn's ear.

"Ah yes, forgive me, the other matter – be quick."

"Lord, it concerns Cian Brydydd Mawr."

"What of him?"

"He feels the hand of death closing around his heart. His apprentices are dead. Everything he passed on to them, in the old way, with the breath of his mouth, is lost."

"You do not have to tell me. It wounds me every time I think about it."

"Lord, he has made a request. He has drawn me aside and asked that certain matters be set down on the page, matters that will otherwise die with him and be forgotten. I am a humble lay brother, little more than a bondsman, I can neither read nor write. If these matters are to survive I will need your help."

Llywelyn's attention was suddenly quickened. He reached across the table and seized Dafydd's hand.

"By God you shall have what help I can give. In the past he disdained the written word. Now he must see that the old ways can hold no longer. Do you know what these matters are?"

"Old stories, he says, that he learned many years ago, older than the Saints. My grandfather, when I was a lad, told fragments of such tales on winter nights – Annwn, Bran, Gwydion – I love them to this day."

Llywelyn smiled at an old, cherished memory.

"I too heard them as a boy – and from the bard himself. When Cian Brydydd Mawr had sung his praises at the high table of the hall, he would come through to my mother's chamber. He would don his old mantle of Cyfarwydd and tell the stories of love and enchantment. I can see us now in my mind's eye: my mother and her ladies seated in the firelight with their hands in their laps, the maidservants lingering in the shadows, the chamberlains pretending they had greater matters on their minds, the children spread-eagled on the floor – all spell-bound by the hanging of a mouse."

Dafydd threw back his head and laughed.

"The hanging of a mouse! I had clean forgotten the hanging of the mouse."

Dafydd and Llywelyn looked into one another's faces, something tender passed between them as though all the layers of caste and fortune had been peeled away.

"But will the old poet live?"

Dafydd nodded.

"He will live long enough. I am sure of it."

Then the scribe coughed.

"Lord, there are matters of importance we must attend to."

Llywelyn exploded.

"Importance!"

He slammed his fist on the table.

"Nothing ..."

Tears were running down his cheeks.

"Nothing could be more important than the hanging of a mouse."

After Compline, when the Sub-Prior came to the feasting hall, he was amazed and outraged to see Dafydd sitting at the high table. He took his place beside Brother Selyf, three tables down.

"What is the meaning of this?"

"I think we will find out before the meal is finished."

Dafydd was seated between the Abbot and the Distain. He was only four places from Siwan. On the table before him was a silver goblet filled with wine. He crossed himself and prayed that he should not be distracted by such allures. When the food was served he ate only bread. Behind Llywelyn a harper was playing an old air. Dafydd remembered his mother singing it. Under the table at his feet, dogs were waiting for dropped morsels.

After two courses had been eaten and cleared, pieces of cheese and slices of honeycomb were brought to the table.

Llywelyn leaned forwards. He peered over the rim of his goblet at the Abbot.

"Father, I have a question."

The boom of his voice silenced the hall.

"What is it, Lord?"

"Is there a monk in the scriptorium at Aberconwy who has both a fair hand and a clear memory?"

"That question is better asked of Brother Selyf, who as Cantor oversees the making of manuscripts."

Llywelyn looked across the hall.

"Well?"

Brother Selyf stood.

"There is one monk, Lord, his name is Brother Iago. He is a young man of great devotion. He has but to hear a psalm or scripture and it lodges in his mind as clear as daylight. And he has a most meticulous hand."

"Then Brother Iago will be the man for the work we have in mind. What about vellum and parchment? Are you well supplied?"

Brother Selyf gestured to the high table:

"Our lay brother, Dafydd, is the vellum master. All our manuscripts are made from his hides at Clynnog Fawr."

Llywelyn smiled at Dafydd.

"You! Then that is settled. We will need perhaps one hundred pages."

"The calves are gone, Lord, for King John's tariff," said Dafydd. "There will be no more vellum. But there is no shortage of sheep and goats for parchment."

The Abbot looked at Llywelyn with approving eyes.

"My Lord, am I to understand that you wish to commission a book? A psalter perhaps, or a missal, or the holy gospels? Or a book of the hours for Lady Siwan? We have brothers who are masters at the art of illumination."

"I am commissioning a book and I will pay you handsomely for it."

"God bless you, Lord."

"And this will be the nature of it. When your lay brother here has prepared the parchment pages. And when Cian Brydydd Mawr is grown strong. Then it shall be written."

Llywelyn cast his eyes across the hall.

"Brother Iago will be fetched from Aberconwy and brought to Clynnog Fawr. He will bring his wax tablets, inks and quills. And as the old poet tells the ancient Matter that he holds so dear, the monk shall set it down on the page."

Three tables down the Sub-Prior sucked his breath through his teeth.

He turned to Brother Selyf and whispered:

"So your lay friend has seen fit to betray us. I had a feeling we should not have brought him with us."

Brother Selyf shrugged.

"It is God's will, brother, let it lie."

But the Sub-Prior was already standing.

"Lord, if I may speak?"

Llywelyn opened his hand in a gesture of approval.

"Lord, this Matter to be set on the page – it is hardly the province of the Holy Church."

The Sub-Prior could not mask his distaste.

Brother Selyf whispered:

"Shhhh."

But there was no stopping him.

"It is but a rag-bag of follies, Lord, from the dim days before the Holy Fathers came to these shores. Our brothers in the scriptorium should not be concerning themselves with such matters. Their work, after all, is prayer. If it must be set down then let one of your scriveners put it to the page."

Llywelyn leapt over the high table. The Sub-Prior found himself seized and shaken for the second time.

"How many lands have I gifted to your Cistercian Brotherhood?"

"Many hundreds of acres, Lord."

"And golden vessels, silver plate?"

"You have been most kind."

"And you wish to keep my favour?"

"We do my Lord."

Llywelyn drew him so close that their noses were touching.

"Then write me my book."

He dropped him. The Sub-Prior fell back onto the bench and wiped the spittle from his face.

Llywelyn returned to the High Table.

"What does our Father Abbot have to say on this?"

The Abbot got up to his feet.

"My Lord, while I understand the concern that has been voiced by my brother ..."

Llywelyn growled, the Abbot hurried on:

"... I think he is mistaken. There is after all a precedent across the water in the kingdom of Ireland. Did not our Sainted Patrick, in the golden age of the Christian Fathers, fall into conversation with the son of Fionn McCumhaill? As I remember, it is thanks to Patrick's pen that Ossian's songs and the tales of the Fianna were set down upon the page. Did Ossian not say: 'For the strength of your love, Patrick, do not forsake the great men of old; bring in the Fianna who are unknown to the King of Heaven?' And Patrick, despite his devotions, did not forsake him."

Llywelyn struck the table with his fist.

"Then there can be no more argument."

Three tables down the Sub-Prior shook his head.

Brother Selyf whispered:

"The Dialogue of the Ancients! Hardly a text that would have received the blessing of Saint Benedict."

Sunday August 21st

It was after Compline the following night that Dafydd reached Clynnog Fawr.

It had been a long day's journey from Aberffraw. They had left Llywelyn's Llys after Vigils and had arrived at the Strait when the tide was low. The Sub-Prior had maintained an angry silence. The only time he had addressed Dafydd directly was when they were kneeling on the shingle for the Eucharist after leaving the ferry at the Bay of Foryd.

Brother Selyf, though, held no grudge. As they parted he had said:

"So, friend, no doubt our paths will cross again before long. Make sure there are more pages of parchment waiting for me than Llywelyn's hallowed hundred."

The monks had gone eastwards towards Aberconwy. Dafydd had

trudged westwards, the height of Yr Eifl and its two lesser peaks showing him the way.

When he got home Brother Deiniol was still awake.

"God bless you, Dafydd, you are safely home."

He led him to the refectory and found him bread and hard-boiled eggs.

Dafydd blessed the food and ate in silence.

When it was finished he said:

"The old bard from Nant Gwrtheyrn, how is he faring?"

"He is still in great pain, but he takes food. He sits up sometimes. His wound has begun to close. The boy nurses him like a mother."

"Good. And the cattle got safely to Bangor?"

"All were counted and handed over. There was some trouble on the way home with vagrant soldiers, but beyond one black eye the brothers suffered no great harm."

"Good. And is there any other news?"

"One thing. We had an old woman here today from Tan y Graig. She was beside herself. She had found her son hanging by the neck from an elder tree. She wanted us to bury him here, but I had to tell her that with the Pope's interdict there can be no burials in sacred ground. Besides, it sounded to me as though he had taken his own life."

"What was his name?"

"His name was Rhys. You might have known him. The one they called 'Broken-nose'. Two Brothers went back with the old woman to bury him at Tan y Graig and offer prayers for his soul. When they cut him down they saw that his lips had been sewn together. They cut the threads and opened his mouth. In it was a leather purse. They pulled it out between his teeth. Inside were thirty silver pennies. What do you make of that?"

Dafydd shook his head, shuddered, crossed himself and said nothing.

2

Brother Iago

Monday November 25th

After Eucharist, when he had taken the Mass, the old poet would walk to the sea-shore. He would stand with his hand on Tomos' shoulder and look out across the water. Every day the ritual was the same, whatever the weather.

This day was no exception. The wind was blowing from the sea. The clouds raced above them. He drank in the salty air. His bony fingers tightened on the boy's arm.

"What is it – the blind beast from before the flood?

Without skin, without flesh,

Without bone, without blood,

It is no older and no younger than it was in the beginning.

Who can say no to it – nobody."

"Tell me more."

"Its breath is wide as the lipless world,

It has never been born,

It has never been seen,

It casts no shadow.

Sometimes it is gentle, sometimes it is wild,

Sometimes it sings, sometimes it shouts,

And yet it cannot speak."[14]

Tomos guessed:

"Is it the wind?"

The old man was silent for a while.

"It is the wind."

He sighed.

"It is the wind that every day cuts colder and deeper."

"But you are mending well master."

"I am mending well on borrowed time. And I am ready now. Go to Dafydd ap Dafydd ap Dafydd, tell him that I am ready."

Tomos nodded:

"I understand."

"Tell him that I have not forgotten his promise."

Dafydd was in the stone barn of the Grange. He was sharpening his knife with a whet-stone. Tomos heard the sound before he saw him. When he entered he saw squared wooden frames stacked against the walls. Inside each of them a scraped skin had been stretched tight between taut thongs.

Dafydd saw him. He dropped his knife, reached down and lifted a coiled parchment from the floor.

"Look at this."

He carried it to the doorway. He stretched it between his hands. A veined yellow light shone through it.

"What do you think? It is newly cut."

Tomos touched the smooth, waxy, translucent surface of the parchment.

"It is hard to believe it was once a sheep."

"It was never a sheep, Tomos, it was a goat."

"Even harder."

"Soon it will be cut into pages, lines will be pricked onto it, and then it will be covered with marks that will mean no more to me than the bleatings of the goat it once was."

"Nor to me."

"But still it is a beauty, and these others too, I hope."

He picked up the knife and turned to the second frame.

Tomos reached for his arm.

"I am come from my master. He says that he has not forgotten your promise. He says he is ready now."

"Ah." Dafydd smiled at the boy. "Good. And so am I, or very nearly."

Half to himself he said:

"I will speak to Brother Deiniol. He must send word to Aberconwy. By the time Brother Iago gets here the pages will be cut and pumiced and he can take his pick of them."

Tomos stood and listened.

"What should I tell the old man?"

"Tell him I have not forgotten."

The boy turned and ran through the open doors of the barn. Dafydd watched him until he was out of sight. Then he turned to his frames.

Dafydd's autumn had been consumed by the preparation of parchment. Huge orders had come from Brother Selyf. More than a hundred skins had been steeped in salt and then in lime. All the lay brothers had helped. When the skins had been stretched on their frames they had scraped away the stinking flesh from one side and the wool and hair from the other with their curved knives.

Every day Dafydd had tightened the skins as they dried. And always he'd made sure that, as well as the pages prepared for Brother Selyf, there was parchment enough for Cian Brydydd Mawr.

Everything was ready now. Only the cutting remained.

Tuesday November 26th

Nobody had expected a visit from Llywelyn and Siwan.

The monks were filing out of the church after Lauds when an outrider came to Clynnog Fawr.

"The Court is making a circuit of Gwynedd. Today it crosses the peninsula to Criccieth. Our Lord, being close at hand, has expressed an earnest wish to visit the poet Cian Brydydd Mawr."

Brother Deiniol was thrown into a panic of preparation.

"Fetch bread, cheese, butter, the little winter apples that are sweetening on the racks. Take the old mead from the pot. Throw sheepskins over the wooden seats and carry them to the old man's cell. Sweep it clean. Throw sticks and charcoal onto his fire. Sweeten the smoke with herbs."

The bell was ringing for Eucharist when Llywelyn's Court reached the little monastery. A company of men and women on horseback, a retinue of armed foot soldiers, wooden-wheeled wagons drawn by teams of horses and oxen – all clattered and trundled to a halt on the rough road. Llywelyn turned to his Distain.

"Go ahead to Criccieth. Leave me only five armed horsemen. We will have caught up with you by nightfall."

The court moved on.

Five soldiers tethered their horses at the churchyard gate. They found a place out of the wind and settled themselves for a game of dice. Llywelyn and Siwan rode to the church door. Two lay brothers took their horses. They entered the cold incense-laden shadows. They kissed the stone that covered the bones of Saint Beuno and knelt for mass. It was the first week of Advent.

'Behold the days come, saith the Lord, that I will raise unto David a righteous Branch; and a King shall reign and prosper and shall execute judgement and justice in the earth. Veni ad liberandum nos, Domine, Deus virtutum.'

When Llywelyn entered the old man's cell, Cian Brydydd Mawr dropped to his knees. His voice was thin and tremulous.

"I would praise my Lord with the nine strands of my art,
with the nine-fold awen, with the nine strains of song.
First I'd sing of the wolf of warfare,
second I'd sing of pleasure in his presence,
third I'd sing of his mead-nourished mercy,
fourth I'd sing of his soul's lofty thought,
fifth I'd sing of his fervour, fierce as a falcon,
sixth I'd sing of his lavish lordship,
seventh I'd sing of his gifts of gold,
eighth I'd sing of his deeds of bright daring,
ninth I'd sing of his Saviour's succour.
But long pain, old age and a back thrice snarled,
A nagging wound, a wooden staff, and a thin throttle
Are come between me and my song."[15]

Llywelyn took his hands and kissed them. He lifted the old man to his feet.

"Sit down, old friend, just to hear the sound of your voice is a sweet medicine."

Then Siwan entered. He was on his knees again.

"Siwan – summer-weather-hued
gold at her throat gorse-yellow ..."

Llywelyn lifted him again and laughed.

"Sit down, sit down. There is no need to tire yourself."

The old man sat down and caught his breath.

Brother Pedr entered carrying a board laden with food and drink. He set it by the fire. He poured mead into cups and set the food onto wooden platters. He blessed it.

"Tomos, help our guests. Take their gloves, cloaks, hats. Lay them on the wooden chest over there."

Brother Pedr lifted a bowl of warm scented water.

Llywelyn and Siwan sat down and washed their hands. The meal was served. They ate.

"Good," said Llywelyn. "Now leave us alone."

Brother Pedr crossed himself and hurried out of the cell. The boy stood behind the old man's chair. Llywelyn turned his glittering eyes on him.

"Go. Go! You heard what I said."

Tomos didn't move. The old man smiled at him.

"Go, son."

Tomos made his way slowly towards the door.

"He is a good boy and I owe him my life."

As he was lifting the latch Llywelyn called him:

"Come here."

Tomos crossed the cell and knelt.

Llywelyn pulled a little iron knife from the top of his boot. It had a bone handle carved into the shape of a horse's head.

"This is a gift for you."

Tomos turned it over in his hand. He grinned.

"Thank you, Lord."

Llywelyn ruffled his hair with his hand.

"I look into your face and I see my own son, Gruffydd. Maybe one day you and he will ride side by side."

There was a pause as his thoughts rested on his hostaged son.

"Now listen. There is a lay brother who came to my Llys at Aberffraw some months since. His name I think is ... "

"Dafydd?"

"Yes, Dafydd, fetch him."

Tomos ran to the door.

When he was gone it was Siwan who spoke. Her voice was hushed for fear of being overheard.

"Brydydd Mawr, Great Poet, Cian, you are well again?"

"As well as old age and a deep wound will allow."

"God be praised. I have never forgotten your songs. Nor how, when my father first sent me as bride to this distant place, I listened to your stories and wept – for Branwen and her speckled starling."

The old man nodded.

"There is solace sometimes, my lady, in the mirrors the old tales hold."

"I spoke no Welsh in those early days, my ladies whispered it into French as you were speaking."

"I remember."

She reached for Llywelyn's hand.

"But my husband was no Matholwch, and I have found what I neither expected nor deserved. And when I peer into the mirror now, it is not Branwen, but Rhiannon's face I see."

The old man bowed his head.

"The Great Queen."

"And my father is become Efnisien, Matholwch, Gwydion and all that is hateful and heartless in this world."

Suddenly she was on her knees.

"Forgive me, forgive me, forgive me, I am no longer John's daughter. I am Llywelyn's wife and the Sovereignty of Gwynedd is ours."

She let go of her husband's hand, reached for the old man's and placed it on her belly.

"Once more I am quickened with its seed."

He could feel that she was swollen with child.

"Do not hold me to account for the sufferings my father has brought upon you."

Cian Brydydd Mawr shook his head.

"There have been those who muttered against you, my Lady. I was never one of them."

Llywelyn leaned forwards.

"Great poet. My wife listens to you and the stories hold up a mirror. I listen and I too see myself reflected, first here, then there, in the twists and turns of a tale. Is it not the same for everyone, king and commoner, nobleman and bondman, servant and slave?"

"It is the very same."

"And are not the stories spread across the face of Wales? They do not only take place in Gwynedd – but in Powys, Dyfed, Deheubarth, Ceredigion?"

"Indeed, my Lord."

"So any Welshman, from any kingdom, might look into this mirror and see the image both of himself and of his native land?"

"Yes."

"By God!"

Llywelyn's sword was out, not in anger but in a sudden exhilaration of spirit.

"By God!"

With the point of his sword he drew an outline of the coast of Wales into the hard-trodden clay of the floor, with its two pointed peninsulas and the curve of the Bay of Ceredigion. He made a triangle for the Isle Môn. He looked down at it.

"There is more to this Matter than I had seen."

There was a timid knock at the door.

"Is all well?"

Llywelyn lifted the sword and pushed open the door.

Brother Deiniol was standing outside looking anxious.

"Is all well my Lord?"

"Away!"

He swung his sword.

"Away with you! Everything is well!"

He slammed the door.

"Is there no peace from these damned monks?"

He sat down and rested the point of his sword between his feet.

He looked at Cian Brydydd Mawr.

"The world has changed. Since our defeat in the summer the winds of fortune have begun to blow a different way."

The old man raised his eyebrows.

"Tell me more."

"First comes an envoy from the Vatican bearing a letter from Pope Innocent himself. He tells me that his Interdict is to punish John – and not the enemies of John. He has lifted it. Gwynedd need suffer no longer. Our dead will be buried once more in hallowed ground, and our brides and grooms blessed by the Holy Church."

"That is good news."

"Listen, there is more. After John returned to England with cattle, horses, hawks, hostages and the best part of Gwynedd tucked under his belt, he ordered his men to start building castles. Fourteen of them. In Bala, Treffynnon, Mathrafal, Rhuddlan, Deganwy – the list goes on."

"How is this good news, Lord?"

"Because it is more than the other Princes can stomach. John does not build his castles in Gwynedd only. He is trying to make all Wales quake under his tyranny. Now the turn-coat Lords who sided with him – Gwenwynwyn of Powys, Maelgwm and Rhys Gryg of Deheubarth, Hywel of Merioneth – are changing their tune. They are lining up at my door. They talk about making common cause against the Normans."

"Do you trust them?"

"You have sung in many Courts my friend. As a Pencerdd you have been honoured by princes. In your heart you must know they are as fickle as foxes. But I have, for a long time, had a dream of a Wales that is united under one Lord. If they will offer me their homage, I will lead them to victory. We go to meet them now."

The old man's head was nodding. His eyes were closed.

"We are tiring you."

"No. I am listening, Lord."

"Then, only two days ago, a letter came from the King of France. He has long hated John. He will support a Welsh uprising with money and men. My friend, you will be singing the Unbeiniaeth Cymru for such a muster as Wales has never seen before. When spring comes our swords will be reddened with English blood."

The old poet's voice wavered into song:

"Man's mettle, youth's years,
Swift thick-maned steeds,
Broad leather bucklers,
Glittering grey-blue blades,
Gold-bordered garments,
And a song that will praise
The blood-soaked field
Before the wedding feast."[16]

66

Llywelyn looked hard at him.

"Perhaps you are losing the taste for war?"

"No, but the margin between victory and lament is as narrow as the edge of a blade."

Siwan leaned across and refilled the goblets with mead. She passed one to the old man. His hand was trembling.

Llywelyn drank and set down his goblet.

"All the kingdoms of Wales united, and I, Llywelyn ap Iorweth, will be the keystone in an arch of princes."

"It is a great and noble dream my Lord, but like all dreams it lacks substance."

"One day, Cian Brydydd Mawr, one day it will become as substantial as the ground we stand on."

He cut a little lump of clay from the floor with the end of his sword. He lifted it and rolled it into a ball between his hands. He pressed his thumb into it.

"And when it does, my friend, we will need a mirror that we can look into and see all of Wales reflected: its people, its places, its memories, its creatures, its dreams and follies, its half-forgotten gods.

This Matter of yours will be that mirror. It must never be forgotten."

It had taken Tomos the best part of the morning to find Dafydd.

Now they were hurrying past the church to the old poet's cell.

Tomos knocked.

Siwan opened the door. She lifted a finger to her lips.

"Shhhh. He is sleeping."

They entered. The old man was stretched out on his pallet. His mouth was open, his hands folded on his chest.

Llywelyn was sitting, leaning forwards, his hands folded over the pommel of his sword, staring into the fire. He turned his head as they approached.

Dafydd and Tomos knelt before him.

"Ah, Dafydd the lay brother – so this is your domain?"

"These are the hills I have always known, my Lord."

"Tell me, how fares my book?"

Dafydd nodded to the sleeping figure.

"The old bard is ready, Lord."

"You must be careful. He is frail. A little at a time. And the pages?"

"They are all but cut."

"And the scribe?"

"Word has been sent to Aberconwy. He will be here in three or four days. By the second week of Advent the work will have begun."

"Good."

Llywelyn stood and stamped his feet.

"Very good."

"My Lord ..."

The old poet's voice was thin and clear.

"... there is one more thing."

"What is that?"

Cian Brydydd Mawr was sitting in the bed with his knees drawn up under the blankets.

"I must have a woman."

Llywelyn looked at Siwan. They both smiled.

"A woman?"

"I cannot tell these stories unless I have a woman."

Llywelyn turned to Dafydd.

"Who is the most senior of the brothers who serve here?"

"Brother Deiniol, Lord."

"Fetch him."

Brother Deiniol was brought to the cell. He knelt warily before Llywelyn. His eyes were on the sword that was now safely in its scabbard.

"Can I help you, Lord?"

Llywelyn's face was solemn.

"Brother, your guest has made a request."

"We will do what we can for him, Lord."

"He needs a woman."

Siwan's hand was over her mouth, she was pinching her nose to hold back the laughter.

Brother Deiniol paled.

From the pallet the old man piped.

"She must be a woman of experience, ripe and knowing, if she's had a child or two it would be no disadvantage, not one of your veiled sisters."

Llywelyn put his hand on the monk's shoulder.

"Do you think you could procure him one?"

Siwan could contain herself no longer. Her laughter shrilled out from behind her hand.

The old poet tottered to his feet.

"The woman could sit here." He pointed to Siwan's chair.

"Dafydd ap Dafydd ap Dafydd could sit here."

He pointed to Llywelyn's chair.

"The boy, Tomos, could sit at their feet."

He gestured to the ground.

"And my audience would be balanced and complete."

He came across to Brother Deiniol.

"My Matter, you see, is as much for women's ears as for men's, and without both it cannot be told."

Llywelyn looked first at Siwan, then at the old man. He grinned.

"You will have your woman!"

He curled his fingers around the hilt of his sword and turned smiling to Brother Deiniol.

"See to it."

The monk crossed himself and hurried out of the cell.

"And now we must continue our journey to my castle at Criccieth."

Friday November 29th

Three days later, Brother Iago arrived at Clynnog Fawr. It was late afternoon, that period between None and Vespers when the brothers were finishing the tasks of the day.

The cold rain had not ceased since the first light of morning. Brother Iago was soaked. His white robes sodden and heavy. The rain ran in runnels down his face and neck. Behind him a lay brother led a mud-splattered pack-horse. Strapped to its back was a dripping writing desk and leather bags of varying sizes.

Brother Deiniol met them at the church door.

"Good day to you."

"May God prosper you."

"Come into the refectory, there is a fire there."

Brother Iago followed him.

The lay brother led the pack-horse to the stable.

Brother Iago stood in the flickering light and stretched his hands towards the flames. Steam rose from his woollen robes.

"Every river is risen. The fords will soon be impassable."

"It must have been a hard journey, Brother. A cell has been made ready for you. There are dry robes."

Brother Iago turned his wet, vehement face to Brother Deinol.

"I have no need of dry robes."

"You will sleep in these?"

"Every hour I am kept from sleep is an hour of prayer. Should not our hearts embrace suffering and endure it without weakening or seeking escape?"

"Very well – but we don't want you succumbing to a fever."

"I am never ill."

Brother Deiniol looked at his tall, spare frame, the skin that shone with a young man's strength and certainty.

"So be it."

At Vespers, Brother Iago, his robes still dripping onto the stone floor, sang the psalms and responses without a glance at the open psalters.

Afterwards, when the brothers sat down to their supper, he went to the stables and unfastened his desk from the pack-horse's back.

"It is a Friday. I never eat on a Friday."

The lay brother from Aberconwy turned to Rhodri as they entered the refectory and shrugged.

"He sups on sunshine and rain, like oats and barley in the field."

"Good luck to him. But, as I see it, if our Saviour himself could break bread and pour wine, then where's the harm in it?"

"I'll drink to that."

They clinked their goblets and tipped the small beer down their throats.

Outside in the sloping rain, Brother Iago was carrying the writing desk from the stable to his cell. He went back and fetched the leather bags. He closed the door, lit a candle, loosened the drawstrings and pulled the bags open. One by one he emptied them. He pulled out bundles of clipped goose-feather quills. He set them on the desk. He pulled out jars of ground oak gall, salmortis, gum-arabic, pumice and vinegar. He opened the lids and sniffed.

"Good."

He pulled out knives and a straight rule. He pulled out two ink-horns and set them in the holes that had been cut into the surface of the desk. He pulled out a box of needles and a reel of linen thread. He pulled out boards and clasps and a bound pile of wax tablets. He reached to the bottom of the last bag and found a sharp stylus.

He laid everything on the desk and ordered it with the careful precision of a man setting out the pieces for a game of chess.

When everything was in order he knelt on the hard floor and prayed until the bell rang for Compline.

After the service Brother Iago drew Brother Deiniol aside.

"Brother, I have a question."

"Ask."

"Is there a cell with a lock to its door?"

"No. All cells here are open. Why?"

"I would sooner no-one entered and ..."

He shuddered.

"... interfered with my writing desk or its implements."

"*Your* writing desk?"

"Not mine of course, as it says in the Acts: 'All things should be the common possession of all, so that no-one presumes to call anything his own.' But even so, Brother, these implements are my tools of prayer, like my lips and tongue. Please. I do not want them touched. At Aberconwy the Scriptorium is always locked after Vespers."

"No-one will touch them, Brother, you have my word. Why should they?"

There was a note of panic in Brother Iago's voice.

"But they might. What then?"

Brother Deiniol saw it was time to steer the conversation to other matters.

"Tell me, did our Father Abbot say anything about the nature of the book you are to make?"

"He said it is for our Lord Llywelyn. He said it will ensure his continuing kindness towards our Cistercian Brotherhood. He said I had been chosen because of the confluence in me of a sharp memory and a tidy hand. I am obedient to our Father's will."

"All this is true, but did he say anything of the content of the book?"

"No. But as we were strapping the writing desk to the horse's back the Sub-Prior came out to me. I can remember his words clearly."

"What did he say?"

"He said: 'Do not be beguiled by the work of the Devil, and sprinkle your pages with the name of God as liberally as you would sprinkle an ailing man with holy water.'"

Dafydd had been busy. After Eucharist, when he had broken his fast, he had made his way out of the monastery. He had walked inland, following the track uphill until he came to the little farm at Careg boeth.

The boys had been killing pigs for the winter. Three of them were hanging by their hind trotters from hooks in the stone wall of the house. Their throats had been slit. There were leather buckets under their snouts collecting blood. An old iron cauldron of water was coming to the boil over a fire. Dafydd guessed it was for scouring. The boys were resting in the firelight, sharpening knives.

"Gwyn! Rhys!"

They stood up and grinned.

"Dafydd! Uncle!"

They came forwards to embrace him.

"Wait, lads, wash some of that blood from your fingers first."

They looked at their hands, nodded and stood back from him.

"What brings you up here?"

"I have come to see your mother. How is she managing? How are you all managing?"

Gwyn narrowed his eyes.

"We're doing alright. She's inside measuring oats."

He pointed with his thumb to the buckets of blood.

"For puddings."

Dafydd nodded.

"God bless you."

He pushed open the door of the house.

The byre was to the left, the kitchen to the right. A ladder led up to the loft where the beds were.

"Olwen."

She was scooping oats from a sack into two earthenware bowls.

She dropped the wooden scoop.

"Dafydd!"

She came across to him and put her hands on his brown-robed shoulders.

"You *are* still Dafydd?"

"It was a good enough name for the greatest of our Welsh saints. Why change it?"

"I think of you when I hear the bell. Who would have thought it? Dafydd on his knees with the Holy Brothers."

"Not on my knees for much of the day. I spend more time managing their livestock than I do in prayer."

She smiled.

"No changes there. But you are happy?"

"Since Angharad and the baby died I have forgotten happiness. I am content. The rhythms of their prayer, their hours, their yearly round were first a solace, and then – I don't know, something else began to happen."

"It drew you in?"

Dafydd crossed himself.

"It became more than a comfort. I had visions. I saw Christ Jesu on his cross. His sorrows were mine. My pain was the pain of the fallen world. He was suffering it on my behalf."

"And there was a promise of heaven?"

"There was a hope – but only if I could renounce the Dafydd I once was, leave him behind and cleave to the holy offices I barely understand. Sometimes, Olwen, I dream of angels."

"And have you left the old Dafydd behind?"

"For a little while I thought so, but in these last months I begin to doubt myself. There is a part of me that lies so deep it will not be denied. I am torn in half. And that is why I am come to you today."

He sat down on the wooden bench. She sat beside him. For a while they said nothing. Then Dafydd turned to her.

"But what of you? How are you coping?"

"It was a strange thing," she said, "a brother and sister dying so close together in time. Your Angharad in childbirth, and my dear Iwan in that skirmish on the borders."

She rubbed her eyes.

"Those who returned said it was an honourable death. But that has been small consolation. The boys have taken their father's part and I am proud of them. You saw them I suppose?"

"I did – good lads both, I could see it in their eyes."

"But the work is very hard. Iwan was a taeog, a bondman as you once were. Being widowed for our Lord Llywelyn's cause does not release me from my rents and obligations. And then there is the loneliness."

"I understand."

She got up and poured buttermilk from a jug into two cups. She gave him one.

"Tell me, Dafydd, why have you come here?"

He drank, and then licked the milk from his lips.

"One of the old court bards, Cian Brydydd Mawr, has come to the monastery. He has not long to live."

"The great poet, I have heard of him."

"He has stories in his head that no-one else remembers. His deepest wish is that they should be written down. But the Holy Brothers hold these matters in contempt."

"What stories?"

"Bran, Pryderi, Manawydan, Blodeuedd – that manner of thing."

"Oh, the old, old tales. I heard fragments when I was a girl."

"As have we all. And from the moment the bard first spoke of them they have called to me from deep in the marrow of my bones. I have felt an allegiance to them. I am torn. The old Dafydd will not leave me in peace."

"And *are* they to be written down?"

"Everything is in place. But Cian Brydydd Mawr will not open his mouth until there is a woman listening. That is why I am here. Will you come?"

"Me!"

She stood and tossed her hair back from her forehead.

"How long will he take?"

"He tires. He will tell a little at a time. Then it must be written down. Three months – maybe more."

"Three months!"

She laughed.

"My holy brother-in-law has been away from a working farm for too long. There is hard graft from dawn to dusk. Then, when the candles are lit, the mending and spinning and weaving begin. I have no time for stories."

She picked up her scoop.

"Go back to your psalms."

"Olwen, I know, I know how hard the work is. But listen, I have a plan. Every morning after Lauds, two lay brothers will come here. Good men. When they arrive you will go down to Clynnog Fawr. They will stay until your return. They will do the work of two husbands."

She sat down, put her hand on Dafydd's hand and sighed.

"All tasks but one."

She looked at him from the corners of her eyes.

"But it is a kind offer."

"What do you say? It will be a rest. You will be a lady of the Court, with no demand on your time but to sit and listen."

Suddenly her head was on his shoulder.

"I have not sat like that since ... since I cannot remember ... since I was perhaps five, six years old ... Dafydd ... I am so weary ... so weary."

"Then you will come?"

"I will."

Brother Iago had returned to his cell for his first night at Clynnog Fawr. Brother Deiniol could hear him pushing his desk against the closed door.

Dafydd's whisper came out of the darkness.

"Brother."

Brother Deiniol turned.

"Brother, I have found a woman for the old poet."

Brother Deiniol was glad of the cover of darkness. His heat under the white robes would pass unnoticed.

"Who is she?"

"She is a widow. My dead wife's dead brother's wife."

"That is a little tangled for me, Dafydd, at this late hour. What is her name?"

"Olwen. You will have seen her at the high festivals. The Nativity, Easter, Pentecost, All Souls."

"From the farm at Careg boeth?"

"Yes."

In the darkness Brother Deiniol feared Dafydd could hear his heart pounding.

"I know who she is."

It was late November, but little beads of perspiration were forming on his forehead.

"I have heard her confession once or twice."

Long after midnight Brother Deiniol would be on his knees, praying to be released from the memory of the deep lilt of her voice, her whispered sins, the clear frank blue of her eyes looking into his.

3

Pwyll

Monday December 1st

It had been a weekend of preparation. In the intervals between the offices, Brother Iago had made his ink. He had infused the oak gall with vinegar, mixed it with salmortis and gum-arabic and poured it into his horns. He had ironed his wax tablets with a hot knife until they were smooth. He had inspected Dafydd's parchment, rubbing each page between finger and thumb.

"These are very good. Bring me a paste of milk, flour and egg-white and I will treat them."

"A batter?"

"A thin batter – without yolk."

He had pricked and ruled the first twenty pages and then painted them with the paste.

After Vespers on Sunday, when they sat down to eat, Brother Deinol had said:

"So tomorrow the work begins."

Brother Iago bowed his head.

"It is God's will."

"Rather it is Llywelyn's will. I pray the two are of one accord."

After Lauds on Monday two lay brothers walked up the hill to Careg boeth. Olwen was waiting for them.

In the monastery Dafydd and Tomos followed the old poet to his cell. Chairs had been made ready. They sat down.

There was bread and water. They broke their fast.

The old man's brow had been newly shaved into the bardic tonsure.

There was a rap on the door.

"Come in."

Brother Iago lifted the latch and entered. Under his arm he was carrying a pile of wax tablets. Cian Brydydd Mawr looked him up and down.

"Good day to you."

"May God prosper you."

"You are our scribe?"

"I am."

"Eat some bread or you won't have strength enough to lift a quill, there's no fat to you."

Brother Iago shook his head.

"Not before the Eucharist."

"What is your name?"

"Brother Iago."

"Yes, but what is the name your father gave you?"

"That name I have left behind. My only father is the heavenly one."

"You have the look of a Tewdwr to me, a bastard perhaps, not one of the pure line?"

Brother Iago's anxious eyes darted to left and right as though he had been trapped in a snare. He took a knife from his belt and sharpened his stylus. He looked up and the old man's eyes were still fixed on him.

"Can we begin now?"

Cian Brydydd Mawr shook his head.

"Not until the woman comes."

"The woman? Nobody told me about a woman."

The old poet sang softly to himself:

"I had a girl one day, we were of a single mind,

I had two, their praise be the greater for it,

I had three and four in a bed of fortune,

I had five, all splendid in the whiteness of their flesh,

I had six without concealing sin,

I had seven and an arduous business it was."[17]

He chuckled to himself.

"Nothing can begin without a woman."

Brother Iago crossed himself and ran out of the cell.

He found Brother Deiniol.

"There is to be a woman, Brother, it goes against all the rules and ordinances of Saint Benedict."

Brother Deiniol led him back to the old man's cell.

"Think of the Desert Fathers, the temptations of Saint Anthony. Do not be beguiled or led astray. Look on it as an ordeal to be overcome."

He opened the door and gently pushed Brother Iago back inside.

The old man looked up at him and smiled.

"I'm remembering now, old Rhys of the Tewdwr line, when he was white as hoar-frost and in his dotage, bedded a fish-wife from Ceredigion. She bore him twins."

Brother Iago closed his eyes and prayed softly to himself.

When Olwen entered the cell the old man got shakily to his feet.

He breathed in through his nose as though a new air had entered with her.

"God be praised you are here and we can start."

She was wearing a dress of blue-dyed wool. It had been lifted through a leather belt at her waist so that it wouldn't drag in the mud. Over her shoulders she wore her only cloak. It was splattered with mud and grease from long usage. On her feet were wooden pattens. Her dark hair had been plaited and fell between her shoulders.

Cian Brydydd Mawr looked at her approvingly, her strong arms and shoulders, the full breasts and hips beneath her woollen dress.

"Please sit down."

She took off her cloak and threw it onto the chest. She looked at the gathered company.

"Good day to you all."

Dafydd showed her a chair. She kissed his cheek and sat down.

Brother Iago's eyes were fixed on the unscratched yellow surface of his wax tablet.

The old man said:

"Your name is Olwen?"

"It is."

"From?"

"Careg boeth."

"Ah, then you must be Iwan's wife, who fell on the banks of the Dyfi."

"I am. How did you know?"

The old man smiled and shook his head.

"It has been sung many times before. I will sing it again."

His voice was thin and gentle.

"Thoughts come in throngs,
my mind is mournful
and my breath faint,
I think of the man,
the noble stag
who once I loved,
who gave his life for a lord's sake."[18]

Olwen went across to the old man. She took his hand and pressed it to her lips. She looked into his eyes and he could see her deep-buried grief.

"Thank you." She said. "Thank you."

She sat down again.

Cian Brydydd Mawr looked at his audience and cleared his throat.

"This is the Matter, as I heard it from old Meilyr many years ago, and as I have told it since."

He turned to Brother Iago. His wax tablet was on his knee and his stylus in his hand.

"You are ready, Iago ap Rhys?"

Brother Iago did not lift his head. His voice was little more than a whisper.

"Speak. I will not forget. The tablets are merely for notes and names."

The old poet began.

"This Matter of mine begins far to the south of Gwynedd, south of Powys, south even of Deheubarth."

"If I could sing, I would sing of Pwyll, lord over the seven cantrefs of Dyfed.

I can see him before me now, my friends, as clearly as I see you sitting here."

The old man closed his eyes.

"It is – as it is today – that chill season between Samhain and Midwinter.

The trees are rimed with frost and the rusty bracken bows and bends. A red sun has risen above the bitter mist. The last yellow leaves of the oaks are steaming in the cold air. The reeds are broken at the lake's edge.

Pwyll has left his fire and the fragrant steam of the cauldron on its hook. He has turned his back on his Court at Arberth.

His heart is yearning for the hunt."

Cian Brydydd Mawr opened his eyes and smiled.

"Just as it is for our Lord Llywelyn, the hunt is Pwyll's delight. He knows the antlered stags will be belling, the dappled hinds and their speckled fawns will be deep in the bramble thickets of Glyn Cuch. Their scent will be strong on the hard white ground and among the fallen leaves.

He has slept one night at Pen Llwyn Diarwya.

He has made a muster of his huntsmen and hounds.

Now the air is thick with the blaring of horns, the barking of dogs, the stamping of hooves, the shouting of men, the creaking of saddles and the rattling of arrows in their leather quivers."

The old man was on his feet. He was staring at his audience as though he could see a vision beyond them. His voice was almost a shout.

"Do you see them?"

Tomos nodded vigorously. Dafydd answered gently:

"Yes, we see."

"Let me sing of Pwyll as the hunt rides out. His four-cornered cloak is billowing behind him. At his shoulder is a clasp of knotted gold. His grey-headed, sturdy-legged, hollow-hoofed mare kicks the hard clods above her head like swallows. Before him run his spotted, white-breasted hunting hounds, keen as the wind, nosing the ground as they bound ahead.

But now, listen, their song has changed.

His dogs are singing with one voice.

The ground is sweet with the scent of stag.

They are away."

The old man lifted his arm and pointed urgently ahead. Then he sat down and caught his breath.

"Headlong, through thicket and thorn, Pwyll's dogs were running with one shared mind, with one shared purpose.

Pwyll reined his horse around and followed them, bruising the steed's grey flanks with his spurs until the cold air flattened his red beard against his throat.

The dogs hurled themselves through the wooded slopes of Glyn Cuch, between oak and ash, between alder, rowan, willow and sallow, through bracken and heather, with Pwyll as close behind on the grey mare as tongue is to thought.

All of his huntsmen were left behind.

The dogs followed the scent and Pwyll followed the dogs until the winter sun had reached its low noon height."

The old man lifted his hand to his ear.

"Then he heard something.

The music of his hounds was mingling with another music. There were other dogs. Somewhere close at hand they too were singing like pipes with the rapture of the chase.

They came to a clearing that the sun's heat had not reached.

Tall tattered oaks surrounded it on all sides.

The grass was stiff and ribbed with white frost.

In the middle, beside a spring, stood a ten-tined stag.

His nostrils were flecked with foam. He snorted and swung his antlered head from side to side. He scraped at the hard ground with his hooves.

Pwyll lifted his horn to his lips and blew.

He urged his spotted hounds to the kill.

But they were hanging back.

Some were whimpering as though they had been struck with a huntsman's leather whip, others curled back their lips and snarled. Not one would run forward to bring the stag down.

And all the time the other music was growing louder.

Then he saw them.

Out of the undergrowth, between the trunks of the oaks, the other dogs came.

They were hounds of a kind Pwyll had never seen before. Each was the size of a wolf, each was furred as white as new-fallen snow, each had ears as red as heart's blood.

One grabbed a hind leg in the trap of its jaws. Another caught a foreleg. The great stag stumbled. The pack poured onto him. Three were hanging from his throat. A dozen were tearing open his belly. The antlered head swayed and sank into the baying clamour.

Still Pwyll's dogs hung back.

They ignored their master's urgent command.

He lost all patience.

He leapt down from the saddle. He seized a broken branch and strode to the fallen beast. He swung it from side to side, driving the dogs from their kill. He beat their backs. He tore their muzzles from the meat. He kicked their hindquarters. He shouted at them until they skulked away from the dripping carcass.

Then he called his own dogs.

They crept forwards with tails curled between legs.

First they licked. Then, grown bolder, they worried the torn skin. They chewed the warm sinew and muscle. Drunk with blood, they buried their muzzles in the steaming gore.

But look. Can you see?

They are being watched.

In the shadows behind the trees a figure is sitting astride a stallion, silent as stone.

The mare sees him. She whimpers with alarm.

Man and stallion watch Pwyll's dogs. They are still as an image carved from grey rock, still as an owl in its hollow."

Cian Brydydd Mawr lifted a cup to his lips and drank.

"The stranger flicked his reins. His stallion stepped silently into the clearing. Like the hounds, it was white with red ears, and as the whiteness of its body shone, so did the redness of its ears glisten.

The man was dressed in hunting garb of grey. His horn was slung about his neck. The fineness of cloth and cut suggested royal blood.

He dismounted.

He stood two spans taller than Pwyll.

His eyes shone golden-brown. They were fixed with solemn gravity on the ravening dogs.

Then without turning his head he spoke:

'Chieftain, I know who you are, and yet I will not greet you.'

Pwyll looked the stranger up and down.

'Perhaps your rank does not require that you should greet me.'

And now the man turned his eyes on Pwyll:

'It is not my rank that prevents me.'

'Then what is it?'

'It is the ignorance of your mind, the discourtesy of your heart and the blunt hardness of your hand.'

Pwyll opened his hands.

'These are my lands to hunt as I please. What fault have you found in me?'

'As great a fault as I have ever witnessed in all the race of man. To drive off the pack that killed the stag, and then to feed your own pack upon it. That was discourtesy indeed.'

The stranger paused.

'I shall not take revenge, but I will be avenged. I will order my bards to make such withering satires that you will be shamed to the value of a thousand stags.'

Pwyll began to tremble.

'Lord, if I have committed a wrong, then I will make peace with you. But I do not know who you are. Tell me, what rank do you hold?'

'I am a crowned king in the country that I come from.'

Pwyll dropped to his knees.

'Lord, tell me, what country is that?'

'Annwn – I am Arawn, King of Annwn.'[19]

Brother Iago put down his stylus and crossed himself. The old man nodded to him.

"See how, just as our Brother blanches, the blood drains from Pwyll's features. Even the thick red curling beard of his face seems to pale. His eyes clench as tight as fists. As you will know, my friends, the cost of offending the denizens of the Other World is always high. And it is the king of that realm that Pwyll has angered."

As though he was in the clearing himself, Cian Brydydd Mawr dropped to his bony knees on the floor of the cell.

'Lord, how shall I make peace with you?'

For the first time, Arawn smiled.

'Here is how. I have an enemy. He makes war upon my people continually. His name is Hafgan. If you could deliver me from his oppression then there would be peace and friendship between us.'

Pwyll drew his dagger from his belt.

'I will kill him gladly, but tell me, how can it be accomplished?'

'Listen. He is protected by spells. There is only one way that he can die. He must be struck once – once and once only – by the hand of one of the race of men. And he must be struck as he stands waist deep in the ford that separates his realm from mine.'

Arawn reached beneath his grey tunic and drew out a wand of rowan.

'Here is how his death will be accomplished. I will make a strong bond between us. You and I will exchange shapes, so that you will have my appearance and I shall have yours. You will return to my kingdom and no-one, neither huntsman nor servant, neither bondman nor chamberlain, neither horse nor hound, shall know that you are not I. My own wife, the fairest woman you will ever set eyes upon, will invite you to bed each night and will sleep, unknowing, in your arms. For one full year you will be the King of Annwn. And when that year is over we shall meet again in this place.'

Pwyll knew he had little choice.

'How shall I find your enemy?'

'I am to meet him in a year's time at the ford. He will not know that you are not me. He will demand single combat. Give him one single blow. However he pleads with you to strike again you must ignore him. The second blow will revive him as surely as the first will lay him low.'

'And what will happen to my kingdom while I am away?'

'Not a man nor a woman in Dyfed shall know that I am not you. I will rule in your place.'

Arawn lifted his wand above his shoulder and struck him.

In that moment Pwyll felt strangely changed.

He looked down and saw that he was dressed from head to foot in grey.

He turned to the stranger and saw himself, red bearded and mantled.

Arawn's white stallion pressed its nose to his neck. He climbed onto its back and whistled. The white hounds lifted their red ears and came running to him.

The stranger – who was himself – lifted his arm and pointed.

'Your path will be smooth and nothing will hinder you.'

Pwyll saw that the frosty clearing bordered a land he had never seen before.

There were woods and green fields. Long-horned cattle were grazing and the trees were heavy with blossom and fruit. The sun was shining on a world that was at once both spring and fruitful summer.

'Over there is my court. This realm will be in your power. There will be no-one who will not recognise and welcome you. Watch and listen, you will quickly learn the customs of my country.'

Pwyll turned his back on himself and rode into Annwn.

He galloped across the green fields. His horn swung from his neck and his dogs ran behind.

He came to the court. Each doorway was carved and decorated with red gold and white silver. There were sleeping quarters, chambers and a feasting hall thatched with reed.

A groom led his horse to the stables.

He strode into the hall.

Seven boys ran forwards to remove his hunting gear and pull off his boots.

Two chamberlains dressed him in bright silks woven with golden thread. He settled on a throne and watched as the fires were lit and a company of warriors – the best equipped he had ever seen – laid down their weapons and took their places at a long table.

Dish by dish, food was carried into the hall. Each dish smelt sweeter than the one before.

Then the women entered.

Pwyll's eyes were dazzled by their beauty. They washed their hands and sat down.

Then came Arawn's queen. As the full moon overwhelms and pales the stars, so she outshone all the others.

She took his hand and led him to a carved seat at the head of the table."

Cian Brydydd Mawr paused. He looked directly at Olwen and Dafydd.

"See how the company sits at the table."

He gestured to Olwen:

"Pwyll has the queen to his left hand."

And then to Dafydd:

"To his right some chieftain among the noblemen of that country."

He lifted his fingers and smacked his lips.

"And the food! It is fragrant and subtle to the tongue. The drink is strong and sweet. The platters are of jewelled gold. At his shoulder a harper is playing airs of exquisite joy.

See how Pwyll turns to the queen and she smiles. Soon they are deep in talk. Her breath is sweet as honey as she leans to whisper in his ear. She is as eloquent in her conversation as she is fine of feature.

And when the food is cleared away, when bellies are full and heads are light with drinking, hear how the company sings, their voices clear and true as daylight."

The old man sighed.

"It seemed to Pwyll that he had entered a place of unimaginable delight.

And that, my friends, wasn't the end of it.

When the songs were over, the queen reached across and seized his hand. She stood up and drew him to his feet.

She led him out of the hall and across the compound to a bedchamber. With deft fingers she unfastened his clothes. She loosened her ribbons and shook off her dress. She drew back the white linen coverlet of the bed and lay down.

He found himself climbing in beside her.

She took his hand and pressed it to her breast, he could feel her red nipple hard against his thumb. She brushed her mouth against his. She slid her other hand down over his belly."

Outside, the midday bell began to ring for Sext. The old man fell silent. He looked at his audience.

"Ah. So now some of us must go to prayer, some must eat, and I must sleep. Give me two sweet hours to rest my head. Come back after None and I will tell you what happened to Pwyll, Lord of Dyfed, during his sojourn in the Kingdom of Annwn."

He went across to his pallet and lay down. Tomos drew up a blanket and tucked it under his chin.

Olwen turned to Dafydd and smiled.

"I too feel as though I am trespassing in some forbidden realm. Is there a place where a woman can sit and eat without causing offence to one or other of the Holy Brothers?"

"Come with me. The food store will do as well as any. Help yourself to apples from the rack. They are wrinkled and sweet."

Brother Iago woke with a start from the dream of the story. The words were still ringing in his ears. He shuddered and crossed himself several times. He put down his wax tablet, hurried out of the cell and knelt for the Sext psalms:

'Mountains and hills shall be levelled; crooked paths shall be made straight, and rough ways smooth. Come Lord and delay not, alleluia.'

Two hours later they were back.

Cian Brydydd Mawr leaned forwards in his seat.

"You will not have forgotten, friends, how Pwyll felt the hand of Arawn's wife sliding down his belly."

Olwen shook her head and laughed.

"We have not."

The old man fixed his eyes on Brother Iago.

"Slowly she ran her fingers through the thickening hair of his groin."

The young monk blushed and, in his thoughts, uttered an urgent prayer.

The old poet paused.

"And in that moment, Brother, you will be relieved to hear that Pwyll, Lord of Dyfed, remembered where he was.

The events of the day came flooding back to him.

He saw himself driving the red-eared hounds from their quarry.

He saw his own dogs feasting on another man's prize.

He saw Arawn, King of Annwn, silent among the leafy shadows.

He shuddered and rolled over.

He turned his back on her.

He lay with his face to the edge of the bed.

He closed his eyes and slept.

And so the time passed.

Days became weeks and weeks became months.

In the daytime there was affection and tender conversation between them. But at night not a word was spoken. There was neither gesture nor touch. It was as though he had laid a sharp sword of polished iron between his body and hers.

The days were spent in a dream of hunting and feasting, of drinking and song. The land was held in a season of endless summer. Joyful swallows darted in the sky and their brisk music encircled every hill. Pwyll was caught in a whirl of enchantment.

And every night he slept with his face to the wall.

And then the allotted day came.

The chief noblemen woke him from his sleep. Chamberlains brought his spear and shield, his sword, axe, bow and sharp-tipped arrows. The seven boys dressed him for battle.

The white stallion was waiting for him, saddled and bridled, its blood-red ears quick to every sound. He put his foot to the stirrup and swung onto its back.

With chieftains to one side and noblemen to the other, the King of Annwn rode to the ford at the kingdom's margin."

Cian Brydydd Mawr stood.

"See how, on the far side of the water, Hafgan watches and waits.

His hand is tight on the hilt of his sword. His feet set a little apart on the green turf of the riverbank. Each muscle of his body is coiled, poised and knotted with the promise of victory. He is sinewed as an old tree, twisted with limbs of ancient strength. The shield on his arm is bronze-bossed, fashioned from nine layers of hardened ox-hide. Behind him his iron-grey warriors eye the approaching company."

He sat down again and caught his breath.

"The King of Annwn reined in his horse and dismounted.

One of Hafgan's warriors spoke:

'Listen and listen well. This confrontation is between two kings. One stakes a claim to the other's territory. The dispute should be settled in the old and honoured way, one king against the other. We should stand aside and leave the fighting to Arawn and Hafgan.'

The King of Annwn bowed his head.

'So be it.'

Hafgan smiled grimly to himself. He drew his sword and waded into the water. He waited for his enemy.

Look!

The King of Annwn has stepped into the river to meet him. He is calf-deep, thigh-deep, waist-deep in the churning ford. The two kings circle one another, each a hand's breadth beyond the reach of the other's blade. Their eyes are locked in a cold courtship.

There was a flash.

A sudden lunge, bright as a kingfisher's flight.

A lifted sword caught the light and buried itself in flesh.

A shattered shield drifted downstream. The river billowed red with blood.

Hafgan doubled into the water, then lifted his dripping head. Incredulity mingled with mortal pain in his staring eyes.

Crimsoned water gushed from his mouth.

'Arawn, King of Annwn – if it is truly him – has no right to my death.'

His eyes fixed on the face of his enemy.

'But I beg you, since you have begun, then finish. Strike me again, and this time kill me.'

But the King of Annwn shook his head.

'Find someone else. I will not touch you.'

Hafgan groaned and turned to his warriors.

'Then carry me away from here. My death is now a certainty.'

The King of Annwn turned.

He waded back to the riverbank. One of his noblemen spoke:

'Mighty Arawn! You rule all the realms of Annwn now! There is no king but you.'

He nodded.

'Ride out across Hafgan's kingdom. Receive everyone who bows to my kingship with gentleness. But force into submission with the sharp edges of your swords anyone who defies my rule.'

And so his noblemen and warriors struck spurs to the flanks of their horses and rode out. By noon of the next day both kingdoms were under his command.

Now it was time for Pwyll to return home.

In the shape of the King of Annwn he rode across the green fields and woodlands until he saw a strange sight. In the heart of the fresh-leafed forest there was a clearing that was white with frost. It was circled by winter oaks clinging to the last yellow tatters of their leaves.

There was a well-spring rimed with ice.

He rode between the trees and felt a sudden chill.

When he looked over his shoulder Annwn had vanished.

He was surrounded on all sides by grey winter.

He dismounted.

At his feet were the bleached white bones of a stag.

He touched his cheek and found the familiar tangle of his red beard.

Ahead of him Arawn was approaching, dressed in grey.

He was leading Pwyll's mare.

He put his hand to Pwyll's shoulder.

'May you be repaid a hundredfold for your friendship. I have already heard rumours of it.'

Arawn turned the antlered skull with his foot.

'I give you my word. All that was broken between us is now mended.'

He handed Pwyll his horse and lovingly took the reins of his own.

Each king mounted and rode through the trees to his own kingdom.

This was how it fared for Arawn.

When he returned to his court his heart soared with delight to see his retinue coming forwards to meet him. They showed no surprise and treated him with an easy deference, as though this was just one in the familiar procession of days.

When food had been brought to the table his wife sat beside him.

His blood quickened. He took her hand and pressed it to his lips.

She showed no great delight at the sight of him.

Indeed, she seemed to Arawn to have cooled in her manner towards him, though her talk was lively enough.

The evening passed in conversation and carousal until the moon was high and the hour had been reached that is more suited to sleep than to song.

They retired to their bedchamber.

They undressed and climbed between the linen sheets.

She was amazed to find herself lying against him, belly to belly, her cheek resting inside the soft crook of his arm.

For a while they talked. She felt his mouth against hers, his hand to the small of her back.

She eased herself around him and they took their urgent pleasure of one another.

And now see how Arawn sleeps.

He is lying on his side, his hand rests on her belly, his nose is to her shoulder, his bent knees to the backs of her knees.

But she does not sleep.

She is lying on her back beneath the soft furs and coverlets, staring up at the dark rafters of the roof.

The candle has not been blown out.

One flickering thought is chasing another through her mind.

He opens his eyes.

'Sleep.'

She does not answer.

When he wakes again he says:

'Blow out the candle and sleep.'

She does not answer.

The third time he reaches for the candle and blows out the flame himself.

Still she says nothing.

He whispers into her ear:

'What is the matter? Why won't you answer me?'

She turns to him.

'Maybe because I am not used to talking. You and I have spoken more in this bed tonight than we have spoken in a full year.'

'How can that be? We have always talked.'

'You know as well as I that for the last twelve months, from the moment we have lain down and gathered the bedclothes about ourselves, there has been neither conversation nor pleasure between us. You have not even faced me – let alone anything more than that – the only firmness you have shown me has been the hard bone of your back. You have never spoken a word.'

Arawn was thinking.

'I have found a unique friend in Pwyll, King of Dyfed, one of the race of men who is truly to be trusted.'

He said to his wife:

'My lady, I swear I am not to blame. It is a full year since I last slept with you.'

She sat up in bed. The blow she gave him sent the little birds that had been sleeping under the thatch skittering up into the night sky. It woke the bleary-eyed chamberlain who had been dozing outside the door of the royal bedchamber."

Olwen chuckled to herself.

"And I would have done the same, by God!"

"Arawn lifted his hand to the side of his head.

'There is a story to be told.'

'Then you had better tell it!'

He told of all that had happened between himself and Pwyll.

His wife shook her head.

'You must have had a strong hold over this king of the race of men, for him to fight away the lures of the flesh.'

'These are my thoughts.'

She lifted a glowing ember from the fire and rekindled the wick of the candle. She peered into his eyes.

'And how did _you_ fare? Does Pwyll of Dyfed have a wife?'

He returned her gaze.

'He is unmarried. For a full year I have slept with the empty air in my arms.'

She smiled and settled back down beside him. She pressed her mouth to his ear and whispered:

'Then maybe we should repay him for his courtesy.'

The old man looked at his audience. He was tired now and his voice was little more than a whisper:

"And you will be wondering about Pwyll?"

They nodded.

"When he returned to his court at Arberth he was curious to know how his kingdom had fared.

He called together his noblemen.

'Tell me,' he said, 'how well would you say I have ruled over this realm in the last year? Have things gone better for you, or worse?'

His noblemen replied:

'Lord, it has been as though you had cast aside your old hot-headed ways. You have ruled us with discernment and wisdom. In manner you have been amiable. Your generosity has been unbounded and you have been eager and ready to share all that you have gained. Your kingdom has prospered as never before.'

Pwyll bowed his head.

'It is not me that you should thank.'

He told them the story of all that had happened between himself and Arawn, King of Annwn.

When his story was finished a great silence fell upon his noblemen. Then one of them spoke:

'Lord, now that you have returned, we hope and trust you will continue to rule in the same manner.'

'You have my word.'

And so a bond of friendship was established between this world and the Other World, between Pwyll, King of Dyfed, and Arawn, King of Annwn. They would meet at the boundary places and exchange gifts: horses, hunting dogs and speckled hawks. They would present one another with treasures of fine-wrought gold and pale silver. Whatever one king thought would delight the eye of the other was freely given and gladly received.

Because of this concord and colloquy between the worlds, the people of Dyfed honoured Pwyll with a new title; they called him 'Pwyll of Annwn'.

But of all the gifts of Arawn and his queen, the greatest was yet to come."

Cian Brydydd Mawr settled back in his chair. His face was ashen with exhaustion.

"That is enough. No more."

His audience stood and stretched They stamped the blood back into their feet. Brother Iago gathered up his wax tablets. Three of them were marked as though birds had scratched and trodden the mud at a stream's margin. The old man looked at him.

"How long to set it on the page?"

The monk's face seemed for a moment to have become young and clear, as though he had allowed himself to forget, for a little while, the harsh demands of his devotions. Then, all at once, he was clouded again with piety.

"With God's grace I will need a full week, maybe more."

"We will meet again in nine days, on Wednesday, in the third week of Advent."

He waved his arm.

"Leave me alone now."

Olwen picked up her cloak and lingered in the doorway.

"I, for one, will be counting the days."

Tuesday December 2nd

Dafydd peered into Brother Iago's cell. He had set his desk in the doorway to get as much of the cold clear winter light as he could.

In his left hand he held a knife to hold the parchment flat and steady, in his right was the quill. He was bowed over a page. Already it was half covered with orderly black script, the letters ranked and clustered like warriors advancing on a field of battle.

Dafydd watched him for a while.

"These letters make no sense to me. But you know that our Lord Llywelyn will understand them. He will expect every word to read true."

Brother Iago stopped to sharpen his quill.

"I am writing it down as I heard it."

He dipped his pen into the inkhorn.

"And once it is written I am praying to forget it. The old man's words fasten on me like a succubus and give me no peace."

Dafydd turned from him and walked away.

"They'll do you no harm lad."

After None he returned with the boy Tomos. Several pages were covered now. The light was beginning to fade. He watched the scratching point of the pen leaving its trail of mysterious marks.

He leaned over the desk.

"Read me that."

He pointed to the middle of a page.

Brother Iago looked at it and read aloud:

"Of all the hunting dogs he had seen in the world, he had never seen dogs the colour of these. Glittering white were their bodies, and their ears were red."

Dafydd shook his head in wonder.

"It is one thing to hear the Latin words spelled into speech. But this is my own native tongue. The old man's living breath is held fast on the page."

Tomos said:

"When he dies, surely the ink will fade away? All will be gone?"

"No. The ink will stay."

Brother Iago put down his quill.

"Just as the words of Christ Jesu are held between the boards of the Gospels, and the songs of David in any Book of Psalms."

Dafydd crossed himself.

Wednesday December 10th

The company gathered as before in the old man's cell.

Cian Brydydd Mawr rocked backwards and forwards in his seat as though he was trying to fill his body with the rhythm he needed to tell his story. When he spoke his voice was trembling on the edge of song.

"If I could sing, I would sing of Pwyll, lord over the seven cantrefs of Dyfed, I would sing of Pwyll of Annwn as he sat at a feast in his court at Arberth.

Three circling years had passed since he had swapped shapes with Arawn.

Now he was sitting at the head of the high table. It was high noon.

His twisted torc of yellow gold was bright about his throat.

The black iron cauldrons were bubbling over the flames of the fires. The steam was rich with the savoury scent of venison.

The tables were piled with bread, sweetened oatcakes, honeycombs, cheese, nuts and eggs. There were jugs and flagons of ale and strong mead.

A company had gathered to enjoy the generosity of their king.

Men and women of high rank were dressed in woven plaid and linen, fur and dyed leather. Like birdsong in the woods at dawn when spring is turning to bright summer, the hall echoed with the shrills and the deeps of their talk.

Pwyll raised a hand.

His servants dipped ladles into cauldrons and filled the wooden dishes with steaming stew. Frothing jugs were emptied into cups.

Horn spoons were lifted to lips.

Talk quietened.

When the cauldrons had been scraped clean and the jugs of

mead had been emptied, refilled and emptied again, Pwyll stood up.

He was unsteady on his feet.

He turned to one of his noblemen, Pendaran Dyfed.

'It has come into my mind that I should like to walk out into the fresh air and climb to the top of Gorsedd Arberth.'[20]

Pendaran Dyfed placed his broad hand on Pwyll's shoulder. He laid such a force of weight upon it that the king was obliged to sit down again.

'My Lord, you know what is said of that place. Any man of noble birth who sits at its summit shall not leave without suffering an injury or seeing a marvel.'

Pwyll's eyes blazed with anger.

'Who am I?'

'You are my King and Lord.'

'Tell me more.'

'You rule over the seven cantrefs of Dyfed.'

'Tell me more.'

'You are Pwyll of Annwn ...'

'... who has ruled the Other World, who has defeated Hafgan, who has no fear of injury and who craves with all his heart to see a marvel.'

He shook off the hand and stood again.

'I will climb the hill of Arberth!'

He gestured to the company.

'And you will come with me, for what is there for me to fear in the midst of such a host as this?'

His noblemen eyed one another.

Their Lord, in his cups, had become the hot-headed Pwyll of old. There could be no crossing him or holding him back from his purpose.

Look.

Can you see the company as it climbs the path that spirals up and around the green slope of the breasted hill?

Pwyll strides ahead, the air filling his cloak like a sail.

He is eager for wonders.

Behind him his company follow, one behind the other, a reluctant procession, their thoughts on the fires of the hall and the comforts of the feast.

Above them a cairn of lichened stones marks the summit of the hill. Below them the lazy white smoke drifts through the thatch of the halls of Arberth.

Pwyll was the first to reach the height of Gorsedd Arberth.

He clambered up onto the cairn. He settled himself on a flat stone.

He gathered his cloak about himself and waited, his eyes scanning the fields and forests and hills, the distant huts and farmsteads, the looped rim of the horizon that marked the borders of his realm.

His noblemen and their wives sat on the grass below him and grumbled.

Hour followed hour, the sun began to sink in the sky.

And then they saw, on the highway that curved past the foot of the hill, there was a woman on horseback.

She was approaching Gorsedd Arberth at a gentle, steady pace.

Pwyll rubbed his eyes and looked again.

She was riding a white horse. Its ears were red as blood. She was dressed in a garment of glittering gold and silk brocade.

For a moment he thought she was Arawn's wife ... but no, her bearing, her flaxen hair, her height were all quite other.

Even though he could barely see her face, there was no doubt in his mind that she was the Queen of Annwn's equal in beauty.

Pwyll was transfixed. Above her head, it seemed to him, there were three birds circling. The song they sang was of love.

He leapt to his feet. The company stood and stared. Everyone was watching her, enchanted by her strange glamour.

His question broke the spell.

'Is there any one of you who knows who this woman is?'

They shook their heads.

'No, Lord.'

Pwyll turned to the youngest of them.

'Run! Run down the hill and meet her. You will catch up with her easily. Ask her who she is.'

The youth turned on his heel and set off headlong down the hill, leaping over the grassy tussocks. When he came to the highway she was just a little ahead of him.

He ran to catch up with her, but she was still ahead of him. He sprinted with all the speed his legs could muster, and she was ahead of him by the same margin, her pace gentle, unhurried.

The youth turned back, he climbed the hill. He was gasping for breath, red-faced with exertion.

'Lord,' he said, 'no-one in the wide world will catch up with her on foot.'

Pwyll nodded.

'There is some magic at work here. It is time to go back to the court. Tomorrow we will return to Gorsedd Arberth – and we will bring a swift horse.'

The next day came.

When the feast was finished and the wooden platters had been pushed away, Pwyll called one of his grooms.

'Go out into the field and choose the fastest of my horses. Make it ready for riding.'

When the groom returned, leading the horse by the reins, Pwyll and all the company were waiting. They made their way to the foot of Gorsedd Arberth. They sat on the grass behind a clump of hawthorn trees that hid them from the road. They tied the horse, bitted and bridled, to a post. Pwyll spoke to the groom.

'If the woman comes again, let her pass and then ride after her. Find out who she is.'

Hour followed hour.

They waited.

Then they heard the sound of hollow hooves clattering against the stones of the highway. They peered through the green leaves. They could see her trotting towards them at the same easy pace.

Pwyll's heart was pierced by her presence.

He nodded. The groom climbed up into the saddle. He lowered himself against the horse's neck to keep out of sight.

She rode past. She was so close they could hear the rustling of her skirts.

The groom straightened himself. He put his horse into an amble, thinking that even at such a steady pace he would easily overtake her. But when he came to the highway she was already well ahead of him and riding no faster than before.

So he gave his horse the reins, and though the woman's pace remained gentle he could get no closer.

So he pricked the horse with his spurs. He urged it to a full gallop. He slapped it hard with the flat of his hand. The horse was straining and frothing at the lips. The rider stood on his stirrups, the air raced into his face, but still he came no closer.

The woman trotted ahead at an easy saunter.

The faster he rode the further ahead she seemed to be.

At last he reined in the horse and turned it round. He rode back to Pwyll.

'Lord, the horse can do no more than you have seen.'

'I have seen,' said Pwyll, 'and maybe it is beyond the skill of any horseman to catch up with her. But I feel in my bones that she is here for a purpose. Tomorrow I will follow her myself.'

The next day came.

Pwyll's groom led his master's mare from her stable, stamping and steaming and champing at the bit. Pwyll fitted his golden spurs to his heels and took his whip down from its hook.

They came to Gorsedd Arberth and waited behind the hawthorn bushes at the road's edge.

As the sun began to sink towards the horizon they heard the sound of the woman approaching.

Pwyll climbed up into the saddle and waited.

As she came level he turned after her and gave his grey-headed, sturdy-legged, hollow-hoofed steed its head. He supposed that at the second or third bound he would be beside her. But her white horse with its red ears ambled along ahead of him and for all his speed he came no closer.

See Pwyll now!

See how he drives his sharp spurs into the horse's flank so that the red blood trickles down its belly.

See him standing in his stirrups and whipping the horse's dappled hindquarters until they smart.

See the horse's lips curled back, the teeth clenched to the bit.

Hear the screaming whinnies as she plunges forwards like a wave breaking on the sea-shore.

Hear her hooves pounding against the hard earth of the highway like the drumming of stones on the sea's hard shingle.

And see the woman, still a stone's throw ahead, her gentle pace unaltered. She's looking ahead, paying no heed to the chase behind, as though it is of no more consequence than the soft breeze among the grasses.

And then Pwyll opened his mouth and shouted:

'Woman! For the sake of the man you love the most, wait for me!'

Immediately she stopped.

He came up beside her.

'I will gladly,' she said, 'and it would have been better for your horse if you had asked me some time ago.'

She drew back a piece of gold-threaded cloth that had blown across her face. She fixed her eyes on his. In that moment he knew that of all the women he had ever seen she was the most beautiful.

'Lady,' he said, 'where have you come from? Where are you going?'

'I am half-way between where I was and where I will be and I have my own reasons for riding here.'

He bowed to her.

'My welcome to you,' he said, 'and will you tell me what those reasons are?'

'I will tell you the chief of them. It is to see you.'

For a moment Pwyll was lost for words.

'That, Lady, is the best of all reasons. Will you tell me who you are?'

'I am Rhiannon, daughter of Hyfaidd Hen of the kingdom of Annwn. I come seeking your help.'[21]

Her eyes searched his. They were blue as thrushs' eggs.

'There is one in that realm who seeks to marry me against my will. But the only man I have ever desired is you.'

She reached across and brushed his hand with her fingertips.

'I will not be his bride unless you reject me. It is to discover your answer that I have made this journey into your world.'

'Then this is my answer,' said Pwyll, 'if all the women of your kingdom and mine were to stand one beside the other, it would be you that I would choose.'

She smiled.

'I am glad. If this is what you want, then before it is too late we must arrange to meet again.'

'The sooner we meet the happier I will be. Tell me the time and the place. Wherever you choose, I swear that I will be there.'

'Very well, we will meet a year from tonight at the hall of my father, Hyfaidd Hen. There we will become husband and wife.

I know that you are familiar with the border where our kingdoms join. A boy will be waiting to show you the way. A feast will have been prepared. Our bridal bed will have been made warm.'

She offered her hand and he lifted it to his lips.

'I give you my word. I will follow the boy.'

She drew her hand away and took the reins:

'Lord, stay well! Remember to keep your promise.'

She shook the reins and rode along the road.

In no time she had vanished from his sight."

Cian Brydydd Mawr lifted his cup to his lips and moistened his throat.

"It was a long year.

Never, it seemed to Pwyll, Lord of Dyfed, had time turned more slowly than in those weeks and months.

Look.

There is a door post that leads to his bedchamber.

On it he has made three hundred and sixty-five marks with a lump of white chalk, one above the other. Every morning he rubs one of them clean with the corner of his cloak.

He watches the long year dwindle. Beltane to Lughnasa, Lughnasa to Samhain, Samhain to Imbolc. The days move as slow and stately as the woman herself whose horse will not be overtaken.

At last there are three marks left, then two, then only one.

Pwyll's servants dress him for his wedding. His linen shirt is pulled over his head. His torc of twisted gold is placed about his throat. A four-cornered mantle of purple cloth is fastened at his shoulder with a golden clasp. At each corner of it hangs a silver apple. His polished sword is hung from his belt. His beard is combed, the white strands plucked from his chin.

With ninety-nine armed men he rode out of Arberth.

They came to the circle of oaks.

Though the buds of the trees were swelling with the promise of green spring, the wind still spoke of winter. A sloping rain had soaked through wool, leather and linen to their skin beneath.

Sitting on a stump was a boy, nine or so years old.

Beside him a shapely little white pony with red ears tugged at the new grass that pushed between the dead leaves.

The boy looked up at Pwyll and, without speaking, mounted the pony and rode out between the trees.

They followed him.

Suddenly they were in high, green, fruitful summer.

The boy led them over rounded hills and through sloping valleys.

A warm fragrant wind blew their clothes dry.

They came to the hall of Hyfaidd Hen. Rhiannon was waiting outside with a great company. She ran forwards and welcomed Pwyll.

She led them all inside.

The tables, the beams, the shelves and the lintels of the hall had been strewn with red and yellow flowers. A thousand candles blazed. Their dancing flames glinted on golden goblets and golden dishes. Somewhere in the shadows a harper was playing.

They were given basins of scented water to wash away the grime of their journey. Their riding boots were pulled from their feet and replaced with slippers of soft leather.

Hyfaidd Hen, white-bearded, showed Pwyll to his place at the high table. The food was served and the wedding feast began.

Pwyll sat with the old man to his right and Rhiannon to his left. Beyond them each man and woman had been placed according to their rank and station. They ate and talked and drank.

One dish followed another in a golden whirl of celebration and delight.

And then the feast was interrupted.

When the last course had been eaten, when the singers were clearing their throats and the guests were refilling their goblets, the doors of the hall swung open.

A tall young man entered.

He was auburn-haired and regal in his bearing. He was dressed in shimmering silk.

He walked the length of the hall until he stood before the high table.

He greeted Pwyll with civility.

'And a warm welcome to you, friend,' said Pwyll, 'come and sit down.'

The stranger shook his head.

'I come as a supplicant, not as a guest. I have a request.'

Pwyll, humoured with food and wine, was eager to bestow gifts.

'Then make your request. Whatever you ask, as far as it is in my power to give, you shall have.'

Rhiannon shuddered, she lifted her hands to her mouth.

'Oh – why did you give such an answer?'

The stranger laughed.

'He has made his offer, my lady, in the presence of a hundred noblemen.'

Pwyll narrowed his eyes.

'So tell me, what is this request of yours?'

The stranger looked him full in the face.

'The woman I love is to sleep with you tonight. My request is this – that you give her to me, along with her wedding feast and all of its preparations. That is my demand of you.'

Pwyll turned pale and stared at the table. For a long time he said nothing. It was Rhiannon who broke the silence.

'You can sit there tongue-tied for as long as you like, never has there been such a half-wit as you.'

'My lady, I did not know who he was.'

She raised her voice.

'This is Gwawl, son of Clud. He is a man of great power. He has many friends and followers. He is the one who would bring me to bed. And now that you have given your word you must let him have me, or you will bring bitter disgrace upon yourself.'

'My Lady, I cannot let that happen.'

Rhiannon put her lips to his ear.

'Give me to him and I will make sure that he never has me.'

'How can that be?'

'Shhh, listen,' her voice was a whisper, 'take this bag.'

Under the rim of the table Pwyll could feel her pressing a piece of cloth into his hands.

'Do not lose it.'

He nodded. She continued.

'This feast is not yours to give, it is mine and my father's. I will promise Gwawl a full wedding feast a year from tonight. I will promise that he will sit at the high table and afterwards take me to bed. Now listen carefully, this is your part. That night you must be waiting with your retinue in the orchard outside. You must be dressed in threadbare rags. When Gwawl is in his cups you must enter, looking like an old beggar. You must ask for your bag to be filled with food. It is no ordinary bag! If all the food of Annwn were put inside, it would still seem empty. When the whole feast has been thrown into the bag Gwawl will say: "Will your bag never be filled?" You must tell him that it will never be filled until a great nobleman treads it down with his feet and says: "Enough." The moment he sets his feet to the food you must pull the bag up over his head and tie it tight. Then call your horsemen in.'

As Rhiannon was whispering, Gwawl was pacing backwards and forwards. Suddenly he stopped and fixed his eyes on Pwyll.

'Come, Lord, I have been waiting too long, it is time that I had an answer to my request.'

Pwyll replied:

'All that it is in my power to give, you shall have.'

Then Rhiannon spoke softly:

'It is not in Pwyll's power to grant you the wedding feast, it was prepared by my father and I, we have chosen to give what's left of it to the horsemen of Dyfed. But a year from tonight I will prepare another feast for you my friend, and afterwards, I promise, you will lie between my friendly thighs.'

Gwawl nodded, turned, and strode from the hall.

Soon afterwards Pwyll, cursing his hasty tongue, took his leave.

His retinue rode behind him, their saddle-bags swollen with food. They followed the boy to the circle of oaks and entered their own world."

The bell rang for Sext.

The old man cocked his head to one side.

"There my friends. We are woken by the bell from a world that knew nothing of Christ Jesu and his mercies. But it was a world that was not without its wonders, and maybe its heaven was closer than ours."

Brother Iago shuddered.

"Every old hen-wife beguiles little children with tales of Annwn. It is no Heaven. Rather it is the primrose path that will charm us into damnation. Arawn is Lucifer himself, Gwawl is surely a demon, and Rhiannon a demoness sent into the world to tempt us into sin."

The old man shook his head.

"Our grandfathers and grandmothers, in the ancient days before the saints came, knew nothing of Heaven or Hell. They built their altars to other gods."

He lifted a cup to his lips.

"And now, Brother, it is time for your prayers and my rest."

After None the listeners returned.

Olwen was the first to come into the cell. Cian Brydydd Mawr was on his seat waiting. Tomos was whittling a stick with his horse-headed knife. The old man looked up at her.

"So, what do you make of my stories?"

She smiled.

"It seems to me that our grandfathers and grandmothers in the forgotten times, though they knew nothing of saints or demons, understood men and women and what passes between them as well as anyone."

She threw her cloak onto the wooden chest and sat down.

Then Dafydd entered.

"What about you, Dafydd, what do you make of my stories?"

"I was helping my father once. We were fishing from his little boat. I fell into the water and an undercurrent sucked me down. I was under the water for so long that I breathed in water. After the terror came a sense of great well-being so that I was angry when he pulled me out and pumped the air back into my lungs. Each time the story begins I resist it like a drowning man, and when you finish I do not want to leave it behind."

"So you would sooner drown than be saved?"

Brother Iago entered. He selected a clean wax tablet and sat by the door.

"These are good answers. Now we can resume.

You will all remember Pwyll's unthinking words at the wedding feast and his return to Arberth with no bride on his arm?"

They nodded.

"Another line of marks was chalked onto his door post, one above the other. And if the year before had been slow, this one dragged its feet as though the ankles of each hour had been shackled with iron chains.

When twelve months were over and the last of the marks had been rubbed away, there were no wedding garments for Pwyll to wear.

Instead his servants, struggling to mask their laughter, dressed their Lord in filthy rags.

They smeared his face with dirt. They wrapped muddy clouts around his feet where his leather boots had been. A donkey skin, rank with mould, was slung across his shoulders and fastened under his chin with twine. Grease was dripped into his red beard.

He hid his hunting horn under his rags and climbed up into the saddle. Ninety-nine men were waiting to follow him, each one armed with sword, knife, spear and a stout cudgel.

This time they needed no guide.

They rode first to the circle of oaks, then over the green hills to the hall of Hyfaidd Hen.

When they arrived the wedding feast had already begun.

Through the closed doors they could hear the sound of music and laughter, the clink of knives against platters and the chime of golden goblets.

Pwyll dismounted and put his eye to a crack in the wall.

He could see, in the glow of candlelight, the company decked in its wedding finery. At the high table he could see Gwawl, with Rhiannon to one side and her father to the other. He could see, under the table, his hand was resting on her leg. It seemed to Pwyll that her flushed cheek was tilted towards Gwawl's shoulder.

He ground his teeth and waited.

Course followed course. Outside in the orchard the hundred horsemen of Dyfed could smell the sweet flavours of the food. Their bellies rumbled and groaned.

And then came the first strains of song.

Gwawl, son of Clud, was leaning back in his seat at the head of the high table. The feast was finished and ahead of him lay the wedding night with its long awaited delights. He closed his eyes and let the swelling music fill his ears.

Then there came a hammering at the doorway of the hall.

The music stopped. He opened his eyes.

A ragged oaf was hobbling across the floor towards him.

He wore a cloak of stinking mottled skin.

He was knock-kneed, cock-eyed, shock-headed, cack-handed.

In one trembling fist he gripped a twisted stick, from the other dangled a cloth bag.

The beggar bowed to the company at the high table.

Gwawl rose to his feet. He was obliged to follow the ancient courtesies of supplication and boon.

'Welcome stranger, how can I help you?'

'Great Lord, I am come to beg a favour.'

'If it is reasonable, then it will be granted.'

'I ask only that ravening hunger be held at bay. Please fill my little bag with food.'

Gwawl nodded to the servants.

'It is a modest request and it shall be granted.'

The beggar opened the neck of the bag and the servants began to fill it with food. They threw cakes and loaves and cheeses into it. They threw joints of meat, racks of ribs and roasted fowl. They threw sweetmeats, biscuits, honeycombs. They poured soups, stews and sauces. All that was left of the feast was fed into the bag.

Still it was less than half-full.

Gwawl began to grow impatient.

'Friend,' he said, 'will your wretched bag never be filled?'

The beggar looked up at him.

'My Lord, it will never be filled, unless a great nobleman treads it down with his feet and says "enough".'

Rhiannon lifted her arm and rested the soft palm of her hand against Gwawl's neck. She spoke to him tenderly.

'Then it must be you, our bed is warmed, let's waste no more time.'

Gwawl stepped down.

The beggar rolled back the sides of the bag. Gwawl stepped inside. He trod the food with his feet and said:

'Enough!'

Cian Brydydd Mawr looked at Tomos.

"What then?"

Tomos reached down with his hands and then lifted them both above his head.

The old man laughed.

"Exactly!"

"See how the beggar, grown suddenly straight, pulls the lips of the bag up and over the auburn head of Gwawl.

See how he ties it with a threaded thong of leather.

And see how the bag is become alive with the man inside, punching and kicking against his soft dungeon of cloth like a hare in a hunter's sack.

Gwawl shouted and cursed.

He threatened and cajoled.

His retinue staggered to their feet.

Sluggish with food and wine they drew their knives.

The beggar wasted no time.

He reached beneath his rags and seized his hunting horn.

He lifted it to his lips and blew.

Ninety-nine warriors of Dyfed bounded into the hall, their swords drawn, their wits sharpened with hunger.

Each of them seized one of Gwawl's retinue and tied him tight with rope. They dragged their victims across the floor and laid them, one beside the other, against the wall of the hall, writhing and twitching in their bonds.

The men of Dyfed came forwards to the high table. One after another they bowed to the beggar and nodded at the bag.

'What's inside the bag master?'

Pwyll replied:

'A badger!'

Each man in turn swung his cudgel and struck the bag a blow.

With each crunching blow Gwawl, son of Clud, groaned.

That is how the game of 'badger-in-the-bag' was played for the very first time."

Olwen shook her head.

"It is a cruel sport. I have seen it."

The old poet nodded.

"Soon enough the bag was seeping blood.

From inside Gwawl pleaded through broken teeth.

'Lord ... listen ... I beg you ... spare my life ... to perish inside this bag would not be a fitting death for me.'

White-bearded Hyfaidd Hen got to his feet.

'He speaks the truth and it is proper that you should hear him. This is too base a death for a man of noble blood.'

Pwyll gestured to his men. They stepped back from the bag.

He turned to Rhiannon.

'I will deal with him as you see fit.'

She spoke then.

'This is what I advise. This man who, until a few short minutes ago, believed himself a bridegroom, should fulfill his duties and obligations. He should give gifts until he has satisfied all supplicants. It is Pwyll who will take me to bed, but it is Gwawl who will give on his behalf. He must also promise that he will seek no vengeance for what has befallen him today.'

From the bag came the broken voice of Gwawl.

'I accept these terms.'

Pwyll bowed his head.

'And so do I.'

Then the leather thongs were untied and Gwawl crawled out of the sack. His silken clothes were caked with food, his hair matted with gravy and blood. He staggered to his feet. One arm hung limp from its shoulder.

'My lords ... I have received many wounds ... allow me to wash myself and tend to my injuries ... my men will make good my duties and obligations.'

Pwyll said:

'Very well, do as you propose.'

Gwawl turned and, holding himself upright, clutching at tables and wooden posts, limped and tottered out of the feasting hall.

A second feast was made ready.

Servants hurried forwards to unfasten Pwyll's rags. They washed him and dressed him in fine clothes. He and his retinue sat as they had done the year before. Meat and wine were served. The horsemen of Dyfed lifted the fragrant food to their mouths and ate with a grateful appetite.

They ate until they could eat no more.

Then, from outside, came a sound of tuneful horns.

The doors of the hall were opened and Arawn, King of Annwn entered with his queen on his arm.

They were dressed in robes of shimmering gold.

Pwyll and Rhiannon stood aside and made space for them at the head of the high table.

The minstrels ran their fingers across the strings of their harps and all throats were opened in song. As the music swelled the Queen of Annwn leaned across and whispered into Pwyll's ear:

'So we have found you a queen. I trust you will not be turning your face to the edge of the bed tonight.'

The old man looked at his audience.

'Eh! What do you think Iago ap Rhys? If Adam had turned to the edge of the bed, where would we all be now?'

Brother Iago crossed himself.

'If Adam had not sinned, the world would not have fallen.'

Cian Brydydd Mawr sipped from his cup and continued.

"See how Gwawl's retinue lie tied and trussed.

All through the long hours of carousal they lie among the shadows by the wall, like flies in a spider's larder.

See how they struggle to break their bonds.

See how, in their gagged and grimacing faces, a single shared thought is written: 'Gwawl may have sworn to seek no vengeance, but no such promise has issued from our lips.'

The time came to seek slumber.

Pwyll and Rhiannon retired to their bedchamber.

They passed the night in long anticipated pleasure and delight.

A king from the race of men coupled with a high-born woman of the Other World. The next morning she woke him with a kiss.

'My lord, it is time to satisfy all the supplicants. Every request must be granted.'

Pwyll got out of bed.

'I will do that gladly!'

He dressed and went through to the feasting hall.

He summoned all the supplicants and minstrels and told them that each would have his every wish and whim satisfied to the full.

He told his men to unfasten the ropes that bound the prisoners.

Bruised and aching, they were made to stand in a row.

Each supplicant stepped forwards and made his demand.

Gwawl's men had no choice but to give whatever was asked:

the silver and gold coins from their purses, the clasps from their cloaks, the shoes from their feet, the clothes from their backs, the horses that were cropping the grass outside the hall.

Piece by piece, on behalf of their jilted master, Gwawl's retinue honoured the duties and obligations of a bridegroom.

They watched the supplicants as they dressed themselves in their own finery and rode away on their own steeds.

Then, barefooted, dressed in their linen shifts, they turned and trudged homewards with dark thoughts in their hearts.

Pwyll turned to Hyfaidd Hen.

'With your permission I will set out for Dyfed tomorrow.'

The old man nodded.

'May your path be a smooth one. And before you leave you must arrange a date for my daughter to follow you.'

'My lord, I swear we will ride together!'

Hyfaidd Hen bowed his head.

'If that is your wish, then it shall be so.'

The next morning they rode away from the hall.

Pwyll and Rhiannon led the way, followed by the ninety-nine horsemen of Dyfed. At the rear trotted a row of sturdy pack-horses, one roped behind the other. They were loaded with a dowry of the finely wrought treasures of Annwn.

They came to Arberth.

The high-born men and women of Dyfed assembled to welcome their new queen. Not one of them went home without a gift fashioned by the craftsmen of Annwn. To some Rhiannon gave rings and brooches, to others precious stones set in gold and silver.

Throughout the kingdom she was welcomed."

The old man closed his eyes.

"And there we will leave her."

Brother Iago got to his feet.

"I will need a week or longer to write it down ... ten days maybe."

"Ten days you shall have ... no, you shall have longer. We will meet again in fifteen days. On the Feast of the Nativity."

He smiled to himself.

"After the Eucharist."

Olwen reached for her cloak.

"I have a request. As it is a feast day we will not be working on the farm. When the beasts have been fed my boys will come down to the church for Mass. Might they be allowed to stay and listen with us?"

"How old are they?"

"Gwyn has seen twelve winters, Rhys seventeen. In the evenings as we make cloth I have told them the stories as best I can."

"Then I will welcome them."

Brother Iago was hovering in the doorway. The old man looked at him.

"Go out or come in, Brother."

"I have a question."

"Ask."

"You say that in the forgotten times our grandfathers built altars to other gods."

"Yes."

"Then why has there been no mention of these gods in your stories?"

The old man nodded.

"That is a good question, and it is one that I remember putting to old Meilyr when he taught me these tales more than fifty years ago."

"What was his answer?"

"He said – and I can see his brown eyes now that were already melting into blindness – he said: 'These *are* the old gods.'"

Thursday December 25th (Christmas Day)

'O shepherds, whom have you seen? Speak, tell us who has appeared on earth!

We have seen the newborn infant, and a multitude of the heavenly host praising God. Alleluia, alleluia.

The mother brought forth the King whose name is eternal; the joy of a mother was hers, cum virginitatis honore: nec primam simile visa est, nec hambere sequentem, alleluia.'

The church was full. Monks, lay brothers, farming and fishing families from the shores and the surrounding hills worshipped together. The people coughed and fidgeted through the long Latin prayers and psalms. They came forwards for the Mass, kissing the stone that covered the bones of Saint Beuno before they knelt at the altar.

A hard frost had been followed by clear winter sunshine. The skies were a luminous blue. After Eucharist Olwen and her sons built a fire outside the monastery gates. They broke their fast with bread and cold mutton. Then they damped the flames with turfs and made their way to the old poet's cell.

The old man beckoned for them to sit. They gave him a little willow basket filled with bread, meat and honey-cakes. He smiled his thanks.

Dafydd entered with a fistful of holly and mistletoe.

"Red as blood, white as milk – it is an old custom."

He hung it from the ceiling above the old man's chair.

Brother Iago came in and settled himself closer than usual to the charcoal fire. He had denied himself a fire in his own cell and was eager for warmth.

Cian Brydydd Mawr cast his eyes on his audience.

"We are ready?"

They nodded.

"If I could sing, I would sing of Rhiannon, Queen of Dyfed.

I would sing of her as I have seen her in carvings of stone.

She is astride the horse that none of the race of men could outpace. She is holding in her left hand the bag that could never be filled (some say it was made of crane-skin). Above her head three birds are circling.

For one year she and Pwyll ruled over the seven cantrefs of Dyfed and the people were prosperous and content. For two years they ruled and the kingdom flourished.

But during the third year the noblemen began to talk behind their hands, muttering and complaining that no child had been born to Pwyll and Rhiannon. A rumour began to spread that the seed of the race of man could never take root in a womb of Annwn.

This was the question they asked one another:

'How can the land prosper with a barren queen?'

It was the feast of Lugnasa when they summoned Pwyll to meet them at Preseli.

'Lord,' they said, 'you are no longer in the first flush of manhood and you can be sure you will not live for ever. We are afraid that you will never get an heir from this wife of yours. Cast her aside and take a woman who will give you sons. We will not tolerate a childless queen.'

Pwyll replied.

'We have not been together for long. Give us another year. If no child has been born in twelve months, then I will abide by your decision.'

Pwyll went to Rhiannon.

'My lady, there is discontent among the noblemen of Dyfed that you have not borne me children.'

She reached for his hand.

'My Lord, listen to me. We have made enemies in Annwn, powerful enemies. They will be eager for revenge. I would rather have no child at all than lose one to Gwawl's men. If my baby came to any harm I could never forgive myself.'

'Gwawl has sworn ...'

'Gwawl has sworn, yes, but he was not the only one humiliated on our wedding night. We must be careful.'

Pwyll pulled his hand away from hers and rested it on the pommel of his sword. His eyes glowed with a fierce fire.

'I will set armed men to every gate and door of my court. I will have women watching in your bedchamber by day and night. I swear that neither you nor your child will be in any danger.'

She leaned forwards and pressed her lips to his.

Two months later it was announced at every hall, highway and marketplace, at every fair and farmstead that Rhiannon, Queen of Dyfed was with child.

By the feast of Samhain her skirts had been loosened. By Imbolc the people of Dyfed rejoiced to see her swollen belly. By the spring equinox she was so big with child she could barely stand.[22]

Pwyll ordered his warriors to wait at every door and gate of his court at Arberth. He ordered five of his most trusted men to guard the door of Rhiannon's bedchamber.

It was not until Beltane-eve that she went into labour.

Six midwives were fetched. They came with bowls of steaming water and rolls of clean white linen. They were told that they were to stay with the queen and keep watch by day and night.

The women gave their solemn word.

At midnight Rhiannon opened her thighs and gave birth to a baby boy. He wriggled into the hands of the midwives, slippery as a fish and gasping for air.

They washed him and bound him in swaddling linen. Around the linen they wrapped brocaded silk.

They gave him to his mother. She lifted the boy to her breast. They watched as she gave him suck.

Then mother and child closed their eyes.

The midwives gently lifted and folded back the coverlets.

They made Rhiannon and her baby comfortable for sleep.

See how the six women settle themselves down.

Two sit at the head of the bed, two at the foot, one to either side.

They have brought sewing to keep themselves awake.

In the flickering candlelight they thread needles and push copper thimbles onto their fingers.

Beyond the door the five trusted warriors are waiting, throwing dice to pass the long hours of night.

Outside more soldiers are patrolling the courtyards, stamping their feet against the chill air.

In the feasting hall, Pwyll sits by the fire and nurses a goblet of warmed wine between his cupped hands. The news of the birth of his son gladdens his blood. Tomorrow he will cast eyes on the boy for the first time.

But look, a strange thing is happening.

There is a shift in the air. It is grown soft and still and weighed with a sweet-scented compulsion to sleep.

Pwyll's head falls forwards.

Outside in the yard his warriors settle on benches and doorsteps, they are overwhelmed by a desire to lie down and close their eyes. The five trusted warriors drop their dice and sink into oblivion.

The six midwives, one by one, set their sewing onto their laps and drift into dreams.

A silence as deep as the womb settles on the court of Arberth.

Birdsong woke them.

The six midwives opened their eyes. The first light of morning was flooding the bedchamber. They looked at one another. They knew that they shared the same guilty secret. They jumped to their feet and ran to the bed. They tore back the coverlets.

Rhiannon was lying fast asleep.

The baby was gone.

Beyond the door the five warriors woke and saw the fallen dice on the floor. From inside the bedchamber they could hear a con-sternation of voices. They lifted the door latch and entered.

The six women came forwards, on each pale face and open mouth the same terrible truth was written.

'The baby is gone!'

'We slept. We couldn't help it. The baby was taken.'

The men nodded.

'We slept also,' they looked at the women, 'our deaths are certain. We shall be hanged, every one of us, or burnt alive for this.'

'Is there anything we can do?'

One of the men said:

'Listen, I have a plan. I have a stag-hound bitch. Two nights ago she gave birth to a litter of pups. If I killed one of them and we smeared the blood on Rhiannon's face and hands, then we could swear, eleven against one, that she has eaten her own child.'

When Rhiannon woke she reached for the boy.

He was gone.

She opened her eyes.

'Ladies, where is my child?'

The midwives looked at her. Their faces were pale with horror.

'Do not ask us for your child.'

They pointed to their wrists and arms.

'Look at these bites and scratches and bruises.'

'We fought to protect him, but never have we seen such ferocity in a woman.'

'There was nothing we could do to stop you. You have eaten your own baby. Do not seek him from us.'

Pwyll was shaken awake by his five trusted warriors.

'My Lord, you must follow us. A terrible thing has taken place.'

Pwyll jumped to his feet and followed them across the compound to the queen's bedchamber. They pushed open the door.

Pwyll, King of Dyfed saw his wife.

She was sitting upright in her bed. Her mouth and neck were sticky and dripping with blood and torn flesh. The pillows and coverlets were stained red. Little chewed bones lay around her.

The midwives ran forwards to him. They were trembling. Their faces and hands were scratched. They were speaking but their words carried no meaning.

The only truth he saw was in his wife's face.

Her eyes were fixed on his in a gaze of unspeakable sorrow.

The news spread like wildfire.

From hall to highway, from fair to farmstead the story

spread that Pwyll's wife, the woman from the Other World, had devoured her own child.

His noblemen summoned him to a meeting.

'My Lord, for committing such an outrage, you must cast aside this queen of yours.'

But Pwyll replied.

'Our agreement was that I should cast her aside if she was barren. She has borne me a child, so I will not.'

'Then she must be punished.'

'If you believe that she is guilty, then you must punish her.'

A punishment was devised.

Rhiannon accepted it as a penance that she must pay.

This was the punishment:

That every day for seven years she must wait beside the mounting block that stood inside the gates at Arberth.

That she must tell the story of her crime to every traveller who came to the gates.

That she must offer to carry him on her back to the doors of her husband's hall.

Look.

Can you see the great queen waiting at the gate?

On her back she's wearing a saddle of leather.

In her hands she carries a bit and bridle.

See how her head is bowed, not with shame, but weighed with the ache of heart and womb and the bitter burden of her loss.

It is a weight heavier than any of the men who mount her back and fit the cold iron bit between her teeth."

The old man turned to Tomos.

"That is enough. Go and see how close we are to noon."

As the boy ran outside to look at the stone sundial, Brother Pedr swung the midday bell.

"There."

The audience were slow to stir.

Dafydd said:

"This is a harsh story to set against our Saviour's birth. And it touches a tender place in me."

"The world is both harsh and tender, Dafydd – as you know – and the story is not yet finished. Come back after None and you will hear what happens next."

They left the cell.

Olwen, Gwyn and Rhys lifted the turfs and blew their fire back into life. They skewered cold meat on sticks and warmed it in the flames.

Olwen saw Tomos and called out to him:

"Come and sit here with us."

By the time None was finished the three boys were flinging pebbles at a pile of stones they had heaped on the churchyard wall.

"Hai! Look at that!"

"Good shot!"

When they saw Brother Iago emerging from the church they gathered again in the old man's cell. He was eager to begin.

"If I could sing, I would sing of Teyrnon Twrf Liant, Lord over the high wooded hills of Gwent.[23]

I would sing of Teyrnon standing in his stable running his fingers through the coarse white hair of his horse's mane.

See how his mare presses her nose against the folds of his neck.

Throughout his kingdom and the kingdoms that lie beyond there is no horse that compares with her. It has been said that she was bred from the snow white horses of Annwn.

But there is a mystery.

Every winter she conceives and carries a foal, but every Beltane-eve, in the dead of night, when she is due to drop it, the foal vanishes.

No-one knows what becomes of it.

No-one has ever been able to watch through the night without falling into the sweet oblivious balm of sleep.

Teyrnon turned on his heel.

He walked out of the stable and across the compound to his high hall. It was Beltane-eve and the red sun was sinking below the hills.

His wife was waiting for him. He said:

'The mare is big again and will drop her foal tonight. No doubt we will lose it. She, like you, seems cursed to remain childless.'

She lowered her head and sighed.

'What can we do?'

'A vengeance on me if I do not stay awake all night and keep watch.'

He told his men to lead the mare into the hall and bed her down with straw. He sharpened his sword. He ordered his carpenters to hammer long nails through the back of his wooden throne, the sharp ends pointing forwards at the height of his head.

When his evening meal had been eaten he sent everyone away.

He settled down on his throne. He rested his sword on his lap.

His mare was tethered before him. She was gently munching oats.

Teyrnon watched and waited. Hour followed hour.

In the dead of night there was a shift in the air. It grew soft and still and weighed with a sweet-scented compulsion to sleep.

Teyrnon's head sank back.

'Aaaargh!'

The nails had pierced the back of his head.

With a jolt he sat forward.

For a second time the urge to sleep overwhelmed him.

The sharp pain woke him with a start.

For a third time his eyelids drifted downwards.

The nails pricked him into wakefulness.

Now, with the warm blood trickling down the back of his neck, he knew there would be no more sleeping.

It was midnight.

The mare was whinnying softly, bending herself for birth.

Then the foal came, slithering out of her body onto the straw.

The mare nudged it with her nose, a banner of bloody ribbons hanging between her hind legs.

The little colt hoisted to its knees and struggled to stand. It lifted its nose to one of its mother's teats. She licked its back.

Teyrnon got up and looked at it. He felt the colt's neck and haunches. It was as beautiful as its mother.

But listen.

There is a rattling at the doors of Teyrnon's hall.

The handles turn and the latches lift.

The hall is flooded with the cool air of the night.

A huge clawed hand comes in through the opened door, then a wrist, then a long arm bristling with red hair.

It feels this way and that until it finds the foal.

The clawed fingers close around its neck.

The mare's lips are curled back from her teeth.

She screams and bites, straining at her tether.

The hand is dragging the little colt across the floor towards the door.

Teyrnon ran forwards.

He lifted his sword above his head.

With one sharp stroke he cut through flesh and bone.

From outside came a piercing cry of pain.

The severed forearm dropped twitching to the floor.

The clawed hand opened and fell still.

The dripping arm withdrew.

Teyrnon's eyes were fixed on the open door.

He rushed out into the night.

Something was crashing through the bushes and disappearing into the blackness of the forest beyond. It was grunting and groaning.

He followed the sound. The night was too dark for him to see.

He remembered that his hall had been left wide open.

He turned and hurried back. He entered and bolted the doors behind him. He came into the glow of firelight.

And there he saw a wonder.

Lying on the straw beside the foal there was a newborn baby. He was wrapped in swaddling linen and brocaded silk.

Child and foal were fast asleep, pressed together.

Above them, standing guard, stood the white mare."

Cian Brydydd Mawr paused. He looked across the cell at Brother Iago.

"So there we have it. A baby asleep in the straw. The son of the Great Queen. Half of this world, half of the Other. No ox or ass looking on, but a mare instead. What do you make of that?"

Brother Iago crossed himself and said nothing.

"Teyrnon reached down and gently lifted the baby in his arms.

He hurried across the courtyard to his wife's bedchamber. Everyone was still sleeping. Guards, servants and soldiers were sitting with their heads in their hands, or stretched out on the hard ground.

He came to the edge of her bed. He whispered:

'My lady, are you asleep?'

She opened her eyes.

'I was deeply and strangely asleep, but now that you have entered I am awake.'

'I have something for you, something you have longed for and never had.'

He passed her the baby. She gently unwound the swaddling bands and saw that he was a boy. She looked up at her husband.

'Lord, tell me what happened?'

'Listen, and I will tell you everything.'

Teyrnon told her of the adventures of the night.

When he had finished she said:

'And he is wound with bands of brocaded silk, he must be the son of noble people.'

She lifted the baby and sniffed the soft creamy crown of his head.

'Lord, it would be a pleasure and the deepest delight – if you would agree to it – for me to take my maidservants into my confidence, and tell them to put the word out that I have been pregnant and now am delivered of a child.'

Teyrnon leaned down and kissed his wife on the forehead.

'I will agree to it gladly for, like you, I have always longed for a son.'

And so they raised the boy as though he was their own.

They gave him the name Gwri Golden-Hair, for his head was soon covered with curls of yellow gold.

The boy grew as no boy had grown before.

By the time he was one year old, he was walking and running like a three year old. By the end of his second year he was as strong as a six year old. Before he reached the age of four he was bargaining with the stable boys to let him lead the horses to water.

Teyrnon and his wife watched him. She said:

'Lord, where is the foal that was born the night the boy was found?'

'I ordered the grooms to take it and look after it.'

'Should we not give the horse to the boy? There will be a bond between them.'

'I do not disagree with you. We will have the horse broken in. And it must be you who gives it to him.'

She smiled.

'Husband, you are a kind man, may you be repaid for it.'

She told the grooms to have the horse gently broken in.

She took Gwri Golden-Hair by the hand. She led him to the stable. She brought the horse to him.

Without hesitation Gwri climbed onto its back. Without instruction, without saddle or bridle, without a word of command, he rode the horse out of the stable and round the compound as though they shared a single mind.

From that moment boy and horse were inseparable.

Time passed.

One day a story reached the high wooded hills of Gwent.

It was the story of a queen's harsh punishment.

Men who had travelled to Arberth told how they had seen the wretchedness of Rhiannon as she waited by the mounting block.

Teyrnon began to enquire about the matter.

He asked when the child had been lost.

'On Beltane-eve some five years since.'

He pondered in his heart. He looked closely at the boy.

As a young man, Teyrnon had served at Pwyll's court. It seemed to him that never had a son so resembled his father as Gwri Golden-Hair resembled Pwyll.

He went to his wife and put his hand to her arm.

'My lady, our boy is indeed the son of noble people. He is the son of Pwyll, King of the seven cantrefs of Dyfed, and his wife Rhiannon of Annwn.'

She looked at him in astonishment:

'You are sure? I have heard their story.'

'I am sure, and it would be a terrible thing to let so great a queen suffer such sore punishment for a deed she has never committed.'

She looked at him. Tears spilled from her eyes. She smiled through them and said in a small voice:

'And I suppose, my Lord, we shall get three things as a consequence. We shall get the gratitude of Rhiannon for her release from grief. We shall get the deep thanks of Pwyll for rescuing and raising his son. And – if he grows to be a gracious man – we shall never be forgotten by little Gwri, who will love us and do his best on our behalf.'

The next day Teyrnon and Gwri set off together.

They rode out of the gates. Teyrnon was on the back of his white mare. Gwri Golden-Hair was mounted on the mare's offspring, the horse that had become his constant companion. Behind them came two noblemen of Gwent.

Teyrnon's wife came out to bid the boy farewell. She pressed his hand to her cheek. She stood in the gateway and watched him ride away until all sight of him was gone.

The four of them rode for three long days.

It was late afternoon when they drew close to the court of Arberth. Look.

Can you see Rhiannon?

She is sitting on the stone mounting block.

Her elbows are on her knees. Her hair has fallen over her face.

The leather saddle is strapped to the small of her back.

She hears the sound of horsemen approaching.

She pulls herself upright as they draw close. She recites the terrible litany of her crime. Her voice is flat and broken with sorrow.

'I am a murderess who has destroyed her own son. Lords, go no further. Leave your horses here. Ride me.'

She holds out the bridle. She opens her mouth and pushes the bit between her teeth. She curtseys and bends forwards. She offers them the saddle.

Not one of the horsemen will touch the offered bridle.

Teyrnon took her hand.

He drew her upright.

'Noble Lady, there is not one among this company who will ride upon your back.'

Gwri shook his head.

'Certainly I will not.'

The noblemen of Gwent said:

'No more will we.'

The two horses, Teyrnon's mare and her offspring, circled around Rhiannon. They sniffed her face and lowered their lips to her hands.

The riders dismounted and walked their horses to the hall.

Pwyll had just returned from a circuit of the seven cantrefs of Dyfed.

A feast to celebrate his homecoming was being prepared.

When he saw his old friend his heart was filled with joy.

'Teyrnon. Welcome. It is many years since we last met.'

He invited the visitors into his hall.

They washed their hands and sat down at the high table.

This was how they were placed:

Teyrnon, as honoured guest, sat with Pwyll on one side, and Rhiannon on the other (it had been decreed that her punishment should cease at sunset).

Teyrnon's two companions sat beyond, with the boy between them.

The food was served and eaten. When the platters and trenchers had been pushed away Teyrnon spoke:

'My Lord and my Lady, I have come with a tale to tell.'

Pwyll motioned for their goblets to be filled.

'My friend, speak and we will hear you.'

Teyrnon told the story of the mare and the child. He told them how he and his wife had raised the boy as their own. He stood up and gestured towards the lad with the curls of yellow gold:

'And here you see your own son.'

The boy got to his feet. He went to Rhiannon. He gently put his arms around her neck.

Teyrnon watched.

'Whoever spread these false stories did Rhiannon a great wrong.'

Rhiannon took the boy's hands in her own trembling hands. She kissed his fingers.

Teyrnon laughed.

'And look at the boy! Can anyone doubt that this is Pwyll's son?'

The company laughed with him.

'No-one doubts it.'

Rhiannon cupped the boy's face in her hands. She kissed his forehead, his eyes, his cheeks. She turned to Pwyll.

'I am delivered at last from care.'

It was Pendaran Dyfed, one of Pwyll's noblemen, who said:

'Lady, you have named your son. From this day onwards he shall be called Pryderi – "Care".'

'But surely he has a name already.'

Teyrnon said:

'We named him Gwri Golden-Hair.'

Pendaran Dyfed shook his head.

'That is a cradle-name. Now he is become Pryderi. Pryderi, son of Pwyll of Annwn.'

Pwyll nodded.

'It is right and lawful that the boy's name be taken from the words his mother spoke when first she saw him.'

It was agreed among the company.

Pwyll turned to Teyrnon.

'You have brought us a gift more precious than any the world could offer. As long as I live I will uphold the welfare of your realm. And if the boy grows to manhood it will be fitting for him to do the same.'

Teyrnon replied:

'My Lord, the woman who raised him grieves for him sorely. It would be a shame if he ever forgot her.'

'He will not forget her. But now he must learn the ways of Dyfed. Pendaran Dyfed will teach him all that a king's son needs to know. You and your wife, to whom he owes his life, will always be cherished in his memory. There will be a strong bond between Gwent and Dyfed.'

The next morning Teyrnon Twrf Liant, lord over the high wooded hills of Gwent, made his farewells to Pwyll and Rhiannon. They offered him their finest horses, their keenest dogs, their swiftest hawks, but he wanted nothing.

He embraced the boy and with his two noble companions he set off for home.

The years passed.

Pryderi, the noble son of the great mother, was raised with loving care. He became the most splendid youth, the fairest and the most accomplished in every feat, of all the young men of Dyfed.

Pwyll, meanwhile, like all born into the race of men, grew old and stooped and grey.

But his queen barely aged at all.

Rhiannon, on her white horse with its red ears, could outride the ravages of time.

When old Pwyll had died, and Pryderi had been crowned Lord over the seven cantrefs of Dyfed, she was as beautiful as she had been on the day she first appeared at the foot of Gorsedd Arberth."

Cian Brydydd Mawr was silent for a while.

'And so ends the first 'Cainc' of the Mabinogi. Bards and scholars can argue – as they always will – whether Cainc means the branch of a tree, the strand of a rope, or the verse of a song. For me, who tells the tale today, it means all three.'

He looked across at Brother Iago.

"I suppose you could describe that first 'Cainc' as being the story of an Advent and a Nativity."

"You would be treading on the margins of blasphemy if you did."

"But the Holy Church does not have the sole right to tales of love, conception and birth."

"The Holy Church does not concern itself with tales. It concerns itself with truth. That is the difference between your story and mine."

"Aha."

"And who is this Pryderi, this Gwri Golden-Hair, that you could dare to compare him with our Saviour, Christ Jesu?"

The old man sighed.

"I make no comparison with the Lord of Mercies, least of all on the high holy feast of his birth."

"But who is he?"

"In truth, Brother, I do not know. All we have left to us are fragments from the ancient tales. Old Meilyr gave me more than most, but they are fragments none-the-less. I piece them together as best I can."

Monday January 5th 1212

After nightfall when the brothers were singing the Vespers psalms, Tomos was helping the old man get ready for bed. He took him out into the cold air for a piss. As they were returning to the cell there came a sound of distant shouting. They could hear drumming and voices raised in song. It grew louder and louder until it drowned the steady chanting of the monks. There were blazing torches processing down the side of the hill.

"What is going on?"

The old man chuckled.

"Look. Can you see her?"

He pointed:

"There."

A figure in the centre of the procession stood head and shoulders above the rest. Its head was the long hollow-eyed skull of a horse. Its body was made of several dappled hides stitched roughly together.

There were dancers under the hides. The horse seemed to have many legs. One of the dancers was holding the pole that bore the white skull.

"Have you not seen her before? She is the Mari-Lwyd, the White Mare."

The crowd came down to the monastery wall. It passed the monastery gate. Tomos thought he saw the faces of Gwyn and Rhys in the torch-light.

"I don't suppose they'll stop here. No they are passing us by. The Holy Brothers would, I suspect, give them short shrift."

"Who are they?"

"It is always the same on Twelfth Night. They carry her from farm to farm. There are riddles and songs and she's brought into the warmth of every kitchen. It would be ill fortune otherwise."

The old man was shivering. They went back into the cell.

"Tell me about her."

"There is an old story. It is written in the Holy Scriptures that on the night Christ Jesu was born there was no room for Joseph and blessed Mary in the inn."

"Yes, I have heard that story."

"Well, it is said that when the inn-keeper led them to the stable, it too was full. There was an ox and an ass. Also there was a mare that was on the point of dropping her foal. Mary's labour pains had begun. What were they to do? The inn-keeper fetched a length of rope. He and Joseph dragged the mare out into the night. There was room then for Mary to lie down on the straw and give birth to our Saviour."

"What happened to the mare?"

"Ever since she has wandered the world searching for somewhere to drop her colt. On Twelfth Night she goes from farm to farm. Each place brings her in from the winter cold. Her blessing brings prosperity for the coming year. She is called the Mari-Lwyd."

"Maybe you should tell the story to Brother Iago."

Cian Brydydd Mawr smiled.

"I could tell him, Tomos, but even if he listened he would not hear."

4

Branwen

Tuesday January 27th 1212

For a fortnight there had been snow. Even Brother Iago had relented and allowed himself a smouldering log or two in his cell.

The track to the farm at Careg boeth had been blocked by head-high drifts. Olwen was unable to get down to the monastery.

Without her presence the old poet refused to speak.

He spent the days in bed, or wrapped in skins and blankets by his fire. Sometimes he sang to himself. Sometimes he would go to the church and kneel for Eucharist.

It was more than a month until his audience was assembled. He was impatient to get started.

"You are ready?"

Brother Iago nodded.

"I am."

"Good. My story moves now from south to north."

"If I could sing I would sing of Bran the Blessed, High King over the Island of the Mighty.[24]

I would sing of Bran whose name means Raven.

I would sing of mighty Bran, son of Llyr, watching the blue sea from the high cliffs of Harlech.

Look.

A golden crown is glittering on his broad brow.

He sits on the soft grass at the cliff's margin.

His legs hang over the edge. His heels are kicking the rock face.

His body, from the root of his spine to the back of his head, is the height of the twisted mountain oaks that stand behind him.

His hands rest on his thighs, each as broad as the spread hide of an ox.

His eyes are fixed on the open sea.

Beside him sit three companions.

They are of human height. The tops of their heads barely reach his rounded belly. These are his brothers.

To his left sits Manawydan, who is a true brother, being a son of Llyr by Penarddun, daughter of Beli.

To his right sit his two half-brothers, Nisien and Efnisien.

Let me tell you about them.

It has been said of Manawydan that there was no craft or skill of which he was not the master.

It has been said of Nisien that he could make peace between two warring armies when their rage had reached its full fury.

And it has been said of Efnisien that he could make hatred between two lovers when their rapture had reached its full height.

Beyond the four royal brothers sat the noblemen of the Island of the Mighty, all of them looking out across the wide blue waters of the sea.

They saw thirteen ships.

Their sails were swollen with the wind. Their prows were slicing through the waves. They were approaching Harlech from the western horizon at a smooth and swift speed.

Bran lifted one of his huge hands to shelter his eyes from the glare of the sun.

'I see ships coming boldly and brazenly to the shores of my kingdom. Take weapons and armour, go down to the sea-shore and find out who these people are and what it is that they want.'

The noblemen and their retainers seized spears and swords and hurried down the winding track from the cliff top. They ranged themselves along the beach below. The white surf broke over their feet.

As the thirteen ships came closer they could see that they were well equipped and finely fashioned. Shapely flags and banners of coloured silk flapped from their mast-heads.

The middle ship sped forwards, leaving the others behind.

The warrior standing in the prow was holding a shield above his head. It was upside down, the sign of peace.

The noblemen of Britain waded into the water. The strangers threw them ropes. They pulled the boat towards the shore.

As the keel touched the soft sand the strangers looked up to the cliff-tops. They greeted Bran.

From high above them the High King spoke.

'Strangers, welcome. What ships are these and who is chief over them?'

They lifted their hands to their mouths and shouted:

'Great Lord, these ships belong to Matholwch, King of Ireland. He has come to ask a boon of you.'

The voice of Bran the Blessed boomed down from the heights.

'What does he want? Does he wish to come ashore?'

'He has a request, and will not come ashore unless you grant him his heart's desire.'

'What is his request?'

'Lord, he seeks to make an alliance between your family and his own. He has come to ask for the hand of your sister Branwen in marriage. If you would give your agreement there would be a bond of blood between Erin and the Island of the Mighty.'

There was a pause. Bran pondered. He loved his sister and the thought of her crossing that width of water weighed heavily on his heart.

'Bring your king to land. Tomorrow we will take counsel and discuss this matter.'

The boat was pushed back into the water. It returned to the King of Ireland. He was waiting in one of the anchored ships.

His men told him Bran's reply.

'Then I will go gladly.'

The sailors lowered little currachs over the sides of the ships.

The Irish king and his retinue clambered aboard and were rowed to the shore."

Tomos had pulled his knife from his belt. He was stabbing at the clay floor beside the glowing hearth. The old poet stopped his story and put his hand on the boy's shoulder.

"What is the matter, son?"

He spoke to the rhythm of the stabbing.

"The – Irish – in – their – ships."

"What of them?"

"I hate them. I hate every one of them."

Dafydd leaned down.

"You are remembering?"

The boy nodded.

"The day they came. The day my father and my mother died."

Tomos stared at the fire.

"It is hard, Tomos. But think of Brother Pedr. Think of Brother Edwen who carved the stone sundial. Both are from Ireland. There is good and bad in every kingdom, just as there is good and bad in every heart."

The boy gazed unblinking at the flames. There was nothing in his pale face to suggest that he was any more at ease with the memory the story was conjuring.

The old man's voice was kind.

"Shall I continue?"

"Yes."

"That night there was a feast.

In the court in Ardudwy a huge assembly was gathered.

Bran the Blessed sat outside under the stars, for a house had never been built that was big enough to contain him. The Irish king and his company mingled with the noblemen of the Island of Britain.

Meat and wine were served. Every belly was filled and every heart brimmed with good will.

Bran turned to his brother Manawydan.

'Go and fetch Branwen.'

Manawydan went to her chamber.

'Come.'

She looked up at him.

'They are waiting for you.'

She took his arm. She had been dressed in a robe of flame coloured silk and around her throat she wore a torc of red gold. From her shoulders hung a cloak of dark blue wool, embroidered with golden thread. Neither the eyes of a mewed hawk nor the eyes of a thrice mewed falcon were brighter than her shining grey eyes.

She was brought before the Irish king.

A great silence fell upon the company.

Rumour had reached Ireland that no maiden of the race of men compared with her in beauty.

Matholwch seized her hand and pressed it to his lips.

He demanded that a counsel be held at first light.

Branwen's eyes moved between the face of her brother and the face of this Irish stranger.

Matholwch's face was ardent, urgent, smiling up at her from the feasting table.

Bran's was kindly, indulgent, smiling down from its height like a full moon rising above shouldered hills.

She wondered what strange destiny might be unfolding beyond the formalities of the feast and the slurred compliments of these Irish guests.

The next morning, as the dawn took its golden throne, a counsel was held on the sea-shore below the cliffs of Harlech.

All the noblemen of the Island of the Mighty were there.

A seat of strong oak had been brought down for Bran the Blessed.

His brothers, Manawydan and Nisien, had taken their places, one to either side of him.

Nisien's silver tongue put the strangers at their ease.

Manawydan's shrewd eye tried to gauge their deeper purpose.

Matholwch and his retinue leaned forwards, eager to make good their proposition.

The sun climbed over the hills of Ardudwy. The air was thick with conversation and negotiation.

But look.

Not all the brothers of Bran are there. One is missing.

Efnisien, the unpeaceful, for whatever reason his twisted heart has given itself for absence, is hunting in the woods above Harlech.

Watch him as he crouches in the shadows and fits an arrow to his bow-string. Look at his face as he narrows his eyes and lets it fly. There is a contrary joy, a smile that flickers on the edge of malice, a dark unreadable intention written into the lines of his forehead.

A scream breaks the silence.

See how he strolls forward and picks up the struggling hare.

See how slowly he twists the arrow from its wracked body.

See how casually he breaks its neck between his hands and drops it into the bag that swings from his belt.

On the beach there was accord.

By the time the tide had covered the sands of Harlech, the counsel had reached its conclusion. Jars of mead were opened. Goblets were filled. Nisien raised his cup.

'Our sister is pledged to the King of Ireland. There will be a marriage feast at Aberffraw. Branwen will sleep with Matholwch. The bond of peace between Ireland and Britain, between Erin and the Island of the Mighty, will be sealed and secured.'

Cups were lifted to mouths. Strong mead moistened British and Irish throats.

But not every throat was moistened.

In the Court of Ardudwy, Branwen heard the clamour of men's voices. She lifted a polished bronze mirror and peered deep into her eyes. She shuddered as though a cold wind had blown across her heart. She turned the mirror over and laid it face down on the table.

Efnisien strode homewards with his bag of kills.

He heard the distant shouting.

He pulled the dagger from his belt and felt its honed edge with the flat of his thumb. He spat onto the ground.

Night came.

The moon rose and fell. The sky brightened with stars.

At first light the Irish company returned to their ships.

They set sail for Aberffraw, navigating the treacherous waters around Ynys Enlli.

Bran the Blessed and his retinue journeyed overland.

They made their way through the mountains and the valleys.

Bran strode ahead. The others followed on horseback.

When they reached the straits of Menai he waded across.

The water barely reached his thighs. His retinue waited for low tide.

They came to Aberffraw. The noblemen of the Island of the Mighty oversaw the making of a tent of larch poles and stretched leather that would be of sufficient height and breadth to accommodate their king.

Inside it, feasting tables and mead benches were constructed.

An enormous oaken throne was set in place.

The Irish anchored their ships in a sheltered cove.

Their horses smelt land. They whinnied and pined for firm ground.

They were roped together and swum ashore. Hurdled enclosures where the pasture was green and sweet had been made ready for them.

Bran's retinue leaned over the fences and admired the Irish horses. There were piebald, skewbald, bay, chestnut, roan and grey mares. There were geldings and stallions.

They were long-necked and sleek as swans.

Matholwch came ashore.

Bran, Manawydan and Nisien stood on the sea-strand and welcomed him as he stepped out of his currach. His retinue followed him.

They were led into the great tent. The floor was fragrant with cut rushes. They were invited to sit at the high table.

This is how they were placed:

Bran the Blessed sat on his throne in the centre. To his left sat his brother Manawydan, to his right sat Matholwch, King of Ireland. Beyond Matholwch Branwen was seated, and beside her Nisien the silver-tongued.

The food was served. The first night of feasting began.

Look.

Can you see how the Irish stranger smiles at his bride?

He offers her sweetmeats from his plate. He lifts fatted crumbs to her lips with his thick horseman's fingers. She blushes at his laughter.

When the platters have been cleared and the harpers have sung their songs, see how he reaches and takes her hand.

He grips it so tight that there can be no shaking it off.

The flushed faces of her brothers speak only encouragement.

See how he pulls her to her feet. He leads her out of the tent.

She stumbles behind him as they cross the starlit enclosure.

The horses watch with indifferent eyes.

They come to the court of Aberffraw.

The door of the bedchamber is open. The marriage bed has been made bright with candles. They enter.

Without releasing his hold he closes the door with the heel of his foot.

With his free hand he's reaching down. He lifts the hem of her bridal dress. He's pulling it up to her waist. His weight is against her. She's falling onto the soft coverlets of the bridal bed. His hips are pressed between her splayed knees.

Hear her sudden cry of pain as he hunches over her and spills his Irish seed into her womb.

And now, grown tender, see how he unfastens every tie of her dress and runs his hands across her pale skin.

See how he licks away the tears that are spilling from her grey eyes and whispers into her ear as though she is a colt he is breaking to the saddle."

Tomos jumped to his feet and ran to the door, knocking the stylus from Brother Iago's hand. He ran outside into the snow. They could hear the sound of his hoarse sobbing, furious in its sudden release.

Dafydd got up to follow him. Olwen caught his robe.

"Wait."

She drew him back.

"Leave him for a while. He has seen too much, that boy."

The old poet looked at her.

"*You* must go to him. He has lived too long in worlds of men. First at Nant Gwrtheyrn then here at Clynnog Fawr. He needs something we cannot give him."

Dafydd nodded to her.

"He is right."

He sat down again. There was quiet for a while in the cell. Outside the sobs continued.

Cian Brydydd Mawr whispered:

"The boy looks into the story and sees his own story, it is always the way."

Olwen got up. She picked up her cloak.

"We will need a little time."

"Come back after None."

She made her way across the snow. The boy was by the gate. His forehead was leaning on the gatepost. His hands were over his face. He was trembling.

She rested the palm of her hand on his neck.

"It was hard for you to listen?"

He said nothing. At her touch his body stiffened.

"It made you remember?"

His voice was as high as a child half his age.

"My mother ..."

He broke into sobs.

"... what they did before she died ..."

He banged his head against the gatepost.

"... the pirates, the Irish pirates when they came."

"You saw?"

His silence told her all she needed to know. She took his shoulders, turned him round and folded him inside her cloak.

The bell rang for None.

Half an hour later the monks came out into the cold light. The woman and the boy were still standing by the gate. The top of Tomos' head was tucked under her chin.

After None, Dafydd was the first to come back to the cell.

He took his place and looked at Cian Brydydd Mawr. The old man could see there was darkness around Dafydd's eyes, as though he had been too long at prayer, or too long awake in the winter night.

"I listen to your stories and wonder. Maybe I too have lived for too long in the world of men."

The poet raised his eyebrows.

"Dafydd ap Dafydd ap Dafydd, maybe you have."

Olwen and Tomos came in together. The boy crossed the room. He lifted a blanket and drew it across the old man's shoulders.

"Thank you, son. You are ready to hear more?"

The boy nodded.

"The story does not get any kinder. It is not a story's job to be kind."

Tomos shrugged. He sat down on the floor by the fire.

Brother Iago arrived. The old man began.

"And so the marriage bond was sealed between Branwen and Matholwch, and with it the bond between Erin and the Island of the Mighty.

For three days and nights the wedding feast was celebrated.

On the evening of the fourth day Efnisien came.

He saw the enormous tent. He saw the ships anchored in the bay.

He saw the Irish horses. Some grooms were deep in talk.

Efnisien approached them.

'Tell me friends, whose horses are these?'

'They belong to Matholwch, King of Ireland.'

'What are they doing here?'

One of the grooms stepped forwards.

'Surely, Lord, you know that your sister has slept with Matholwch. They are become husband and wife. These are the horses he brought with him from Ireland.'

Efnisien's voice dropped to a whisper.

'So they have given her away, and have not sought my blessing.'

He turned and melted into the shadows.

That night Efnisien returned.

The feasting was finished and the revellers were asleep in their beds.

There was a full moon shining in the sky.

All of Aberffraw was illuminated: the currachs pulled up onto the sand, the towering tent, the thatched roofs and the standing horses. Everything was black and grey and silver in the moonlight.

Efnisien jumped over a hurdle and entered the enclosure.

The horses turned their heads towards him. They snorted.

He pulled his glinting knife from his belt.

He seized one of their heads by its mane and plunged the blade of his knife into its mouth. He cut the lips back to the teeth. He cut off its ears.

He caught hold of another horse's combed tail. He severed it close against the rump.

The next horse he blinded, cutting through its eyelids to the bone.

One by one he maimed them.

Then he slipped away into the night.

The horses were shrieking, screaming and rolling their heads in the grass. They were galloping, blind and frantic, against the hurdles that held them. They were splattering each other with their streaming blood.

Matholwch was asleep.

Dawn had not broken when two of his noblemen burst into his bedchamber. He was lying in the bridal bed with Branwen beside him.

They woke him with their urgent whispers.

'My Lord, you have been bitterly insulted.'

He sat up in bed.

'How?'

'Come with us.'

They led him out of the court to the hurdled enclosure.

He stood in the first light of morning and stared at his ruined horses. For a long time he had no words for what he saw.

'I do not understand.'

He turned to his men.

'If they wanted to insult me, why did they first give me a woman of such beauty, of such high rank, and so beloved by her family?'

His men shook their heads.

'My Lord, an insult is an insult. We must return to our ships. We must sail home to Ireland.'

The King of Ireland had no choice.

One by one his retinue were shaken awake.

Silently they slipped away from the court of Aberffraw.

When they came to the cove they dragged the currachs down to the water. They rowed out to the anchored ships. The sails were unfurled and the clanking iron anchors were lifted.

Matholwch turned his back on Branwen, his bride of four nights, and set his face for home.

Bran was woken with the story of the blinded horses.

He lifted his huge hands to his head and pondered.

Then he spoke:

'Send messengers to the cove. There may still be time to avoid disgrace.'

Two fleet-footed messengers ran to the rocks above the cove. Their names were Iddig and Hyfaidd Hir.

The Irish ships were making ready to sail.

The messengers shouted across the water:

'Lord Matholwch! Great Bran wishes to know, why are you leaving?'

One of the little boats was lowered. The King of Ireland climbed into it. He was rowed across to the rocky outcrop where they stood.

'Tell Bran the Blessed that if I had known how deeply he would insult me, I would never have come. No man has ever embarked on such an ill-fated expedition as this.'

The messengers replied:

'Lord, it was never our king's will, nor the will of his noblemen, nor of any who gathered at the counsel on the shores of Harlech, that such an insult should be perpetrated. If this act of violence is bitter to you, we give you our word that it is a hundred times more bitter to Bran the Blessed.'

'Maybe,' said Matholwch, 'but an insult remains an insult, and no word or gift or act of recompense could ever undo what has been done.'

He nodded to his men and they dug their oars into the blue water. They turned the little boat around. The currach made its way back to the thirteen waiting ships.

The messengers returned to Bran with Matholwch's words on their tongues. He shook his great head.

'Matholwch is insulted. Our sister is disgraced. There is nothing to be gained by the Irish leaving our shores in anger. We must not allow it.'

He summoned Manawydan.

He rested his broad hand on his brother's shoulder.

'Go to the sea-shore. Offer him whatever terms will bring him back to the feasting table.'

Manawydan made his way to the rocky outcrop.

He drew breath and bellowed:

'Lord Matholwch! Listen to me! I am Manawydan, son of Llyr, brother to Bran the Blessed, brother also to your wife.'

Matholwch leaned over the rails of his ship and listened.

'The High King of the Island of the Mighty offers these terms.

For every one of your ruined horses he will give you a sound one of strong mountain stock, nimble-footed and swift as the wind.

As an honour price for the insult you have received he will give you a rod of pure white silver as thick as his thumb and as tall as he is.

He will also give you a golden plate as broad as his face.

The maiming of your horses was an act that ran contrary to all his wishes and intentions.'

The words of Manawydan rang clear across the water. Matholwch turned to his noblemen.

'How should we receive this offer?'

'Lord,' they said, 'if we refuse it, not only will you have been insulted, but also you will have received no recompense. You should accept and return to the table.'

The King of Ireland and his retinue came back to the great tent at Aberffraw. Bran invited them to sit at the high table. They were arranged as before, with Branwen between her brother and her husband.

But where there had been good cheer before, there was a sullen silence now. A grey cloud had cast its shadow across the feast.

See how uneasily Branwen sits.

Her eyes are torn. To her left is the huge face of Bran, flushed and eloquent with mead, eager to mend the misunderstanding and make all well. To her right Matholwch's eyes are downcast. He turns his food over with his knife, eating little, saying less. He has the air of a gambler who has lost at the dicing table. The noblemen of his retinue are silent also, chewing their food as though there's more gristle than meat to it.

Branwen turns to her husband. Her body has not forgiven his bruises nor forgotten his unexpected tenderness. She turns to the brother who has given her away. She knows that, as a king's sister and one cursed to beauty, she must fulfil her destiny. Bran leans down and kisses her brow, whiter than the petals of the marsh trefoil. She smiles. She cannot love him any less for what he has done to her.

Nisien the silver-tongued gets to his feet.

He walks to the throne of Bran the Blessed.

'Brother.'

Bran turned to him.

'A word in your ear.'

Bran leaned down. Nisien whispered:

'Brother, it seems to me that the Irish king is unhappy. You must offer him something more or it will not go well for our sister.'

Bran bowed his head. He said to Matholwch:

'Lord, your tongue is slow to speech. I feel the weight of your grief. If you are still slighted and you feel that the honour price is not high enough, then I shall increase it.'

Matholwch grunted. He did not look up from his platter.

'Tomorrow I will replace all your wounded horses with spirited British steeds.'

Matholwch shook his head.

'These you have already promised.'

'And,' said Bran, 'there is something else. I have among my treasures a certain cauldron ...'

For the first time the King of Ireland looked up. His face quickened with interest.

'... it is no ordinary cauldron. It has a very particular property. If a dead warrior is thrown into it, he will be restored to life. He will rise up in the full vigour of his youth. But he will have no speech. He will have become as silent as the grave.'

Matholwch seized his drinking cup. He raised it to Bran. His eyes had brightened.

'That might be a double blessing! If you were to give me such a gift I would be restored to happiness and my compensation would be complete.'

He turned to Branwen. For the first time since his return, he pressed his lips to her cheek. She neither inclined towards him nor away.

He reached for her hand and drew her to her feet.

The Irish noblemen watched their king's back as he led the woman out of the tent. They kept their counsel.

The next morning, compensation was paid.

Matholwch was given the rod of silver and the plate of yellow gold.

He was given all of Bran's horses that were stabled in Aberffraw. When they had been counted it was found there were not enough.

So they journeyed to another commot where he was given colts to make up the full tally.

Ever since, that part of Môn has been called Talebolion, which means 'the payment of the colts'.

The horses were led to the sea-shore. They were roped to the currachs and swam behind. They were lifted aboard the Irish ships and bedded down with straw and hay.

When the sun had set, Matholwch and Bran sat down for the last night of the wedding feast. The two kings fell into conversation.

'Lord,' said Matholwch, 'tell me about the cauldron that you have promised me. How did it come into your keeping?'

'I was given it,' said Bran, 'by a man bigger than I am. I suppose you would call him a giant. He had come across the water from your country. As far as I know that is where he found it.'

'What is his name?'

'His name is Llasar Llaes Gyfnewid. He came here with his wife Cymidei Cymeinfoll. They walked out of the waves and up the slope of the sea carrying the cauldron on their backs. They told us a story about a house made of iron. It surprises me, Lord, that you know nothing about these matters yourself.'

Matholwch smiled.

'Indeed I do, and as soon as you spoke of the cauldron I had a feeling in my bones that this must be the one. Listen and I will tell you all that I know of it.

There is a lake in my kingdom that is called "The Lake of the Cauldron". Beside it stands a green mound with a stone cairn at the top of it. One day I had been hunting and I stopped to rest. I hobbled my horse and climbed the hill. I sat and looked out across the wide blue water of the lake.

I hadn't been there for long when I saw a wonder.

First a shock of red hair – I took it for weed – appeared on the surface of the lake. Then came a craggy brow, a twisted nose and a red beard that dripped water. A giant of huge proportion was striding out of the lake towards me. On his shoulders, which were as wide as two stallions standing nose to nose, he was carrying a bronze cauldron. With each swing of his step it slurped water down his back. His body was bowed with the weight of it.

Then I saw that he was not alone. Behind him another head had appeared. This time there was no beard. Instead I saw bare shoulders, two swinging breasts, a belly, and hips as broad as any stable door.

And Lord Bran, if he was big then she was twice his size, and if he was ugly, one glance from her would have soured a jug of milk.

When they had come out of the lake they saw me.

He put the cauldron down at the water's edge and made a great show of bowing to me. I greeted them:

"Strangers," I said, "how goes it with you?"

The giant replied:

"This is how it goes with us, Matholwch, King of Ireland. Every six weeks my wife conceives and gives birth to a son. He drops out of her womb fully grown, fully armed and fierce as a wild boar. Matholwch, you have two choices. Friendship or bitter enmity. Either you can offer us hospitality and take us into your household, or you can turn us away. What do you say?"

Well, Lord, I had no choice. I took them to my court and for one full year I maintained them. I treated them like honoured guests. Day and night my servants sweated over boiling pots to satisfy their raging appetites. My brewers toiled to slake their thirsts. Every six weeks another son was added to their number, and each one hungrier than the one before.

For the first four months they kept themselves to themselves, but then they began to range far and wide. They pestered, molested and mocked my noblemen and their wives. They picked quarrels. They stole cattle. After half a year they were loathed and unwanted in the land. When ten months were past my people could stand it no longer. They petitioned and begged me to get rid of them.

They told me that if I could not rid my realm of this race of giants, then my kingship would be at an end.

But it is no easy thing to dispose of guests like those. Nothing would persuade them to leave, and nobody – such was their strength and ferocity – could force them to go.

As they feasted at my expense and availed themselves of my hospitality, my advisers began to hatch a plan.

They invited all the blacksmiths of Ireland to come together and construct a chamber of iron. It was to have an iron floor, an iron roof and four walls of iron. In one of the walls there was to be an iron door with iron bolts.

For weeks the air was riven with the sound of hammering.

When the chamber had been finished, the blacksmiths fetched charcoal. They piled it around the walls and over the roof until only the door was left uncovered.

My servants carried tables and benches into the iron chamber. They lit candles. They set out wooden platters and knives and bronze goblets. They piled the tables with food. Sides and haunches of meat were prepared, whole cheeses, enormous pats of butter, loaves of bread, one piled on another. Rich stews steaming in their iron cauldrons were set on the floor. Baskets of eggs and nuts and dripping honeycombs were hung from hooks overhead. Barrels of ale and mead and wine were rolled into the chamber, each one well seasoned and ready for tapping.

When everything was ready I approached the giants.

'Friends,' I said, 'it is now a year since our paths first crossed at the Lake of the Cauldron, and to celebrate I have prepared a feast in your honour.'

I led them to the chamber of iron. As always they brought their cauldron with them; they would never part with it.

When they saw the feast they wasted no time.

Llasar Llaes Gyfnewid, his wife Cymidei Cymeinfoll and their eight ferocious sons bounded into the chamber and gorged themselves. They crammed the food into their open mouths, seizing the bread and meat from each other's hands. They lifted the iron cauldrons to their lips and gulped the stews. They tipped the barrels of strong liquor down their throats.

In no time there was nothing left but chewed bones and empty vessels. They stretched themselves out on the iron floor that was awash with grease and gravy.

They closed their eyes and slept.

It was then, Lord, that we closed the iron door and pulled the iron bolts into place. All the blacksmiths of Ireland pushed the iron noses of their leather bellows into the charcoal. When it had been set alight they pumped so that the heat spread and the chamber began to glow.

Inside the giants had woken. We could hear them roaring but we showed no mercy. The blacksmiths pumped until the hill of charcoal was shimmering with heat. They pumped until the chamber was red-hot and its molten walls were beginning to sag and bend.

By now we were sure they must have perished, but a strange thing happened.

Llasar Llaes Gyfnewid burst through one of the walls of melting iron. He was carrying the cauldron on his back. He leapt clear of the furnace, kicking away the bellows with his bare feet.

Several blacksmiths were trampled to death.

With enormous strides he ran across Ireland. Close behind his wife followed, sweating like a reaper in high summer.

When they came to the sea they waded in. The water boiled and hissed around them like ale around a mulling iron. The grey waves closed over their scorched heads.

Their sons had perished, but these two had set their faces towards the Island of the Mighty.

And I suppose, Lord Bran, it was not long afterwards that you encountered them?'

'Indeed I did,' said Bran the Blessed, 'we met on the sea-shore and they gave me their cauldron.'

'What sort of welcome did you give them, Lord?'

'I welcomed them with all my heart. I gave them lodging, and as their numerous sons were born I dispersed them across my kingdom. They prosper everywhere and strengthen my armies with the ferocity of their fighting and the cunning of their craftsmanship.'

The two kings called for their cups to be filled, and filled again.

They feasted until deep into the night. The air was thick with the sound of their talk. When the hour was reached that is more suited to sleep than to song, they retired to their beds.

The next morning Branwen walked down to the sea-shore.

Behind her a line of servants were staggering under the weight of her dowry, packed into wooden chests that had been bound with bronze and iron. The cauldron, the great golden plate and the rod of silver were carefully loaded into the boats.

Three brothers stood at the water's edge.

Bran the Blessed dropped to his knees on the sand and opened his arms to Branwen. He embraced her. He drew her cheek against the soft folds of his enormous woollen tunic and spread his hand over the length of her back. Manawydan tenderly kissed her forehead and Nisien the silver-tongued kissed her hands.

As to the fourth brother, Efnisien, I do not know whether he watched his sister climb into the currach beside the Irish king. I do not know whether he watched her turn her face towards the open water so that her tears would not be seen. I do not know whether he watched, from some hidden place, and rocked from heel to toe with his own twisted sorrow.

I do know that the thirteen Irish ships lifted their anchors and made ready to sail for home.

When they came to Ireland the new queen was welcomed.

The noblemen and their wives had heard rumours of her beauty. They came to the court of Matholwch and none were disappointed. Branwen gave them gifts of gold. She gave them brooches, rings and precious stones.

And then her belly began to swell.

Her dresses would no longer tie. There was rejoicing throughout the kingdom. The king's seed had rooted in fertile soil. A fecund queen means a fruitful land.

Matholwch made sure she was tended and cared for. She was never without a companion from among the noble women of Ireland.

When her time came the midwives were fetched and a fine son was born. He was given the name Gwern."

"Enough. I am tired now. Tomos make my bed ready, I need to lie down."

He looked at Brother Iago.

"How long?"

"As before, a little more than a week."

"Then we will meet in ten days."

Dafydd and Olwen spoke in unison:

"Lambing has begun."

They looked at each other and smiled.

Dafydd continued:

"The farm is busy. We have plenty of lay brothers and herd-boys. But even so there are times when I will need to go out and take my turn."

She said:

"The boys should manage ... and with the extra help I will hope to be with you ..."

"Good. I need you all – every one of you. I cannot do without you. This story is something we make together."

Brother Iago was the last to leave.

"I do not understand. Why could you not dictate your Matter to me alone? It would save time. And then I could return to Aberconwy and continue the work of God."

The old man closed his eyes.

"Iago ap Rhys, do you think I could tell these stories in the way that I have told them if I was speaking to you alone? This Matter is fed by its listeners, just as a tree is fed by the soil in which it grows. Every Cyfarwydd sends out his roots and draws sustenance from his audience; because you cannot see them does not mean they are not there."

"Then your Matter might be different another time?"

Cian Brydydd Mawr smiled.

"It might Brother. Now go. Leave me in peace."

Monday February 2nd

Olwen and Rhys were in the lambing enclosure when the bailiff came.

One of the ewes was struggling to give birth. Olwen was on her knees. She was reaching for the slippery front feet of the lamb that would not come. Rhys was holding the ewe steady. With a sudden groan the lamb came slithering and coughing into the cold light. It struggled to pull itself to a wobbling stand. Rhys let go of the ewe. It turned and licked the lamb's face. Olwen picked up a fistful of hay and wiped her arms clean.

The bailiff had been sitting astride his horse, watching in silence.

"A healthy beast I'd say."

Olwen looked up at him. She knew he never came without a reason.

"Yes, it'll live."

"How many lambs so far?"

"Sixteen."

He scratched marks onto his tally stick with a knife.

"That'll be four for the tithe."

"I know."

"How old is the boy?"

"Seventeen winters."

"He'll have to go then, when the summer comes. He'll have to serve his time away."

Rhys came forwards. Olwen nodded.

"We have been expecting it. Where will he go?"

"There will be harvesting on our Lord's fields in Môn. There will be building at Dolwyddelan. I do not know yet."

He paused.

"And, between you and me, there will also be war."

Olwen paled.

"You are sure?"

"There are whispers of a great uprising. Llywelyn is eager to regain his losses. If that is the case, every strong young man," he nodded to Rhys, "will be wielding a sword, not a sickle or a mattock. Our Lord will be swelling his teulu into a war host."[25]

Olwen reached forwards. She put her hand on the neck of the bailiff's horse.

"Do your best for him. I have lost one man already. I could not bear to lose another. He has many skills, but he is a farmer not a soldier."

The bailiff reined his horse around.

"If the lad could fight as nobly as his father, then he would be a source of pride to us all."

"Yes, and he would also be dead."

"It is not in my power to help you. Just remember, the boy's age has been noted."

Mother and son watched him as he struck spurs to his horse's flanks and rode down the slope of the hill to the next farm.

Saturday February 6th

"Come in, come in. Sit down."

The old poet's audience was complete.

"If I could sing I would sing of Branwen, daughter of Llyr.

I would sing of Branwen as she crooks her arm so that her child's head is lifted to her white breast.

172

She looks down at him as he takes succour from her body.

All hiraeth, all her longing for her native land, melts away into the milk he swallows. She has found a place in the king's orchard.

Soft furs and cloths have been thrown across a wooden seat.

The sunlight is dappled by the shifting leaves.

Gwern's head falls away from her, his mouth is open, his eyes closed. The blue-white milk is dribbling from his lips.

In this moment there is nowhere she would rather be.

She has not heard the muttering voices.

Matholwch's retinue had not forgotten the maiming of their king's horses. The story had been passed from mouth to ear. It had been whispered across the kingdom of Ireland.

As the rumour spread, the people began to look askance at their British queen. Was not the culprit her own half-brother? What punishment had he received? What recompense was a fistful of flattened gold, a silver rod and a cauldron of bronze?

Did the British colts compare with the ruined Irish horses?

The whispers became a muttering.

The muttering became an outcry.

A deputation of people and poets approached the Court.

They told Matholwch that unless he sought revenge, they would bring his kingship to an end. They told him that if he let the matter rest, his name would be satirised the length and breadth of the realm. They told him that revenge must be taken on the cursed British queen whose family had allowed the mutilation of his horses and the humiliation of Ireland.

Branwen saw her husband approaching the orchard.

He came to where she sat.

He stood before her and looked down. His head was tilted to one side as though he was trying to read her thoughts. He was dressed in his robes of court – his cloak, his torc, his golden-hilted sword.

He reached towards her.

She passed the sleeping baby to a maidservant and lifted her hand. He seized her wrist and pulled her to her feet.

She turned to the maidservant and shook her head, as if to say 'there is no need to come with us'. The servant curtseyed gravely, lifting her skirt with her one free hand. Both of them understood that there were no choices. This was what had to be endured.

She stumbled behind him as they crossed the courtyard.

They came to the royal bedchamber.

To her surprise they did not enter.

He pulled her past its closed door. They were going somewhere she had never been before. The air became hotter. The smell of smoke tickled her throat.

Outside the kitchen door twelve noblemen were waiting.

All of them were familiar from the feast at Aberffraw.

Her husband held her shoulders as they unfastened her clothes.

They tore away her silks and linens and soft woollen garments.

One of them was holding a dress of sack-cloth.

It was filthy with grease and ashes. He pulled it down over her head. He tied it round her waist with coarse twine. Another pushed a wooden ladle into her hand. She looked at Matholwch.

'What will happen to our son?'

His narrowed eyes looked beyond her, as though he was staring into a strong sun.

'He will forget you.'

The kitchen door was opened and she was shoved inside.

She staggered and slipped on the slimy flagstones.

When she opened her eyes the door had been slammed shut.

A cook pulled her upright and led her to a kneading trough.

'We need another pair of hands. There's bread to be baked for the royal table.'

The dough was set before her. She saw she had no choice.

She pushed her hands into it and set to work. All day she kneaded one loaf after another until her arms were aching.

When the bread was baking in the domed ovens, the other scullions hurried home to their hovels.

But for Branwen the day's ordeal was not yet over.

A butcher came across to her. He had been cutting meat for the cauldrons. His hands were red and sticky with blood.

He looked at her as though she was another beast to be felled.

He struck her on the ear with the full force of his fist.

Branwen crawled across the floor to a pile of rags by the fire.

She lay down and slept.

The butcher went outside to the well and washed his hands clean.

Every day was the same.

Branwen, daughter of Llyr, one of the three chief maidens of the Island of the Mighty, was condemned to knead bread for the royal table, and then to be struck by a butcher's bloody hand.

This was the way the noblemen of Ireland avenged the maiming of their horses.

They went to Matholwch.

'Lord, you must place a prohibition, so that no Irish ships cross the water to Britain. Likewise you must ensure that anyone from that country who sets foot on Irish soil is cast into prison. We must make a secret of your wife's humiliation. Her brothers should never come to hear of it.'

The King of Ireland saw he had no choice. The prohibition was placed.

Three long years passed.

Nobody could have guessed that the slattern who kneaded the bread, with her filthy hair, her swollen hands and her face as disfigured as a three-quarter moon, had once been the Queen of Ireland.

But Branwen did have one forlorn hope.

There was a starling that flew down to her kneading trough.

Every morning it stole the crumbs that fell to the floor.

She sprinkled flour onto her hand.

It hopped up and swallowed it.

She lifted her hand to her lips and whispered to it.

The little bird cocked its head to one side and listened.

Slowly, over weeks and months, she taught it to speak.

She told it about the mountains and valleys of her native land.

She told it about her brother, great Bran the Blessed, so tall that no house could hold him.

She told it of the life she had lost, of the son she never saw.

She told it of the bed of rags and the butcher's bloody hand.

She poured out her heart to the little bird.

One morning she whispered:

'Now go! Fly across the water! You know how to recognise my brother, the High King of the Island of the Mighty.'

She made a map of Wales with the peaks and the troughs of dough.

She pointed with her finger.

'This is where you will find him, in Caer Seint, in Arfon.

Tell him my story. Spare no detail. Go!'

The speckled starling opened its wings.

It beat them against the air and rose up into the rafters.

It flew out of the kitchen and was gone.

There is not time to tell of the buffetings, the salty winds and sea sprays, the long lonely acres of water, the mockery of gulls, the aching struggles of that flight.

At last the little bird saw mountains looming over the grey horizon. It tasted land on the shifting currents of the air.

When it settled on firm ground it eased its hunger with a feast of insects. Then it followed the long shingled shoreway to Caer Seint.

Look.

There is Bran the Blessed.

See how his shadow is cast over the assembly of the noblemen of Britain. They are gathered round him like foothills around a mountain.

He leans forward to listen to their words.

He considers and plans. He passes judgement. He offers his counsel.

His voice has the rich, rumbling resonance of a deep bronze bell.

Now he has launched into a speech of such eloquence that the assembly has slipped into spell-bound silence.

His tongue has reached its height of oratory.

There is a flapping in his face.

He brushes the bird away with his huge hand.

It is back. It has caught hold of his beard with its claws and is pecking at his cheek. He flicks it with his finger. It circles around his head and lands on his ear.

One of the nobleman's sons is fitting a stone to his sling.

To his amazement Bran hears a torrent of chattering speech.

He reaches forwards and seizes the sling. He casts it aside.

He raises his finger to his lips.

'Shhhh.'

The bird is pouring words into his ear.

Every feather is trembling with the vehemence of its message.

Bran listens with his full attention.

See how the blood is draining from his cheeks.

See how the hot salt tears are streaming in runnels from his eyes.

See how he trembles with rage.

See how he throws back his head and bellows. The sound echoes from valley to valley, over and over. Then settles into silence.

Bran's face is a mask of iron resolve.

The speckled starling flies up from his ear.

It beats the air with its wings and is gone.

'What have you heard, Lord?'

Bran told them.

Messengers were sent to the one hundred and fifty-four kingdoms of the realm. Every Lord and Lesser King mustered his warriors, made his ships ready, prepared for battle.

The lowlands of Arfon became a sea of soldiers.

Bran strode among them like a man wading knee deep in water.

One of those Lords we have met before.

Pryderi, son of Pwyll, Lord of the seven cantrefs of Dyfed, was among the host. He had been recently married to Cigfa, daughter of Gwyn Gohoyw.

It had been a hard and tender parting.

She'd watched her newly wed husband ride from his court at Arberth.

Beside her had stood Rhiannon.

Like wives and mothers everywhere they'd watched their man ride out to war. Then they'd turned indoors, not knowing whether he would ever warm his hands at their fires again.

'Not for nothing was he named Pryderi – Care.'

Behind him had ridden a thousand noblemen and warriors. Each man armed with sword, spear, bow and a quiver full of arrows; each dressed for battle with helmet, shield and battle vest.

Every heart had been eager for war."

Olwen stood up.

"There we have it," she said. "Every boy should be christened Pryderi. Every mother's son, every wife's husband. I know that journey from gateway to empty hearth. I have made it myself. It is strewn with ashes."

The midday bell rang.

"And soon I must make it again."

Cian Brydydd Mawr bowed his head.

"We will stop there for a while."

Outside it was raining. Olwen wrapped her cloak around herself.

She hurried across to the food store to eat the cheese and coarse bread she had brought for her midday meal. The monks' voices drifted from the church. She finished her food, chose an apple from the rack and sank her teeth into its sweet, sharp flesh. She ate it to the core. The rain was streaming from the thatch onto the wet ground outside. The sound of psalms and running water mingled in her ears.

She fell into a reverie that was bordering on sleep.

The door latch clicked. She woke with a start.

Brother Deiniol came in. He crossed the floor. He reached up and took a string of onions from a hook. He hadn't seen her.

Should she say something or keep still?

Maybe he wouldn't see her among the shadows. She held her breath.

He was humming to himself. Then he turned.

"HOLY MARY!"

He dropped the onions and hurled himself through the door.

"Christ Jesu and all the Saints!"

He ran to the church and dropped to his knees before the altar.

Olwen hurried out. She found an ash tree to shelter beneath.

She didn't see Brother Deiniol creeping back. She didn't see him pushing open the door and peering inside. The store-room was empty. His voice was a whimper.

"There's nobody here!"

He shuddered and crossed himself.

When they came back to the old man's cell, Olwen said to Dafydd:

"I think maybe the store-room is not such a good place for me to eat my dinner."

"Why not?"

"I have given one of the brothers a terrible fright."

"Which one?"

"Is he your Abbot? Brother Deiniol?"

"He is not our Abbot, but he is the most senior of the Brothers at Clynnog Fawr."

Brother Iago was breathless when he came in from None.

"I am sorry if I have kept you waiting. There was a collapse. Brother Deiniol, when we spoke the words 'they have dug a pit for my soul', fell onto the floor in a swound. We could not wake him."

"How is he now?"

"He is revived, but will not cease from prayer."

Cian Brydydd Mawr looked at Olwen.

"It seems you are become Eve, Bathsheba, Delilah, Magdalen ..."

She shrugged.

"And yet, when I lean over the edge of the well, I see only myself."

"You will remember how the lowlands of Arfon were become a sea of warriors.

Bran the Blessed left seven trusted men behind. Together they were to rule over the Island of the Mighty while he was away.

They would be caretakers until his return from Ireland.

These were the seven:

Caradawg (who was his own son),

Hyfaidd Hir,

Iddig, son of Anarawg the Curly-Haired,

Ffodor, son of Erfyll,

Wlch Minasgwrn the Lip-Boned,

Llashar (one of the many sons of the giant Llasar Llaes Gyfnewid),

Pendaran Dyfed (who had been Pryderi's foster father).

Caradawg was to be the chief among them.

Each one of these seven was renowned as a rider and breeder of horses. The place where Bran bade them farewell is still called Bryn Seith Marchawg, 'The Hill of the Seven Horsemen'.

The Irish Sea was shallow.

The great inundation that would fill the Bay of Ceredigion to the brim had not yet taken place. The water was never deeper than two or three fathoms, except where two ancient rivers – Lli and Archan – had eaten away the sea bed.

Bran the Blessed waded through the water.

He carried all of his harpers on his shoulders.

Sometimes the water was knee deep. Sometimes it lapped against his shoulders.

Gathered around him – before and behind – were the ships of the Island of the Mighty. Their sails billowed like swollen bellies. Their prows sliced through the blue waves. Every ship was crammed with warriors. Every warrior had slaughter in his heart.

The green hills of Ireland began to rise above the blue horizon.

Look.

Can you see the shepherds of Matholwch?[26]

They have brought their flocks down to the sweet, tender pasture at the sea's edge. They are squatting together as their sheep range over the green sward. They are sharing bread and cheese. They drink water from a stream that winds down the hill towards the sea. The sun is warm. The sky is clear. They stretch out on the soft grass. They close their eyes.

One of them is keeping watch.

'Wake up!'

They were startled by a shout.

'Over there!'

The watcher was pointing across the water.

His hand was shaking. The others sat up and stared.

A vision was approaching, a strange sight that was beyond their understanding.

They leapt to their feet. They left their flocks and ran to the court of Matholwch.

The King of Ireland was in counsel with his noblemen and advisers. They burst into his hall.

They dropped to their knees.

'Lord, may you prosper.'

Matholwch stood up.

'Do you bring me news?'

'Lord, we do. We have seen a wonder. We have seen a vision that we cannot comprehend.'

'What did you see?'

'Lord, we saw a forest of trees moving across the waters of the sea.'

Matholwch paled.

'Did you see anything else?'

'Lord, we did. In the heart of the forest there was a mountain. It too was moving.'

The king's voice grew shrill.

'Anything else?'

'At the summit of the mountain there was a ridge. To either side of it there were lakes of red water.'

The king's hands began to tremble.

'Anything else?'

'From the moving mountain there came the strains of music.'

Matholwch looked from one nobleman to the next; his eyes were flickering with agitation.

'Can any of you read this vision?'

They shook their heads.

Bards and men of learning were fetched. They were told of the vision. One of them spoke:

'Lord, there is only one person who could read this wonder – your wife Branwen.'

Matholwch ordered that Branwen be brought from the kitchen.

She was dragged before her husband. Her hands were still sticky with dough.

The shepherds told her what they had seen.

Matholwch dropped to his knees before her.

'Lady, unriddle this vision if you can.'

Branwen narrowed her eyes. She pointed to her swollen face, her rags, her filthy hands.

'Lady! I am no longer a lady. But I can tell you what the vision means.'

'Then tell us.'

Branwen looked down into his face with scorn.

'The trees are the masts and the yard-arms of the ships of Britain moving across the water. Every ship is crammed with warriors with hatred in their hearts.'

'Tell us more.'

'The mountain is my brother, Bran the Blessed. He is wading through the water. The ridge is the bridge of his nose. The two red lakes are his eyes. They are blazing and bloodshot with fury at my bitter humiliation.'

'Tell us more.'

'The music is the sound of his minstrelsy, perched on his shoulders, singing of the downfall of Erin at the hands of the hosts of the Island of the Mighty.'

Matholwch turned to his noblemen.

'What are we to do?'

'Retreat, Lord ...' was their reply, '... retreat beyond the River Shannon. Destroy every bridge behind you. There are magical lode-stones in the bed of that river that will drag any ship, vessel or swimmer down to its depths. They will not be able to follow you.'

Matholwch ran from the hall. They shouted after him:

'And, Lord, take the woman with you.'

The King of Ireland ordered all of his fighting men to retreat to the far side of the River Shannon.

He followed them with his retinue.

Branwen was taken to a bath-house. She was washed and cleaned and combed. Healing ointments were rubbed into her face. She was dressed in silks and fine linens. Her hands were bound behind her back and she was hurried across the river to the camp where her husband was waiting for her.

Blazing torches were carried down to every bridge that spanned the River Shannon. Soon the waters were alive with the reflection of red and yellow flame. All night the bridges burned until the starry sky was smeared with black smoke.

Look.

Bran the Blessed is striding up the slope of the sea.

His armies disembark and wade ashore. The sun is setting in the west. They light fires. They slaughter the sheep they find wandering un-shepherded on the grassy slopes. They eat.

A whole ram has been roasted for Bran. He holds the head with one hand, a hind leg with the other and with his teeth he tears the sweet flesh from its bones.

Some men sharpen swords and stretch taut strings across their bows. Some boast of battles they have fought.

Some stretch out in the firelight and sleep.

Bran lies on his back and listens to the sounds of his army as it makes ready for warfare. He hears whet-stone on iron, stamping hooves, eager talk, grunts and snores, crackling flames.

He smiles for the first time since the starling came.

He closes his eyes.

'Tomorrow there will be a reckoning.'

It was still dark when they breakfasted.

At first light the army of the Island of the Mighty set off across Ireland. Bran strode at its head. Behind him his horsemen followed at thigh height, and his foot soldiers at calf height. As a farmer will lead his sheep and geese to the marketplace, Bran crossed the kingdom of Erin.

When they came to the banks of the Shannon they saw that all the bridges had been burnt.

Manawydan rode to his brother's side and shouted up:

'You know what has been said of this river? There are lode-stones in its depths that will drag any ship or swimmer down?'

'These things I have heard.'

'Every bridge is broken. We can advance no further.'

'We will cross it.'

'How?'

Bran the Blessed looked down at his army, massed and restive on the riverbank. His voice rang out:

'He who would lead, let him be a bridge.'

He stood at the water's edge and fell forwards like a toppled tree. He stretched himself out. He rested his forehead on the far bank and his feet on the near side. The back of his head, his neck, his back and the backs of his legs made a crossing place. Planks were laid over the length of his body.

Manawydan was the first to ride across. After him came horsemen in pairs and foot soldiers in ranks of three. All day the army crossed the river and gathered on the far side. When the last warrior was safely on the far bank the planks were lifted. Bran crawled on his knees through the water. He stood upright. He towered over his army, dripping mud and water onto their heads.

The words of the High King of the Island of the Mighty have never been forgotten. They have become a proverb that is on the lips of men and women to this day – 'He who would lead, let him be a bridge.'"

Cian Brydydd Mawr paused.

"As our Lord Llywelyn is a bridge."

Olwen sighed.

"And across it march men and boys who will never come home."

"The news that Bran and the host of Britain had crossed the River Shannon reached the ears of Matholwch.

Branwen was brought before him.

'Lady, what are we to do?'

She looked at him. Her heart was rejoicing.

Her grey eyes were cold as stones.

'I will utter no word until you give me my son.'

The boy was brought to her.

He was dressed as a man, with cloak and woollen breeches. At his hip there was a little wooden sword. Gwern looked at his mother with solemn eyes, as though she was a stranger.

'Gwern! My son!'

At the sound of her voice a memory stirred.

'Gwern.'

He ran to her and pressed his face against her breast.

Branwen turned to her husband.

'Untie my hands.'

The ropes were cut. She held her son. She held him for a long time. No word was spoken. When she broke the silence her bruised cheeks were wet with tears.

'These are the terms you must offer my brother. Tell him that to make good the injury I have suffered at your hands you will give the throne of Ireland to our son. Tell him that Gwern will be crowned King of Ireland in Bran's presence. And tell him that you, Matholwch, are to be treated as he sees fit, either here or in the Island of the Mighty.'

Matholwch turned to his noblemen.

'What do you say to this?'

They shrugged.

'Lord, his army is approaching. You have no choice.'

A messenger was sent.

A while later he returned. He stood pale-faced before Matholwch.

'Well?'

'Bran the Blessed says it is not enough. He wants more. Lord, the army of Britain is advancing. Soon you will hear the thundering of their hooves against the turfs of Ireland.'

Matholwch turned to Branwen. His eyes were those of a stag with dogs at every quarter.

She laughed in his face.

'There is a way to save yourself. My brother has never been inside a house or a hall. If you were to construct a thatched building in his honour, if it was made large enough to hold him and his retinue, as well as you and all your noblemen. If, beneath the roof beams of that house, you were to crown little Gwern ... and if you were then put yourself at his mercy.'

She turned away from him.

'If you were to offer all these things – maybe he would consider making peace with you.'

Matholwch remembered the tent of skins at Aberffraw. He nodded to his messenger:

'You heard the terms. Go!'

Bran saw the messenger galloping towards him.

He lifted his arm and the host of Britain halted.

He squatted on his haunches and peered down at the Irishman.

'So, what does your king have to say for himself?'

The messenger stood on his stirrups and looked up at the huge face that was scrutinising him:

"Lord, Matholwch, King of Ireland offers you these terms ...'

He delivered his message.

As he spoke he became aware that it was raining.

Huge drops of water were landing on his shoulders, his face, and the top of his head. The rain tasted of salt.

He saw that Bran the Blessed was weeping.

Tears were pouring from his eyes.

'These words you speak do not come from the mouth of Matholwch. They come from the lips of my dear sister. She knows that my deepest and most secret wish has always been to sit beneath the beams and the rafters of a house.'

Bran held a counsel with his brothers and his retinue.

They agreed to Matholwch's terms.

The host of the Island of the Mighty set up camp and waited while Matholwch ordered his men to build a tremendous house.

Oaks were felled and trunks spliced together.

Reed-beds were harvested. Dung and clay was trodden for daub.

Huge timbers were lifted upright.

Roof beams were slotted and lashed into place.

A hundred thatchers worked by day and night.

Iron-hinged doors, wide and tall enough for Bran to walk through, were hung from the door-frames.

The hall towered high above the tree tops.

The point of its thatched roof pierced the sky.

Matholwch's noblemen drew their king aside.

'Lord, come with us.'

They pushed open the enormous oaken doors and led their king inside. A fire had been lit. The smoke was drifting through the thatch.

'Do you see how the walls are at such a distance from the fire that they are cast into shadow?'

'I do.'

'Do you see the hundred pillars that carry the weight of the roof?'

'I do.'

'Lord, if we were to hang two leather sacks from each pillar, they would melt into the shadows and not be seen.'

'Tell me more.'

'If in each sack there was an armed warrior, with a sword and a sharp knife ...'

Matholwch smiled.

'I understand. Set the shoe-makers of Ireland to work. Tell them to stitch two hundred bags of ox-hide. Choose two hundred of our fiercest warriors.'

Soon, in the shadows against the wall, two hundred bags were hanging from the wooden pillars.

Matholwch sent word to Bran the Blessed.

When Bran saw the hall his heart was filled with delight.

He walked round it.

He looked up at the new thatch stretching high above his head. Its yellow reeds caught the golden light of the sun.

Matholwch approached him.

'Great Bran, I, your kinsman, your sister's husband, welcome you with all my heart. To show that we have no evil intentions, we will leave our weapons outside the hall.'

The King of Ireland, his noblemen and warriors, unbuckled their swords and knives and threw them onto the ground.

Bran turned to his company and nodded. They did the same.

Two heaps of discarded weapons lay outside the hall. There were bossed shields, leather scabbards, swords of bronze and iron, gold-hilted daggers, ash-wood spears.

For the first time in his life Bran the Blessed walked upright beneath the lintel of a doorway. He entered the hall. He lifted his arm and with wonder he traced the length of a roof beam with his finger-tips.

Matholwch followed him. Behind them came their retinues and all the noblemen of Britain and Ireland.

The two armies waited outside.

All of Bran's brothers were there.

Manawydan and Nisien the silver-tongued had been with him since the outset.

But another brother had appeared. While the hall was being built Efnisien had stepped out of the shadows. With no word of apology or explanation he was suddenly among them.

His brothers had shared food with him. He had lifted the meat to his mouth and offered them no clue as to the twisted reasoning of his heart.

Now he was entering the huge hall of Matholwch.

With hard, merciless eyes he peered about himself.

The fire was blazing. He saw Matholwch was seated on one side of it. On the other side Bran was resting on an oaken bench.

Beyond and around them their retinues were filling the hall.

Then he saw, among the shadows below the thatch, there were leather bags hanging from pegs. He turned to an Irish nobleman and pointed to one of them.

'Tell me, what is in this bag?'

The Irishman smiled.

'Flour, friend.'

Efnisien walked across to it. He reached up with his hands and felt the bag. He pressed it with his fingers. Beneath the leather he could feel bent legs and a long back. He could feel the shoulders, neck and head of a man. He could feel a hard, narrow scabbard. He wove his fingers together and cupped the head between the palms of his hands. Slowly, as though he was cracking a nut, he brought the heels of his hands together until he felt the bone break. Through the leather he could feel warm brains sagging out of a splintered skull.

Around him cups were being filled with mead and wine.

The company was settling itself down for the crowning ceremony.

He went to the next bag.

'What's inside?'

'Flour, friend.'

He felt for the head, cupped it in his hands and cracked it. Slowly he worked his way round the hall, playing the same game with each bag until only one man was left alive.

'What have we here?'

'Flour, friend.'

The skull shattered with a dull crack and red blood trickled through the leather seams of the sack.

Efnisien smiled and sang softly to himself:

'There is, in these sacks, flour of a sort,
milled from the skulls of skirmishers,
bitter the battle they would have fought.'

There was a blaring of horns.

Every face turned towards the entrance.

Branwen was standing in the light.

She was dwarfed by the height of the doorway. She was holding Gwern's hand. They walked into the shadowy hall.

Her eyes were peering to the left and the right. As soon as she saw her brothers she reached down and lifted the boy into her arms.

She ran across to Bran the Blessed.

The High King scooped them both up in his hands. He held his sister close, as though she was a child herself and he a nursing mother. She buried her face against his neck and her hot tears soaked his throat. The boy clambered out of his mother's arms. He scrambled up onto his uncle's shoulder.

Bran set them both gently on the ground.

Mother and son walked around the fire to Matholwch.

The boy knelt before his father.

Matholwch reached up. He lifted the golden crown of Ireland from his own head.

A drum sounded.

It was the sound that should have brought the waiting warriors from their bags.

The Irish noblemen shifted weight from foot to foot.

No warriors came. The King of Ireland saw he had no choice.

With trembling hands he lowered his crown. It went over the boy's head and rested on his shoulders so that his eyes peered over its fine-wrought points and decorations.

Bran's voice bellowed:

'Gwern, King of Ireland.'

He was echoed by the host of Britain:

'Gwern, King of Ireland!'

'And peace between Erin and the Island of the Mighty.'

Branwen tenderly lifted the crown from the boy's shoulders.

Gwern ran back to Bran. The High King put him onto the palm of his hand. He lifted him high above the watching crowd and pressed his lips to the boy's cheek. Gwern looked down at the upturned faces and laughed.

Gwern ran to Manawydan who kissed his forehead. He ran to Nisien who kissed his hands.

Then Efnisien spoke:

'Why doesn't my sister's son come to me? Even if he were not the King of Ireland I should still want to show him the affection of my heart.'

Nissien held Gwern tight, but Bran turned to him.

'Let the boy go.'

Nissien opened his hands and Gwern ran gladly to his fourth uncle.

Efnisien whispered to himself:

'Now I swear I shall commit an outrage beyond the expectation of anyone in this high hall.'

He embraced the little boy. His grip tightened on his nephew's shoulders. He lifted him above his head and flung him into the heat of the fire.

Look. Listen.

There is the appalled moment when the world pauses.

It is an eternity and the fleeting blink of an eye.

Its only sound is the scream of a child.

Its only sight is a child engulfed in flame.

Its only smell is a child's burning flesh.

And then there is a mother's anguish.

See how Branwen flings herself at the little flaming figure as it sinks into the shimmering heat.

See how she wades into the fire to seize its drowning hand.

Her dress is blazing. Her face is pale and passive in its resolve. Her only pain is the one engulfing agony of loss.

And now something is pulling her back. Something is dragging her away from her son. A huge hand has reached into the fire and curled its fingers around her waist.

She tries to break its grip. She tears at it with her fingernails.

It has lifted her blazing body from the ground and drawn her away from the heat. Another hand comes. It wraps her in a cloak and stifles her flames. It tips cold water over her.

Bran the Blessed lifts his stricken sister and, rocking backwards and forwards, he holds her to his heart."

Nobody spoke.

The mid-afternoon bell rang and fell silent.

Cian Brydydd Mawr looked across at Brother Iago.

"Ten more days?"

Brother Iago nodded.

"We will meet on Ash Wednesday."

Saturday February 14th

The roads had been cleared and the fords were crossable again. On Friday the Cantor, Brother Selyf, had completed the journey from Aberconwy with two pack-horses. He had come to Clynnog Fawr to collect new parchment for the Scriptorium.

After Eucharist, when they had broken their fast, he and Dafydd walked across the fields of the Grange towards the stone barn.

Brother Selyf unfastened the hurdles of a gate.

"Are you well, friend? You seem to have lost some of your old red-cheeked robustness since I saw you last."

Dafydd closed the gate behind them.

"It has been a busy winter, Brother. We've been hard at work – as you'll soon see."

"Is that all?"

"No, there is something else. Though I don't know whether I should be speaking of it now or in the confessional."

"Maybe it should wait."

"Maybe it should, but then again I'm not sure whether or not I have sinned."

"Tell me more."

Dafydd was silent for a while.

"I have not lost my faith, but something has happened."

"What is that?"

"I took my vows and renounced the world – but whichever way I turn the world is still in front of me."

He pointed at Yr Eifl, at Bwlch Mawr and Gyrn Goch, at the sea and the narrows of the Menai Strait.

"It is under my feet. It is overhead. It is in every sound. I close my eyes and it is in my blood, my dreams."

"These are the promptings of doubt. You must not listen to them Dafydd."

"I do not feel doubt, Brother, but certainty. The old poet's stories have confirmed it. I cannot deny who I am."

Brother Selyf snorted.

"Those! They are delusions my friend, they are sheep tracks that entice you from the true path. They will lead you nowhere."

"The bread and wine of the Mass taste no less true for having heard them ..."

Brother Selyf crossed himself.

"... and when I turn to face the Virgin Mary after Compline it is a woman's voice that I hear calling me back into the world."

"The Devil can speak in the voice of a woman, and often does."

"No, Brother, it is something else I hear. The voice is true, as true as the Mass. I denied it when my wife died, now I am compelled to answer to it."

"Compelled?"

"I have no choice."

"Why?"

Dafydd kicked a stone. He was reluctant to give voice to what he felt he was being urged to say.

"Because, it seems to me, at the heart of the world is ... something ... something that happens between a man and a woman. I cannot deny it any longer."

"This *is* a matter for the confessional. We will speak no more of it. Show me your parchment."

They walked the rest of the way in silence.

When they came to the barn, Dafydd moved the stones from the wooden boards. As the weights were lifted the parchment pages underneath found their original undulations. The boards sprang up. He took one of them and leant it against the wall. Several pages toppled onto the floor.

"Here they are – no vellum, as you know."

Brother Selyf picked up a page. He sniffed it. He held it to the light of the doorway. He ran his fingers across it.

"This is excellent. I have never seen better."

He picked up another.

"How many?"

"Four hundred or so."

"And how many will be needed for Llywelyn's folly?"

Dafydd smiled and patted Brother Selyf's shoulder.

"Be easy – Brother Iago has all the pages he will need."

Brother Selyf's eyes showed only appreciation, there was no shadow of condemnation.

"God bless you, Dafydd. It would be an ill day if we lost you."

"You will not lose me."

Wednesday February 18th (Ash Wednesday)

'Let them praise His Name with a dance, with timbrel and harp let them play before him. For the Lord delighteth in His people, He crowneth the humble with triumph. The just exult in their glory, they shout for joy on their beds. With the praises of God in their mouth, and two-edged swords in their hands. Ad faciendam vindictam in nationibus: increpationes in populis ...'

Brother Iago was hungry when he came from the Eucharist to the old man's cell. This was the first day of his Lenten fast. He was allowing himself food once a day, between Vespers and Compline. He had more than eight hours to wait. He watched Tomos and the old man breaking up a loaf and sharing it with Dafydd and Olwen.

He raised his hand and shook his head when they offered him a hunk.

His whispered prayer competed with the rumbling of his stomach.

Cian Brydydd Mawr licked the crumbs from his beard.

"You will remember what had just taken place?"

Olwen looked across at him.

"It would be hard to forget."

"The burning boy. Yes. It does not go away."

"The British and Irish noblemen fell upon one another.

They fought with bare fists. They swung blazing brands.

Heads butted heads. Thick fingers throttled throats.

Outside the hall the two waiting armies heard the sound.

They seized their weapons. A terrible battle began.

Bran, Manawydan, Nisien, Efnisien and all the lords of the Island of the Mighty staggered outside into the light of day.

They grabbed swords and shields from the heap of weapons and fought with ferocity. Bran wielded his blade with one hand. With his shield he sheltered Branwen from the fray. He bellowed:

'Hounds of Gwern, beware of him whose thigh will one day be pierced!'

With every swing of his sword he severed heads.

The furrows of the fields ran red with spilt blood.

The battle spread like floodwater.

In every settlement there was pillaging and slaughter. Soon the kingdom of Ireland was engulfed from shore to shore in a crimson tide of bitter warfare.

The army of Bran the Blessed had the upper hand.

The victory would have gone to the warriors of the Island of the Mighty had they not forgotten, in their battle fury, that

Matholwch had a weapon they could not match.

The cauldron of Llasar Llaes Gyfnewid was dragged into the huge hall. It was set over the flames of the fire and filled with water. The steam began to billow.

Soon the Irish were hurling the bodies of the slain into it.

One warrior would hold the feet, another the shoulders.

They would swing each corpse into the boiling water.

And each dead man, as he sank beneath the surface, shuddered into life. He clambered out of the cauldron. Dripping and steaming he seized his weapons and returned to the fray, his eyes unblinking, his lips sealed, his ferocity increased.

Tirelessly, by day and night, the living hurled the dead into the cauldron. The army of Matholwch renewed itself over and over again. Death only served to increase the vigour of the slain.

No valour on the battlefield could vanquish it.

The tide of war began to turn against the army of Britain.

Efnisien crouched behind a clump of bushes.

The doors of the hall were wide open.

He saw the dead carried in and the living leaping out.

He saw the steaming cauldron swinging over the fire.

He felt a sensation he had never known before.

It was a slow tug on his heart, a weight on his belly, a welling of harsh remorse. He lifted his hands and covered his face.

'Shame on me to have caused so many deaths. And bitter shame if I cannot make good this desolation.'

Moving from shadow to shadow he entered the hall. He lay down among the heaped corpses of the dead. He stiffened himself and stared with the blank eyes of the slain. The stench of decay surrounded him. The blood of other men's wounds soaked him to the skin. He waited his turn.

Two bare-arsed Irish foot soldiers seized him, one by the ears, the other by the feet. They swung him. They flung him into the steaming red soup. He sank into the depths of the cauldron.

He straightened himself and stretched out his arms.

With his clenched fists he pushed against one side, with the soles of his feet he pressed against the other. With all his strength he strained against the enclosing bronze walls of the cauldron. His muscles tensed and trembled. His lungs ached for breath. He strove to burst his bounds with every sinew of his body.

There was a deafening crack.

The cauldron flew apart. Its riveted sides sprang open.

Its bloody water doused the fire. Clouds of scalding steam seared the skin of the Irish soldiers.

Efnisien's heart burst also. He fell dead onto the hissing sodden ashes.

The tide of war turned.

Fortune began to favour the army of Bran the Blessed.

Warrior by warrior, the Irish army was destroyed.

Acre by acre, the kingdom was overwhelmed.

Matholwch was cornered and killed.

But it was a hollow victory.

Of all the warriors of Britain who had crossed the water, only seven survived. Of all the kingdom of Ireland, five pregnant women lived to tell the story of that terrible war.

And look.

Bran is coming crawling towards the seven survivors.

Like an enormous beast he comes on hands and knees.

His body is torn and scarred and weeping with wounds.

Trailing from his thigh is a barbed spear.

Branwen runs forwards.

She calls for poultices and hot water. She twists the point of the spear and pulls it from his flesh.

His cry is the trumpeting of a bull with a butcher's axe in its neck.

His arms give way. He is lying with his cheek on the grass, his vast body splayed and shaking. His drumming feet make the sound of a marching army.

His sister sponges his face. She kisses his cheek.

No tender concern can ease the passage of the poison that courses through his veins.

Bran lifts his hand and beckons to his brother.

Manawydan comes. He stands before the High King's twisted mouth. The whispered words are urgent and faltering:

'Take my sword ... cut through my neck ... carry my head across the water to Harlech ... then bring it to the island of the strong door, the island of Gwales ... stay there until the closed door is opened ... then carry it to London, bury it in the White Hill.'

Bran the Blessed closes his eyes and falls silent.

See how Manawydan walks down his brother's flank until he comes to the hip. See him curl his fingers round the hilt of the sword and draw the blade from its scabbard. See how the edge cuts a furrow in the ground as he drags it. See how he strains to lift it, how he holds it high above his head.

Then watch it fall.

See how the blade cuts a silvered arc out of the air.

See how it slices through skin, flesh, bone.

See how the High King's head rolls away from his shoulders.

It lies still. Its cheek is in the dirt. Its neck is spurting blood.

Look. It is opening its mouth. Words are coming. They are clear and deep as the ringing of a bell of bronze:

'Brother, take me home to Harlech.'

Branwen and the seven survivors bow their heads.

They stand silent until the night has cloaked them with shadow."

Tomos looked up.

"Five pregnant women remained?"

The old man nodded.

"Yes, and they are the ancestresses of all the peoples of Ireland, a grandmother for each of the five provinces."

"I wish they had been killed too – then my mother and father would be living now."

"Come, come." Cian Brydydd Mawr reached down and stroked the boy's shoulder, "You cannot condemn a whole people for the actions of a handful of cut-throats. I do not condemn the population of Gwynedd for the actions of the broken-nosed one ..."

"Rhys Drwyndwn," said Dafydd.

"Yes. Who destroyed the Bardic School for a purse of money."

Tomos nodded.

"And besides, old Meilyr used to say that in the oldest songs the war was not with Ireland at all, but with the Other World. There was a fragment he would sometimes sing:

'Is it not the cauldron of the King of Annwn,
With a rim around its edge of pearl?
It will not boil the coward's portion.
To him will be brought the bright flashing sword
Wielded by the hand of Lleminawg.
Before gates of ice we will kindle horns of light.
When we went with the High King in his splendid labours
None but seven came home from that campaign,
Seven only returned from Caer Vediwid.'[27]

The old man paused.

"Make of it what you will."

The midday bell rang.

As the monks were celebrating None, Tomos helped the old man up from his bed. He wrapped a blanket over his shoulders. Gave him bread and cheese and water. The boy asked:

"Have you forgiven the killers who came to Nant Gwrtheyrn?"

Cian Brydydd Mawr shook his head.

"It is the Holy Brother's way to forgive. It is the way of the Christ. It is an honourable way."

"But have you?"

"No. I have not."

One by one the audience returned.

"If I could sing, I would sing of the head of Bran the Blessed.

I would sing of the head of the High King as I have seen it in carvings of stone.

The deep-set eyes rest on that threshold where two worlds meet. They peer both inwards and outwards. The mouth is open.

The tongue is made eloquent by what the eyes have seen.

Its speech is song.

The head of Bran was set on a wooden frame that rested on the shoulders of the seven survivors. They carried it across the blackened, blood-soaked wastelands of Ireland.

Branwen walked behind.

As they journeyed, the head opened its mouth and sang to them.

It sang lullabies and the gentle songs that a mother might sing to ease the fears and the troubles of the world.

These were the seven who survived:

Manawydan, son of Llyr,

Pryderi, lord of the seven cantrefs of Dyfed,

Glifieu Eil Taran,

Ynawg,

Gruddyeu, son of Muriel,

Heilyn, son of Gwyn Hen,

Taliesin the bard (for without him this story would have been forgotten).

They came to the place where their ships were moored.

They waded out to one of them. They gently lowered the head of Bran onto the deck. They lifted the anchors and set sail for home.

Branwen stood in the prow of the ship.

The wind blew into her face. She peered at the horizon for a glimpse of the mountains of her native land. She scanned the sea's edge for the peaks she had ached for during her long exile.

At last she saw them. She saw the old familiar summits looming over the blue line of the water.

But they did not fill her heart with joy.

She understood that this could be no triumphant homecoming.

Of all the great hosts of the Island of the Mighty that had crossed the water for her sake, only seven were returning. They had nothing to show for their victory but the severed head of her beloved brother.

She looked over her shoulder.

Behind her were the blackened hills of Ireland.

She saw a kingdom laid waste, a realm steeped in blood.

Her womb ached for her lost son.

Every thought was bruised by the horrors and humiliations she had witnessed.

'A curse on the day that I was born. Two good islands have been destroyed for my sake, and the world has broken all its promises.'

Her sorrow was beyond tears.

She dropped to her knees.

She folded her head down to her lap.

And her heart burst in her breast.

When they came to the Island of Môn the seven survivors carried the body of Branwen to the banks of the river Alaw.

They made a four-sided grave for her and laid her to rest.

They set her head towards the mountains of Wales and her feet towards the coast of Ireland.

They wept for her.

Then they lifted the head of Bran the Blessed onto their shoulders.

They carried it across the straits of Menai.

They carried it through the valleys and over the hills to Harlech.

As they journeyed the head sang to them.

It sang songs of strength and consolation.

As they approached Harlech they met an old shepherd.

Manawydan spoke to him:

'Old man, what news here in the Island of the Mighty?'

'No news. No news at all, save only that my sheep grow fat.'

'Old man, why do your sheep grow fat?'

'Because the grass grows so thick and green there, on the side of the hill.'

'Why does the grass grow thick and green?'

'Because of the blood that was spilt on it.'

'Whose blood was spilt?'

'The blood of six of the seven who were left by Bran the Blessed to rule over Britain while he waded through the water to fight the Irish.'

'Old man, how did they die?'

'Caswallawn, son of Beli, came in a cloak of invisibility. As they climbed the hill he attacked them. Only his sword could be seen. It stabbed and sliced and struck them down. Bran's son, your nephew Caradawg, watched them fall to the ground. He could not help them. He died from grief. Only Pendaran Dyfed escaped. He ran away into the woods.'

'So Caswallawn is become king?'

'Yes. Caswallawn rules over the Island of the Mighty. And the world turns. There's nothing to tell ... save only that my sheep grow fat.'

The seven survivors came to Harlech.

Great quantities of food and strong drink were prepared for a feast. They sat and ate together. The head of Bran was set upon the table.

It spoke and sang.

As they listened the survivors forgot their sufferings.

The sorrows of their homecoming were lifted from their hearts.

Bloodshed and treachery melted from their memories.

Another sound came.

The seven looked out across the waters of the sea.

Three birds were circling and singing.

The birds were far away, but if they closed their eyes it was as though they were perched on the severed head of their king.

These were the birds of Rhiannon.

One sang of victory in defeat.

One sang of defeat in victory.

The third sang of the freedom of the heart from bondage.

All the songs the seven survivors had heard before were harsh and coarse compared with that music.

Time dissolved like honey stirred into white milk.

Whether they sat for seven hours, seven months or seven years they did not know. They were held in a thrall of delight that was beyond the confines of joy and sorrow.

The song ended.

A sweet silence settled on the air.

The seven survivors looked at one another and nodded.

They lifted the head of Bran onto their shoulders and set off for the island of Gwales. They journeyed southwards, following the margins of the sea.[28]

On the island they found a tall, thatched hall.

They entered. It had three doors; two were open and one – facing southwards towards Cornwall – was closed.

Manawydan lifted his arm and pointed:

'See over there. That is the door we must not open.'

They set down the head.

It opened its mouth and sang.

The birds flew in through the open doors.

Look.

Can you see the head on its wooden frame?

From neck to crown it is the height of a full-grown warrior.

Its eyes are open.

They are the eyes of a man who walks in his sleep.

They look into an unfathomable place that is both here and distant as the summer stars.

The tongue and lips shape words of unutterable sweetness, melodies that bewitch and beguile.

The three birds of Rhiannon fly among the rafters.

One is blue with a crimson head, one is crimson with a green head, the third is speckled with a golden head. Their music mingles with the words of Bran, weaving strands of silver in and out of the deeper strains of his song.

The seven survivors are sitting before the head.

Their eyes are closed, their faces enraptured.

The sorrows of the world have disappeared.

Time is no more. Each moment is an eternity.[29]

'Shame upon my beard if I do not open the door and see whether there is any truth in what has been said of it.'

It was Heilyn, son of Gwyn Hen, who broke the spell.

He got to his feet and crossed the floor of the hall.

He lifted the wooden latch of the third door that faced Cornwall.

The birds vanished.

The head fell silent.

There was a sickly-sweet stench of decay upon it.

The other six opened their eyes.

They looked at one another.

In that moment they remembered the two ravaged kingdoms.

They remembered the hills and heaps of corpses, the fields soaked with blood. They remembered the friends and kinsmen who had been killed. They remembered the death of Branwen. They remembered their wounded king.

It was as though they were witnessing these things for the first time. Where there had been unspeakable joy there was bitter grief. Tears coursed down their cheeks.

It seemed that a lifetime of bliss had been interrupted by the world and all of its attendant sorrows. They lifted the head of Bran the Blessed onto their shoulders and set off on the long journey to London.

They came to Gwynfryn, the White Hill.

With spades and mattocks they dug a deep hole and buried the head of their king. They made a grave for him in the place where the White Hill rises above the banks of the River Thames.

They turned his face, the flesh now falling away from the bone, towards the south as a protection against invasion.

They knew that as long as the head of Bran the Blessed was in that place, no oppression would ever reach this island from across the sea."

Cian Brydydd Mawr lifted his cup and cleared his throat with water. "That is why the burying of the head of Bran is known as one of the 'Three Fortunate Concealments'."[30]

He smiled.

"And it was Arthur, whose stories are so beloved by our Norman enemies, who removed it. It did not seem proper to him that the Island of the Mighty should be protected by any strength but his own. His pride has cost us dearly. That removal is known as one of the 'Three Unfortunate Disclosures'. But even though the head is gone, Bran is not altogether forgotten. I'm told there are ravens still on the White Hill.

So, to conclude my story, when the last wish of Bran the Blessed had been fulfilled, the seven survivors parted company and returned to their courts.

Pryderi, son of Pwyll and Rhiannon, tried and tested by the turmoil of war and its sweet and bitter aftermath, turned his face to the seven cantrefs of Dyfed.

In Ireland the five pregnant women, who had been hiding in a cave, gave birth to five sons. All were born on the same day.

In time they grew into young men.

They became the founding fathers of the five Provinces of Ireland.

When their thoughts turned to women they slept with one another's mothers. Their children began to populate the country. Wherever battles had taken place they found tin, bronze, gold and silver.

With the passing of time they became wealthy and powerful.

And that is how, Tomos my friend, the people of Ireland are all descended from five mothers. Of all that population one ship-load of pirates have a blood price on their heads; maybe one day they will pay it."

Tomos narrowed his eyes.

"I can still remember their faces."

"The rest, my son, you can forgive – their only crimes are the dark deeds of their ancestors, and which one among us is innocent of those?"

The old man opened his arms to his listeners.

"And so ends the second 'Cainc' of the Mabinogi."

Brother Iago gathered his wax tablets and stood up.

The old man turned to him.

"Tell me, Brother, what sense does a Cistercian make of the Assembly of the Severed Head?"

Brother Iago looked at the ground. There was a pale smile on his lips.

"I owe that episode in your strange and profane story a debt of gratitude."

"Why is that?"

"It brought into my thoughts a book that we have in the library at Aberconwy. I have copied parts of it myself."

"Tell us more."

"It contains the writings of Dionysius the Areopagite. He writes: 'The mysteries of God's word lie simple, absolute and unchangeable in the brilliant darkness of hidden silence. Amid the deepest shadow they pour overwhelming light on what is most manifest. Amid the unsensed and unseen they fill our sightless minds with treasures beyond all beauty.'"

"Aha! Then maybe there is not such a gulf between the old ways and the path of Christ."

Brother Iago crossed himself and hurried out of the cell.

5

Manawydan

Saturday February 21st

It was the gap between Lauds and Eucharist.

Brother Selyf was ready to leave. The pages of parchment had been bound tightly together and packed into leather bags. The pack-horses had been fed and soon the bags would be slung across their backs. He was planning to set off after celebrating the Mass. It was a cold, clear day. The mud on the roads would be frozen firm.

He saw, in the half-light, that the door to Brother Iago's cell was open. He wandered across and peered inside.

"Good Day."

Brother Iago was making ready for the day's work.

"May God prosper you, Brother."

Brother Iago set a half written page on the desk. He lit a candle from his fire and began to mix his ink. In the corner of the cell a pile of completed pages were held between the wooden boards that would one day make the covers of the book.

"It has been an undertaking, this writing."

"It has been a penance for a sin I did not know I had committed. But our Father Abbot sent me, and so I came."

Brother Selyf nodded to the pages.

"Is it nearly finished now?"

"I don't know, Brother. The old poet shows no sign of ceasing. I write it down and then fight away the spell it casts with prayer. It will be a full winter spent and wasted. I could have been copying the Scriptures."

Brother Iago looked up. His eyes were welling with tears.

"And now it is Lent. I fast and keep vigil ..."

He wiped his cheek with the back of his hand.

"... and am distracted by page after page of feasting, war, enchantment and the endless love-play of men and women. It is the work of the Devil."

Brother Selyf put his hand on the young man's shoulder.

"Then the time is not wasted. Every word you write is a lesson on the lures and temptations of the fallen world. Remember, you have renounced that world. Do not let yourself become entangled in its nets and snares. Stay with your Lenten prayers. Our Father Abbot was right to send you here. There is a teaching in your struggle."

After the Eucharist, Brother Selyf walked across to the stables. Brother Deiniol followed him.

"Brother!"

Brother Selyf turned.

"Brother, before you go. I have a request."

"How can I help?"

"Will you hear my confession?"

"I have been here a week. Why did you not ask me before?"

Brother Deiniol sighed.

"It has taken me time to find the courage."

"Very well."

Brother Selyf patted one of the horses and said to Rhodri:

"Load them up. Be careful the bags don't chafe."

The lay brother set to work. The two monks returned to the church. Brother Deiniol knelt.

"Brother, I have sinned. I do not know what to do."

"How?"

"It is my old affliction. It is why our Father Abbot sent me here. There is a woman."

"You have lain with her?"

Brother Deiniol began to tremble. He crossed himself several times.

"No, no, no. Though, God knows, I have dreamed of it."

"How did it begin?"

"A year ago I heard her confession. She is a widow. She has two sons but has lived for some years without a man. She confessed to how, in her solitude, she staves off her loneliness ..."

He covered his face with his hands.

"I gave her a small penance. It seemed a little venial sin for a young widow to commit. But Brother, the thought of her gives me no peace. I am plagued by phantasms. I ache to make good what she lacks."

"Do you see her often?"

"She is the one who comes to hear Cian Brydydd Mawr. Our Lord Llywelyn insisted upon it."

"I glimpsed her on Ash Wednesday."

"Brother. I glimpse her all the time. I see her when she is not there. I went to fetch food from the store. I turned and she was in the shadows."

"You are sure she was not there?"

"I went back – there was nothing."

Brother Deiniol shook his head.

"I have prayed and prayed. The thought of her possesses me."

Brother Selyf whispered, half to himself:

"It seems our poet has set several red-eyed wolves prowling among the placid, grazing flocks of Clynnog Fawr."

He looked sharply into Brother Deiniol's eyes.

"You are constructing a woman from your own fevered dreams. She is an ancient demon and she has haunted us all. She must be fought again and again. Prayer alone is not enough. Your penance is this. For the duration of Lent you must kneel for an hour after Vigils and again after Compline. Punctuate your prayer with the lash – across bare shoulders. It is the only way."

Wednesday February 25th

The bailiff was back. He struck the door of the farmhouse.

"Where's the lad?"

Olwen was grinding barley-grain into flour. She came out and brushed away the dust.

"He's with the sheep."

"Tell him there's to be a muster. He's listed to fight."

Olwen paled.

"When is he to go?"

"The week after Easter. They will be expecting him at the Maerdref of Caernarfon. He will train in swordsmanship, the skills of the bowman."

Her voice was sharp.

"So you pleaded on my behalf then?"[31]

The bailiff shrugged.

"It's not my business to plead on anyone's behalf. Every young man is to be called."

"How am I to manage without him?"

He turned and called over his shoulder:

"You should find yourself a husband. Any other woman would have done so long ago."

He rode away.

Olwen went inside. She threw some sticks onto the fire. She sat silently and warmed her hands.

"Any other woman!"

She spat into the embers.

"But any other woman would have been wedded to any other man."

She thought about the muster. She rocked backwards and forwards on the wooden stool.

"Rhys ... my Pryderi ... I have no choice ... I must watch you go."

When the boys returned from the fields she was still there.

Monday March 2nd

The old man was getting frailer. Winter was taking its toll. The wound in his shoulder ached. He could hardly bear to go outside into the cold.

When the door of the cell opened he was impatient.

"Come in. Close it behind you."

His eyes and hands had a life that the rest of his body lacked.

"Sit down. Where's our scribe? Ah good, here he comes. Are you ready?"

"If I could sing I would sing of Manawydan, son of Llyr, brother of Bran the Blessed.

I would sing of Manawydan, the last survivor of his dynasty.

I would sing of him as he turned on his heel and walked away from the White Hill where his brother's head had been buried.

You will remember that the throne of the Island of the Mighty had been seized by Caswallawn, son of Beli.

By all rights the kingship belonged to Manawydan, but he had no appetite for war. He had seen enough bloodshed to last him for the rest of his life. He had also glimpsed a bliss that was beyond the petty squabblings of kings.

As he looked across the thatched rooftops of the settlement of London he was seized with a deep sorrow.

'Why should I, of all the seven survivors, be the one who has no home to return to?'

It was Pryderi who overheard him. He came across and put his hand on Manawydan's shoulder.

'Lord, don't be downcast. Caswallawn has seized the throne. He has wronged you. He has overthrown your brother's son. But you have rights. You should make a claim from him. Are you not one of the prime chieftains of this land? Nobody, not even he, could deny you some dominion.'

But Manawydan shook his head.

'I cannot go. I could not bear to see him sitting on my brother's throne. To spend any time under the same roof would be a bitter torment to me.'

'Then,' said Pryderi, 'will you take some other advice?'

'Tell me more.'

'I am lord over the seven cantrefs of Dyfed. They were left to me by my father, Pwyll. While I have been away my lands have been ruled by my widowed mother, Rhiannon and my wife, Cigfa, daughter of Gwyn Gohoyw. What I propose to you is this: that you take my mother as a wife and rule over the seven cantrefs as though they were your own. The realm will be mine in name, but the enjoyment of it will be yours. I assure you, there are no finer cantrefs in the Island of the Mighty. I, for my part, have gained more land by my marriage – the seven cantrefs of Seisyllwch – and our dominions will border one another. What do you say? You may not be eager for power and wealth, but perhaps you will accept that.'

Manawydan smiled.

'I am not eager for such things – but I am grateful for your friendship.'

'The best friendship I can give is yours if you want it.'

'I do want it and I thank you. I will go with you and cast my eyes over your lands ... and make the acquaintance of your mother, Rhiannon.'

'I tell you my friend, she is as fine looking a woman as you will ever meet, and in conversation and discourse there is nobody to match her.'

Look.

Can you see them?

The two veterans of the Irish war are making their way southwards. They ride side by side.

They have fought together through the iron hail of the battlefield, through the red sleet of slaughter. They have been battered by the same storms.

Look at them, a young man and an old man.

Pryderi has the flush of youth on his cheeks, though his skin is not without its scars. There are no grey hairs among the golden curls that spill over his shoulders. See how he spurs his horse into a gallop.

Manawydan rides at a steady trot. His beard is grizzled and his eyes quiet. His large, thick fingered, nimble hands rest on his horse's neck. Both have been cursed with stories too terrible to be told, and blessed with the knowledge that they hold them in a shared silence.

At last they came to the court at Arberth.

Cigfa and Rhiannon had prepared a feast to celebrate their home-coming. Wife and mother welcomed Pryderi with all the shy and joyful solemnity of long separation.

When horses had been stabled and the dust of the road had been washed away they sat down together at the high table.

This is how they were placed.

Pryderi sat in the centre with Cigfa to his left and Rhiannon to his right. Beyond Rhiannon sat Manawydan.

Course followed course.

As goblet after goblet was emptied and filled again, Manawydan fell deep into conversation with Rhiannon.

The more they talked the more they were drawn to one another.

Each was delighted by the other's discourse. By the time the feast was finished they were smiling into one another's faces.

Manawydan reached for her hand. She closed her fingers around his fingers. He called across the table:

'Pryderi, I agree to your proposal!'

Rhiannon turned to her son.

'What proposal was that?'

'Mother,' said Pryderi, 'I proposed to Manawydan that he make you his wife.'

She laughed.

'It is a curious thing. My son makes a proposal on my behalf, and I find that my heart cannot refuse it.'

Manawydan lifted her fingers to his lips.

'I am honoured,' he said, 'and may good fortune reward the mother and son who have given me such generous friendship.'

That night Rhiannon took him to her bed. She cast aside the long years of widowhood in the urgency of her embrace. He forgot all his sorrows in the oblivion and sweet release of love.

They slept in one another's arms.

The next morning Pryderi said:

'Enjoy yourselves here in Arberth. Feast to your heart's content. I must travel to England and tender my homage to our new High King, Caswallawn, son of Beli.'

'My son,' said Rhiannon, 'Caswallawn is in distant Kent! Why travel so far? Soon his royal progress will bring him somewhere closer to home. Stay here with us.'

Pryderi bowed his head.

'Very well. I will wait. And while I wait let's show our friend the delights of the seven cantrefs of Dyfed.'

It was agreed. Preparations were made. Hunters were alerted. Hounds were unleashed. Horses were saddled. Hooded hawks were set on wrists. Carts were filled with provisions and clothes.

Pryderi, Cigfa, Manawydan and Rhiannon rode out of Arberth.

The warm spring air was filled with the sound of their talk.

Manawydan saw that this was indeed a place of plenty. The hunting grounds were thick with deer, hare and wild boar. The rivers were silver with trout and salmon. There were bees' nests dripping with sweet golden honey. Crops grew in abundance and orchards were white with scented blossom.

It seemed to him that the place had been blessed by the denizens of Annwn.

As the circuit continued and the talk deepened, the four became such firm friends that they sought only each other's company, by day and by night.

Then word came that Caswallawn was holding court in Oxford.

Pryderi went to him and made his homage. He was received with great courtesy and thanked for his allegiance.

Manawydan made no such journey.

He stayed in Dyfed and kept his counsel.

When Pryderi returned there was a feast.

After the platters had been empied he got to his feet.

'Friends, it occurs to me that I should like to stretch my legs and climb Gorsedd Arberth.'

Cigfa turned to him.

'My Lord, you know what is said of that place. Any man of noble birth who sits at its summit shall not leave without either suffering an injury or seeing a marvel.'

'Then we shall go!' said Manawydan, 'and seek marvels.'

Rhiannon lifted her golden goblet to her lips and said nothing.

The four friends threw cloaks over their shoulders and made their way out of the court. They left their noblemen and servants behind. They climbed the path that spiralled up and around the green slope of the breasted hill. When they came to the cairn of lichened stones they found places to sit. They settled themselves and waited. Their eyes scanned the verdant fields and forests, the farms and barns, the distant hills and the blue-green lip of the horizon.

Then everything changed.

From the clear skies there came a crash of thunder.

Drums were sounding in the heavens above and far below in the roots of the hills. They covered their ears with their hands.

The ground trembled. Loose stones from the cairn clattered down the slopes of Gorsedd Arberth.

A white mist came.

It was so thick that they could no longer see one another.

They could no longer see the ground at their feet.

The pounding sound hammered the air.

Then it was quiet.

A light suffused the mist so that it glowed like pearl.

Their eyes were dazzled by its strength. They could see nothing.

Then the mist cleared. They saw one another.

Cigfa threw herself into Pryderi's arms. Manawydan reached for Rhiannon's hand. They cast their eyes across the kingdom and it seemed to them for a moment that nothing had changed.

But look.

The landscape is emptied.

Where there had been thatched farmsteads, barns and yards there is nothing but long rough grass and tangled brambles.

The pastures that had been grazed by shambling cattle and flocks of fat sheep are become empty moors. There are no women with leather milking pails, no men with hunting dogs at their heels, no shouting children.

The seven cantrefs of Dyfed have been returned to wilderness.

Only Pryderi's court at Arberth remains.

They look down at it.

There is no smoke rising from the thatch, no sign of guards or warriors or scuttling servants.

The four friends hurry down the slope of the hill.

They make their way through the gates.

Everything is silent. Their footsteps echo against the stone walls.

They push open doors. Tables, benches and beds are intact.

Empty cauldrons swing over cold ashes. Spears and swords are stacked in ready piles, but there are no hands to lift them.

Everyone is gone. Every animal is gone. Every crumb of food is gone. Neither in the mead hall or the kitchen is there anything but hollow emptiness.

Manawydan broke the silence.

'Where is the court and all its retinue? Noblemen, bards, minstrelsy, soldiers, servants, cooks, grooms – all are gone.'

The next morning they began to search.

At the first light of dawn they set off on foot.

Each journeyed in a different direction, travelling towards the four quarters of the kingdom. They met nothing but woodland, moor, marsh, rushing water, packs and herds of wild animals, flocks of wild birds.

It was as though men and women had never set foot in the land.

At dusk they returned to Arberth.

They had no choice but to become hunters.

They set traps and threw nets into the rivers. They stalked deer, and with long spears they killed wild boar. They smoked bees from their nests and scooped out the sweet honey.

The empty court of Arberth became a hunter's lodge where skins were cleaned and cured. They dragged firewood into the courtyard and chopped it with their own hands. They smoked meat in the thatch of the mead hall. Their bronze cauldrons steamed with stews of pike and salmon, of snipe, duck, goose and curlew.

For a year they delighted in this life, unconstrained by the formalities of the court. Their friendship sustained them, so that they wanted for no other company.

Then a second year passed.

One day Manawydan looked across at Pryderi, Cigfa and Rhiannon. The two women were skinning a deer. Their faces were dusky from wood smoke and their arms splashed with blood. Their clothes, that had once been of the finest, were patched and worn. There was dirt under their fingernails.

Pryderi was crouching by the hearth, coaxing damp wood into

flame. Manawydan looked down at his own ragged cloak, his mud-splashed arms grown lean and strong.

'Friends,' he said, 'we cannot live like this for ever.'

They took a skin bag and filled it with some of the treasures of the court. The silver was tarnished. The jewelled gold had become smoke-blackened.

They set off on foot.

They crossed the seven cantrefs of Dyfed and the seven cantrefs of Seisyllwch. When they reached the borders of their realm they found themselves surrounded by an unchanged world. There were villages and farms. Men and women were busy about their work.

They traded some of their treasure for horses.

Look.

Rhiannon is taking the reins into her hands.

Two years have passed since she set eyes on a horse. See how it dances around her like a foal, tossing its head and uttering little whinnying cries of transport and delight. See how she whispers into its ear and quietens it with a word.

See how the other three horses watch her with spelled eyes, barely noticing the bits that are slipped between their teeth or the saddles that are strapped to their backs.

See how she mounts her steed as though she and it are of one mind. She shakes the reins and her horse trots forwards.

The others follow.

They rode to Henffordd.[32]

Manawydan said:

'Friends, we will be saddle-makers.'

They traded their treasure for new clothes and leather, needles and waxed thread, moulds and metal.

They set up shop in the marketplace.

Manawydan had learned from the sons of the giant Llasar Llaes Gyfnewid how to make blue enamel. Now he set about using his skill on the pommels of the saddles. While the others cured, softened, shaped and stitched the leather, he fashioned luminous blue pommels.

Their saddles were set on display.

When the people saw them they turned their backs on all the other saddle-makers. They emptied their purses into the hands of Rhiannon and Cigfa. Soon every horse in Henffordd had its sky-blue pommel. Any saddle that had not been fashioned by the strangers seemed tawdry and ill-made in comparison.

The other saddlers began to suffer.

They were losing all their trade. They muttered among themselves. Things went from bad to worse. They held a meeting. They decided to murder Pryderi and Manawydan and burn their workshop to the ground.

They sharpened their knives and lit blazing brands.

It was Pryderi who first saw their torches and guessed their intent.

He called the others.

'Listen to me,' he said, 'Manawydan and I have fought before, and against greater odds. Let them come. We will kill the churls, every one of them. There will be nobody left to envy us our skill. The market will be ours.'

But Manawydan lifted his fingers and touched Pryderi's lips.

'Friend, enough. Have you forgotten already? It is always the same. One bloody deed leads to another. If we kill these men, more will come and in greater numbers. We would be better advised to find another town and start again.'

The four friends slipped away.

They hurried through the streets and out of the city gates of Henffordd.

They came to another town and set themselves up again.

This time they made shields.

They purchased wood, leather and metal. They cut and shaped their materials. They made them light on the arm, but with strength enough to withstand a battle-axe.

Once again Manawydan decorated them with blue enamel.

As soon as the people saw them they wanted them.

Throughout the town no shield was bought unless it had been fashioned by the strangers. They worked quickly. Money exchanged hands faster than it could be counted. Soon every arm bore its buckler of dazzling blue enamel.

But the other armourers began to grind their teeth. They hatched a plan. They would slit the throats of these strangers and throw their bodies into the river.

This time it was Manawydan who overheard their whispers.

'Pryderi, these men intend to kill us.'

'Let them try,' said Pryderi, drawing his knife, 'we can give as good as we get. It'll be their blood that will fill the gutters of this town, not ours.'

Manawydan put his hand over his friend's hand and pushed the point of his dagger back into its scabbard.

'No. It will only bring ruin. Caswallyn will hear of it. He will think you have broken your word. His soldiers will seek revenge. What then? Let's go to another town and start again.'

They journeyed on.

When they came to the next place, Pryderi said:

'Which craft should we set our hands to now?'

'Shoe-making,' said Manawydan. 'Cobblers are a timid breed. They will not have the courage to fight us.'

So they bought the finest leather and set to work.

Manawydan made friends with the goldsmiths of the town. He watched them making buckles. When he understood their craft he started to fashion them himself.

Soon their fine-stitched shoes, each with its glittering golden buckle, were the talk of the town.

The other shoe-makers saw their trade was dwindling away. They held a counsel.

'We may be humble cobblers,' said one, 'but we have our pride.'

They dug out cudgels and rusty swords and set off to kill the strangers.

Pryderi saw them coming.

'This time we stand our ground!'

'No,' said Manawydan, 'there is no advantage in spilling blood. We will return to Dyfed.'

They spent their earnings on hounds and horses.

With gold to spare, they journeyed homewards.

The land was as wild as before.

At the empty court in Arberth they built fires. They ate the fine food and wine they had brought with them. Soon it was gone.

They returned to a life of hunting and trapping."

The bell rang.

The old man closed his eyes.

"And there we must leave them for a while."

The listeners left him to his rest.

Outside the sun was shining. Olwen found a place against the wall that was out of the wind. She sat and closed her eyes. She soaked the warmth into her skin. She was woken by a voice.

"Can I sit with you for a while?"

She patted the grass.

"Sit down, brother-in-law."

Dafydd settled down beside her.

"You are not going to Sext?"

"No."

She unpacked her bundle of food.

"Try this."

She cut him a lump of cheese. He bit into it.

"Mmmm, very good."

They ate in silence. She turned to him.

"I could envy them."

"Who?"

"Manawydan and Rhiannon, Pryderi and Cigfa."

Dafydd nodded.

"Yes."

"Man tempered by woman, youth tempered by experience. There is something perfect in their friendship."

"It is a story. We can be sure it will not last."

"Nothing lasts – but as an ideal, a possibility of happiness."

"I agree."

"Even you agree, who have taken your vows and renounced the love of women."

"I have not forgotten it, Olwen."

She looked at him from the corners of her eyes.

"You can set your hand to most things, Dafydd; you were a bit of a hot-head once as I recall. Now you're grizzled, and harsh experience has battered you into some sort of wisdom ... you wouldn't make a bad Manawydan."

Dafydd stared at the ground. He said nothing.

Suddenly she was on her feet. She was as surprised as anyone by the sudden anger that possessed her. Her shout startled the brothers from their psalms.

"It's a pity you've damn well gelded yourself with prayer."

Dafydd knelt for None.

He whispered to Brother Pedr:

"Please translate, Brother."

Brother Pedr's measured Irish voice spoke the text:

"Marvellous mystery, that Mary, a maiden, should bear us a Saviour, the Lord of Creation. At Jordan, John saw Him and cried to the people: 'He is God's Lamb. On him shall be laid the sins of the world.'"

When the service was over Dafydd hurried across to the old man's cell. The words were still ringing in his ears as he took his place by the fire.

Olwen leaned across and whispered in his ear:

"Forgive me."

"You will remember that the four friends had returned to Arberth.

One morning Manawydan and Pryderi unleashed their dogs and mounted their horses. The dogs ran ahead barking and yelping and sniffing at the air. They came to a thicket of tangled brambles and thorns. The dogs picked up a scent and their barks became one song. They ran in among the bushes like the many rivulets of a single stream.

From deep among the leaves there was a sudden shriek of pain.

Two dogs came crawling out. One was dragging its entrails over the dead leaves. The other had lost the skin of its back. It was licking the white cage of its panting ribs.

The rest of the pack followed. They were whining, their bellies lowered to the ground, their hackles up, their tails curled between their legs. They were shaking with fear.

Pryderi turned to Manawydan.

'Friend, let's enter the thicket and see what's inside.'

They dismounted and waded in among the brambles. They slashed with their swords. Ahead of them something started. It hurled itself between them, knocking them to the ground. It hurtled headlong out of the thicket. They glimpsed it for a moment and then it was gone. An enormous wild boar. It was white as snow, its ears as red as blood."

Cian Brydydd Mawr lifted his arm and pointed.

"Look, there it is!

Its tusks are sharp as crescent moons, each of them sticky and dripping with gore. See its bowed bristling back, the hairs as thick as wires. See its broad shoulders tapering into neck and narrow head. See its wet snout, its yellow teeth. See its hard little glittering eyes. See its pricked scarlet ears. See how it tears away the thorns and kicks up the earth with its cloven feet. See how it crashes into the light snorting with rage.

'Whoaaa! Follow!'

Pryderi's horn was on his lips. They leapt up onto their saddles.

They whipped and urged their horses and dogs to the chase.

The white boar ran ahead.

Whenever they drew close it stopped and rounded on them.

One of the dogs was tossed into the air. It plummeted and lay still.

A leg had been bitten clean off.

'Whoaaa!'

Each time the dogs backed away and the boar ran again.

All day they followed it.

They came to the edge of a forest. The boar held its ground. Another dog was gored. It hurled itself into the shadows between the trees.

'Whoaaa!'

Dogs, horses and men set off at full tilt.

Manawydan and Pryderi ducked to avoid the low branches.

They came to a clearing.

It was edged by a circle of tremendous oak trees.

Inside there was a high round wall of stone.

Though they had been in the forest many times they had never seen it before. The stone was newly cut. The wall was freshly built.

It had one wooden doorway. The door was open.

The white boar ran through and the dogs followed.

The door closed.

Manawydan and Pryderi reined in their horses and waited outside.

There was no sound from within.

Time passed.

Pryderi dismounted. He spread his hand against the cool stone of the wall.

'I will go inside and see what has happened to the dogs.'

Manawydan shook his head.

'Friend, that is not a good idea. We have never seen this place before. Take my advice – do not enter. It is my opinion that whoever put a spell on the land has caused these walls to appear.'

'I will not forsake my hounds.'

Pryderi lifted the latch. The door opened.

He drew his sword and entered.

It closed behind him.

He looked about himself.

There was no sign of the white boar or the dogs.

There were no buildings, neither house nor hall.

The grass was close cut as though it had been cropped by sheep or deer. In the centre there was a well-spring that bubbled out of the ground with a sweet music.

Beside the well was a flat slab of white marble stone.

Above the stone was a golden cauldron. It was hanging from four chains that rose up and up and disappeared into the sky overhead.

Pryderi gasped. He thrust his sword into its scabbard and walked around it.

It had been worked with silver and jewels, decorated with images of men and beasts, birds and plants. Some were strange, some familiar.

He stepped onto the white stone and peered closer.

He reached forwards and touched it. The gold was cold against his palm. He tried to draw his hand away.

It would not come.

He was held fast by the cauldron. He lifted his other hand to push himself free. It stuck. He tried to lift his feet. They were fixed to the white stone. He opened his mouth to shout. No sound came.

Outside, Manawydan waited.

The afternoon darkened to evening. Pryderi did not return.

The first stars began to brighten in the sky overhead.

Still there was neither sight nor sound of him.

He waited until midnight then turned away.

He rode out of the wood, leading Pryderi's horse by the reins.

All night he journeyed.

When he came to Arberth the dawn was breaking in the east.

Rhiannon had been waiting and watching.

When she saw Manawydan returning home with no dogs and a riderless horse she ran out to meet him.

'Where is my son? Where are the hounds?'

Manawydan swung down from the saddle. He took her hands.

'My Lady, listen, this is what has happened ...'

He told her the story.

She listened. Her eyes filled with tears.

'Again he has been taken from me. And a poor friend you have proved, to have lost my only son and come home alone.'

She took the reins of Pryderi's horse. She swung up onto the saddle.

It was easy for her to follow the trail that had been left the day before. There was a spoor of destruction where the white boar had trampled the ground.

When she came to the forest she followed the broken branches and torn bushes until she came to the circle of oaks.

She knew this place.

She dismounted and tied the horse's reins to the trunk of a tree.

She circled the wall. The wooden door was open.

She walked through. It closed behind her.

She saw her son.

He was half embracing, half wrestling with the golden cauldron.

It was swinging on its four iron chains.

To Rhiannon his twisting gyrations were a mystery.

If it hadn't been for his mask of anguish she might have laughed at his antics.

She ran forwards.

'My son,' she said, 'what is the matter?'

He mouthed at her with no sound.

She stepped onto the white stone.

He shook his head with all his might. She didn't understand.

She reached forwards and touched the gold.

Her hand was stuck fast. Her feet rooted.

She opened her mouth. Silent words came.

There was a crash of thunder.

Drums sounded in the heavens above them and in the ground below. A white mist enveloped them.

They could see nothing.

Then there was silence.

A bright light suffused the mist.

The circling walls were gone.

The wooden door was gone.

The white stone, the chains and the golden cauldron were gone.

Rhiannon and Pryderi had vanished.

The circle of oaks remained.

In the heart of the clearing the bubbling well-spring sang."

The old man's head dropped forwards. He had slumped into sleep.

Tomos looked across at Dafydd.

"Could you help me please?"

Together they lifted Cian Brydydd Mawr and laid him gently on the bed.

"He sleeps a lot these days."

They covered him.

"And says very little. It is only when he tells the stories that the life comes back to him."

"It is strange."

The old man opened his eyes and whispered:

"Not strange, Dafydd ap Dafydd ap Dafydd. The Matter is all the breath I have left. It rides me into the ground."

Friday March 6th

The wind had grown stronger as the week progressed.

Rhys and Gwyn had been out ploughing with the two oxen. They had worked from dawn to dusk. Two of their yew-wood shares had splintered in the stony ground. When they drove the beasts home at the end of the day they were exhausted. They forgot to secure the doors of the byre.

In the night Olwen was woken by a crash.

She ran outside. The wind had lifted one of the doors from its hinges. It lay broken on the ground. The other was swinging on one hinge.

She woke the boys. They roped the swinging door as best they could.

The next morning they inspected the damage.

"Those iron hinges. They cost your father a foal. They're half torn from the wood. I pray they aren't skewed."

They tried to lift the door.

"It's solid oak. It's too heavy."[33]

Olwen sat down to catch her breath.

"Go down to Clynnog Fawr. Find your Uncle Dafydd. Tell him what has happened. Maybe he could bring the two lay brothers who come on the story days. Between them they'll have the measure of the place."

The boys ran down the hill.

By the end of the afternoon the doors had been mended and lifted onto the pins of their hinges.

Dafydd swung one of them gently backwards and forwards between his hands.

"I've set the hinges higher than they were before. The wood

was torn where Iwan hung them. But they'll serve you well enough."

He stroked the door posts.

"There's another hundred years in these."

Olwen stepped towards him.

"Thank you. I'm sorry to have wasted your time."

The bell of Clynnog Fawr rang faintly below them.

"You could have been at prayer."

Without thinking Dafydd lifted a strand of Olwen's hair that had been caught by the wind and tucked it behind her ear.

He met her gaze and smiled.

"You are forgiven, Olwen. You are always forgiven."

The three lay brothers turned and walked down the hill. Their brown robes flapped in the wind. She watched them until they were out of sight.

Wednesday March 11th

'They who formerly were sated have hired out themselves for bread, and they who were hungry are satisfied. The lord maketh poor and he maketh rich; he humbleth and he exalteth. He raiseth up the needy from the dust, and lifteth up the poor man from the dunghill, that he may sit with princes and hold a throne of glory ... Pedes sanctorum suorum servabit, et impii in tenebris conticescent ...'

Brother Iago's lips moved to the Canticle of Anna. Beside him on the wooden pew were the wax tablets and the stylus for the day's work ahead. He had ironed away the names and places he had noted down from previous tellings, but they were not altogether gone. Out of the corner of his eye he saw the ghost of a scratched word: 'Gorsedd Arberth'. He shuddered and crossed himself.

"If I could sing I would sing of Manawydan, son of Llyr."

The old man broke into a fit of hoarse coughing. Tomos patted his back and gave him a cup of water. He gulped it down and surveyed his audience with eyes that seemed feverishly bright beneath their hooded lids.

"I would sing of Manawydan, the man of deep resource.

I would sing of Manawydan, whose hands are quick to any craft, whose mind is not bound by the shackles of pride.

All day he and Cigfa waited in the court at Arberth.

When the sun set, Pryderi and Rhiannon had not returned.

At dawn there was still no sign of them.

They rode out together.

When they came to the circle of oak trees they found the tethered horse. The high wall had vanished. There was not so much as a worked stone on the mossy ground.

In the heart of the clearing the well-spring bubbled.

They called and shouted:

'Pryderi!'

'Rhiannon!'

They were answered by the sounds of the forest.

Cigfa buried her face in her hands and shook with sobs.

'What is to become of me? In all the seven cantrefs of Dyfed and the seven cantrefs of Seisyllwch only you and I have survived. And now I suppose, like all men, you will press your advantage. You will take me to your bed and shame me. What difference if I live or die?'

'Lady,' said Manawydan, 'you are grievously mistaken if you weep for fear of me. I swear that you will never find a truer friend. Even if I were in the first flush of youth I would remain true to

238

Pryderi – and to you too. For as long as we are destined to endure these sorrows, I will be your loyal companion.'

She looked up at him and her face brightened.

'Then I thank you with all my heart. I never should have doubted you.'

They untied the tethered horse and rode back to Arberth.

As they were drawing close Manawydan turned to her.

'Well my friend, there is little to be said for staying here. We have lost all our hounds. There are only two of us now. It will be hard for us to support ourselves by hunting. Will you travel with me across the border and make a living there?'

'Gladly, Lord,' she said.

They took a bag of golden coins and travelled until they came to a town they had not seen before.

As they entered, Cigfa said:

'I suppose we must set our hands to another craft. Which one will it be? Nothing too dirty or demeaning I hope.'

'I have set my heart on shoe-making, as I did before.'

'Shoe-making! You the rightful High King of the Island of the Mighty, and I the Queen of fourteen cantrefs are to become cobblers again. It is too humbling for a man of your rank and status.'

Manawydan shrugged.

'That is what we will do.'

With the golden coins he bought the finest leather. She had no choice but to cut and stitch and he made golden buckles. Before long their shoes were the envy of the town. They were bought as soon as they were made. The other cobblers watched their custom falling away.

By the end of a year the old familiar pattern had repeated itself. Angry words were whispered and sharpened knives drawn.

Cigfa said:

'Lord, why should we have to endure such behaviour from these churls?'

'We will not endure it. We will leave this town and return to Dyfed.'

Manawydan had a plan. Before they crossed the border he exchanged their hard-earned gold for grain. He bought as many sacks as could be slung across the backs of their two horses. He bought a pair of sturdy oxen for ploughing. He bought a cart-horse and a wagon. He bought an iron plough and two sharply honed sickles. He bought hoes and spades and mattocks.

Cigfa looked at him.

'Are we to become peasants now and stain our hands with soil?'

Olwen snorted.

"Peasants! It would be a fine thing if the high-born got blisters on their fingers from time to time. If they understood the meaning of hard work they might be a little kinder with the tithes and taxes they demand."

"They returned to Dyfed, the country they had shared with Rhiannon and Pryderi. They trapped the meat and fish they needed.

At the same time they cleared three fields.

They dug out brambles and briars. They cleaned the ground of thistles and tares. They worked until their hands were hard and calloused."

"Good!" said Olwen.

"Manawydan yoked his oxen to the plough.

The new-turned earth was rich and dark.

Field by field he sowed his grain. He drove away crows.

The first tips of young wheat began to green the ground.

Manawydan tended his three fields. Every day he walked their margins. He hoed them free of weeds.

He watched his crop with the pride of a father with growing sons. Between finger and thumb he felt the grain swelling in the ears.

When high summer came the wheat paled and stiffened.

He drew a whet-stone across the blade of his sickle.

'Tomorrow we will harvest the first field.'

In the grey light of dawn, Manawydan and Cigfa harnessed the horse to the cart. They led it to the fields.

The red sun rose into a clear sky.

They gasped.

There was a crop of naked stalks.

Every swollen ear had been broken and stolen.

The wheat stood tall but was worth no more than its weight in straw.

They looked at the ground.

There was not a single dropped grain.

There was nothing to be gleaned.

Cigfa wept. Manawydan ran to the second field.

It was ripe and ready.

'We are not completely ruined. We will harvest this field tomorrow.'

They returned to Arberth.

The next morning when they came to the second field it was the same story. Where each ear joined the stalk the wheat was broken.

The grain had been stolen away.

Manawydan said:

'Someone or something is trying to destroy us. And the land is ruined too.'

He went to the third field. The wheat stood tall and fine. Its ears were fat and swollen.

He told Cigfa what he had seen.

'Well,' she said, 'what is your plan?'

'Shame on me if I do not keep watch. We can be sure that whoever carried away the wheat will return for the last of it tonight. I will find out who they are – and they will wish they had never been born.'

They went back to the court of Arberth.

He gathered what he needed for the night: a long sword, a short sword, a battle-axe, a spear, a bow and a quiver full of sharp arrows. Weighed down with weapons he returned to the field.

He found a hidden place and waited.

The sun set below the western hills and a full moon rose up into the sky.

Listen.

There is a sudden clap of thunder, a drumming above and below.

Look.

A white mist is rising from the ground. It veils the field from the light of the moon.

Manawydan can see nothing.

A rustling sound comes, like the wind among dry reeds.

The mist clears.

The field is alive with an army of mice.

They are silvery grey in the moonlight. They are running this way and that. They are climbing up the stalks of wheat and nibbling them through. They are scuttling away with ears between their teeth. They are gathering every dropped grain, thieving away the fatness of the land.

Manawydan roars with fury and runs in among them.

With a sword in either hand he swings and lunges. He stabs

and strikes at the stalks with all the strength of his arms.

He may as well be cutting at a cloud of gnats in the air.

See how the mice run about and rejoice in their robbery. They scamper over his feet and pay him no mind.

He throws down his weapons and tries to catch them in his hands.

Their work is done. They stream out of the field.

The wheat is stripped. Every golden grain is gone.

Manawydan follows. He snatches at the empty air.

They dart ahead, quicker than thought.

But one mouse can't keep pace.

It is plumper than the rest and slower on its feet.

Manawydan stretches out his arm. He dives forwards to catch it.

His fingers close around its little body. He closes his fist.

It is struggling and squealing pitifully in his hand.

All the rest are gone. He pulls off his leather glove and drops the mouse inside. He ties the mouth of the glove with twine.

Holding it tight he strides back to the court at Arberth.

Cigfa is awake.

Without saying a word he hangs his glove from a peg.

She watches him.

'What's in the glove, Lord?'

'A thief.'

The bell rang.

Cian Brydydd Mawr seemed to shrink into himself. It was as though, when he stopped speaking, he was cast into shadow.

His audience left the cell quietly.

When they were outside Olwen said to Dafydd:

"These story days, when the old man speaks, are so precious. I do not want them ever to end. I am both rested and fed."

"You feel like one of the seven survivors, beguiled by the Head of Bran?"

"No. It is not that. I do not forget the world. I am taken deeper into it."

"Yes."

She settled down among the leaning daffodils by the church door.

"Will you sit with me?"

"No. I have work to attend to."

She ate her food alone.

After Sext the monks came out of church. Brother Deiniol was the last to leave.

"Brother."

He saw her and quickened his pace.

"Brother Deiniol!"

She got up and ran after him. She caught his arm with her hand.

He had no choice but to stop.

"You are trembling. Are you unwell?"

"No, no. I am not unwell."

"I wanted to apologise. For frightening you. In the food store."

His trembling increased.

"You *were* there."

She laughed.

"Of course I was there. I was sheltering from the rain."

She saw there were sores at the base of his neck.

"You are sure you are well?"

"Yes, yes. It is Lent."

He crossed himself.

"We suffer with Christ Jesu."

"That is why I wanted to speak to you. It is Lent. It is time to make confession. Will you hear me?"

Brother Deiniol paled. His knees weakened so that, for a moment, he thought he would crumple onto the ground. Then he understood. This was a trial. Like Christ in the Wilderness he was being sorely tested.

"Come on Friday. After the Eucharist."

He turned and hurried away.

After None the old man was eager to begin again.

"You will remember, friends, the mouse in the glove."

Dafydd, Olwen and Tomos nodded.

Brother Iago sighed with impatience.

"Good ink, good parchment, precious time – and all for the sake of a mouse in a glove."

Cian Brydydd Mawr smiled tenderly at him.

"Maybe one day, Iago ap Rhys, in a world you cannot imagine, people will thank you for a mouse in a glove."

He sipped from his cup.

"Cigfa raised an eye-brow.

'What sort of thief could you fit inside a glove?'

'Listen,' said Manawydan, 'and I will tell you everything.'

He told her the story of the night.

'One of the mice was fatter than the rest so I caught it and kept it in my glove. Now it is to be hanged.'

'You would hang a mouse!'

'If I could have captured the rest of them I would have hanged them all. But yes, what I have caught I will hang.'

'So the rightful heir to the throne of the Island of the Mighty has been a hunter, a saddler, a shield-maker, a cobbler and a peasant – and now he is to become a hangman and execute a mouse!

It is hardly proper for a man of your status to bother with such creatures. Do the honourable thing and let it go.'

'It will hang for its crime!'

She turned away from him and sighed.

'I have no interest in the creature. I only want to prevent you from further disgracing yourself. Do as you see fit.'

Manawydan smiled.

'If it had been in your heart to seek a pardon for the mouse, maybe I would have listened. But, as you know, I pay scant regard to status or disgrace. The thief will hang for its crime.'

He snatched the glove and strode out of the hall.

He made his way to Gorsedd Arberth.

He took his knife and cut two sticks from a hawthorn tree. He shaped them until each was long and straight with a fork at the end.

He cut a third to be the cross-piece of the gibbet.

He climbed to the top of the hill. When he came to the cairn he crouched down beside it and pushed the two straight ends into the ground until the forks were level. He laid the cross-piece between them. He took some twine from his pocket and knotted it into a noose. He began to untie the glove.

Suddenly he was aware that he was not alone. He looked over his shoulder and saw a young Cerddor, dressed in a coat of patches, climbing the hill towards him.

'Lord,' he said, 'good day to you.'

'And welcome to you,' said Manawydan, 'where have you come from?'

'I have come from beyond the border, where I have been singing in the courts of the powerful. Why do you ask?'

'Because for seven years I have not seen a living soul in the seven cantrefs of Dyfed or the seven cantrefs of Seisyllwch save only its king, his wife and his mother – and two of them are vanished – and now I see you.'

'Well, Lord, I am just passing through on my way to my own country, but tell me, what is it that you are doing here?'

'I am hanging a thief that I caught stealing from me.'

'What sort of a thief can hang on a gallows that is not a knee's height from the ground?'

'A mouse.'

'A mouse! Lord, I can see by your bearing that you are a man of high status, and yet you lower yourself to such a degree that you would hang a mouse. Are you become a killer of vermin or a common rat-catcher? Let it go!'

'I will not. I caught it stealing and am punishing it according to the statutes of the law.'

'Lord, it pains me to see you demean yourself in this way. Look, I have a golden coin here that I was given for my song. I offer it as a blood price for the mouse's life.'

Manawydan shook his head.

'I will not sell it or let it go.'

'As you wish.'

The Cerddor turned and was gone.

Manawydan pulled the mouse from his glove. He held it tight with one hand, and with the other he secured the noose around its neck. He was oblivious to its squeals.

Then there was another voice behind him.

'Good day.'

He turned and saw a Bardd Teulu riding up the slope of Gorsedd Arberth. He was seated on a fine horse.

Manawydan saluted him.

'May good fortune prosper you. It is a curious thing to meet two strangers in a single day when for seven years I have seen no-one.'

The bard tilted his head to one side.

'Lord, what are you doing?'

'I am hanging a thief.'

'I see only a mouse.'

'It stole from me, and so it is to be punished.'

'Lord,' said the bard, "rather than watching you making a laughing stock of yourself, I will pay a ransom for the mouse and save you from disgrace.'

He reached into his saddle bag and pulled out a bag of gold.

'All this will be yours if you set it free.'

Manawydan shook his head.

'I want no ransom, I only want to see this scoundrel hang by the neck until it is dead.'

The Bardd Teulu shrugged.

'Do as you please.'

He rode away.

Manawydan tightened the noose around the mouse's neck. He looped the twine over the cross-piece of the gibbet and fastened it. He cupped the weight of the mouse in his hand. Its legs were kicking. He was on the point of letting it swing when there came a pounding of hooves.

A Pencerdd was approaching, and behind him a retinue of ten men. All were dressed in shimmering silk.

'Good day,' said the Pencerdd, 'what are you holding in your hand?'

Manawydan looked up and smiled.

'Strange how this hill has become such a highway! It is a mouse, Lord. And it is about to die.'

'Why?'

'As you will know, it is the penalty for theft.'

The Pencerdd climbed down from his saddle and put his hand on Manawydan's shoulder.

'It pains my heart to see a man such as you stooping so low. My fellow bards will sing satires of "The Rodent and the Rope" and your name will be shamed for seven generations. Let me save you from disrepute. Set the mouse free and I will give you ten bags of gold.'

'No, it will hang!'

'Twenty-four bags.'

'No! Even if you doubled your ransom I would not spare the mouse.'

'Then I will give you all the horses of my retinue and the loads of baggage they bear upon their backs.'

Manawydan withdrew his hand and the mouse began to swing and kick frantically.

'Stop!' the Pencerdd's voice shrilled.

Manawydan cupped his hand and took the mouse's weight again. The Pencerdd was ashen-faced.

'Name me your price.'

'The release of Pryderi and Rhiannon.'

'You shall have it.'

'That is not all.'

'What else?'

'The lifting of the enchantment from the seven cantrefs of Dyfed and the seven cantrefs of Seisyllwch.'

'You shall have it. Now please release the mouse.'

'That is not all.'

'What else?'

'That you tell me who this mouse is.'

'She is my dear wife. If she had been any other, I would never have come three times in disguise seeking her release.'

'Why did she come?'

'She came to steal. Listen and I will tell you my story. I have come from Annwn. My name is Llwyd, son of Cil Coed. I was one of the retinue of Gwawl that night many years ago when he was humiliated at his wedding feast. I have never forgotten how I was tied and trussed. I have never forgotten how I watched my lord beaten with cudgels in the game of 'badger-in-the-Bag'. I have never forgotten that long night on a hard floor, writhing and twitching in my bonds, or how we paid the minstrels and supplicants with the clothes from our backs. And when my lord swore that he would seek no vengeance, I vowed that I would. And so did my companions.

One of them stole Rhiannon's son, but lost an arm for his trouble.

As for me, I waited. Pwyll was dead by the time I laid my enchantment on this land. But his wife was no less guilty than he. I stole them both, the mother and her son, Rhiannon and Pryderi. They will not forget my retribution.

And when I saw you growing wheat on ground that I had made wilderness I sent my war band, in the shape of mice, to destroy your fields. Two nights they came. But on the third night my wife and the ladies of my court begged to join the sport. I agreed, and they too were transformed. But my wife is with child, she is not as quick as the others, and now you have caught her.

I have answered your questions, it is time for you to release her.'

'I will not.'

'What more do you want?'

'I want you to swear that there will never again be an enchantment upon the seven cantrefs of Dyfed or the seven cantrefs of Seisyllwch.'

'I swear. Set her free.'

'I will not'

'What more?'

'I want you to swear that you will never be avenged on me, or Rhiannon or Pryderi or Cigfa, or any of the generations that are born to them.'

'I swear. And you have struck a shrewd bargain, for if you had not asked for that I would have made sure a heavy affliction fell upon their shoulders.'

'Yes,' said Manawydan, 'that is what I had surmised.'

'Now, free my wife.'

'Not until I see Rhiannon and Pryderi with my own eyes.'

'Look, here they come! And they are wearing the emblems of their imprisonment.'

Manawydan turned. He saw his wife and his friend climbing the slope towards him. Rhiannon was wearing a leather harness stuffed with straw over her shoulders. Pryderi had the heavy iron lock of a door hanging from his neck.

When they saw him they shouted with joy and ran forwards.

'Now will you give me my wife? Everything you have asked for has been given.'

Manawydan gently loosened the noose and pulled it over the mouse's head.

'I give her to you gladly.'

He passed the mouse across to Llwyd, son of Cil Coed.

Llwyd took the creature and set her tenderly on the ground. He reached beneath his cloak and pulled out a wand of rowan.

He touched the mouse's head – and she was transformed into a woman of surpassing beauty, her belly rounded and full with the child she was carrying in her womb. She threw her arms around her husband's neck and kissed him.

Llwyd gestured with a sweep of his hand.

'Look around you,' he said, 'your land is restored.'

Rhiannon, Manawydan and Pryderi looked out from the height of Gorsedd Arberth and they saw that everything was as it had been before. Stretching away below them there were green fields, walls of stone and wooden fences, thatched farms, homesteads and barns. There were fat sheep and grazing cattle. There were women scattering grain for hens and geese. There were men on horseback and children clambering high among the branches of trees. And when they turned their eyes on the court of Arberth they saw that it had become busy with guards, warriors and hurrying servants.

For a long time they gazed outwards at the land.

And when they looked back they saw they were alone.

Llwyd, son of Cil Coed and his wife were gone.

They returned to the Court of Arberth.

Cigfa ran out to welcome them.

They told her how Manawydan had bargained for them with a pregnant mouse and a gallows made of twigs.

A feast was prepared and they ate.

When it was finished Manawydan said:

'Tell me friends, where were you taken when the enchantment carried you away?'

Pryderi was the first to speak:

'Whether it was a for a long time or a short time that I was held in the darkness of the house of stone, I do not know. But the lock I bear is the lock that bound me.'

Then Rhiannon said:

'Whether it was for a long time or a short time that I hauled hay with the working horses, I do not know. But the harness I wear is the harness that held me.'

The old man was silent for a while, and so were the listeners.

"And so ends the third 'Cainc' of the Mabinogi."

Brother Iago leaned forwards.

"Tell me more about the three disguises that Llwyd took."

There was impatience in the old man's voice.

"They are the three orders of Bard, of course."

"I have never been to court."

"Never been to court – and you the son of old Rhys Tewdyr!"

"I was born the wrong side of the bed. A little purse of coins was all we ever saw of our royal blood."

Cian Brydydd Mawr shook his head.

"Such is often the way, I am sorry, Brother. I was hasty."

He thought for a while.

"I suppose that in your world the disguises might have taken the form of scholar, priest and bishop – had they had such things in the distant days before the holy fathers came."[34]

6

Gwydion

Friday March 13th

"Brother, I have sinned."

Brother Deiniol's back was sore. The scabs cracked and wept when he leant forwards. At the sound of Olwen's voice his heart pounded. He was grateful to be sitting in shadow.

"How have you sinned?"

"I have desired a man who is unattainable."

He tightened his closed eyes. He struggled to keep his voice calm.

"He is married?"

"No, he is not married."

"He is nobly born?"

"No."

"Then how is he unattainable?"

"He has taken holy orders and is sworn to celibacy."

Brother Deiniol gripped the sides of the little desk he knelt at. His head was swimming.

"It is not just that I have desired him, Brother. I have fallen in love with him."

"He is a brother here, at Clynnog Fawr?"

Her eyes were frank and there was pain in them.

"Yes."

"Does he know?"

She shook her head.

"I think not."

Brother Deiniol was in turmoil. Dread of mortal sin was wrestling with the hope that it might be him. His cock pressed against the rough wool of his robe.

She whispered:

"There is something else."

"What is that?"

"Even if he were to renounce his vows, he would be unattainable."

"Why?"

"He is my dead husband's dead sister's husband."

Brother Deiniol knew straight away – it was Dafydd.

A sharp twisting jealousy mingled with a deep gratitude to have been released from the torment of temptation. He took a deep breath.

"That, at least, is not a sin. You have no blood in common."

He paused. He could feel the burden of guilt dissolving and diminishing in his blood.

"But the first sin must be atoned for."

She nodded.

"You can hear the bell ring, I think, at Careg boeth?"

"I can."

"Whenever it rings, between today and Easter Sunday, you must drop to your knees and pray for mercy and deliverance from the promptings of the flesh."

"Even at Vigils."

"Even at Vigils if it wakes you."

"Thank you, Brother."

She got to her feet.

"I fear it will not cure me."

"It is the effort that releases us from sin."

Brother Deiniol watched her cross the church. She closed the door behind herself. He kissed his bible.

Tomorrow he would start praying for Dafydd.

Saturday March 21st

Brother Iago was becoming skeletal with fasting and prayer.

The old man watched him take his accustomed place by the door of the cell.

"You are racing me to the grave, my friend."

Brother Iago shook his head.

"'Man shall not live by bread alone, but by every word that proceedeth out of the mouth of God.' I am sustained by psalms and prayers."

Cian Brydydd Mawr got to his feet. He tottered across to him and put his hand on the monk's shoulder.

"Iago ap Rhys, I'm afraid that this Lententide it is I who have become the Tempter. You are not sustained by every word that proceeds from my mouth."

"No, I am not."

The old man gestured to the hearth.

"What if I could turn these stones into bread?"

Brother Iago allowed himself a smile.

"I would not eat them."

"My story moves again from South to North.

The kingdom of Gwynedd – that once had been the domain of Bran and the sons of Llyr – is ruled by a new Lord now.

If I could sing, I would sing his name – Math son of Mathonwy.

I would sing of Math, who is steeped in the sciences of magic, enchantment and spell-craft.

I would sing of grey-bearded Math, High King of a new dynasty. Look.

He is seated on his golden throne in his hall at Caer Dathyl.

His eyes are half-closed as though he is listening with intent concentration to some secret the air is carrying to his ears.

He is alone, save only for a girl who sits on a stool before him and cradles his naked feet in her skirts."

The old poet looked directly at his listeners.

"You see, my friends, Math suffered from an affliction.

He would fall into a mortal sickness unless his feet rested upon the soft lap of a virgin.

He could never leave his hall. He could stand only for a little while.

Even so he ruled the land with an astute attention. His ears were so fine-tuned that no whispered word escaped his notice.

He had two nephews.

Their names were Gwydion and Gilfaethwy.

He ordered them to ride out with his retinue and make circuits of the kingdom on his behalf. Everything they saw they reported back to him. In this way, despite his strange malady, he held his realm in the palm of his hand.

The only time the curse of his affliction was eased was when Gwynedd was at war. Only then was he able to jump to his feet, leave his hall, and lead his army into the turmoil of the battlefield.

The name of the lap-maiden was Goewin, daughter of Pebin.

She was the fairest woman in the kingdom of Gwynedd.

She had not escaped the notice of Gilfaethwy.

From the moment he first set eyes upon her he lusted after her.

She consumed his dreams. Whenever he was in her presence his mind's eye was stripping her naked. His every thought was of her warm skin against his.

Cradling her Lord's feet in her lap, she blushed at his fierce scrutiny.

He ached for her. But she was always with Math.

He was beside himself with a desire that only she could satisfy.

He began to forsake his meat. He grew pale and lean. His eyes were bright and feverish with the heat of his obsession. The flesh fell away from his face so that it became hard to recognise him.

Gwydion said:

'Brother, what has happened to you?'

'Why do you ask?'

'You are losing your colour and becoming thin and grey as a wolf in winter. What is the matter?'

'I cannot tell you.'

'Why not?'

Gilfaethwy's voice dropped to a whisper. He gestured with his thumb towards Caer Dathyl.

'Because he will hear. He hears everything.'

'Only when there is a breeze. When it is still he can hear nothing.'

They waited until there was no breath of wind.

Gwydion said:

'I have guessed your thoughts. You desire Goewin.'

'Shhhhhhh.'

Gilfaethwy sighed with a great weariness. He rubbed his fingers against his eyes.

'I cannot live unless I have her.'

'There is no use in sighing, brother. It will cure nothing. Listen, the only way to get her is to start a war. Math will ride out with his army and she will be a ripe fruit for the plucking! Leave it to me, I have a plan.'

Look.

See how Math's nephews, Gwydion and Gilfaethwy, the two sons of his sister, Danu, approach their uncle's throne.[35]

Gwydion walks ahead.

He is measuring the mood in the hall as a fox will sniff at the air.

His face is subtle and alive to every sense. His forehead is high and furrowed with thought. His eyes are cold and clear as water in a deep well.

Gilfaethwy follows.

His face is ravaged by appetite. It is scarred and hungry, lean and eager, furtive and bold.

The lap-maiden sees them coming.

A chill deep inside her body makes her shudder.

Math looks up at the two brothers and smiles. He loves them both. Gwydion is showing great promise. He has no reason to doubt them.

'Well my lads, how can I help you?'

Gwydion kisses his uncle's hand.

'My Lord, you will have heard of Pryderi.'

'Why should I not have heard of old Pryderi, son of Pwyll. He is lord over twenty-one cantrefs in the south.'

'But Lord, have you heard of the creatures that he owns? Their like has never been seen before in the Island of the Mighty.'

'Tell me more.'

'They are smaller than sheep and naked of all but a few bristles.

They are cousin to the wild boar, but their meat is sweeter and more plentiful. They thrive on what is thrown away. They can loosen the most intransigent ground. And they can be kept in a yard, as tame as any dog. It is said that their flesh is better than beef.'

'What are they called?'

'They are called 'moch' my Lord.'[36]

'How did old Pryderi come into the possession of such miraculous creatures?'

'There has, since the days of his father Pwyll, been conversation and colloquy between Dyfed and Annwn. I understand, Lord, that the creatures were a gift to Pryderi from Arawn.'

There is a pause as Math ponders.

Something in the jut of his lip reveals his thought.

Gwydion reads it. He knows his uncle has taken the bait.

Math looks him hard in the eyes.

'Well, how can we get some of them from him?'

'I have a plan. I will go with eleven men disguised as bards. We will ask Pryderi for the creatures.'

'He could refuse you.'

Gwydion's cold eyes meet his uncle's gaze. His mouth curves into a sudden smile.

'He won't.'

Gwydion and Gilfaethwy disguised themselves as travelling bards. They took ten trusted men. They were dressed in robes, with only knives at their belts. Between them they carried four harps.

They journeyed southwards to Rhuddlan Teifi where they knew Pryderi was holding court.

He was an old man now. His face was creased and wrinkled with the joys and sorrows of a lifetime, scarred from a thousand skirmishes.

He welcomed the company of bards.

They were invited to sit at the feasting table. This was how they were seated: Pryderi sat at the head of the table. Gwydion was to his left and Gilfaethwy to his right. Beyond Gilfaethwy sat old Cigfa. And beyond Gwydion sat Rhiannon, twice widowed. She was still a handsome woman with no streak of grey in her hair.

When the feast was finished old Pryderi turned to Gwydion.

'Well, it is time one of your young men entertained us with a story or a song.'

Gwydion shook his head.

'Our custom Lord, when we come to the court of a great man, is that on the first night it is the Pencerdd who should perform. I would be delighted to tell you a story.'

'Very well.'

Cian Brydydd Mawr paused.

"I do not know know which story Gwydion told that night. It has been said that his uncle had taught him the arts of enchantment, and that of all the tellers in the world he was the most accomplished. Let us imagine that he told this one, for it is dear to my heart and I would not want it forgotten.

'Lord,' said Gwydion, 'you and your friend Manawydan were two of the survivors of the terrible war against Matholwch, King of Ireland.'

'Indeed we were.'

'I should like to tell you the story of another of the seven who returned. You will remember the poet, Taliesin.'

Pryderi bowed his grizzled head.

'I remember him well.'

Two of the harps struck up a melody.

'This is the story of his birth.[37]

Lord, there was once a lake. In the lake there was an island.

On the island there lived a woman of power and her name was Ceridwen.

She had two children.

She had a daughter whose name was Creirwy. It was said of her that the poppies of the field tried to imitate the creamy whiteness of her brow. They failed so miserably that they have blushed bright red ever since.

She also had a son. He was of such impenetrable stupidity and such unsightly ugliness that he was given the name 'Afagddu', 'utter darkness'.

Ceridwen made a cauldron and filled it with water. She set it over the flames of a fire and began to gather the ingredients for the enchantment she was shaping. She gathered herbs and minerals according to the shifting phases of the moon and the turning seasons of the year: moonwort, comfrey, cassia, vervain, honey, wheat, mercury, silver and salt.

The cauldron was to boil for a year and a day.

Then three distilled drops would rise to the surface.

They would be charged with prophetic knowledge and poetic insight.

They were to be put onto the tongue of Afagddu.

They would dispel his stupidity.

Ceridwen kidnapped a little boy from a village at the lake's edge. His name was Gwion Bach.

He was given a long wooden spoon. He was told to stir by day and by night without ceasing. The boy did what he was told.

By the light of the sun and the stars he stirred.

He was enchanted by the strange dark beauty of the woman.

He watched her coming and going. Her arms were filled with herbs and minerals. He did not know – such was the secret nature of the ingredients of the cauldron – that his throat was to be slit when the year and its day were ended.

The time passed.

Three months, six months, nine months passed.

The boy stirred without ceasing. A year passed.

Then it was the day beyond the year.

A dark bubble formed on the surface of the cauldron. It burst.

Three drops landed on Gwion Bach's finger.

They were scalding hot.

Without thinking he dropped the wooden spoon and lifted his finger to his mouth.

Everything changed.

It was as though his thoughts had been polished and infused with light. It was as though all past and future had no horizon any longer.

With his inner eye he saw the death that had been planned for him. With his outer eye he saw Ceridwen striding towards him, her face exploding with rage.

He turned and he ran.

She was close behind him. She was so consumed by her fury that she had become a crone. Her eyes were red and swollen, her black tongue lolled to her chin.

Gwion Bach ran and ran. In his thoughts he was a hare, leaping and bounding into the space before him. He became a hare.

She became a greyhound.

The hare was swift but the greyhound was swifter.

Gwion Bach ran to the water's edge. He leapt. In his thoughts he was a trout, twisting and straining into the space before him. He became a trout.

She became an otter.

The trout was swift but the otter was swifter.

Gwion Bach jumped out of the water. In his thoughts he was a crow, beating his wings against the wind. He became a crow.

She became a hawk.

The crow was swift but the hawk was swifter. The hawk swooped down and dug its talons into his neck.

Gwion Bach became a grain of wheat. He slipped between her talons and fell down to the ground.

She became a black hen.

She flapped and fluttered down out of the sky. She scratched and pecked until she found the one grain among the many.

She swallowed it.

The little grain of wheat in the crop of the black hen began to grow.

It swelled for three, for six, for nine months. Ceridwen became big and heavy with child.

Her waters broke. She lay on her back. She opened her thighs and gave birth. The child lay wet and gasping on the ground.

She took a dagger.

She was going to slit his throat.

Then she looked into his face. He was beautiful. His forehead was shining with light. He was her own son.

She could not bring herself to kill him.

She scooped him into her arms. She wrapped him in animal skins. She made a little coracle of withies, leather and pitch.

She put the baby into the coracle and carried him across the lake. She carried him through valleys and over mountains until she came to the edge of the cold, grey sea.

She flung the coracle into the tide.

It was carried, spinning and tossing, by the currents and winds of the ocean. For days, weeks and years, for hundreds of years the little boat was carried by the waves.

In all that time the baby, wrapped in skins, did not age by a single day.'"

The bell rang.

The old man smiled.

"Gwydion paused. His harpers struck up an air."

He took a sip of water.

"Gwydion lifted a cup of wine and moistened his throat."

He gestured to Dafydd, Olwen and Tomos.

"Pryderi, Rhiannon and Cigfa were leaning forwards in their seats. They were enmeshed in the enchantment of the tale – and there we will leave them."

He straightened himself slowly.

It was Tomos who broke the silence.

"Must we stop there?"

"Yes. I need to rest now."

The listeners left.

Two hours later the old man was ready to start again.

"Gwydion's story was not finished yet."

"There was a prince whose name was Elphin.

He was a drunkard and heavily in debt.

One Beltane-eve, he thought he'd try his luck with some nets across the river Dovey.

'Perhaps,' he thought to himself, 'the salmon will be running, or maybe some piece of good fortune will come floating in with the tide.'

Elphin stretched his nets from bank to bank. He sat on the grass beneath the stars and waited. With the first crack of dawn he waded into the water to see what he'd caught.

There were no fish – but there was something.

There was a little coracle tangled in the nets. It was encrusted with limpets and barnacles. It was slimy with seaweed.

Inside there was something wrapped in skins.

He carried it to the river's edge. He set it down on the soft grass and began to unfold and unwind the skins.

The skins became warm.

Inside there was a newborn child. His purple birth-cord was still moist against his belly. He was beautiful. His forehead shone with light.

Elphin leaned forwards and lifted the child in his arms.

'I will call you Taliesin, "Shining Brow".'

He climbed up onto his horse's back and set off for home.

But as he rode his mood began to change. His heart sank in his breast. He saw the thin cattle in his fields. He saw the tattered, crumbling outline of his hall. He thought about his debts and the lack of fish in his nets.

The tears began to trickle down his cheeks.

One of them splashed onto the baby's face.

The baby opened his eyes, opened his mouth and spoke:

'Dry your tears sweet Elphin, never in any river was such good fortune as this. I am Taliesin, I sing perfect metre that will last until the end of the world.'

Elphin stared at the child.

'What are you? Man or spirit?'

The child smiled.

'Gwion Bach I once was, and evermore am Taliesin.'

Elphin spurred his horse onwards. As he drew close to his hall, his wife came out to meet him.

'Well, Elphin, what did you catch? How many fish?'

'I didn't catch any fish – but I did catch a poet!'

She turned away from him shaking her head.

'You drunkard, you wastrel.'

Elphin jumped down from the saddle. He thrust the baby into her arms.

'Look!'

She took the child and he spoke again:

'I am Taliesin,

I sing perfect metre that will last until the end of the world.

I know why there is an echo in a hollow.

I know why breath is black, why liver bloody,

and why silver shines.

I know why a cow has horns and why a woman loves.

I know why milk is white, why holly green,

why sea is salt, why ale is bitter and why berries red.

I know of the beasts at the sea's bed.

I know how many spears make a confrontation

and how many drops a shower of rain.

I know why fishes have scales

and why swan's feet are black.

I have been a blue salmon.

I have been a stag, a dog, a roebuck on the mountain,

a stock, a spade, an axe in the hand,

a hare, a trout, a crow in the air.

I fell to the ground as a grain of wheat.

I was pecked and swallowed by the black hen.

For nine months in her crop I lay.

I have been dead. I have been alive.

I am Taliesin.'

Elphin and his wife were amazed.

They looked after the miraculous child, and he grew as any child would grow.

But in language and knowledge he was beyond all learning.

It was as though his tongue and the breath that moved over it was as old as time itself.

It was a wonderful thing to see the baby, sitting in his cradle, singing to his parents of the mysteries of creation.

It was a wonderful thing to see him on a little stool in the orchard, speaking of time beyond time, time upon time, and once upon a time.

And from the moment the baby was found, Elphin's luck took a turn. His sheep began to grow fat. Cream dripped from the swollen udders of his cattle. His harvests were good. His granaries were stacked with bulging sacks of grain.

Soon his debts were paid and his crumbling hall rebuilt.

The miraculous child became the greatest poet ever to have walked the face of the earth.

'I am Taliesin,

I sing perfect metre that will last until the end of the world.

I am Elphin's chief bard.

I have been on the white hill a year and a day in stocks and fetters.

I have been on the windy cross with the merciful Son of the Great Mother.

I am a wonder whose origin is not known.

I have danced on the galaxy at the heart of order.

I have spoken before receiving the gift of speech.

I have been teacher to all intelligences and it is not known whether my body is fish or flesh.

I have been for nine months in the womb of Ceridwen.
Gwion Bach I once was, and ever more am Taliesin.'"

The old man sighed.

"Of course Pryderi was entranced by Gwydion's tale."

"Who wouldn't be?" said Olwen.

'He looked at the Pencerdd with gratitude and wonder.

'Many times, during the Irish war, Taliesin roused our spirits with stories and songs, but never once did he tell us of his own birth.'

Gwydion was adept at lying and flattery.

'Lord, for seven years I studied with Taliesin in the Bardic Schools. From him have I learned a thousand tales of miraculous births and youthful exploits, of elopements and adventures, of voyages and deaths. A year of nights would not exhaust my repertoire. And, Lord, already Taliesin sings of the Irish War. He has immortalised the name of Pryderi, son of Pwyll, in song.'

Pryderi got up to his feet.

'We are honoured to have you here in our hall. How can we pay for such enchantment and delight as we have received this night?'

'Lord,' said the Pencerdd, 'could anyone articulate a request better than I?'

'No, yours is a most accomplished tongue.'

'Then I will tell you. You have in your keeping certain creatures that were given to you by Arawn, King of Annwn. I plead for them in exchange for my song.'

Rhiannon plucked Pryderi's sleeve. She shook her head.

She leaned across the table and whispered urgently into his ear.

Pryderi said:

'I am sorry. It would be the easiest thing in the world to give them to you, were it not for a promise I have made my people concerning them.'

'What promise is that?'

'That I will not give or sell any of them until they have bred double their number in my land.'

The Pencerdd lowered his voice.

'Lord, do not refuse me yet. Tomorrow I will return to your hall. When you see what I bring, I'll wager that you will think again.'

The twelve bards bowed and left Pryderi's hall.

When they were out of sight, Gwydion grinned.

'Men, we were never going to get the pigs by asking for them.'

'So,' said Gilfaethwy, 'what ruse do you have up your sleeve?'

'Watch me. I will make sure we don't leave without them.'

He told his men to trap twelve rats and twelve mice.

Look.

Gwydion is reaching beneath his cloak and taking out his wand of rowan. The rats are held in wicker cages. He pokes the tip of his wand into each cage. He touches each rat. The wicker flies away as they swell and burst their bonds. Paws become cloven hooves. Legs lengthen. Necks grow long and slender. Faces narrow.

With all the skills of his art he transforms the rats into twelve lithe horses with golden saddles and golden bridles.

He touches each mouse. They become black hunting dogs with golden collars and long leashes of leather.

He walks out into the fields and gathers twelve wide, white mushrooms. At the touch of his wand they are transformed into golden shields.

The next morning they returned to Pryderi's hall.

Each bard was leading a horse and a dog.

The Pencerdd bowed.

'Good day, Lord.'

Pryderi welcomed them.

'Lord,' said the Pencerdd, 'yesterday you said that you had promised your people neither to give nor sell your pigs until you had bred double their number. But you said nothing about exchanging them. Look. I would give you all these horses and hounds, with their golden saddles, collars and bridles in exchange for the new creatures.'

Rhiannon shook her head. Pryderi said nothing.

The Pencerdd nodded to his bards. They left the hall. Soon they returned bearing the shields.

'And also, Lord, I throw in these twelve golden shields. Surely there was never a fairer exchange than this.'

'I will hold a counsel and discuss the matter with my noblemen.'

They were dazzled by the craftsmanship. Rhiannon urged them to refuse, but she was over-ruled. Pryderi bowed his head.

'Very well. The pigs are yours.'

Horses, dogs and shields were handed over.

The bards were led across the yard.

'Here they are.'

The doors of the sties were pulled open. The air was filled with grunts, snorts, squeals, and a sweet-sour smell they had never known before.

The bards rounded up the strange naked beasts.

They began to drive them northwards.

Gwydion laughed aloud.

'There's no time to waste! The enchantment will only hold from one day to the next. It has less staying power than a story. When Pryderi discovers how he has been hoodwinked we can be sure he'll seek revenge. Keep these creatures trotting at a steady pace!'"

"I will stop there."

Cian Brydydd Mawr closed his eyes.

Dafydd said:

"Less staying power than a story! Does anything have *more* staying power than a story?"

The old man smiled.

"It depends on who tells it and why. Sometimes a story can be true, sometimes it can be no more than diversion and distraction. The world is full of Gwydions ..."

He looked across at Brother Iago.

"... who would turn stones into bread that could not sustain us."

"Or bread into stones?"

"That too."

Olwen was uneasy.

"But the story of Taliesin, surely that was more than a distraction."

The old man reached forwards and put his hand on her knee.

"Who was telling it, me or Gwydion?"

She looked at him and did not answer. He whispered:

"If it was me, then it was the truest story I know."

Thursday March 26th

For four days, Cian Brydydd Mawr had not got out of bed. Occasionally Tomos would hold a bucket and he would relieve himself into it.

When he heard the brothers leaving the church after Eucharist he beckoned to the boy.

"Go and fetch Brother Deiniol. I would like to speak with him."

When he had broken his fast Brother Deiniol came to the old man's cell. He knocked on the door.

"Come in. Come in. Sit down."

He settled himself into a chair. The old man turned his head on his pillow. His voice was little more than a whisper.

"No fainting fits recently I trust."

Brother Deiniol blushed.

"God has been merciful."

The old man chuckled, then fell into a fit of coughing. Tomos lifted his head and pressed a cup of water to his lips.

"Thank you."

Brother Deiniol leaned forwards.

"You wanted to speak with me?"

"Yes. I have been wondering about our Lord. What news is there of Llywelyn?"

"Strange news."

"Tell me more."

Brother Deiniol frowned.

"It is difficult to understand. Barely eight months have passed since the humiliation of Gwynedd. And yet our Lord Llywelyn and Lady Siwan have ridden to Cambridge with their retinue. They are to celebrate the Easter festival with King John. It is as though he has all but forgotten his defeat and its bitter aftermath."

The old man scratched his cheek.

"And yet, the widow Olwen tells me, her son Rhys is to join a muster at Caernarfon on Easter Monday."

"That is what I struggle to understand. While Llywelyn prays and feasts with his father-in-law, every man in the kingdom who is aged between fifteen and thirty winters will be preparing for war. And I have heard rumours from my brothers in the south that the same is happening in other kingdoms also."

The old man closed his eyes and smiled. It was as though he was basking in the news that had been brought to him. Brother Deiniol, thinking he had fallen asleep, got to his feet and crossed the floor of the cell. As he was lifting the latch of the door Cian Brydydd Mawr whispered:

"There is a fashion among the Normans for animal stories. I have heard them even in the Welsh courts. Their king, of course, is the lion. Then there is Isegrim the wolf, Bruin the bear, Grimbard the badger, Curtois the hound, Tibert the cat. All are vying for power."

Brother Deiniol smiled.

"I have heard of them."

"But the one who outwits them all, the one who gains the upper hand every time is Reynard the fox."

"Aha, Llwynog. So you are saying Llywelyn is our Llwynog?"

"I am saying that if the fox and the lion are kneeling together at the altar-rail, we can be sure the fox has a plan."

Friday April 3rd (Good Friday)

'For the enemy pursueth my soul, he treadeth my life to the ground. He maketh me dwell in darkness, as those who are long dead; my spirit is afraid within me, my heart within me is disconsolate. Memor fui dierum antiquorum, meditates sum in omnibus operibus tuis: in factis manuum tuarum meditabar.'

The altar was bare. The candles had been extinguished. The psalms were spoken. There was no Mass. Today there would be no food at all.

Brother Iago had been awake all night in vigilant prayer. His eyes were dark hollows. The skin was stretched over the bones of his face. The roots of his teeth ached. In the back of his mind he was counting the hours until Easter Sunday and its promise of release from suffering.

When he came to the old man's cell the others were already gathered.

There was concern in Cian Brydydd Mawr's voice.

"Are you strong enough, Brother? We could meet on another day."

"I am strong enough."

His hand trembled as he sharpened his stylus.

"But my memory is suffering. The story Gwydion told, the Taliesin story, I struggle to remember the verses. They are too oblique."

The old man smiled.

"They would challenge the memory of the most accomplished bard. Set them aside Iago ap Rhys. Another day I will spell the story out to you. When you have food in your belly."

"You will remember that Gwydion and his brother were driving Pryderi's pigs towards Gwynedd.

All day they journeyed.

When the night came, they had reached the place that is still to this day called Mochdref, 'Swinetown'.

The next day they travelled on. They made their way northwards until they reached a commote that still bears the name Mochnant, 'swine-brook'.

From there they drove the creatures through Rhos and stopped at another place that still bears the name 'Mochdref'.

By this time word had reached the two brothers' ears that Pryderi was mustering an army.

'We must not stop moving until we come to Gwynedd.'

They drove the pigs to the highest township in Arllechwedd

and penned them. The place still remembers those creu or pens, its name is 'Creuwryon'.

When the pigs were secured the two brothers went straight to Math's hall at Caer Dathyl.

They saw a great gathering of warriors.

Striding among them was their grey-bearded uncle. He was dressed for war. In his hand he was holding a long ash-wood spear.

Gwydion dug his fingers into Gilfaethwy's ribs.

'Look! He's on his feet. Everything is going to plan. A few more hours and your lap-maiden will be yours.'

They pushed through the ranks of soldiers until they came to Math.

Gwydion spoke:

'Uncle. What is happening here?'

'Have you heard nothing? Pryderi has marshaled twenty-one cantrefs. A huge army is on the move.'

Gwydion raised his eyebrows, as though this was news he had not heard before. Math's voice was raised so that it echoed in the hall.

'They have been pursuing you. It is strange that it should have taken you so long to get here.'

Gwydion smiled.

'These new creatures have many virtues, but speed is not one of them. Each has its own mind. They do not run together like sheep or cattle.'

'Where are they now?'

'We have made a pen for them in Arllechwedd.'

At that moment there came a sound on the wind.

The valleys were echoing with the distant blaring of war horns, the shouting of men, the neighing of horses, the thundering of hooves and the clattering of swords against shields.

277

'They have arrived!'

Math leapt onto his horse's back. He lifted his spear above his head and galloped to the front of his army. He led his war host through the valleys to Penardd in Arfon.

Gwydion and Gilfaethwy ran into the hall. They seized weapons and shields. They saddled fresh horses and followed.

At Penardd they set up camp.

As darkness settled they could see the fires of Pryderi's army flickering in the distance. They stretched from one edge of the horizon to the other.

Math, Gwydion and Gilfaethwy held a council of war.

'Tomorrow we will find ourselves a position of advantage. We will wait for them in the fastness of Gwynedd, between Maenawr Bennardd and Maenawr Coed Alun. We must be constantly on our guard.'

Their uncle got to his feet. He stretched and yawned.

'And now we will sleep.'

As he turned away, Gwydion nodded to Gilfaethwy and winked.

They slipped out of the camp, mounted their horses and rode back to Caer Dathyl.

Look.

There is a mood of high holiday in Math's hall.

With their lord and his warriors away in Penardd, see how grooms, servants, minstrels and handmaidens sit together at the feasting tables in an easy fellowship. The fires are blazing in the hearths. The air is alive with talk and the laughter of women.

The doors are thrown open.

The two brothers enter. Their swords are drawn.

Gwydion's shout cuts through the babble of conversation like a sharpened blade.

'On your feet!'

They turn their heads towards him.

'Every one of you, on your feet!'

Slowly they stand. One of the grooms feels the flat of Gilfaethwy's sword across his back.

'You heard what he said!'

Another reaches to empty his goblet. It's struck out of his hand. It clatters to the floor and splashes wine onto the ankles of the women.

Gwydion lifts his sword and gestures to the door.

'Out!'

Gilfaethwy swings his blade and rounds them up like cattle.

'Every one of you. Out!'

Men and women shuffle through the doors, one after another.

'Not you!'

Gwydion has seized Goewin by the arm. She cries out like a frightened animal. She tries to shake herself free.

He's thrown down his sword and twisted his other hand in her hair. He pulls her back from the other maidens.

She begs for help.

They hurry away, not daring to turn their heads.

He drags her to his uncle's bedchamber. Gilfaethwy follows.

Beside the bed Gwydion holds her fast as his brother, starting at the throat, tears open her clothes. She stares at him in a silent, breathless horror.

When she's naked Gwydion lets go of her.

He walks out of the bedchamber and gently closes the door.

With sword drawn, he stands guard outside.

He hears her pleading, her screams, her sobs, her cries of animal pain and then, for a long time, her silence.

Two hours before dawn he hammers on the door with the pommel of his sword. Gilfaethwy opens it. He's buckling his belt.

On the bed the girl is lying in a crumpled heap among the bloodied linen.

'Better?'

Gilfaethwy grins and puts his hand on his brother's shoulder.

'Much better!'

'Perhaps you'll eat something now.'

They stride out of the hall, straddle their horses and ride back to Penardd."

"That is behaviour beyond forgiveness."

It was Olwen's voice that interrupted the story. She reached across and rested her hand on Tomos' shoulder. The boy lifted his hand to hers. She could feel he was trembling.

Cian Brydydd Mawr looked at them.

"I am only recounting the story as it was told to me. With Gwydion and his tribe a new magic had come into the world. It was shallow, dark and very clever."

"At first light Math's army moved up into the rocky heights between Maenawr Bennardd and Maenawr Coed Alun.

It was there that Pryderi attacked them.

The warriors of the south climbed the slope and loosed a volley of arrows. Many warriors of Gwynedd fell.

Then Math's army came down from the heights.

It fell upon Pryderi's men. There was terrible slaughter.

Math drove them down into the valley.

They retreated to Nant Coll.

There they rallied and made a stand.

Again the two armies met. There was killing beyond measure. Pryderi retreated again to the place called Dol Benmaen.

He sought a truce. He offered twenty-four noblemen's sons as hostages to the peace. Among them was Gwrgi Gwastra.

Math accepted the truce and the hostages were delivered.

Pryderi's army began to make its way southwards.

But the foot soldiers of Gwynedd could not restrain themselves.

All along the way they killed stragglers with arrows, spears and knives. When they reached Y Felenrhyd, Pryderi ordered his warriors to halt again.

He sent messengers to Math, son of Mathonwy.

'Too many good men have been killed. This matter should be resolved between the man who is wronged and the man who has wronged him. Pryderi, son of Pwyll, challenges Gwydion, son of Danu, to single combat. The two armies can stand aside and watch as one man sets himself against the other. Only in this way will the dispute be settled.'

When the messengers came, Math said.

'If Gwydion will accept the challenge, the two men should fight.'

Gwydion shrugged.

'I accept it gladly. Why should the warriors of Gwynedd fight on my behalf when I could set my own body against the body of Pryderi?'

The messengers returned to Pryderi.

A place was set for them to meet at Y Felenrhyd on the banks of the river Dwyryd.

Gwydion sauntered down to the water's edge.

He carried a shield on his arm, a spear over his shoulder. A long sword swung from his belt.

He had no interest in Pryderi. The only purpose of this war had been to entice Math away from his lap-maiden.

Gilfaethwy's itch had now been scratched.

The pigs had been secured.

A quick clean death would bring the business to a close.

He thrust the butt of his spear into the moist ground and waited."

The bell rang. It had been muffled with cloth for Good Friday.

"Enough. You must go to your bare altar now, and I to my sleep."

Olwen beckoned to Tomos. When the old man was settled he followed her out of the cell.

"Come and eat with me."

She had bread and hard-boiled eggs. They sat together under the ash tree. She looked at him.

"Are you alright?"

The boy shrugged.

She said:

"The old poet is failing. I'm afraid he has not long to live."

"I've done my best for him. He was very kind to me when they took me in at Nant Gwrtheyrn, like a grandfather. "

"You have repaid him."

"Every day he gets weaker. When he dies I don't know what will happen to me."

"You would not stay here?"

"No. I could never be one of the brothers. Maybe I could become a warrior – and one day avenge my mother and father."

"They will not take you yet."

"I know."

They ate for a while in silence.

"I will have a bed to spare when Rhys goes. And Gwyn would be glad of a companion when the flocks and herds go up to the summer pastures."

"You would take me in?"

"It would be hard work."

"I don't mind that."

She reached across and put her arm around his shoulders. She drew him to her. Tomos was surprised to find that he was crying.

"Thank you. Thank you."

"I hear the muffled bell, Tomos, I listen to the stories, I see my son prepare for war – the world needs all the kindness it can muster."

After None the listeners gathered.

Cian Brydydd Mawr began:

"Pryderi strode down to the river's edge.

He had been dressed and armed for combat.

He wore helmet, shield and a battle vest of close-linked iron.

He carried a spear and a battle-axe. A long sword and a short sword hung from either hip.

He looked across the water at the man who had made a mockery of his hospitality, tricked him with his enchantments and robbed him of his pigs. The man who had lured his army into the mountains of the north, and then slaughtered them.

There was a price for such a humiliation.

Gwydion's blood would pay it."

At that moment Tomos noticed that Brother Iago's head had fallen forwards. His stylus had dropped to the floor. He was fast asleep. Tomos scraped a piece of clay from the floor. He rolled it into a ball.

"They hurled spears over the water.

Pryderi was the older man by more than twenty winters, but

his throw was deadly. The point of his spear split Gwydion's shield and cut a slice from his cheek.

Gwydion's spear glanced from Pryderi's mailed shoulder.

He was unscratched.

With a shout Pryderi drew his sword and waded into the water. Gwydion knew that this was his moment.

He threw down his broken shield and jumped from the grassy bank into the river.

Waist deep the two men pushed through the dragging current towards each other. Their eyes were locked together.

They advanced until they were almost at striking distance.

Gwydion scooped up a handful of water.

He flung it into Pryderi's face.

It was an ancient simple spell.

The old man blinked.

When he looked again there were three Gwydions.

They were all raising their swords.

They were shieldless, unprotected.

Only one of them was flesh and blood.

It would be the easiest thing in the world to pierce him to the heart – but which one? He lunged for the figure in the middle.

His blade went through empty air.

He fell forwards, face-down in the water.

There was only one Gwydion now and his sword was merciless. Again and again he hacked the back of Pryderi's neck. He cut through bone and flesh until only a strip of skin at the throat held body and head together.

The river was red with billowing blood.

Gwydion waded back to the riverbank. He flung his sword into the air. It spun four times round, flashing in the light.

He caught it and thrust it into its scabbard."

The ball of clay struck the shaved crown of Brother Iago's head. He woke with a start.

"There was a keening shout of grief.

The men of the South ran to the edge of the Dwyryd.

Their Lord had been dragged down to the bed of the river by the weight of his battle vest. They plunged into the water.

They lifted him in their arms.

They lashed together their ash-wood spears and made a bier.

They carried his dripping body on their shoulders from Y Felenrhyd to Maentwrog.

All night they sang his praises.

They sang of his miraculous birth and abduction, his boyhood as Gwri Golden-Hair, his fostering by Pendaran Dyfed and his youthful exploits in the Irish Wars. They sang of his courtship of Cigfa. They sang of the assembly of the severed head and the enchantment of Dyfed. They sang of the friendship of Manawydan. They sang of the long years of kingship and of how he had held his kingdom safe against all invaders. They sang of his death at the hand of Gwydion, son of Danu.

He was buried in Maentwrog.

The stone that marks his grave is still there to be seen.[38]

The men of the South began their long journey homewards.

They lamented the loss of their lord.

They lamented their defeat, the deaths of their fellow fighters, the destruction of their horses and weapons.

When they came to Arberth the news of Pryderi's death was carried to Cigfa and Rhiannon.

The two women wept bitter tears."

Cian Brydydd Mawr looked across at Brother Iago.

"And so the Son of the Great Mother is dead, like Christ Jesu on his Cross."

The monk gathered his wax tablets and straightened them on his lap.

"And there the similarity ends. There will be no resurrection for Pryderi, no ascension, no place on the right hand of God Almighty. There has not even been the promise of a place in Paradise."

"No." The old man sighed. "Our grandfathers, it seems, were denied such consolations."

He took a sip of water.

"But there is a little story that might suggest otherwise. It is a fragment that I remember old Meilyr mentioning once. Do you have time to sit for a little while longer?"

The listeners nodded. Brother Iago put all but one of his tablets down again.

"Put them all down, Brother. Just listen."[39]

He did as he was told.

"My story concerns the one who is called Mabon, son of Modron, the 'Son of the Great Mother'."

Dafydd said:

"There are those who call Christ Jesu 'Mabon'."

"There are."

The old man sipped again.

"The Son of the Great Mother, Mabon, son of Modron, was lost to the world. He was held captive in a place so deeply concealed that nobody could find him and bring him back to the light. A company set off to find him. They were led by Gwrhyr

Gwastad Ieithoedd, who was an interpreter of tongues. He could understand the speech of the birds and the beasts.

They journeyed until they found the Blackbird of Cilgwri.

'Ancient Blackbird,' said Gwrhyr, 'do you know anything about Mabon, son of Modron, who was stolen from between his mother and the wall?'

'When I came to this place,' said the Blackbird of Cilgwri, 'an iron anvil stood here. Every evening I would sharpen my beak upon it. Now it is no bigger then a nut. In all that time I have heard nothing of the man you seek. But there is a creature that is far older than I am. Follow me and I will lead you to him.'

The Blackbird led them to the Stag of Rhedynfre.

'Ancient Stag,' said Gwrhyr, 'do you know anything about Mabon, son of Modron, who was stolen from between his mother and the wall?'

'When I came to this place,' said the Stag of Rhedynfre, 'my antlers had only one tine apiece and the only tree here was a little sapling. It grew into a mighty oak with a hundred branches, then it tumbled and rotted away until all that is left today is its red stump in the ground. In all that time I have heard nothing of the man you seek. But there is a creature that is far older than I am. Follow me and I will lead you to him.'

The Stag led them to the Owl of Cwm Cawlwyd.

'Ancient Owl,' said Gwrhyr, 'do you know anything about Mabon, son of Modron, who was stolen from between his mother and the wall?'

'When I came to this valley it was a wooded glen. A race of men levelled it to the ground. Another forest grew and it was levelled again. The forest that you see before you is the third. In all that time I have heard nothing of the man you seek. But there is a creature that is far older than I am. Follow me and I will lead you to him.'

The Owl led them to the Eagle of Gwernabwy.

'Ancient Eagle,' said Gwrhyr, 'do you know anything about Mabon, son of Modron, who was stolen from between his mother and the wall?'

'When I came to this place,' said the Eagle of Gwernabwy, 'there was a mountain here. From the top of it I could peck the stars each night. Now it is the size of a clenched fist. In all that time I have heard nothing of the man you seek. But once, in the days when the mountain stretched up into the clouds, I sank my claws into the back of a salmon. He dragged me down to the depths and I barely escaped with my life. I made peace with him by removing fifty barbed fish-spears from his back. He is far older than I am. Follow me and I will lead you to him.'

The Eagle led them to the Salmon of Llyn Llyw.

'Ancient Salmon,' said Gwrhyr, 'do you know anything about Mabon, son of Modron, who was stolen from between his mother and the wall?'

'I will tell you what I know,' said the Salmon of Llyn Llyw. 'With every tide I swim up river. Once, when the tide was strong, it carried me to a wall of stone. From behind it came such sounds of bitter grieving as I had never heard before. If you do not believe me, climb onto my back and I will take you there.'

Gwrhyr climbed onto the Salmon's back. They travelled until they came to the wall. They could hear lamenting and groaning.

'What man cries out from the House of Stone?'

'It is Mabon, son of Modron, who is held here. No-one has been so cruelly imprisoned as I have been, not even Llud Llawereint silver-hand, nor Greid, son of Eri.'

'Could your release be secured with gold and silver?'

'Nothing of me will be released, except by harrowing and warfare.'

Gwrhyr Gwastad Ieithoedd returned to the world of men.

He told them what he had heard.

An army attacked the House of Stone. Two champions rode the Salmon's back and laid waste the wall from the depths of the river.

Mabon, son of Modron, the Son of the Great Mother, was set free.

He came out of the House of Stone with the lock that had held him on a chain at his throat. And he returned to the Light of Day."

Cian Brydydd Mawr lifted an arm.

"Now go!"

He let it fall limply on his lap.

The listeners made their way out of the old man's cell.

Brother Iago beckoned to Tomos. The boy followed him outside.

"Don't tell him I fell asleep."

Tomos laughed.

"I won't."

"And answer me this, how did Pryderi die?"

"Gwydion killed him of course – with strength and enchantment."

"Ah, thank you. That is all I need to know."[40]

Sunday April 5th (Easter Sunday)

The church was packed for the Easter Eucharist.

The brothers, the lay brothers, the families from the surrounding farms and villages were there. Cian Brydydd Mawr, wrapped in blankets, sat on a bench beside Tomos. Olwen, Rhys and Gwyn stood with the rest of the congregation. The air was thick with the warm smell of old wool, sweat, dung, smoke and incense.

'Now upon the first day of the week, very early in the morning, the women came unto the sepulchre, bringing the spices which they had prepared.'

Brother Iago mouthed the Latin words as they were spoken. His whole body was trembling.

'And they found the stone rolled away from the sepulchre. And they entered in and found not the body of the Lord Jesus.'

Dafydd needed no whispered translation for this story.

'And it came to pass, as they were much perplexed thereabout, behold two men stood by them in shining garments: And as they were afraid, and bowed down their faces to the earth, they said unto them, Why seek ye the living among the dead? He is not here, but is risen ...'

After they had taken the Mass, the greater part of the congregation shuffled out into the light. Olwen lingered for the final psalm. She saw the old poet was still sitting on his bench. She went across and sat down beside him.

'Praise ye the Lord. Praise God in his sanctuary: praise him in the firmament of his power. Praise him for his mighty acts; praise him according to his excellent greatness.'

Cian Brydydd Mawr reached across and took her hand in his. He stroked her palm with his thumb.

'Praise him with the sound of the trumpet: praise him with the psaltery and harp. Praise him with the timbrel and dance: praise him with stringed instruments and flutes.'

His hand was as cold as stone.

'Laudate eum in cymbalis benesonantibus: laudate eum in cymbalis iubilationis ...'

He leaned across and whispered in her ear:

"These days there is winter in my blood, but once, Olwen, once upon a time ..."

He lifted her hand and pressed it tenderly to his lips.

"... I was a lover of women."

290

He kissed it again.

"Don't wait too long."

He nodded at the statue of the Virgin Mary.

"There's no great virtue in denial, whatever the holy brothers may teach."

Monday April 6th

There were eleven lads from the neighbouring farms who were joining the muster. They had decided to journey together to Caernarfon. Olwen walked down the hill with Rhys.

The bailiff made a head-count.

"All here."

The air was full of their talk. They were eager to be off.

Olwen put her hands on Rhys' shoulders.

"You have your water-skin?"

"Yes."

"Your knife, a blanket, a change of clothes?"

"Yes."

"Food for the day?"

"Yes."

The others were beginning to walk away.

"Your crucifix?"

"Yes, yes."

He broke away from her.

"Rhys, God bless you. Be careful."

She grabbed his cloak and pulled him back. She kissed him and let him go. He ran to catch up with the rest. She heard his laugh. Then his voice was lost in the babble of young men's voices. He was gone.

She walked back up to Careg boeth.

Gwyn was waiting for her. He had a piece of wood for a sword. He was making thrusts and parries.

"I wish I was old enough to go."

She looked at him steadily.

"You will be."

Thursday April 9th

Dafydd came up to Careg boeth after Lauds. Olwen was plucking a chicken, throwing the warm feathers into a basket at her feet.

She was surprised to see him.

"Olwen, would you have time to come down to the monastery this afternoon?"

"Why?"

"Cian Brydydd Mawr has asked to see us, you and I alone."

She raised her eyebrows and smiled.

"Something that is not suitable for the ears of Brother Iago."

Dafydd shrugged and laughed.

"He hasn't spared him so far."

"Poor Iago ap Rhys! I can feel his shudders and blushes from the far side of the cell."

"I have no idea what the old man wants. But there was an urgency in his asking."

"Yes. I will come."

Dafydd reached down and pinched some feathers between his fingers and his thumb.

"And your Rhys – he is gone by now?"

"Gone."

She looked into his eyes and did not spare him the emptiness of her heart.

"Gone."

She stood up and put the half plucked chicken onto the bench behind her. Dafydd opened his arms and she stepped towards him. He held her. She buried her face in his robes. Then she broke away from him.

"Pray for us."

"Sit down."

The old man gestured to the accustomed chairs.

"I want to speak about my death. It is not far away."

He was quiet for a while.

"I have often had gold and brocade
From mortal lords for singing praise,
But songs are gone, my powers fail,
Stripped of wealth my tongue falls silent."

He turned to Dafydd.

"Dafydd ap Dafydd ap Dafydd, you once made me a promise and you kept your word. Would you make me another?"

"What is it?"

Cian Brydydd Mawr turned to Olwen.

"Olwen, when I look into your face, something true looks back at me. If you made a promise I know you would not break it."

"What is it?"

"I had always hoped that I would spend my last weeks in a cell on the holy ground of Ynys Enlli. Long ago I composed a poem expressing that wish:

"May I dwell awhile awaiting the summons
In the cell with the tide beside it:

Secluded it is, undimmed its fame,
With its graves in the breast of the sea.
Christ, his cross foreknown, will know me also,
Will lead me past the pains of hell,
And the Maker who made me will greet me
In the fair acre of Enlli's faithful." [41]

Dafydd nodded.

"The Island of Saints."

The old man smiled.

"Yes, but it is more than that. Old Meilyr always told me it is the Westernmost Isle, The Isle of Apples, where the Thirteen Treasures of Britain are buried."

He sipped from his cup.

"I will die here at Clynnog Fawr, not there. But I ask you this – that you carry my bones to Ynys Enlli and bury them in that soil. Both of you. Together. A man and a woman. It is my deepest wish."

Dafydd and Olwen's eyes met. Without turning away from her Dafydd said:

"I promise."

"Good."

The old man looked at Olwen.

"You?"

"I have a farm, a son ... it is not an easy journey."

Her eyes were fixed on Dafydd. His gaze was unwavering.

"Yes." She said. "Yes, I promise as well."

"Then it is settled. Thank you. You have set my heart at ease."

He closed his eyes.

"I am tired now."

Dafydd said:

"Before we go, tell us, what are these thirteen treasures that lie alongside the hallowed bones of the saints of Ynys Enlli?"

The old man intoned. His voice was barely audible.

"Dyrnwyn the Sword of Rhydderch the Generous,

The Hamper of Gwyddno Garanhir,

The Horn of Bran the Niggard,

The Chariot of Morgan the Wealthy,

The Halter of Clydno Eiddyn,

The Knife of Llawfrodedd the Horseman,

The Cauldron of Dyrnwch the Giant,

The Whet-stone of Tudwal Tydflyd,

The Coat of Padaen Red-coat,

The Chessboard of Gwenddolau ap Ceido,

The Mantle of Arddhu of Cornwall,

The Crock and the Dish of Rhygenydd the Clerk."

His head fell forwards and he seemed to be asleep.

Dafydd and Olwen got up to leave. Suddenly Cian Brydydd Mawr lifted his head. His eyes were shining.

"I will be in good company."

Wednesday April 15th

When Brother Iago came into the cell the old poet looked at him with satisfaction.

"Iago ap Rhys! There is a flush to your cheeks, a little flesh to your bones. Maybe you will live to finish my book after all. And if not, at least you won't be a disappointment to the worms."

Brother Iago smiled and sat down.

"Now that Pryderi is dead, I was hoping that your story might be drawing to its close."

"Brother, there is always more."

Brother Iago sighed and sharpened his stylus.

The old man closed his eyes.

"One army's defeat is always another's triumph. Listen."

"If I could sing, I would sing of the warriors of Gwynedd.

I would sing of them returning home drunk with victory.

I would sing of every man as he crossed his threshold.

I would sing of a father's pride, a mother's welcome and a wife's warm embrace.

Gwydion spoke to Math:

'Lord, should we not release the hostages? The twenty-four who were handed over by Pryderi?'

Math bowed his head.

'Let them be released.'

Gwrgi Gwastra and the other twenty-three sons of noblemen were set free. They returned to the South.

Math began to weaken.

When Pryderi's broken army had crossed the border he could feel himself falling into his old affliction.

He knew he must return to Caer Dathyl.

He called for Gwydion and Gilfaethwy.

'Make a circuit of Gwynedd on my behalf.'

He watched them ride away with their retinues.

He set off for home, bowed in the saddle, his head drooping, the reins slack in his hands.

Look.

He is entering the doorway of his hall.

He has been lifted down from his horse's back.

He stumbles into the firelight with a groom to left and right.

They lead him to his throne. His arms are over their shoulders.

His teeth are chattering. His eyes are bloodshot. His hands tremble.

They lower him gently. He curls his fingers around the arms of the throne. He settles himself.

Then he looks down at the foot-stool.

'Where is the lap-maiden?'

His voice is high-pitched and thin, querulous on the air.

Grooms, servants and handmaidens exchange anxious glances.

His shout wakes them into action.

'Bring me Goewin!'

The servants scuttle away. They return with the girl.

Math smiles.

'Sit down child. Take off my boots. Wash my feet. Dry them with a cloth and cradle them in your lap.'

See how Goewin approaches him and shakes her head.

'Look elsewhere for a virgin, for I am a virgin no longer.'

He looks at her more closely.

He sees that her face is swollen, her wrists bruised.

Her eyes are fixed on his, unwavering in their stare.

'I am a woman now.'

'What does this mean?'

'That is a question you should put to your nephews, the sons of Danu.'

Math narrows his eyes, reaches for her hand.

'Tell me more.'

Now the tears spill from her eyes.

'Lord, they came when you were away at war. Gwydion and Gilfaethwy, the sons of your sister. They took me by force. I did not go quietly. There was nobody in this court who did not hear my cries. They dragged me to your bedchamber. And there, on your bed, I was mercilessly shamed.'

There is a long silence.

Math strokes the back of her hand.

It is as though the hall itself is holding its breath.

When he speaks his voice is a whisper.

'I will do what must be done. First of all you will have full recompense for your suffering. I will make you my wife and put all my possessions and my kingdom under our shared authority.'

The silence deepens.

He is peering into the hollowness of broken trust.

His words are mouthed, barely audible.

'And then I shall seek recompense for myself.'

Math sent out messengers.

They rode to all corners of the kingdom.

Every hall and household was told that there was a ban on Gwydion and Gilfaethwy. Neither of them was to be given food, drink or shelter.

Any man found guilty of aiding or abetting them would be hanged. Any man who brought them alive to Caer Dathyl was promised a reward in yellow gold.

The two brothers lived as outlaws on the wooded slopes.

Then the winter came.

The mountains and valleys were white with snow.

The rivers and lakes were frozen hard. There was thin hunting.

The brothers could not light fires for fear of discovery. The nights were bitterly cold. No trickery of Gwydion's could conjure meat from thin air or bread from stones.

They had a stark choice.

Either they starved among the icy crags of Arfon or they

returned to Math and faced the full force of his fury.

The sons of Danu came to Caer Dathyl.

They were thin and pinched with hunger.

Their cloaks were threadbare, their boots broken.

With bowed heads they approached the throne of Math.

They dropped to their knees.

'Lord, good day to you.'

His eyes brimmed with contempt.

'I suppose you are come to make amends?'

'Lord, we are at your will.'

Math leapt to his feet.

Gwynedd was at war with itself. Suddenly his strength was restored.

'Will!'

His bellow boomed among the rafters of the hall.

'What is my will to you? Was it my will that my warriors should go to battle and be slain? Was it my will that Pryderi should be robbed, humiliated and killed? Was it my will that the army of the South should be destroyed?'

The brothers shook their heads.

'And what was the cause of this bloodshed?'

He paused.

'It was your will, your hot will. Forced upon my lap-maiden in my absence – and upon my own bed.'

The brothers said nothing.

'You cannot compensate me for my shame.'

Math nodded to his guards. They seized Gwydion and Gilfaethwy by the upper arms.

'But since you have submitted yourselves, I shall begin your punishment.'

He reached beneath his cloak and drew out a wand.

He raised it above his shoulder.

'No!'

Gilfaethwy fought to free himself.

The guards locked his arms behind his back and forced his forehead to the floor.

Math struck the back of his head.

In that moment his neck lengthened. His hands and feet became hooves. His arms became long slender legs. His clothes fell away from him. His skin was turned to dappled hide.

He was become a hind.

Gwydion shouted with horror. He broke the grip of the guards and ran towards the door. They followed him, felled him and dragged him back.

Math struck him with the wand.

A crown of forked antlers burst from his head. His face lengthened and narrowed. His arms were arms no longer. He dropped onto cloven hands and feet. He was become a stag.

Math looked at his nephews.

'Since you two have become so closely twined, you will run together for a full year as stag and hind. You will couple in the manner of wild animals. When they give birth so will you. When twelve months are over you will return to my hall. Watch out for traps and hunters – we would prefer not to eat you.'

Every dog in the hall was barking and straining at its leash.

The two deer were driven out of the hall.

They bounded away from Caer Dathyl and disappeared into the shadows of the woods, leaving a trail of hoof-marks in the white snow.

For a full year they lived with the wild herds.

When the year was over they returned.

One of the guards came to Math.

'Lord, there is a great clamour at the gates. A stag and hind with a fawn are standing outside. They will not be driven away.'

'Tie up all the hounds. Open the gates and doors so that they can come into my hall.'

The three animals came and stood before Math's throne.

He got to his feet and looked closely at the fawn.

It was pressed against its mother's flank. He reached forward and it shied away from his hand. It was a pretty, speckled, sturdy creature. He drew his wand from beneath his cloak and struck it between the ears.

In the place of the fawn stood a little boy.

'He will be called Hyddwn, "pale stag".'

Math lifted him and sat him gently on the edge of his throne.

He turned his attention to his animal nephews.

'And as for you – the one who was male this year shall be female next, and the one who was female shall be male.'

He struck the stag. It shrank. The dappled hide became coarse with red-brown bristles. The nose was a snout. The belly sagged. The tail curled.

Gwydion was become a wild sow.

Math struck the hind. Sharp yellow tusks burst from its mouth. Its back was ridged with thick hair.

Gilfaethwy was become a wild boar.

'Go! Whatever is the nature of wild pigs is your nature now! The boar will mount the sow and when a year is passed you will return.'

He seized a spear and drove the creatures out of Caer Dathyl.

They rooted among the thickets of Gwynedd. Their only companions were the wild herds.

A year later they returned.

'Lord, a wild boar and sow with a little piglet in tow are standing at the gates of Caer Dathyl.'

'Bring them in.'

The animals entered.

Math picked up a piece of sweet honey-cake. He offered it to the little pink piglet. It trotted forwards and pressed its wet snout into the palm of his hand. It gobbled.

Math struck it with his wand.

A boy stood in its place, he was big for his age and his mouth was full of cake.

'I will call him Hychdwn, "pale boar".'

He looked at his nephews.

'And as for you –'

He struck the boar.

Where there had been hooves there were clawed paws. Where there had been bristles there was a shaggy grey pelt.

The sagging belly tightened. The drooping ears quickened.

The tusks shrank and the mouth filled with fangs.

Gilfaethwy was become a wolf-bitch.

He struck the sow. Gwydion was become a wolf.

'You will run with the pack as wolf and bitch. You will mate and give birth as wolves. In a year you will return.'

He turned to his men.

'Let loose the wolf hounds!'

His men unfastened the leashes.

Already the wolves were gone.

For a full year they ran as dog and bitch with the wolves of Gwynedd.

Then one morning a woman was drawing water from the well when she saw a wonder. She ran to her lord.

'There is a wolf at the gate to Caer Dathyl. A shaggy brute he is, as big as a pony, with a mouthful of teeth as sharp as knives. And with him a bitch with swollen paps. And a cub as pretty as a puppy. They're sitting on the step, Lord, and whining like tame dogs at table.'

'Open the gates and let them in.'

The wolves bounded into Math's hall and stood before his throne.

He pulled a leather gauntlet onto his hand and reached towards the cub. It growled in mock play and bit him.

In his other hand he was holding the wand. He struck.

There stood a strong, stocky boy.

'His name will be Bleiddwn, "pale wolf".'

He looked at the wolf and bitch.

'Three sons of wicked Gilfaethwy,
     Two champions has he mothered, one fathered:
     Bleiddwn, Hyddwn and Hychdwn Hir.'

He struck the two wolves with his wand.

The brothers stood before him. They were stark naked and filthy. Their skin was scratched and scarred.

The hair of their heads was alive with fleas and lice.

'Nephews, you did me a great wrong. Now you have received full punishment. To have been mounted by your brother, to have conceived and given birth, is a shame that matches the shame you have inflicted. It is over now.'

He called his servants.

'Have these men bathed. Wash and comb their heads. Dress them in robes fitting to their rank and station.'

When they had been thoroughly cleaned and clothed in the finest linen, wool and leather, they returned to Math's hall.

He looked at them and smiled.

'Now, friendship is restored between us.'

The old man paused.

"We will rest now."

Two hours later he was ready to resume.

"If I could sing, I would sing of Gwydion, son of Danu.

I would sing of him as I have seen him in carvings of stone.

He is sitting cross-legged in the shape of a man.

His head is crowned with a rack of forked antlers.

He is surrounded by the animals he has known and been, the animals he has fathered and mothered – wolf, boar and deer.

One day Math summoned Gwydion.

'Now that there is friendship between us; now that the kingdom of Gwynedd is at ease with itself, I feel my old affliction returning.

I am in need of a virgin. Tell me, of all the handmaidens in my hall, who should I choose to cradle my feet in her lap?'

Gwydion cast his eyes to left and right.

His gaze fastened on his sister.

His mouth curved into a sudden smile that had no echo in his eyes.

'Lord, you should choose Arianrhod, daughter of Danu, your niece.'

She gave him a piercing glance. Her eyes brimmed with a fierce hatred.

'Bring her to me.'

She had no choice but to step up to Math's throne.

'Maiden, tell me the truth, are you a virgin?'

'To the best of my knowledge, I am.'

Math reached beneath his cloak and drew out his wand.

'To the best of your knowledge! Either you are or you are not – and I will find out the truth.'

He reached down and held his wand low against the ground.

'Step over this. If you are a virgin I will know it.'

Arianrhod came forwards.

Look.

She is scooping up her skirts and lifting her left foot.

Her face is fixed into a mask. Her smile is a shield against humiliation.

She is straddling the wand.

Something falls.

Her left foot meets the ground. She lifts her right.

Something has been left behind.

A loud cry tears the air.

She has dropped a boy, a naked yellow-haired boy.

Arianrhod does not look back. Her steps become strides.

She is running towards the doors of the hall.

All eyes are on the newborn boy as he rolls over onto his belly and scrambles to his feet.

All eyes are on the boy – except for Gwydion's eyes.

He is watching his sister.

She crosses the threshold and leaves the hall.

Something else is falling from beneath her skirts.

A little thing, a kernel of flesh has been left behind.

See Gwydion cross the hall. He crouches down and lifts it.

He wraps it in a shred of silk and tucks it tight beneath his cloak.

Then he turns and watches with the rest.

The little yellow-haired boy is wailing, staring up at the circle of faces that surround him.

Math reaches down and lifts him.

'The name I give him is Dylan.'

The baby is still slimy with the waters of his mother's womb.

He kicks and struggles. Math loses his hold.

The boy drops to the ground.

See how he runs.

He runs out of the hall. They are following him.

He runs until he comes to the sea-shore.

He runs into the waves.

They stand on the sea-strand and watch him.

See how he takes on the sea's nature. See how he swims, as sleek and supple as any fish of the water.

No wave breaks over him.

Math says:

'We will call him Dylan Eil Ton, "Dylan son of Wave".'"

Cian Brydydd Mawr lifted a cup of water to his lips and sipped.

"And what, you'll be wondering, became of the little kernel of red flesh?"

"Well, Gwydion hid it.

He put the little thing into a wooden chest that he kept at the foot of his bed. He wrapped it in coverlets of silk and woven wool. He closed the lid and left it.

Weeks and months passed.

One night he was woken from his sleep by a muffled cry. It was coming from the chest.

He climbed out of bed and lifted the lid.

Inside there was a baby boy. He was flailing with his arms and kicking with his legs, shaking the coverlets aside.

Gwydion reached down and cradled the child in his arms.

From the moment he set eyes on the boy he loved him.

The next morning he found a woman who was suckling her baby at her breast. She had milk to spare.

Gwydion hired her as a wet-nurse. The boy began to thrive.

At the end of a year he was of such a size that people would have been surprised at his sturdiness had he been a two year old.

At the end of two years he thanked his nurse and left her.

He came to Caer Dathyl.

He found his way to Gwydion and stood before him.

'I am your son.'

From that day onwards Gwydion raised the boy himself.

For two years he fathered him.

He showed him the ways of the wild animals, the courtesies of the court, the sleights of spell-craft.

By the time he was four he could have been mistaken for an eight year old.

One morning Gwydion said to the boy:

'Come with me.'

They walked together until they came to the sea-shore.

The tide was low.

They could see Caer Arianrhod, the hall of Gwydion's sister. It stood on a rocky island.

When the sea was high it could only be reached by boat.

But now that the water was low the two of them were able to splash towards it through the rock pools and over the banks of smooth ridged sand.

Arianrhod saw the figures, man and boy, approaching her hall.

She came out to welcome them.

Then she recognised Gwydion. Her eyes narrowed.

Gwydion raised an arm.

'Good day to you!'

She knew that any word of his rode on a tide of intrigue and dark appetite.

'What do you want? And, tell me, who is the boy?'

'This boy is your son.'

She shuddered.

'My son ran into the water. I see him sometimes, sporting in the sea like a porpoise, Dylan Eil Ton.'

Gwydion shook his head.

'This is the other one.'

He came forwards and touched her cheek with his fingertips.

He mouthed words for fear of Math's hearing.

She read his lips and paled.

'For pity's sake, brother, what possessed you to keep him – unless it was to plunge me into a deeper disgrace and an unfathomable shame?'

Gwydion reached for the boy's hand, he raised his voice.

'If you are ashamed to be the mother of such a fine lad. If you are ashamed that I have raised him – then your shame is a thing of small substance.'

'What is the boy's name?'

'That is why we have come. He has no name.'

'You are daring to ask me to name him?'

Gwydion looked into her eyes.

'I am.'"

Cian Brydydd Mawr took another sip of water.

He looked at Tomos.

"Boys with spears will sometimes hunt wild cats for their skins."

"That is a thing I have never done."

"When the creatures are cornered they will turn and spit and strike with their claws. Arianrhod's whispered words tore with the same sharp fury.

'Never! I curse him now. My shame shall never have a name unless he be named by me – and I shall never name him.'

Gwydion turned away from her.

'You are a wicked woman. And I swear, whether you want it or not, the boy shall have a name.'

He strode across the shallows with the boy running to keep up with him. That night they returned to Caer Dathyl.

The next morning they returned to the sea-shore.

This time the tide was high.

Caer Arianrhod was circled by the sea.

Gulls were perched on the ridges of its thatch.

Gwydion gathered seaweed. He made a heap of dulse and wrack at the water's edge. He took a piece of driftwood and plunged it upright into the middle.

He lifted his wand of rowan and struck it.

In its place a little boat appeared. It had an upright mast, a folded sail and wooden oars lying on its bilge boards.

He gathered seaweeds of different colours – reds, yellows, browns and greens. He struck them with his wand.

They became lengths of coloured leather.

Gwydion smiled at the boy.

'Today we will be shoe-makers, you and I.'

They pulled the boat down to the water and climbed aboard.

Gwydion unfurled the sail. The wind carried them over the waves towards Caer Arianrhod.

As they drew close he changed their appearance. They became an old cobbler and his apprentice. From his pocket Gwydion took waxed threads and sharp needles. He dropped anchor.

They started stitching, leaning over the leather, intent on their work.

Arianrhod saw them. She called to her servants.

'Who are the people in that boat?'

They went down to the shore of the island. They peered across the water at the strangers.

'They are shoe-makers.'

'Row out to them. Find out what kind of leather they are using, and what is the quality of their craftsmanship.'

A boat went out.

The servants saw that the old cobbler had made a pair of delicate slippers. He was stippling green leather with gold.

They returned.

'Madam, the older man is a master, the boy is his apprentice. Their leather is the finest Cordovan. Their workmanship is beyond compare.'

Immediately Arianrhod was possessed by a longing to own a pair of their slippers.

'Good.' She shook off her shoes. 'Measure my feet. Go out and tell them they are to make me slippers of red leather.'

They knelt before her and measured from toe to heel.

They rowed out again.

The shoe-makers set to work. They cut and stitched the slippers. The servants returned.

Arianrhod took them in her hands. She smiled. They were soft and shapely. She leaned down to pull them onto her feet.

They were too big.

'I will pay them for their handiwork. But tell the shoe-makers that my feet are smaller than these. They must fashion a second pair.'

The shoe-makers made new slippers.

When Arianrhod tried them they were too small.

She threw them onto the floor.

'These do not fit either.'

The servants returned to the old cobbler.

When he heard the woman's complaint the old man shook his head.

'It is no good,' he said, 'I will make her no more slippers until I have measured her feet with my own hands.'

Arianrhod was told.

'Very well, I will go out to him.'

She was rowed across the water. She climbed into the little boat.

The old man was chalking a design on the back of a length of leather. The boy was stitching. The cobbler looked up.

'Good day, Lady.'

'Good day to you, I am surprised that you were not able to shape and proportion slippers according to my measurement.'

He pulled the shoe from her foot and cradled her heel in his hand.

'I could not,' the old man smiled at her, 'but now that I have your true measure, I will shape something that will fit you perfectly.'

Look.

Gwydion is making a little gesture with his hand.

It conjures a wren out of the air.

Arianrhod doesn't see the gesture. But she sees the wren.

She watches it fluttering down from mast to stern, its pert tail cocked. She sees its tiny black eyes, its quick restless flurries of flight.

She hears its sharp, stabbing song.

The boy lifts the knife that he's using to cut the leather.

With one deft flick of the wrist he throws it. The blade spins.

It strikes the wren.

It cuts its left leg clean through between tendon and bone.

The little claw falls down onto the bilge boards and the bird flutters up into the air. It cries out in a sudden upsurge of pain and alarm.

Arianrhod looks at the boy and smiles.

She reaches down and picks up the wren's claw between her finger and thumb.

'It is with a skilful hand (llaw gyffes) that the fair-haired one (lleu) has struck the bird!'

The old shoe-maker turns to her and smiles.

'Indeed. And now you have given the boy a name. From this day onwards he will be Lleu Llaw Gyffes, "the fair-haired one with the skilful hand".' [42]

See how boat, sail and leather melt into seaweed.

They roll and sink beneath the waves.

The tide is ebbing away.

They are standing waist deep in water. The boy is up to his chin.

Arianrhod looks across at the shoe-maker and his apprentice.

'You will be punished for making a high-born lady suffer in this way.'

The old cobbler laughs.

'You have not suffered – yet.'

He throws a handful of water into her face.

She rubbed her eyes.

When she opened them she saw Gwydion standing before her.

Beside him was her son. She shook with anger.

'If one curse is broken, then I lay another upon him. This boy, my shame, will never bear arms unless I arm him with my own hands – and that I shall never do.'

Gwydion and Lleu turned away from her.

'Whether you like it or not, your son will be armed.'

They waded through the retreating tide.

They made their way up the slope of the sea to the shore.

She returned alone to Caer Arianrhod.

Dripping and shivering she called on her handmaidens to peel away her sodden clothes and rub her skin dry.

Years passed.

Lleu Llaw Gyffes grew from a boy into a fine youth.

He was given his own hall at Dinas Dinlleu.

Gwydion trained him in all the accomplishments.

He became a skilled horseman and a master in the hunt.

He became adept at law and eloquent in speech.

In form and physique he outshone all others.

But he was not happy.

He longed to bear weapons.

Arianrhod's curse prevented him from carrying sword or shield. Skirmishes, cattle raids and tournaments were denied him.

He could not achieve his proper manhood.

Gwydion looked at him. He stroked his chin.

'Tomorrow,' he said, 'we will go on a journey, you and I.'

The old man looked at his listeners.

"Though what journey that was must wait until we next meet."

"Dinas Dinlleu," said Dafydd, "I have stood there myself when the tide was low and seen the rocks of Caer Arianrhod."

Olwen smiled.

"And the Dylan Stone, I remember Iwan lifting the boys up onto it when they were small – though its name was all we knew of it." [43]

The old man leaned back in his chair.

"We can walk these places, touch them with our hands, speak their names with our tongues. This Matter is their secret life, it is how they dream."

Monday May 4th

Cian Brydydd Mawr had been too ill to get out of bed. Tomos had made a mash of bread and milk and fed it to him with a horn spoon. Sometimes he had broken an egg into the mixture. For several days the old man would only drink water.

This morning he had sat up for the first time in ten days.

His voice was a hoarse whisper.

"Fetch me Brother Deiniol."

After Sext the monk came to the old man's cell. He bowed his head.

"God prosper you. Are you recovered?"

"Age is gnawing at my bones."

"Is there anything I can do? I could bring the wine and host to your bed-side."

Cian Brydydd Mawr shuddered.

"I am not ready for your last rites yet."

Tomos drew a blanket over his shoulders.

"Tell me, what news of our Lord Llywelyn?"

Brother Deiniol knelt beside the bed. He lowered his voice.

"The war hosts are on the move. No sooner was Llywelyn home from Cambridge than the orders went out. King John is distracted by troubles in Scotland and France. Our Lord, it seems, is seizing the moment. My guess is that all of John's castles – Bala, Treffynnon, Mathrafal, Rhuddlan, Deganwy and the rest – will soon be under siege. And word is coming from our brothers in the south that the other princes are following suit. The Pope has given his blessing and is calling it a 'Holy War'."

The old man chuckled.

"God be praised. Reynard even has Innocent on his side."

"And Philip of France."

Cian Brydydd Mawr reached across and seized the monk's arm.

"But you must pray, Brother, for the boys that are held hostage. Pray for them with all your heart. When John hears of this, it will only be a divine intervention that will save them. He has a dark and a shallow heart."

"We are praying."

"Good."

Brother Deiniol stood.

"There is something else. It concerns Brother Iago. He is growing impatient. Your ill health leaves him stranded here with no purpose. He chafes to return to his scriptorium."

"Tell him to stay and sharpen his quills. Tomorrow I will continue with my Matter."

He closed his eyes.

"It cannot wait any longer."

Dafydd found Brother Deiniol.

"Brother, I would like to speak with you."

Brother Deiniol searched Dafydd's face with his eyes.

"Ah, Dafydd, I had wondered when you would come. Is it a confession you are seeking?"

"No. I do not wish to speak about sin."

"Where shall we sit?"

"Under the tree, over there."

They settled down under the ash tree. Its black buds were bursting into green flower and leaf.

"What is it then?"

Dafydd met his gaze.

"I am minded to renounce my vows."

Brother Deiniol shook his head.

"You would become an apostate? That would be a grave decision."

"I am not complete here. I thought I was, but I was wrong."

The monk was careful with his knowledge. He weighed his words with caution.

"Is it a woman?"

Dafydd paused.

"It is a woman, but it is more than a woman."

"More?"

"I cannot live in denial any longer."

"Denial of what?"

"Of who I am ... and of the world I come from."

"It is a fallen world, Dafydd."

Dafydd broke a twig from an over-hanging branch.

"Our grandfathers, before the Saints came, had no notion of sin."

"And they are all in Hell."

"Are they?"

"Of course they are. And this woman – she may be flesh and blood – but it is an idea of her that consumes you, a thing without substance, a phantasm conjured by the Devil. Do not let it rule you. Come to confession. Defeat it. I will help you. I have wrestled with similar demons."

Dafydd smiled.

"She is no phantasm, Brother. I have known her for the best part of my life."

He looked across at the church.

"I have searched my heart. I have prayed and watched in the night. I have partaken of the Mass. I cannot find the voice that convinces me it is a sin to love a woman ..."

Brother Deiniol crossed himself. Dafydd did the same.

"... and neither have I heard anything in the teachings of Christ Jesu."

Dafydd paused.

"And then there is Cian Brydydd Mawr ..."

Brother Deiniol snorted with irritation.

"I feared he might have played a part in this."

"... in his Matter he speaks all the time of men and women ..."

"No doubt he does."

"... there is love and honour, there is lust and rape and betrayal. There is no shortage of what you and I would brand as sin. The Matter is a mirror. It does not pass judgement. But, over and over, it shows that what happens between man and woman is what drives the world. It is the axis on which everything turns. I do not want to live apart any longer."

"And the Holy Church?"

"Is there some precept or law that would prevent a married man who honours his wife from kneeling for the Mass?"

Dafydd looked down. He was silent for a while.

"Anyway, I do not know if she would accept me."

Brother Deiniol closed his eyes. He struggled to distance himself from all that he knew, all that he felt.

"It would be the asking that would sever you, Dafydd. There could be no return after that."

He stood up.

"Weigh these questions in your heart. I will pray for you."

Tuesday May 5th

Cian Brydydd Mawr was in bed when his listeners arrived. He was propped up with rolled sheepskins and had a blanket drawn across his shoulders.

"Sit down, sit down."

They took their places.

His voice was thin, but slowly, as the story possessed him, it increased in strength.

"You will remember how Lleu Llaw Gyffes had been given his name, but was cursed so that he could not bear arms until his mother armed him."

"We remember."

"Gwydion and Lleu set off on horseback.

Dinas Dinlleu, as you know, is a stone's throw from the seashore.

The tide was low. The horses picked their way over the barnacled stones, over the banks of seaweed and sand.

They came to Caer Arianrhod.

Gwydion changed their appearance so that they seemed to be travelling bards. They were dressed in robes. Lleu carried a harp. Both of them had the look of young men. Gwydion was the Pencerdd.

They came to the gate of Arianrhod's hall. Gwydion said:

'Porter, go inside and tell your mistress that bards are waiting at the door. We have travelled from Morgannwg and we would exchange entertainment for food and lodging.'

Arianrhod heard the news. She clapped her hands with delight.

'What are you waiting for? Invite them in!'

The two bards were brought inside. Their horses were stabled. With great joy she led them into her hall and sat them at the high table.

When they had been given their fill of meat and drink, she said:

'Now, perhaps you will entertain us with a story or a song.'

Cian Brydydd Mawr sipped from his cup.

"I do not know which story Gwydion told that day. I will tell you this one because it is ancient and I would not want it forgotten.

The Pencerdd said:

'Lady, in your good opinion, what are the three things that make for a happy and a contented realm?' [44]

'The answer is simple and everyone knows it,' said Arianrhod, 'the sovereign wisdom of its lord, the ferocity of its warriors, and the fecundity of its land.'

'Lady, listen. There was once a time when all three were under threat.'

The second bard lifted the harp onto his knee and struck the strings.

'There were once two brothers.

Their names were Llud and Llefelys.

Llud was High King of the Island of the Mighty.

It was Llud who founded and built the city of London.

Llefelys was the younger brother. He was a wise and prudent man, versed in magic and diplomacy.

Llud loved him above all others.

One day news came from across the water that the King of France had sickened and died. He had left only one heir, a daughter of surpassing loveliness.

The thought came to Llefelys that if he could win her hand, not only would he become the King of France, but also there would be peace and prosperity and ease of passage between the two kingdoms.

Llud agreed and sent Llefelys across the water with a fleet of ships bearing horses, treasures, noblemen and warriors. A counsel was held and the noblemen and lords of France agreed to the marriage.

There was a feast and Llefelys slept with the princess.

They became king and queen.

The fleet returned.

Many, many years passed.

Then the Island of the Mighty was visited by three terrible afflictions.

The first was this: a race of beings called the Coraniaids appeared in the realm. They were evil and had only their own interests at heart. Like our Lord Math they had the power to hear any utterance that was made on the face of the land, but they did not use their knowledge for the common good. They used it for their own wicked purposes.

Any command that Llud gave, any strategy he planned, any law he pronounced, any counsel he held, they would hear and subvert. All sovereign power was undermined.

The king's word counted for nothing.

The second affliction took the form of a shout.

Every Beltane-eve it echoed across the kingdom.

It was of such deafening loudness, of such ear-splitting pitch that any man who heard it lost his courage.

Warriors paled and grew fearful in battle.

Husbands became impotent.

Farmers lost the strength of their arms.

Women too suffered. They miscarried and became barren.

The boldness in the blood of the realm was gone.

The third affliction was this: however much food was stored away for safekeeping, only as much as could be eaten in one night would survive. The rest would be stolen. A year's provision of salt-meat, grain and dried fruit would vanish after the first feast had been consumed. The fat of the land was wasted and the winter months became a time of bitter hunger.

The three afflictions ravished the realm.

King Llud was in despair.

Then he remembered his brother.

Maybe Llefelys, in his wisdom, would be able to relieve the suffering of the people of Britain.

A fleet of ships set sail for France. Llud stood in the prow of the leading ship. He held his shield upside down.

When Llefelys saw the ships approaching at full sail he thought they were threatening war.

He led his own fleet out to meet them.

Then he saw his brother. He saw the shield.

Two ships sailed forward leaving the rest behind.

The two brothers met. They threw their arms around each other's necks. When they had shared food and wine Llud told Llefelys about the three afflictions.

"Ah," said Llefelys, "then we must be careful."

He went down into the hold of the ship and returned with a long, hollow, bronze horn.

"If we speak through this they will not hear us."

Llud lifted one end to his ear. Llefelys spoke into the other.

Every word Llud heard was hateful and hostile.

He threw down the horn and drew his sword.

"I thought we were brothers, but now I see we are enemies."

Llefelys raised his hand.

"Wait, something contrary is mangling the sense of my speech."

He poured wine into the horn. A little twisted imp fell from the other end onto the deck of the ship. They pierced it with knives and flung it into the water.

"Now let's try again."

Llefelys spoke into the horn. This time the words were clear.

"Dear brother, listen carefully. For the first affliction I will give you a box of crawling insects. They are bitter poison to the Coraniaids.

You must break them up with a pestle and mortar and tip them into a vat of water. Invite your people and the Coraniaids to an assembly. When they are all gathered together in one place, take the charged water and sprinkle them from the vat. The Coraniaids will be utterly destroyed. Your people will be unharmed."

Llefelys passed a wooden box to Llud. Its lid was tightly sealed with wax.

"For the second affliction you must measure the length and breadth of your kingdom. When you find the dead centre you must dig a hole. Wait until Beltane-eve and watch. Something will fly up into the air. Put a cauldron filled with the sweetest, strongest mead in the bottom of the hole. Cover the cauldron with a length of silk. Then you must wait. Whatever is trapped in the cauldron must be put into a stone chest and buried deep in the ground."

"I understand."

"The third affliction can only be mended by wakefulness. When the harvest has been brought in, you must have a feast. At a certain moment sweet music will flood the air. Everyone will fall into a deep slumber. You must not succumb. Have a tub of icy water at hand. Whenever you feel sleep approaching you must jump into the tub. If you can stay awake you will see who or what is stealing your stores and winter supplies."

"Brother, I thank you with all my heart."

Llud and Llefelys embraced. They parted.

Llud returned to Caer Llundein.

He told his men to open the wooden box. It was teeming with tiny black insects. They tipped them into pestles and ground them with mortars into a sticky black paste. The paste was stirred into a vat of water.

Llud called an assembly. He invited his people and the Coraniaids. When the charged water was thrown onto them, the Coraniaids crumpled and crumbled into dust before his eyes.

They never troubled Llud again.

He ordered his men to measure the length and breadth of his realm. The dead centre was at Oxford.

They dug a hole.

On Beltane-eve he waited and watched. Out of the hole burst two dragons, a red and a white. They rose up into the air and began to fight, biting and tearing at one another's flesh with their teeth. The red dragon threw back its head and shouted. Llud plunged his fingers into his ears.

Then he lifted the cauldron and lowered it into the hole. He filled it with mead and covered it with a length of silk brocade.

All night they fought ferociously in the sky overhead. They changed shape. They became the creatures of the constellations – bulls, serpents, bears, wolves, horses, eagles.

At first light they sank down exhausted from the heavens.

As they plummeted to earth they took the shape of two piglets. They plunged into the hole. They sank into the cauldron. They dragged the silk down with them.

They drank the mead and fell into a deep sleep.

Llud called his men.

Gently they took the four corners of the silken cloth and lifted the two sleeping piglets out of the cauldron.

A stone chest had been made ready. They were put inside. The lid was fastened and held down with brackets of iron.

The chest was carried to the mountain that is known as Dinas Emrys. At that time it was called Dinas Ffaerraon Dandde.[45]

A deep shaft was cut into the rock and the stone chest was lowered into the depths.

It was covered with boulders.

Llud was never troubled by the scream again.

He waited until harvest. When the food had been gathered and stored away for winter he ordered his servants to prepare a feast.

Beside his throne he told them to set a tub of cold water.

Lumps of blue-white ice from the high mountains were floating in it.

Course followed course. When the tables had been cleared a sweet soft music came. It was the sound of a tender lullaby. It had the power to lull and beguile the most hardened warrior into the sweet sleep of childhood. Cooks slumbered beside their fires, scullions by their sinks, guards at their gates, noblemen at their tables. Women dropped their distaffs and dogs lowered their noses to their paws.

Llud's head began to nod. With eyes half sealed he clambered into the tub. He was awake.

He climbed out shivering and stood before the fire.

He was possessed by an overwhelming urge to curl up in the warm ashes. He plunged back into the icy water.

He was awake again. And now he could hear footsteps.

He ran outside and butted his head against a knee.

He looked up.

A man of enormous stature was striding towards his grain store. He was carrying a leather bag. He opened the neck of the bag and filled it with sack after sack of barley-meal, oats and wheat. From the meat store he took carcasses, smoked and un-cured. From the dairy he took a winter's worth of cheeses.

The leather bag remained half-full.

Llud drew his sword.

"Stop! However much you have taken, you will take no more, unless your prowess proves you to be stronger than me."

He swung his sword and cut through the ligaments in the backs of the giant's knees.

The giant dropped his sack and drew his knife.

They fought until the sparks flew from their blades.

Llud dodged and hacked until the giant toppled to the ground. He pressed the point of his sword into the giant's throat. The giant gurgled. Blood trickled from the corners of his mouth.

"Show me mercy."

"Why should I show you mercy when you have inflicted such loss and injury on my kingdom."

"I give you my solemn word, everything I have ever taken will be restored. From this day onwards I will be your vassal and humble servant."

Llud accepted. He was never troubled by the giant again.

And so it was, my lady, that the Island of the Mighty was freed from its three afflictions. And Llud, with help and advice from his brother Llefelys, ruled over a happy and contented realm for the rest of his days.'"

Cian Brydydd Mawr looked at his listeners.

"A sovereign lord, a fierce war host and a fecund land – what was true in the ancient times is true today. King John would do well to remember it."

Olwen smiled.

"And a fecund queen. They say Siwan has given birth."

The old man nodded.

"Our grandfathers would have made no distinction between the two."

"The only sounds were the sweet strains of the harp and the distant murmurings of the sea. Arianrhod shook away the enchantment of the evening's entertainment. She got to her feet.

'The story is a good one and this bard is gifted with a golden tongue. But now it is late and the time has come to seek slumber.'

The two visitors were shown to a bedchamber.

The silence of deep sleep settled on Caer Arianrhod.

But Gwydion did not sleep.

Long before dawn he slipped between the dozing guards at the gates of the hall. He made his way to the sea's edge.

The tide was high.

From beneath his robes he drew his wand of rowan. He made a spell that stretched his power to its limit. He conjured a deep and complicated magic. He crept back to bed.

At first light there was a hammering at the door of their bedchamber.

They could hear Arianrhod's voice.

'Open up! Open up!'

Lleu got out of bed. He pulled back the bolt and opened the door. She strode into the room.

'Men, listen, we are in a very bad situation.'

The Pencerdd sat up.

'We heard the sound of shouting and battle horns. What is going on?'

Arianrhod's face was pale.

'We cannot see the colour of the sea for ships. A huge fleet is bearing down upon us. Each ship is crammed with warriors. Soon they will be wading ashore and reddening their swords with our blood. What shall we do?'

The Pencerdd jumped out of bed.

'Lady, we have no choice. We must shut ourselves inside your hall and defend it as best we can.'

'Thank you, thank you,' she said, 'there is no shortage of weapons. Whatever you need will be at your disposal.'

She ran out of the room.

Soon she was back. With her were two maidservants. They were carrying weapons and armour for two men.

The Pencerdd had been standing at the window. He turned.

'Lady, there is no time to waste. They are dropping anchor. Quick! You arm my friend. The maids can arm me. I hear the splashing of men jumping overboard.'

'Gladly.'

Arianrhod fastened a helmet onto Lleu's head. She buckled a battle vest over his body. She pressed a shield onto his arm and thrust a sword into his hand.

The bard said:

'Is he armed yet?'

'He is.'

'Then you can take his armour off again. He will have no need of it.'

'What are you talking about? We are under siege.'

'There is nothing.'

She ran to the window. A cold grey sea was sucking the shingle at the water's edge. The ships had vanished.

'I do not understand. What sort of host was that?'

'It was assembled,' said the Pencerdd, 'to break a curse.'

Gwydion and Lleu returned to their proper shapes.

She recognised them instantly.

'Now,' said Gwydion, 'you have armed your son with your own hands.'

She looked at her brother and spat.

'Is there no fibre of your body that is not steeped in malice and deception?'

Then she turned to her son.

'And as for you – I curse you again. You will never have a wife. Of all the races of mankind, no-one has borne or ever will bear the woman who will be your bride.'

Gwydion rested his hand gently on Lleu's shoulder.

'To inflict such suffering upon your own child is a wicked and a shameful thing. But, I give you my word, the boy will have a wife.'

They left the hall, took their horses and rode through the shallows to Dinas Dinlleu.

Weeks, months and years passed.

Lleu Llaw Gyffes took arms and rode out with the warriors of Gwynedd. He grew to manhood. He mastered the arts of war.

In stature and beauty there was nobody to match him.

But he was not happy.

He longed for a wife.

He longed to lie between the thighs of a woman.

He longed for her to swell with his seed.

He longed for love as a counter-spell to his mother's curses.

Gwydion watched Lleu.

The magic that was needed was beyond his power.

He went to Math. He was careful with the truth.

'Lord, may I speak to you about the boy I fostered, my sister's son?'

His uncle bowed his head.

'You have shown him great kindness.'

'But his mother has not. She has cursed him, and though I have some skill in enchantment, this is beyond my knowledge.'

'What is the curse?'

'That Lleu will never have a wife. That of all the races of mankind, not one has borne or ever will bear the woman who will be his bride.'

Math sucked the air between clenched teeth.

'It is a harsh curse.'

He closed his eyes and pondered in silence.

He opened his eyes and fixed them on Gwydion.

'We will make him a wife.'

He smiled.

'We will make him a wife who is not of the race of mankind.'

'What must we do?'

'Fetch me flowers. Gather the yellow flowers of the broom, the green flowers of oak and the white of meadowsweet.'

Gwydion made his way out of Caer Dathyl.

He returned with his arms full of flowers. He set them down at Math's feet.

'Now fetch me the yellow flowers of the primrose and the white flowers of apple and bean.'

Again he fetched them.

'Now gather the yellow flowers of iris and chestnut and the white of hawthorn.'

They were set on the floor.

'Now we have nine.'

Math arranged the flowers into the shape of a woman.

He knelt at her head.

'You must stand at her feet.'

They raised their wands.

Math closed his eyes. He whispered words. Sweat broke from his brow. His body trembled. He gripped his wand with both hands.

He broke it.

The flowers had become a woman.

Her skin was white as apple blossom, her hair as yellow as broom. She blinked. She sat up. She smiled.

She was the fairest woman they had ever seen.

Gwydion reached forwards and took her hand.

He lifted her to her feet.

'She is of the flowers,' said Math, 'we will call her Blodeuedd.'[46]

The bell rang and the old poet closed his eyes. Tomos settled him down on the bed and covered him with blankets.

Olwen, Dafydd and Brother Iago tip-toed out of the cell.

"He has made a woman out of words," whispered Olwen, "it has exhausted him."

Dafydd went to the church for None. He beckoned to Brother Pedr.

"Tell me the psalm."

"Thou shalt eat the labour of thine hands: happy shalt thou be, and it shall be well with thee. Thy wife shall be as a fruitful vine by the sides of thine house; thy children like olive plants around thy table. Behold, thus shall the man be blessed that feareth the Lord."

Cian Brydydd Mawr was sitting on his chair when they returned.

"The Matter is breathing its life back into me."

He turned to Brother Iago.

"Iago ap Rhys, I would like to see your pages."

"I will bring them to you."

"Good."

He sipped.

"Now we return to the woman made by Math."

"If I could sing, I would sing of the woman of flowers.

I would sing of Blodeuedd.

Her scent is the sweetness of apple and bean, the musk of hawthorn and chestnut.

Her flesh is firm as oak, soft as meadowsweet and wanton as the pale primrose.

Her tangled curls are the yellow allure of iris and broom.

I would sing of Blodeuedd whose heart is ruled by the stirrings of sap and sunshine."

"She is a man's dream of woman," said Olwen.

The old man turned to her.

"The moment Lleu set eyes on her he loved her."

"Of course he did."

"A wedding feast was held at Caer Dathyl.

This is how they were seated: at the head of the high table sat Math and beside him his wife Goewin. Beside Math sat Gydion and beyond him his brother Gilfaethwy. Beside Goewin sat Lleu and beyond him Blodeuedd.

The woman of flowers ate and watched.

She tried to follow the signs and signals that passed between one person and another in the pitch of a word or the incline of a gesture. These were languages she did not understand.

When the feast was finished Lleu took Blodeuedd by the hand and led her to the bridal chamber.

He stroked her skin and she was at ease.

This was speech she could follow. His tongue was the probing of a bee. She willingly received his seed. His murmurings of love were a soughing in her ear like the wind. They made no sense. She yawned and closed her eyes until his other language stirred her again.

She turned to him as a flower will lean towards the light.

Meanwhile Gwydion was speaking to Math.

'It is not an easy thing for a man without territory to support himself.'

Math nodded in assent.

'It is not. So I have devised two wedding gifts for Lleu. First I will give him the best cantref that a man could have.'

'Which cantref is that, Lord?'

'Cantref Dinoding.'

Gwydion could not hide his delight.

'That is a generous gift, Lord. And what is the second?'

'I have charmed him against death.'

'Against death? How?'

'There is only one way that he can die. Come closer and I will whisper. No-one should overhear me.'

Gwydion put his ear to Math's lips.

As he listened he smiled. Then he laughed aloud.

The next morning Lleu was summoned to Math's throne.

The two gifts were given.

In the upper part of his territory Lleu built himself a court at Mur

Castell. He and Blodeuedd lived there and ruled over the land. There was no-one in the cantref who was unhappy with Lleu's lordship. [47]

Time passed.

Slowly Blodeuedd began to understand the strange unspoken laws that govern the ways of men and women.

Her ears and tongue unravelled the twisting subtleties of their talk. She found herself flourishing on this new soil.

But what was the meaning of the marriage she had been grafted onto? Where was the nourishment in Lleu's touch, his whispered words? Something warm and restless was stirring in her blood.

Some part of her was becoming human.

One day Lleu went to visit Math at Caer Dathyl.

Blodeuedd and her handmaidens were walking on the slope beneath Mur Castell. She heard the sound of a hunting horn.

She turned her head and saw a stag.

Its head was back. Its antlers were against its shoulders.

It was gasping at the air and frothing at the mouth.

A pack of singing hounds was running close behind.

Then she saw huntsmen on horseback, shouting for the kill.

Then came men on foot with spears and knives.

Blodeuedd said:

'What men are these?'

One of the maidens answered:

'Lady, this is the hunting party of Gronw Pebyr, lord of Penllyn.'

They watched the hunt until it vanished from view.

It was on the banks of the river Cynfael that the stag was brought down. Gronw Pebyr ordered that the beast be skinned and butchered. He baited the dogs with the bones and offal. By the time the meat had been cut and packed into leather bags the afternoon sun was sinking into the west.

It was dusk when the hunting party made its way homewards. They passed close to the gates of Mur Castell.

Blodeuedd saw them.

She saw the sated dogs and weary riders. She saw the stumbling men carrying the folded deerskin and the severed antlers and the bloody bags of fresh meat. It was a slow, footsore progress.

She turned to her handmaidens.

'What should I do? The hour is late. If we do not invite Gronw and his company to pass the night here, might we not be satirised for our lack of hospitality?'

'Lady,' they said, 'the proper thing is to invite them in.'

She sent a messenger to Gronw.

He gladly accepted her invitation.

The hunting party climbed the hill to Mur Castell. The dogs were kennelled and the horses stabled. The footmen were given food and shelter. Gronw and his retinue shook off their bloodied, sweat-stained clothes. They washed. They were dressed in fresh robes. They came to the feasting hall.

Blodeuedd invited Gronw Pebyr to sit beside her at the high table. Look.

Gronw is lowering himself into Lleu's chair.

She turns to him. See how her pale cheek is suffused with blushes. Something new is filling her body. Her eyes rest on his face.

Her pulse is quickening. She knows that she wants him.

Her head, heart and flesh are commanding her to love.

A servant fills their cups with wine.

He smiles. Their eyes meet.

He is consumed by her strange beauty.

They talk and are awakened to one another, so that even before the meat is eaten they have confessed their love.

Long after his noblemen have retired to their beds, see how Gronw sits with Blodeuedd.

Servants and handmaidens have been dismissed.

See how their fingers are entwined, their eyes shining.

She does not delay. She brings him to her bed.

His desire is hers. They are one flesh.

His whispered words are the promise of her need.

She gathers him into herself.

The next morning Gronw ordered his men to prepare for their departure. Horses and dogs were fed and led out of the gates.

He went to Blodeuedd.

'Lady, I seek your leave to depart.'

She looked into his eyes.

'You would not leave me alone tonight?'

He went outside and told his men to ride on ahead.

That night they lay together.

They began to talk of how they might become husband and wife.

'There is only one way,' said Gronw, 'we have no choice.'

'What way is that?'

'Lleu Llaw Gyffes must be killed.'

She sat up in bed.

'That is not possible. He is protected by spells. He is charmed by Math, charmed against death.'

'There is no magic that does not have its counter-charm. You must pretend a wifely concern and find out from him how we may bring about his death.'

He stroked her breast with his fingers.

'It is the only way my love.'

She sank into his arms.

The next morning he made ready to leave. As he was saddling his horse she came to him.

'Lady,' he said, 'may I depart now?'

She pressed her hand to the small of his back and smiled.

'I do not advise you to go today.'

He turned and kissed her lips.

'If you do not advise it, then I will not go. But is there not a danger that Lleu may return?'

'Tomorrow I will let you depart.'

That night they lay together.

The next morning he asked for her leave to return home.

This time she did not refuse him. She came to say farewell.

Gronw Pebyr said:

'Do not forget what I told you. Speak to him with all the affection and concern of a loving wife. Find out how his death might come to pass. As soon as you have his secret – send me word.'

That day Lleu returned.

Blodeuedd ran out to welcome him.

She had ordered the servants to prepare a feast in Lleu's honour. They sat at the table and ate and talked. There was carousal and music. When the hour was reached that is more suited to sleep than to song, they retired to their bed.

She let her husband have his will with her.

Then she rolled onto her side. When he spoke to her she made no reply. She sighed and shook with sobs. No tender word could console her. Lleu said:

'What is the matter? Are you unwell, have I offended you or hurt you in some way?'

'No, it is none of those things.'

'Then what is it?'

She rolled over and looked at him. Her face was wet with tears.

'While you were away I have been haunted by the thought of your death.'

He shook his head and laughed.

'My death! That is one thing you have no reason to fear.'

'But if you were to be killed and I were to be left alone ...'

'It will not happen.'

'But Lleu, everybody must die.'

'I am not easy to kill.'

She wriggled into his arms.

'Tell me how it could happen. My memory is better than yours. I will make sure that it never comes to pass.'

She pressed her mouth to his. Lleu whispered.

'I can only be killed by a spear. It must have been a year in the making, and all the shaping and sharpening done on the first day of the week.'

'You are sure?'

'I am certain. When it has been made, I can neither be killed indoors nor out of doors, neither on horseback nor on foot.'

'Then you are right – you cannot be killed.'

'There is one way. First a bath must be prepared for me on the bank of a river. Over the bath a roof frame must be constructed. On it there must be a snug thatch of reeds. Beside the bath a billy-goat must be tethered.'

'All these things must be set in place?'

'Yes. And if I were then to stand with one foot on the side of that bath and the other on the back of the goat, half out from under the thatch, and if I were to be struck by the spear of a year's making – then, and only then, would I be killed.'

Blodeuedd laughed.

'Then you are safe! Such a fate will be easy to avoid.'

Gronw Pebyr had sent a messenger.

He was hiding among the thickets below Mur Castell.

At first light, Blodeuedd slipped out of bed.

She found him and told him everything. He returned to Penllyn.

Gronw set to work.

He shaped a long ash-wood shaft. He moulded and cast a spearhead of hard, sharp iron. He fitted head to shaft. He worked only on the first day of the week.

The spear was a full year in the making.

When it was finished his messenger returned to Mur Castell. Blodeuedd had been watching. She went to where he was hiding.

'Lady,' he said, 'the weapon is ready.'

'Good. Stay there.'

She returned to the hall. She whitened her face with chalk. She came to Lleu. Her voice was an anxious whisper.

'My love, I am still worried about your death. If I were to prepare a bath on the bank of the Cynfael river and tether a goat beside it, would you show me how you must stand? My mind would be at ease then. I would know what we are to avoid.'

Lleu shrugged.

'Very well, it can do no harm.'

She went to the messenger.

'Tell Gronw to come tomorrow. He must hide in the shadow of the hill that is called Bryn Cyfergyr, 'the hill of the blow'.'

The messenger returned to Penllyn.

Blodeuedd wasted no time.

She took servants to the river's edge.

They made a bath from flat slabs of black slate. They sealed it with clay. Over it they built a wooden frame. They thatched it with long reeds. They found a goat and penned it beside the bath.

Blodeuedd cast her eyes over the preparations.

Everything was in place.

She returned to Mur Castell and waited until morning.

Look.

She is leading Lleu down to the river's edge.

Boiling cauldrons are hanging over blazing fires.

They are emptied into the bath and cooled with river water.

She helps him out of his clothes. She holds his hand as he lifts his foot and steps inside. Pale and naked he lowers himself into the steaming water. See how she leans over the side of the bath and washes him as though he was a child. She rubs his back and neck, his shoulders and arms.

'Lord,' she says, 'the animal you mentioned ...'

'The billy-goat?'

She points at the pen.

'Is this what you meant?'

'Yes, it must stand beside the bath.'

A rope is thrown around the goat's neck. It tugs and butts. It is pulled out of the pen and tethered to a post.

'Lord, show me how you would have to stand.'

See how Lleu rises from the water. He is naked, clean, glistening. His body is steaming. He steadies himself and lifts his foot.

He sets it on the edge of the bath.

He pulls himself up.

The other foot feels for the soft back of the goat.

He sets his weight behind the creature's shoulders.

See how he's stretching out his arms.

He balances, half under and half beyond the thatch.

'Look! Like this!'

"We will leave him there, in the certain knowledge that Gronw Pebyr is watching from the slopes of Bryn Cyfergyr."

The old man closed his eyes.

"I am weary now."

Friday May 7th

Cian Brydydd Mawr heard the brothers coming out of the church after Vespers. Then there was a knock at the door of his cell.

Tomos opened it. Brother Iago was standing outside. In his arms were two wooden boards roped together. Between them were held the pressed pages of the book.

"I have brought all but the page I wrote today – the ink on it is not yet dry."

The old man was in bed.

"Prop me up, son."

Tomos lifted him into a sitting position.

"Show me, Iago ap Rhys."

Brother Iago set the boards down on the floor beside the bed. The old man reached across and rested his hand on them.

"It is all here? The whole Matter?"

"All of it."

"God bless you."

Brother Iago lowered his eyes.

"God has had little to do with it."

The old man smiled.

"Do not underestimate God, my friend."

"Shall I show you?"

Cian Brydydd Mawr nodded. The monk knelt down and untied the rope. He lifted the upper board to show the first page with its neat script across the scored lines. The old man lifted the parchment and held it before his eyes. He turned to Tomos.

"Here is my breath, held fast."

He put the parchment back on top of the pile. He ran his fingers along the edges of the pages and pulled one out.

"Read me this."

Brother Iago took it and read aloud:

"At the edge of the well there was a golden basin fastened to four chains. The chains reached up into the sky, he could not see where they ended. He was filled with rapture at the workmanship of the basin and the fineness of the gold. He came to it and grabbed it. As soon as he did so his hands stuck ..."

"Enough! I have heard enough. It is there. It will not die."

Brother Iago pushed the page back into place.

The old man grabbed his hand.

"I have mocked you, Brother, and pricked at your devotions, but you have done me a great service."

"I was only doing what my Father Abbot demanded."

"It has been a great work."

The old man closed his eyes and was silent. Brother Iago loosened his hand and began to retie the boards of his book. Suddenly he was aware that he was being watched.

"I have one last request."

"What is it?"

"That, when it has been cut and sewn and bound, you should be the one who presses it into the hands of our Lord Llywelyn. He will love you for it."

Thursday May 14th (Ascension Day)

Dafydd and Olwen came to the cell at the same time.

He held the door for her. He could see that she had not slept. As she passed him she whispered:

"The bailiff came. I have news of Rhys. He is gone with the war-host to Bala."

"That is all?"

"That is all I know."

The old man was waiting for them. He was dressed and sitting on his chair. He looked directly at them, first Olwen, then Dafydd.

"The matter we spoke of – the journey to Ynys Enlli."

"We have not forgotten."

"It may be difficult."

He reached beneath his cloak and pulled out a purse.

"This is to ease the journey."

He passed it to Dafydd.

"Take it. There was a time when I travelled with horses and a full retinue. A time when Lords honoured me and filled my saddle-bags with gifts of gold. This is all that remains.

Before my back was bent I was eloquent:

acclaimed by women for wonders,

and maintained by men for subtle metre."

Dafydd pulled open the strings of the purse and looked inside.

"It is more money than we shall need."

"Whatever is left is for Tomos. He is a good boy and has tended me like a mother."

Brother Iago hurried from the church with the words of the day echoing in his mind: 'While they were beholding him going up to heaven, they said alleluia. Lifting up his hands, he blessed them and was carried up to heaven, alleluia. Exalte regem regum, et hymnum dicite Deo, alleluia. While they were looking on he was raised up and a cloud received him ...'

"Sit down Iago ap Rhys, you are in a dream!"

The rest of the company was gathered and waiting.

"I am ready."

He set a wax tablet on his knee. The old man surveyed his audience.

"You will remember that Lleu Llaw Gyffes was standing with one foot on the side of a bath, the other on the back of a goat."

"Already the spear of a year's making was singing through the air.

Gronw Pebyr had risen from the shadow of Bryn Cyfergyr.

With one knee on the ground, the other bent before him, he had drawn back his arm. He had narrowed his eyes and hurled his spear.

His aim was true.

The sharp iron point split Lleu's skin.

It splintered his breast.

It buried itself in the bones of his back.

He threw back his head and screamed.

Blodeuedd and all those standing at the water's edge lifted their hands to their ears.

Look.

Lleu's arms are sprouting red-brown feathers.

Soft feathers are bursting from his breast.

His mouth is curving and hardening into a beak.

He is become an eagle.

He topples forwards and beats his feathered arms against the air. Slowly he rises into the sky.

The spear juts from the bloody wound in his breast.

Higher and higher he flies until he is a speck against the blue of the heavens. Then he is gone.

Gronw is making his way down from Bryn Cyfergyr.

Blodeuedd seizes his hand.

They climb the hill to Mur Castell.

She leads him to her bed.

But nothing escapes the ears of Math, son of Mathonwy.

The sound of Lleu's death reached Caer Dathyl.

Math buried his face in his hands.

He told his nephew.

And Gwydion wept for his son.

For a full day his grief was beyond words.

Then he said:

'Lord, I will not rest until I find my sister's son.'

Math replied:

'Go out and search for him. You will need strength and good fortune.'

Gwydion set out on foot.

He walked the length and breadth of Gwynedd and Powys.

He climbed hills and mountains. He followed valleys and the margins of lakes and rivers. He trudged across open moors.

He asked every man and woman he met for news of Lleu Llaw Gyffes.

He was answered by shaken heads. Nobody knew what had become of him.

When it seemed there was no yard that he had not trodden he came to a farmstead in Maenawr Bernnardd. It was late and he was tired. He demanded lodging for the night.

The farmer welcomed him. Food and drink were brought to the table. He was invited to sit down. One by one the household joined them – cowherds, shepherds, dairymaids. The last to sit down was the swineherd.

The farmer turned to him.

'Boy, has the sow returned?'

'Yes master, she has just come back to her sty.'

Gwydion leaned forwards.

'Tell me about the sow,' he said. 'Where does she go?'

'Lord,' said the farmer, 'it is a mystery to us. These new beasts are strange and wonderful creatures. Every morning she jumps over the wall of her sty. She can't be caught. She vanishes as though she had melted into the earth. And when she returns her belly is bulging. She turns up her snout and disdains any morsel we offer her.'

Gwydion listened intently.

'Tomorrow,' he said, 'wake me before first light. I will come with you and follow this sow.'

The next morning he waited beside the sty. At dawn the sow woke. She shook away the straw. She sniffed the air. She scrambled over the wall and set off at a brisk run.

Gwydion pursued her.

She came to a river and ran upstream. He was close behind. She came to a valley – it is still called the Nantlleu Valley – and her pace began to slow. He saw she was approaching the foot of an oak tree.

He crouched behind a clump of bushes and watched.

Look.

The sow has lowered her snout to the ground.

She is eating something. She is snorting and guzzling.

Gwydion rubs his eyes and looks again.

The ground beneath the tree is littered with red-brown feathers and rotten flesh. The pig is gorging herself.

Gwydion peers up among the boughs and limbs of the oak.

On the topmost branch an eagle is perched.

Hanging from its breast is a spear.

Every time the eagle stirs or shakes itself, flesh, lice and feathers slake away from its body. They rain down through the green leaves. The sow gobbles them as they land.

Gwydion opens his mouth. He sings to the eagle:

'An oak grows between two lakes,
> dark the sky and dark the valley.
If I'm not wrong this darkness comes
> from nine flowers plucked for Lleu.'

The eagle heard the song. It cocked its head to one side and swayed on its branch. It loosened its grip and slipped down through the leaves. It perched in the middle of the tree.

'An oak grows on a high hill,
> not burnt by sun nor soaked by rain.
It has witnessed nine-score torments.
> At its summit Lleu Llaw Gyffes.'

When it heard the song the eagle dropped again.

It plummeted through the tree and perched on the lowest branch.

'An oak grows on a steep slope,
> home it is to a high-born prince.
If I do not tell a lie
> Lleu will fly into my lap."

The eagle launched itself from the tree.

With weary wings it flew to Gwydion. It fell into his lap.

Gwydion drew his rowan wand from beneath his cloak.

He struck the bird.

In its place lay Lleu Llaw Gyffes.

He had the appearance of a man who has been dug from his grave. His body was grey. His flesh was wasted. His bones jutted out beneath his skin. His eyes were blank. His hair was alive with lice. The haft of the spear was sunk into a wound that festered with maggots.

He was not dead.

Gwydion lifted him tenderly in his arms.

His son had no more weight than a dead bird.

He carried him to Caer Dathyl.

Math and Gwydion summoned the doctors of Gwynedd.

They treated Lleu with herbs, leeches, potions and all the skills of physic. The spear was charmed from his body. Broths were tipped down his throat with horn spoons. Marrow fat was rubbed into his skin. Spells were spoken. Slowly he began to regain his strength.

With a mixture of medicine and magic the vigour returned to his limbs.

After three months he could take his first tottering steps.

After six months he could hurl a spear.

After nine months he could outride any horseman in the realm.

When a year was over, Lleu said:

'Now it is time for me to be avenged on the man who has caused me so much suffering.'

Math bowed his head.

'That time is come. He cannot be allowed to rule Cantref Dinoding when he owes you such redress.'

Messengers rode out across Gwynedd. Every man took up arms. A mighty army was mustered.

Lleu, Math and Gwydion rode at its head.

Behind them followed rank upon rank of horsemen and foot soldiers. The air was filled with the sound of the blaring of battle horns, the clashing of swords against shields.

They advanced into Dinoding.

They approached Mur Castell.

Blodeuedd and Gronw heard the sound.

They came out of the hall and saw Math, Gwydion and Lleu at the foot of the hill.

Gronw ran to the stable. He saddled a horse and rode out of Mur Castell. His heart was intent on reaching Penllyn.

Lleu and Math saw him.

They shouted. They dug spurs into their horses' flanks and set off in pursuit. As a hunt will follow a fox or stag, so the host of Gwynedd hounded Gronw Pebyr.

As for Gwydion, he had seen Blodeuedd.

He had seen her slipping through a back gate of the court of Mur Castell.

She was ducking down to stay out of sight.

Her handmaidens were with her.

He saw them lifting their skirts and running down the slope of the hill. He saw them hurrying through the broom and furze.

He leapt from his horse's back and ran after them.

The women were hurrying towards the mountains.

They heard the sounds of pursuit. They looked over their shoulders and saw Gwydion.

They climbed higher and looked again. He was getting closer.

They scrambled higher still. They could hear the clinking of his battle vest, the chinking of his scabbard against the buckle of his belt.

They looked behind.

Gwydion was striding towards them.

He was drawing his wand of rowan from beneath his cloak.

They ran, stumbling over rock and heather. They heard his shout.

Wreaths of white mist rose from the ground.

They lost their way. They lost their footing.

The handmaidens tripped and fell into a lake.

Their sodden linen dragged them down. Every one of them was drowned. The lake is called Llyn y Morynion, 'The Lake of the Maidens'.

Only Blodeuedd remained.

Gwydion shouted again and the mist was gone.

He came to her.

She dropped to her knees.

'Spare my life.'

'I won't kill you,' he said.

He struck her with his wand.

Look.

She is staring up at him. Feathers are forming around her eyes.

A circle of fine feathers is sprouting from the margins of each eye.

Two round, feathered circles are looking up at him.

Her nose and mouth are become one hard, curving, merciless beak.

'You will go in the form of a bird.'

Her yellow hair is falling from her head. Out of the bald skin feathers form.

'Your wanton will has won you the hatred of the other birds.'

Her clothes fall to the ground. Feathers are pushing out of her breasts and her belly, out of her back and her legs.

'You will not dare to show your face by day for fear of their persecution.'

Long flight feathers burst from her arms. Her toes curl into sharp talons.

'But you will never lose your name. You will always be Blodeuedd, "flower-face".'

She opens her beaked mouth – the sound she makes is a long, loud, shuddering hoot. She is become an owl.

She beats her wings against the air and flies over the lake."

Cian Brydydd Mawr sipped from his cup.

"We have all seen her, mobbed by the little birds."

"Gronw Pebyr came to Penllyn.

He knew every hill and hollow, every scar and scarp of his realm. With his horse buckling at the knees, he came to his high hall.

He rode inside.

He told his men to bolt the doors.

Math and Lleu Llaw Gyffes and their warriors came to the hall.

They surrounded it. They set up camp. A siege began.

When night came, Gronw looked out.

He could see a thousand flickering fires.

He knew defeat was inevitable. He sent a messenger to Lleu:

'Gronw Pebyr asks if you want land or territory, gold or silver as recompense for his crime?'

Lleu replied:

'My demand of Gronw is this. He must stand in the place where I stood when I was struck. I will stand on Bryn Cyfergyr. It is my turn to cast the spear.'

The messenger returned.

When Gronw heard Lleu's terms he turned to his men.

'Is there any one of you – my loyal nobles, my retinue, my foster-brothers – who will take this blow on my behalf?'

They all shook their heads.

350

'We will not.'

Outside, the men of Gwynedd were lighting fire-brands. They were hurling them at the thatch of his hall.

He had no choice. He rode out.

Lleu's warriors seized him and carried him to the Cynfael river.

The bath was filled. His clothes were torn from his back.

He was plunged into cold water.

Naked, he was forced to climb up onto the edge of the bath.

He curled his toes against the hard slate.

He could see Lleu Llaw Gyffes.

He was standing in the shadow of Bryn Cyfergyr.

His arm was raised.

He was holding the spear of a year's making.

Gronw shouted:

'It was for a woman's sake that you suffered. Now, for the same woman, I suffer also. In the name of pity I beg you, set that stone between me and the blow I am to receive.'

He gestured with his arm to a boulder that lay at the river's edge.

From the hillside Lleu replied:

'I will not refuse you that request.'

The stone was rolled and set upright between them.

Lleu lifted the spear again.

He drew back his arm and flung it with all of his strength.

It flew through the air and struck the boulder.

Its iron head cut clean through stone.

It struck Gronw Pebyr.

It pierced his body and broke his back. He crumpled and fell.

He floated face-down in the bath.

The water billowed red with his blood.

The boulder, with a hole clean through it, can still be seen on the banks of the River Cynfael. It is called Llech Gronw, 'Gronw's Stone'.

Lleu returned to Caer Dathyl.

With Math and Gwydion he feasted until deep into the night.

He took possession of Cantref Dinoding and ruled it from Mur Castell.

Years later, when Math and Gwydion were dead, Lleu Llaw Gyffes became Lord over all of Gwynedd."

Cian Brydydd Mawr closed his eyes.

"And so ends the fourth 'Cainc' of the Mabinogi.

Bards and scholars can argue – as they always will – whether Cainc means the branch of a tree, the strand of a rope, or the verse of a song. For me, who tells the tale today, it means all three."

He looked at his listeners.

"Come back after None. Now I must rest."

Brother Iago got to his feet. He could not mask his anxiety.

"There is more? Another branch?"

"Iago ap Rhys, I have told you before, there is always more."

The mid-day bell rang. Brother Iago hurried across to the church for Sext.

Dafydd and Olwen sat together.

"A siege, torched thatch, a hurled spear and billowing blood, these stories do not set my mind at rest."

"You know with certainty that John has built a castle at Bala?"

"I do, and why would Llywelyn be sending his war host there if not to destroy it?"

Dafydd leaned across and rested his hand between her shoulders. It was the simple gesture of a brother. It filled them both with the aching pain of unwanted distance.

"All we can do is pray for his homecoming."

"You are praying, Dafydd?"

"Of course I am."

After None the listeners gathered in Cian Brydydd Mawr's cell. He had not got out of bed. He turned his head on the pillow and looked up at them.

"Dafydd, Olwen, Tomos, Iago ap Rhys, I am tired."

He sighed.

"The Matter possesses me for a while, then leaves me broken."

He lifted his knees beneath the blankets.

"Sit me up, son, there is more to tell."

Dafydd helped Tomos lift the old man into a sitting position. He weighed no more than a child. They pressed the rolled skins behind his back.

"Good. That is better. Now you will remember that Lleu had become Lord over all of Gwynedd?"

"We remember."

"If I could sing, I would sing of Lleu Llaw Gyffes.

I would sing of Lleu, Lord of Gwynedd.

I would sing of Lleu, cursed by his mother and betrayed by the woman of flowers.

I would sing of Lleu as he made a circuit of his realm."

Cian Brydydd Mawr paused. He closed his eyes. He was silent for a long time. Tomos pressed a cup of water to his lips. He drank.

"Thank you, son."

The listeners waited.

The old man slumped sideways.

His head hit the earthen floor with a thud.

Dafydd and Olwen ran forwards. They lifted him and laid him gently on the bed. She curled her fingers around his wrist. There was no pulse. Dafydd listened at the open mouth. There was no trace of breath. He pressed on the ribs to bring some new air into the lungs.

The body shuddered. Then it was still.

Olwen ran her fingertips across his face, from the shaved brow to the chin. The old man's mouth had fallen open. She turned to the room. Her face was stricken.

"He is dead."

Brother Iago crossed himself and hurried out of the cell.

"The days of man are short and the number of his months is with thee ..."

He ran to fetch Brother Deiniol.

"... Thou hast appointed his bounds which cannot be passed. Recede paululum ab eo ..."

The boy buried his face in his hands and shook with sobs.

Olwen leaned down and closed the lids of his eyes.

Dafydd was kneeling beside the bed.

"A world is come to its end."

When Brother Deiniol appeared in the doorway with chalice and wafers for the last rites he was too late.

7

Ynys Enlli

Monday May 18th

Brother Iago crossed the fields and came to the barn.

Dafydd was sitting cross-legged in the light of the open door. He was stitching two large hides together, piercing the holes with the point of an awl. He looked up.

"Greetings."

"God prosper you. What are you making?"

"I am stitching a leather shroud for the old poet. He has a journey to make."

"Then you will not bury him here?"

"We are taking him to Ynys Enlli. It was his wish."

"He is to be buried with the Saints! Will the Holy Brothers take him?"

Dafydd looked at the young man with steady eyes.

"You forget, Brother. He was the greatest poet of his age."

Brother Iago was silent. He sat down in the doorway. His voice wavered.

"So you think he will be welcomed into Paradise?"

"That is a matter for God and his Angels."

He pulled his needle through the leather.

"All I know is that he was alive, and I have been made more alive by sitting in his presence."

"And that is enough?"

"It is enough for me."

Dafydd stitched in silence. The monk watched him.

"How will you get him to Ynys Enlli?"

"There's a fellow in Caernarfon who has a boat. He trades up and down the coast. When the wind is right he'll take us there. But he has to be careful. It's a treacherous reach of water."

"So I have been told."

Dafydd measured the lengths of the two stitched hides.

"Do you think the shroud will be long enough to hold him?"

"It is hard to say. He was stooped, but would have once stood tall."

Dafydd folded it over and lifted it.

"The body is still by the altar?"

"Yes."

"I will lay it alongside."

Brother Iago stood.

"Before you go, one thing."

"What is that?"

"Three more days and the old man's Matter will be written down."

"Good, good."

"Then the book must be made."

"Do you have what you need?"

"I have knives, threads, needles and boards. But I am lacking a good cured skin to stretch over the boards."

Dafydd dropped his bundle.

"I have the very thing. I've been keeping it hidden."

From the shadows behind the door he pulled a tied roll.

"It is the last of my calf-skins. It was to have been a gift for Brother Selyf." He dropped his voice to a whisper. "But he and I are no longer of one mind."

He held out his arms.

"Take it – I cannot think of a better use for it."

Saturday May 23rd

The trading boat dropped anchor off the coast of Ynys Enlli.

It swung this way and that with the tug of the currents.

"You'll have to cover the last stretch by currach."

The little skin boat was lowered down to the water. It bucked and dipped with the swell.

"You'll need the strength of your arms."

Olwen and Tomos clambered down and sat side by side.

Dafydd passed them an oar.

"You share this one. I'll take the other."

He lowered himself and sat behind them.

"Pass down the body."

The sailors leaned over the side and lowered the stiff leather shroud.

"That's been dead awhile. It's ripening like an old cheese."

Dafydd laid it along the wet bottom of the boat.

"Still, it'll serve you as ballast."

They pushed the currach with poles.

"Awaaaay. We'll pick you up on our way home."

Dafydd shouted:

"PULL!"

They pulled at their oars and the boat began to spin.

"TOgether and TOgether and TOgether."

They found a rhythm. Slowly the little boat nosed forwards. When they reached the shallows they jumped overboard. They lifted the currach and carried it to the black seaweed of the high tide line.

"We'll leave the old poet here. First of all we must find the Brothers."

The Culdees were at prayer. Dafydd and Olwen sat outside the squat church and waited. Around them was a scattering of stone walled cells with turf roofs. They had lost track of time. [48]

"The sun is on its way down. It must be Vespers."

They sat for a long time. The psalms showed no sign of ceasing. Dafydd whispered:

"I know nothing of the Companions of God – I've heard they endure harsh lives here."

"The winters must be cruel. There are almost no trees. How do they keep warm?"

"Driftwood maybe, driftwood and prayer."

"And yet many come, and see out their last days here."

Tomos appeared. He had been clambering on the cliffs.

"I've never seen so many seals. And look."

He opened his leather shoulder bag. Inside was a clutch of gulls' eggs.

"They are nesting everywhere. We could bake them in the ashes."

"If we could find a fire."

"And there's a little hidden valley full of apple trees. They're all in blossom. And there are bee skeps."

The church door opened. The Brothers filed out in silence.

Dafydd, Olwen and Tomos followed them past the cells to a sunken fire pit. The Culdees sat on the ground in a circle. One of them blew into the embers. Another brought an armful of driftwood. As the fire rekindled they hung a pot over it.

When it was hot the stew was ladled into bowls.

One of the Brothers beckoned to the strangers.

"Eat."

They were given the food – herring stew with celery and spinach, then little pieces of dry bread dripping with honey.

The Brothers ate in silence. Their eyes were open, hardly blinking. Their gaunt faces were weathered and they had a stone-like calm. Tomos pushed the gulls' eggs into the ashes with a stick. The Culdees watched him impassively. When they had eaten they put down their bowls and chanted a prayer. Then they dispersed.

One stayed behind. He came across to the strangers. He crouched beside them.

"Why have you come?"

"We have brought a corpse. It was his dearest wish to be buried here."

"Who was he?"

"His name was Cian Brydydd Mawr."

The Culdee started, then he crossed himself.

"Many come. We do not deny them their repose. Carry him to the church and lay him with his feet towards the altar. Tomorrow we will dig a grave."

"When?"

"After the Mass."

Tomos raked the eggs out of the ashes. He picked one up and threw it from hand to hand until it was cool enough to eat. He offered it to the Culdee. He raised his palm in refusal. His smile was radiant.

"No. Christ Jesu bless you. I can see that you are kind."

Sunday May 24th

'Behold, thou desirest truth in the inward parts: and in the hidden part thou shalt make me to know wisdom. Purge me with hyssop, and I shall be clean: wash me and I shall be whiter than snow. Make me to hear joy and gladness; that the bones which thou hast broken may rejoice. Averte faciem tuam a peccatis meis: et omnes iniquitates meas dele.'

The stitched leather shroud lay in the aisle before the sanctuary. Candles burned at its head and feet. On one side of it a Culdee was swinging a smoking censer. On the other, holy water was being sprinkled from a wooden bowl.

Dafydd and Olwen knelt, with Tomos between them.

After the Absolution the body, which had been laid on a wooden board, was carried out into the light. They followed it to the graveside. Again it was incensed and anointed. It was lowered slowly into the grave. Each of them took a handful of earth and threw it onto the shroud.

"May his soul, and the souls of all the faithful departed, through the mercy of God rest in peace."

Two of the Culdees lifted spades and began to fill the grave. The rest walked away. Dafydd and Olwen stood side by side. They watched Cian Brydydd Mawr disappear beneath the rough stony earth. The only sound was the scraping and scattering of soil, the breaking of waves and the crying of gulls.

She reached across and took his hand.

Their fingers intertwined so that he could feel the warmth of her palm against his. Then she was lifting his hand to her lips. She was holding the back of his hand to her mouth. She kissed it again and again.

He summoned the courage to turn to her. Her face was streaming with tears. She looked at him and smiled.

"Yes."

He understood. It was an answer and a question, a challenge and a truth.

Tomos' eyes were fixed on the grave. He would not turn away from it until it had been filled. Then the three of them walked out of the cemetery together. They threaded their way between the unmarked mounds.

When they came to the gate they saw a figure approaching them. He had a stick in either hand and was hobbling over the stony ground. His back was bent and they could hear the quick rasping of his breath. His white hair had fallen over his face. He was dressed in a green cloak and woven breeches, not the grey robes of the Culdees.

He stopped and looked up at them. They saw that his forehead was shaven.

"Too late, too late. I try to never miss a burial, but my legs have let me down."

His eyes were eager.

"Who was he?"

"A poet, like yourself."

"Was he by God, what was his name?"

"Cian Brydydd Mawr."

The old man bowed his head.

"So I have outlived the Great Poet."

He crossed himself.

"And it is too late now to out-sing him – not that I ever could have done."

"Did you know him?"

"I knew him alright. We were boys together in the Bardic School. He was the hope and despair of his elders. He would take the old tales and weave them into something new and alive, when all they wanted to hear was an echo of their tired old voices. And then, when he mastered the metres, there was nobody who could touch him. He suffered some beatings, but in the end, by God, he bested them all."

Tomos looked at the old man.

"So you must have known Meilyr."

"Who?"

"Old Meilyr, the bard who told the stories to Cian Brydydd Mawr."

The old man shook his head.

"Meilyr was already fifteen years dead when we came to the Bardic School. We never knew Meilyr."

He chuckled.

"But your mention of that name is bringing me a memory."

His ancient face was suddenly beaming with merriment.

"I have not thought of this for sixty years but now it is coming back to me. Cian and I had barely seen ten winters – we were younger than you – we caught a fox cub. Cian kept him as a pet in a hole under his pallet. We'd let him run at nights. In the end his stink gave him away. We called him Meilyr."

The old man turned to Dafydd.

"Maybe in his last days his mind became muddled."

Dafydd put his hand on the poet's shoulder.

"Old man, he was frail. He had been wounded to the bone. He struggled to climb out of his bed. But of one thing I can assure you – his mind was quick-silver to the last."

"Good. I would have expected no less."

Tomos was angry.

"So you are telling us he was a liar?"

The old poet turned towards the gate.

"No, by God, I am not. Cian Brydydd Mawr never told anything but the truth. And now he is gone."

He hobbled into the cemetery.

"Soon I will be joining him."

When they came down to the stony bay it had started to rain.

Dafydd said:

"The trading boat will be returning from Harlech early tomorrow morning with a load of carcasses and timber. If the wind and the waves are kind they will pick us up. We should be ready for them."

Tomos said:

"And what will we do when we come to Caernarfon?"

"There will be a bed for you at Careg boeth."

Olwen put her arm around the boy's shoulders.

"Gwyn is eager for your arrival, and so am I."

Tomos looked at Dafydd.

"And what about you? You will go back to Clynnog Fawr I suppose?"

Olwen smiled.

"There is a bed at Careg boeth for him too, if he wants it."

The rain had become heavy. It had darkened the pebbles of the beach. There were several boats above the high tideline. They had been turned over to keep them dry. Dafydd walked across to the currach. He lifted one side and propped it up with a couple of large rocks.

"Tomos, here's a roof for you. Sleep under the boat, you'll be dry as a bone."

The boy crawled inside and stretched himself out. The rain rattled against the stretched skin and pitch. Dafydd pulled away the rocks and lowered it.

"How's that?" said Olwen. "Snug?"

"Better than any tent."

The rain was falling in torrents. Further along the bay was an up-turned wooden fishing boat. Dafydd ran across and lifted one side of it. Olwen crawled underneath. She lay down and reached out her arm. She caught hold of his ankle.

"Don't go."

He found himself propping up the boat with a sodden log.

Then he was crawling under.

He was answering her 'yes' with his own affirmation.

She took his hand and drew him down beside her.

Her breath was warm. Her wet hair fell into their faces.

"You are not going to turn to the edge of the bed?"

The rain was so loud against the clinker timbers that it was hard to speak. He lifted his mouth to her ear.

"Never. Never again."

He pushed away the log so that the boat dropped down and enclosed them. It was dry and completely dark.

She reached and caught hold of the hem of his brown lay brother's robe. She tugged it upwards. He lifted his back and then his shoulders so that she could pull it over his head. They rolled apart and she spread it over the hard pebbles.

"That's better."

They rolled back onto its soft warmth and into each other's arms.

Monday May 25th

'Thou rejectest all who depart from thy judgements, because their thoughts are wicked. All sinners of the earth I regard as liars; therefore I love thy testimonies. Confige timore tuo carnes meas: a iudiciis enim tuis timui.'

Brother Iago was kneeling for the last time in the little church at Clynnog Fawr.

In the stable outside, a pack-horse had been loaded with the tools of his trade. Above the bulging leather bags, his writing desk had been securely tied in place.

He smiled to himself. Soon he would be back in the monastery at Aberconwy and his long ordeal would be behind him. Brother Deiniol had received word that Llywelyn was holding court in his Llys at Aberconwy. It would be no great journey to find him.

He reached to his right. His hand rested on soft calf-skin. He ran his fingers against the trimmed parchment pages and the cold silver clasp. It was the one thing he had not yet loaded. It was lying on the bench beside him. He knew that pride was a sin, but he knew also that he had made something beautiful. Whatever its content, he had used the skill that God had given him and crafted his first complete book.

After Eucharist, when the other Brothers filed out of the church, he lingered behind. It was heavy. He needed both hands to lift it. He carried it to the altar and laid it down. He knelt.

"Lord God and Christ Jesu, I commend this book, the work of my own two hands, to you. And I pray that the matter it contains – the stories of our grandfathers and grandmothers before they came to Christ – leads nobody into sin. Amen."

Brother Deiniol was waiting outside the church door.

"So, it is done."

Brother Iago was holding the book against his chest.

"Yes. Now, God-willing, I need never again be distracted from the true word."

They walked together to the stables.

"I should have liked to read it."

Brother Iago shook his head.

365

"Better to leave it clasped shut, Brother. Once it is opened you would struggle to close it. Even now I am trying to forget. That is the trap the devil sets in a story. Once you've heard it, it is too late."

Thursday May 28th

Thousands of warriors were camping along the edge of the Conwy River. Llywelyn's host had driven the Normans out of Bala. Now they were waiting for orders. There were fires and makeshift shelters all the way from the monastery to the Llys.

Brother Iago threaded his way between them.

The air was thick with the smell of sweat, horse dung and roasting meat. His ears were filled with the sound of talk and the clanking of blacksmiths as they knocked the dents from shields and helmets.

Brother Iago was aware of the curses melting away from men's mouths when they saw a Holy Brother in his white robes.

On his back he was carrying a leather pack. Inside it was the book.

"Brother Iago!"

He was surprised to hear his name.

"Brother Iago."

One of the warriors was approaching him. He was a young man, with a fresh scar across his cheek.

"Brother Iago. Do you remember me? I am Rhys. I came to the monastery at Clynnog Fawr on the Feast of the Nativity – to hear the stories. I am Olwen's son."

"Of course. Now I see who you are."

"How is my Mother?"

"She is well. She is gone to Ynys Enlli to bury Cian Brydydd Mawr."

"So ... he died."

"Yes."

"And Uncle Dafydd, how is he?"

"He is gone too."

"God bless them. I think about them."

He looked at the monk.

"And what happened to the old man's Matter?"

Brother Iago lifted his hand and patted his pack.

"It is here. I am taking it to our Lord Llywelyn."

"Good."

Rhys reached forwards and gripped Brother Iago's arm.

"Brother, will you take a message to my mother?"

Brother Iago shook his head.

"I will not be returning to Clynnog Fawr. But give it to me and you have my word, I will make sure it reaches her."

"Tell her I am alive. Tell her that I have had a dream. I heard my father's voice. He told me I'd be home for harvest."

Llywelyn had been sitting in a counsel of war with his Distain and the leaders of his war host. They were making a strategy to retake the Perfeddwlad. Several times during the morning a chamberlain had distracted him. First he had whispered something about a Cistercian standing at the gate.

"Let him stand. It'll make a change from kneeling."

Then the chamberlain had returned an hour later.

"Lord, the monk says he has brought you a book."

"A book! What are we to do with it? Throw it at Norman heads?"

An hour later he'd returned again.

"Lord, the monk ..."

"Damn the monk. What does he want this time?"

"He told me to say three words ..."

"Which words?"

"Cian Brydydd Mawr."

"What?"

"Cian Brydydd Mawr."

"Why didn't you tell me before?"

He hit the table with his fist. Then he turned to his men.

"We will have a rest and eat. Give me an hour."

Then he shouted to the chamberlain:

"Bring him in!"

Llywelyn and Siwan were sitting side by side when Brother Iago was led into the hall. A wet-nurse was suckling their son by the fire.

He dropped to one knee before them.

Llywelyn looked him up and down.

"So you are the Brother with a good memory and a steady hand."

"By God's grace, Lord."

"And the book is finished?"

"The old poet had more to tell, but the days of man are short. Death intervened."

Llywelyn and Siwan crossed themselves. She leaned forwards.

"So that most eloquent of tongues is stilled."

"It is, my Lady. He is buried on Ynys Enlli."

Llywelyn whispered:

"Then he is with the Saints ..."

He paused. His eyes filled.

"... and the Treasures of Britain – though I could not name them."

Siwan reached across and took his hand.

For a while neither of them spoke. The baby cried. Llywelyn was startled from his thoughts. His voice had grown tender.

"In God's name show us the book."

Brother Iago untied the pack. He lifted it out and passed it across with both hands.

"It is heavy."

Siwan took it and rested it on her lap. Llywelyn brushed his fingertips over the calf-skin.

"It is a handsome thing."

She released the catch of the clasp and opened it. She turned the pages.

"Look at the writing. It is measured and orderly, like a tended garden."

Llywelyn looked at her and smiled.

"But the proof of the pudding – as your Norman forebears would say – is in the eating. Read."

Siwan settled on a page and read aloud in her lilting Welsh with its French intonation:

"'Well,' she said, 'I will go to him.'

She came to the ship. The shoe-maker was drawing a design and the boy was stitching.

'Lady,' he said, 'good day to you.'

'May God prosper you,' Arianrhod replied, 'I am surprised that you are unable to make shoes that fit.'

'I couldn't before,' he said, 'but now I can.'

At that moment a wren perched on the deck of the ship. The boy lifted his knife and threw it. He hit it in the leg between the tendon and the bone. She smiled.

'God knows, with a fair and skilful hand has the boy hit the bird!'

'Well,' said Gwydion, 'God's curse upon you. The boy has now got a name, and a good enough name it is. From this day onwards he is Lleu Llaw Gyffes.'

Then everything vanished into seaweed."

Llywelyn slapped his hand against the arm of his throne.

"Very good. There are more mentions of God's name than I recall, but the story is intact and true. Read me more."

Siwan closed the book and opened it again:

"The Irish had a plan. They fixed a peg on either side of the hundred columns in the hall. From each peg they hung a bag with an armed warrior inside it.

Efnisien entered the hall ahead of the host of the Island of the Mighty. He cast a hard, merciless glance about himself. He saw the hide bags hanging from their pegs.

'What's in this bag?' he asked.

'Flour, friend.'

Efnisien felt the bag. He found the head. He squeezed it until the bone cracked ..."

"Excellent!"

Llywelyn was beaming with delight.

"Cian Brydydd Mawr is dead – and yet he is not dead."

He fixed his eyes on Brother Iago.

"And neither will you be, as long as these pages are read."

Brother Iago paled.

"Lord, this Matter is not of my making. Nor, to be truthful, is it to my liking ..."

"Nonsense! Is it not writ in your hand?"

He lifted the book and kissed it.

"And whether you like it or not – it is at the very heart of who we are."

Brother Iago saw that his argument was best not pursued.

He bowed his head and said nothing.

Siwan had been watching him. She leaned over and whispered in Llywelyn's ear.

"My wife says she would like you to make her a Psalter. She says that in return, when we win back the Perfeddwlad, she will give your holy foundation more land than you Father Abbot can ride on a long summer's day."

Llywelyn shouted for a scribe.

He came running with quill and parchment.

"And I will give you my guarantee of it – here and now."

Siwan offered Brother Iago her hand.

He kissed it.

"God bless you my Lady. I thank you in Christ Jesu's name."

He was surprised to discover that he was weeping.

When the Distain and the leaders of the war host returned to the hall, Llywelyn was waiting for them. On the table before him there was a book bound in calf-skin.

"So, your Cistercian did bring you his book, my Lord."

"Indeed he did."

The Distain peered at it.

"What is it?"

Llywelyn stood. He lifted his hand. He set it on the book with the solemn gravity of a man who is making an oath.

"Here is all Wales."

Epilogue

King John was in Durham in the summer of 1212 when he received news that there was a Welsh uprising. Llywelyn had crossed the Conway and reclaimed the Perfeddwlad. He had destroyed all of John's castles (only Deganwy and Rhuddlan held out against him). Further south, Gwenwynwyn of Powys and Rhys Gryg of Deheubarth were attacking English castles and towns in their lands.

John hurried southwards. He sent letters to the sheriffs of thirty shires ordering a huge mobilisation of troops and labourers. He demanded 8,430 men. Knights from all over England were summoned. A further thousand men came south from Scotland. Markets were closed by royal order so that there would be food enough to feed the troops. John was going to conquer Wales completely and build the castles that would keep it suppressed.

A vast army began to gather at Chester.

John travelled to Nottingham. He vowed he would touch no food until he had seen all his Welsh hostages executed. He watched as, one by one, they were hanged from the castle walls. They were boys aged between eight and fourteen. Then he ate his breakfast. Only Llywelyn's bastard son Gruffydd was spared.

Then John lost his nerve.

He received letters from the King of Scotland, and from his

daughter Siwan, warning him that he would be killed if he ventured into Wales. He was spooked by a hermit called 'Peter of Pontefract' who also foretold his death. He knew that Pope Innocent had told the English barons that to obey him was to offend God.

On 16th August 1212 he cancelled his orders and disbanded his army.

Meanwhile Llywelyn grew more and more powerful. In 1216 there was an assembly of Welsh princes at Aberdyfi. The reconquered territory was shared among them. The other princes did Llywelyn homage. By 1230 he was titled 'Prince of Aberffraw and Lord of Snowdon'. He established himself as feudal overlord of the other kingdoms, and became the undisputed leader of native Wales. A series of shrewd marriages of his sons and daughters to powerful Marcher families ensured a (mostly) peaceful border with England.

Although he owed fealty to the English king his principality was essentially independent. For a brief period Llywelyn's vision of a united Wales became a reality.

Everything would change with Edward I's invasion of Wales in 1284 (but Llywelyn had been dead for forty years by then).

Siwan's shrewd mediation between her natural father, John, and her husband were central to Llywelyn's success. It seems to have been a fruitful marriage. They had five children.

As the unwilling child-bride of an arranged marriage she might, at first, have identified with Branwen.

Later, as mother and matriarch, she might have identified with Rhiannon.

Finally, as unfaithful wife, caught in her husband's bedchamber with William de Braose, she must have recognised parallels with

374

Blodeuedd's story. It is a testimony to Llywelyn's affection for Siwan that he forgave her (though William was hanged).

Siwan died in 1237 at Llanfaes Priory on Anglesey. Her coffin can be seen in the porch of Beaumaris church. Llywelyn died in 1240 in the monastery at Aberconwy. His coffin is now in Llanrwst church.

The Four Branches of the Mabinogion have survived as copies made by scribes in the late fourteenth century. They are contained in two books: The White Book of Rhydderch which is now in the National Library of Wales at Aberystwyth (dated 1350), and the Red Book of Hergest which is in the Bodleian Library in Oxford (dated 1382). Scholars seem to agree that the first written composition, drawn from oral sources, would have been made in the late twelfth or early thirteenth century. The place of composition is controversial. One contender is Clynnog Fawr.

Along with the 'Four Branches', the collection of stories that have come to be called the Mabinogion also contains material from a later courtly tradition. I have used only what I consider to be the archaic narratives: the Four Branches, Llud and Llefelys, and parts of Culhwch and Olwen. From other sources I have drawn from the Legend of Taliesin, The Spoils of Annwn, the Battle of the Trees, and the Triads.

Notes

1. The monastic day is divided as
    follows:

    Vigils (3.30 am)
    Lauds (7.00 am)
    Tierce/Eucharist (8.00 am)
    Sext (12.15 pm)
    None (2.15 pm)
    Vespers (5.30 pm)
    Compline (7.30 pm)

    Times would have been much
    vaguer in the thirteenth century
    and determined by a sundial. At
    Clynnog Fawr the sundial can still
    be seen outside St Beuno's chapel.

2. The original 'Clas' at Clynnog
    Fawr, founded by St Beuno, was
    sacked by Vikings in 978. The
    churchyard we see today would
    have marked its boundaries.

    The first Cistercian settlement
    in Gwynedd was at Rhedynog-
    felen (a few miles away). It was
    founded in 1186. Soon afterwards
    it moved to Aberconwy.

    There is a tradition (John
    Leland mentions it in the early
    1500s) that there was a Cistercian
    house at Clynnog Fawr. I imagine
    it must have been a 'grange' – a
    farm estate belonging to the
    monastery where food and skins

    were produced. It would have
    been a replica, on a reduced scale,
    of the 'Mother House', with a small
    community of monks and lay
    brothers. It would have been ruled
    by the Abbot of Aberconwy.

    The Cistercian church might
    have stood where St Beuno's
    chapel is today.

3. Today there is a Welsh language
    centre at Nant Gwrtheyrn.

    Above it there is a ruined farm-
    house with a long field, marked on
    the map as containing an ancient
    homestead, hut-circle and field
    system. This is where I imagine the
    Bardic School might have been.

4. Pope Innocent 3rd had placed
    England under an Interdict in 1208
    because John refused to accept
    Stephen Langton as Archbishop.

5. Cian Brydydd Mawr is an invented
    poet. He is in the tradition of the
    'Poets of the Princes' and the
    poetry he recites is drawn from
    that period – the high flowering
    of the Welsh Bardic tradition
    (between the 11th and 13th
    centuries). In translation it is a pale
    echo of the original. Gwyn Jones
    describes the awdl (ode) 'with its

end rhymes, sections, connections, repetitions, vocabulary, figures and tropes, alliteration and internal rhymes, woven into a rhetorical or musical pattern of song, sonorous, powerful and directed very much at the ear'.

6 The poetry in this book is all adapted from Welsh court poetry of the early medieval period. I am indebted to Gwyn Jones' wonderful 'Welsh Verse in English'. This fragment is adapted from 'Exultation' by Hywel ap Owain Gwynedd.

7 There was a hierarchy of bards.
Pencerdd – a master bard, eleventh in order of precedence in the royal hall, he sat next to the heir apparent at table. Not bound to any one royal household.

Bardd Teulu – a household bard, linked to one lord, he would sing at table and also entertain the queen's household. He would ride with his lord to war and sing before a battle and afterwards as the booty was being shared.

Cyfarwydd – a storyteller with a vast repertoire.

Cerddor – a minstrel/jongleur.
There is some evidence that a Pencerdd would have 'risen through the ranks' as Cyfarwydd and Bardd Teulu before becoming a master bard.

I am indebted to an online lecture by the Welsh scholar Dr Gwilym Morus-Baird on the great bard Cynddelw Brydydd Mawr for clarifying these distinctions (for more of his insights visit welshmythology.com).

8 Adapted from 'Poem on his Deathbed' by Meilyr Brydydd.

9 Môn is the old Welsh word for Anglesey.

10 The site of Llywelyn's Llys (court) at Aberffraw is north of the village church, on the site now occupied by the Maes Llywelyn housing estate.

11 A Distain is a Seneschal. At this time the Distain of Gwynedd would have been Ednyfed Fychan ap Cynwrig. He killed three English lords in a battle against the Earl of Chester and carried their severed heads to Llywelyn. As a reward Llywelyn granted him a coat of arms displaying three heads.

12 Adapted from 'The Battle of Tal Moelfre' by Gwalchmei.

13 Hywel Dda (Hywel the Good), 880 – 950, was a king of Deheubarth who codified Welsh traditional law. He also, at the height of his reign, ruled nearly all of Wales. Llywelyn admired him on both counts.

14 Adapted from 'The Wind', attributed to Taliesin.

15 Awen is the Welsh (and Cornish and Breton) word for inspiration. It shares a root with the Welsh word 'awel' meaning 'breeze'.
This poem is adapted from 'In Praise of Owain Gwynedd' by Cynddelw Brydydd Mawr and 'Hateful Old Age' (anon).

16 Adapted from 'The Goddodin' by Aneirin.

17 Adapted from 'The Poet's Loves' by Hywel ab Owain Gwynedd.

18 Adapted from 'The Goddodin' by

Aneirin.

19 Annwn is a name for the Celtic Otherworld. It is derived from 'an' meaning 'inside' and 'dwfn' meaning 'world'. Literally 'inside world'.

20 Gorsedd is a mound or barrow. The most visually convincing site for Gorsedd Arberth is at Crug Mawr, a hill just to the north of Cardigan, with a stream called Nant Arberth running at its foot. Unfortunately it doesn't chime with the other place names mentioned in the tale. We can assume Arberth is Narberth in Pembrokeshire.

21 Rhiannon's name may derive from Rigantona the Celtic goddess 'Great Queen'. She has also been identified with the Romano-Celtic horse goddess Epona (from whom we derive the word 'pony').

22 The Celtic seasonal festivals are celebrated as follows:

Imbolc (1st February) marks the start of the growing season.

Beltane (1st May) marks the start of summer.

Lughnasa (1st August) marks the start of harvest.

Samhain (1st November) marks the start of winter.

Each season is divided by the quarterly festivals of midsummer, midwinter and the two equinoxes, making the year a wheel with eight spokes.

23 Teyrnon's name may derive from the Celtic god Tigernonos, 'Great Lord'.

24 The Island of the Mighty is Britain, or 'Prydain'. Bendigeidfran translates as Bran the Blessed. Bran means raven. Branwen means white raven. She could originally have been Bronwen, 'white breast'.

Manawydan's name may derive from Manannan mac Lir, the Irish god of the sea. Their father Llyr is probably a sea god also, derived from the Irish Ler.

25 'Teulu' means 'household'.

26 In the original these are swineherds. But as pigs appear for the first time, as a gift from Annwn, in the Fourth Branch, I have made them shepherds. (If, as Cian Brydydd Mawr later suggests, Ireland is really Annwn, then it does make sense for them to have been swineherds. See note 19.)

27 This verse is taken from Preiddeu Annwn, 'The Spoils of Annwn'. It is found in the Book of Taliesin, now in the National Library of Wales. It was set on the page in the thirteenth century. It recounts an incursion made into the Otherworld to retrieve a cauldron. Only seven return. It is clearly an archaic ancestor of the Branwen story.

The cauldron would become, in the Christian imagination, the Holy Grail.

28 Gwales is the island of Grassholm, off the coast of South West Wales.

29 This section of the story is known as the 'Assembly of the Noble Head'. In it are traces of the cult significance among the Celts of the severed head, and the magical properties associated with it. The Celts were known in the ancient

world as head-hunters.

30   Here are two examples of Welsh 'Triads'. Triads are similar events from myth, legend and ancient history that are grouped together in threes under a heading. They were used by the bards as a mnemonic device.

    The other two 'fortunate concealments' were: the dragons that were concealed in Dinas Emrys by Llud, and the bones of Gwerthefyr the Blessed that were concealed in the chief ports of Britain.

31   A Maerdref was a regional centre, run on manorial lines. Each had its Llys.

32   Henfordd is Hereford.

33   The Welsh word for oak is 'derw', it is also the root of the word 'door'.

34   Cian Brydydd Mawr tells the stories without a Christian overlay. I am imagining it is the scribe (Brother Iago, and whoever copied the stories again in the fourteenth century) who identifies the three encounters on the top of Gorsedd Arberth with the hierarchies of the church.

35   In the text Gwydion and Gilfaethwy are the 'sons of Don'. This is clearly derived from the Celtic mother-goddess 'Danu' (who gave her name to the river Danube). I've reverted to Danu.

36   Mochyn is Welsh for 'pig'; its plural is 'moch'.

37   The Taliesin story and the cauldron of Ceridwen are referred to in Bardic poetry and in the Book of Taliesin. The story was not written down, however, until the mid sixteenth century (by Elis Gruffydd). I am imagining that it was a core myth among the bards. Cian Brydydd Mawr would have wanted it included in his 'Matter'. Poor Brother Iago, light-headed with his Lenten fast, couldn't hold it in his memory.

    I am indebted to Robin Williamson (as close as we've got to a contemporary bard) for introducing me to this story. My version of it carries traces of his.

38   The stone can be seen just to the west of the porch in Maentwrog church. According to more recent tradition the stone was thrown by Saint Twrog to destroy a pagan altar (hence the village name 'maen' meaning stone and 'twrog'). This is clearly a Christian overlay.

39   The story of Mabon son of Modron is lifted and adapted from another Mabinogion tale 'Culhwch and Olwen'. Several Celtic scholars (notably WJ Gruffydd and Patrick Ford) have seen the Pryderi myth as a relic of ancient belief. His mother is Rhiannon (Great Queen/Horse Goddess). His true father should be her consort Manawydan (God of the Sea). Pryderi's adoptive father Teyrnon (Great Lord) – whose epithet is 'Twrf Liant' or 'roaring wave' – is another manifestation of the god of the sea. The disappearance of Pryderi – son of two deities – brings about the desolation of the land and the humiliation of his mother. His return restores fertility, life